The Midnight Prince

FOILED STARS
BOOK TWO

JENNIFER ASCIENZO

Stag
Beetle
Books

Prologue

GUILLERMO RAMON SAT HUNCHED over the edge of his only daughter's perfectly made bed. He held a folded piece of looseleaf and struggled to catch his breath. Fingers trembling, he reviewed the note again and again

He should've known.

Autumn's behavior the day before had been peculiar, even for her. The way she spoke and looked at him as if she'd been hiding something. As if she wanted to tell him more.

He fell to his knees and punched the floor, wincing with every bone-crunching blow. His silver wire frame glasses fell from his face and shattered against the hardwood floor. The cops would be there shortly to make sense of this catastrophe.

Or at least, he *hoped* they would be. They'd been useless every step of the way.

Eyes fogging with tears, he peered at the letter once more:

Dear Dad,

By the time you find this note, I'll already be gone. Don't bother to come looking for me. It will be easier this way for both of us if you forget all about me and move on with your life. Try

harder to find someone to make you happy, the way Mom did. At least one of us should be happy.

Just so you know, I didn't have a choice. Dante chose for me. He's an alien, and he's taking me back to his planet. Sorry to tell you this way. I know this sounds crazy.

Love you always and forever,

Autumn

Guillermo crumpled the letter, twisting and turning the paper between his fingers. His daughter had *lost* it. Either that, or Dante had kidnapped her and forced her hand. Whatever the case, he wouldn't let Dante get away with this. He'd strangle him if it meant getting his daughter back.

Dante is dangerous.

Guillermo no longer gave a damn. He'd lost the two people in his life he loved more than anything: his wife and his daughter. He had nothing left to lose.

PART ONE

Surge

One

AUTUMN LOOKED *like an angel sealed inside of an icy tomb.*

She laid slumbering, her breast gently heaving. The apples of her cheeks pinkened, as her fanned lashes rested against their soft peaks. White mist swirled against her lips.

Dante pressed his fingers against the glass of the sleep chamber that his Little Moonlight had slumbered in for the last four hundred and five days. He'd barely moved or slept since they'd left Earth. All he could do was watch, wait, hope, and dream of her.

It'd been so long; he'd almost forgotten the sound of her voice. What he couldn't shake however, were the feelings of hatred she bore for him after everything that had taken place. Her resentment for him emanated even in this dreamlike state. He inhaled a trembling breath.

She was justified.

He'd separated her from her only living family member.

But for good reason.

Dante took a seat next to the tank and winced. The fluorescent lights flickered overhead. Although his missing tail stub had since been cauterized, he recollected the sharp phantom pain of it being severed from his body. The sensation shot down his lower back and legs. He could still smell the nauseating metallic scent of his own blood pouring out. His stomach knotted.

Keyserike. If anyone discovered Dante had murdered his former superior in cold blood, he'd be dead.

He spit on the floor, droplets of saliva rolling along the metallic tiles. *Good riddance.*

He crossed his legs as he held one of the books he'd discovered in Autumn's belongings: *Dracula.*

Dante licked a finger and turned the page, resuming his place. It seemed like an awfully familiar tale. A creature of the night, thriving on the blood and suffering of others.

He glanced at Autumn. *Why would she be interested in a story like this?* He had to know, had to understand every little bit of her thought process. Dante needed to know what made her tick. Maybe then he could get her to *love* him again, and everything would be different.

His chest hollowed. When did he become so *weak*? A year ago, he would've found any sort of weakness infuriating.

The medical ward shuddered, and a soldier came stumbling into the room. He fell into a deep, waist-bent bow. He was one of the fortunate ones who hadn't witnessed the massacre with Keyserike, so he'd been permitted to keep his life.

"Authorization to speak, sire," the soldier stammered.

Dante glanced up from his book. "Speak."

"We land on Surge in thirty minutes."

Dante nodded, then waved at him dismissively. The soldier left without another word. He rose and tucked the book beneath his arm.

He admired Autumn one final time before they landed. His dark purple cape fluttered behind him as he exited the room. Determination burned through him at an all-time high. He'd win her back and protect his realm no matter the cost.

Two

IN THE PITCH DARKNESS, Autumn laid as still and silent as the dead. Her eyelids weighed as if they were sewn shut, and her body trembled from lack of muscle usage. Her limbs disobeyed as she tried to lift her head, unable to rise more than an inch before crashing against the pillow with a silent thud.

How long had she been asleep? A hundred years? More importantly, *where was she?*

Glancing sidelong, she laid atop a table. The metal was frigid against her naked backside. She didn't remember falling asleep.

She vaguely recalled a sharp pinch in her elbow pit, cool gusts of white smoke, followed by *darkness.*

Scattered memories of the senator's daughter's wedding clouded her mind. The fear in Iain's dark brown eyes, and the way that Dante had hurt Caleb. She could still hear his bones snapping and his insides sizzling to mush. She shuddered. Even though Dante had apologized, she was disgusted by his behavior.

A deal had been struck, and she bid her dad and former life farewell forever.

Her dad.

She heaved a dry breath and a single warm tear rolled down her cheek. *She'd never see him again.*

Autumn tried once more to sit up, but her muscles fell slack. She groaned and drifted into the shadows of her mind.

* * *

When she opened her eyes again, she glanced at her right arm. A needle pierced her vein. A slow IV drip trickled cool, cerulean liquid into her bloodstream.

She tensed when she beheld a shadow-veiled figure sitting beside her. Long, dark, wispy tresses framed its face. Based on the hair length, Autumn assumed it was female.

Autumn opened her mouth to speak but her vocal cords were scratchy. Two swollen glands sang in pain.

"Where am I?" she asked in little more than a whisper.

The figure didn't respond. It occurred to Autumn that the woman spoke a different language.

When she scanned the deepest corridors of her mind, she discovered a second language that'd been tucked away for safe-keeping. *Ivarkian. How was she familiar with this foreign tongue?*

She asked the question again.

The shadow stroked its long, bony fingers against her scalp. Tingles descended her spine.

"Surge."

"How long was I out for?"

"Four hundred and five days."

Autumn gasped in disbelief. She'd missed a birthday and then some.

The flicker of a dull blue light shining behind a white

gossamer sheet caught her eye. With a lazy blink, shadows glided across the floor, reminiscent of skaters drifting over the Monroe Ponds. Then they vanished into the wall.

Her body succumbed to the pull of darkness.

* * *

The next time Autumn woke, she found herself in a blinding, fluorescent-lit room. Her heart skittered. *Was this another one of Dante's dreams?*

Her muscles relaxed as her fingertips pressed over the tender skin of her elbow pit. A cotton ball had been applied where the IV needle pierced.

"Ouch," she murmured as her fingers grazed against her sore arm.

A throat cleared, followed by the scent of cinnamon.

Autumn whipped around. Dante was with her. Her eyes narrowed as she watched him lounging back in a chair, legs crossed. His royal-purple cape draped behind the seat.

When his mouth curved, her blood boiled.

A warm breeze blew by, and she glanced down. She was naked beneath the sheet. Her cheeks turned to fire.

He snorted, but when she opened her mouth to scold him, her voice cracked, and she swallowed hard.

"Water."

"For a moment I thought you were going to tell me how glad you are to see me." His dark lashes brushed against his prominent cheekbones. "Or perhaps a thank you for sparing you the length of the trip would be more appropriate."

She glowered. A thank you for kidnapping her and separating her from everyone and everything she held dear in life? *Not likely.*

"Go to hell," her voice cracked.

Dante rose from his seat and strode from the room. A

woman with her dark hair secured in a sleek high ponytail replaced him. Autumn did a double take. Her skin wasn't blue like Dante's; it was a golden, burnished hue.

A heather-gray bodysuit hugged her curves. For a moment, she wondered if this entire ordeal was a nightmare and she was back on Earth, until the woman turned her head, revealing sharp, pointed ears.

No, she was as alien as the rest.

The woman handed Autumn a cool, crisp glass of water that she gulped down greedily.

The liquid proved to be too much for her system.

In a matter of seconds, clear vomit erupted from her mouth, splattering all over the floor.

She wiped her lips over the sheet until they were dry. "Sorry."

"It's the sedative," the woman stepped over Autumn's mess. "It's still coursing through your system. And there's no need to apologize; this is my station."

Autumn nodded slowly and pointed to her cosmic backpack at the far end of the bed.

The woman leaned over and grabbed the handle, passing it to her. Inside, Autumn discovered a clean pair of jeans, a black T-shirt, and a fresh pair of undergarments she'd packed before the voyage. They still smelled of Tide laundry detergent.

With the woman's assistance, she changed, pulling on her clothes one trembling sleeve and pant leg at a time. In the process, her eyes gravitated toward a faint, jagged scar on her left wrist. She couldn't for the life of her recall how she'd gotten it.

She grabbed her black Converse and uttered an obscenity when she discovered only one sock.

"Thank you," Autumn straightened her spine.

The woman's lips curved but she didn't bother with a response. She curtseyed and left as Dante re-entered the room.

He glanced at the pool of liquid Autumn had left on the floor before meeting her glower.

"Allow me to assist you," he approached and offered her an onyx-gloved hand that she shoved away.

With wobbling legs, she attempted to stand on her own but slid to the floor, almost sitting in the puddle of her own vomit.

Dante knelt beside her, placing a hand on her arm. "Let me help you."

"Get away from me," she hissed. "You've done enough damage."

He nodded and left her there struggling to stand on her own. She'd be damned if she accepted his help after everything he'd put her through.

She slung her bag over her shoulder and took baby steps as he led her toward a stream of golden, glowing light.

Three

AUTUMN STUMBLED behind Dante into an open field. The weight of her backpack challenged her unused muscles with each step. Her eyes took a minute to adjust to the light as she'd been in the darkness for the last *four hundred and five days*.

When her vision finally cooperated, what she beheld was both beautiful and magnificent all at once.

A warm breeze gusted, swaying the tall grass surrounding them. Only it *wasn't* green. Rather, it shimmered the rich hue of cobalt.

The fragrance of lavender overwhelmed her senses, reminding her once more of everything she'd lost on Earth and everything she'd left behind. Her vision clouded, but she willed away the tears.

Not here, she scolded herself.

She had to keep her wits about her. She'd arrived on an *alien* planet.

The sky shined blue like on Earth, but there wasn't a single cloud. When she turned her head, she saw a white dome-like structure. It might've been a base, but she couldn't be sure.

In the distance spanned a metropolis filled with *countless* buildings, identical to the vision Dante had given her. Her heart sped. Thankfully, there was no forest with dark, laden trees.

However—

Most unsettling of all were the hundreds of helmeted figures aligned in perfect horizontal rows, clothed in pure obsidian. They carried all too familiar metallic rocket launchers.

She gulped, recollecting how they'd vaporized the men on Earth—into dust.

Without thinking, she grabbed Dante's hand but immediately brushed it away. *Crap.*

"At ease," Dante commanded. They placed their guns at their hips in a single fluid motion. Metal clanked against the ground as they fell into deep bows.

Once again, she comprehended Ivarkian. *What the heck?*

Dante strode toward two disc-shaped vessels, each sectioned into eight sleek triangular units. She ambled close behind, legs working overtime to keep up with him in her groggy condition.

After passing through a gap between a row of soldiers, they boarded through one of the segments to take their seats. Her heart accelerated.

"Wait," she shouted at Dante, not wanting to speak with him but having no choice under the circumstances. "Where's my other bag and my snow globes?"

"They're at Sanguis," he muttered.

"Sanguis?"

"The palace," he clarified.

That's right, Dante did mention that he's a crown prince. However, she couldn't recall the rest of the conversation. Her brain was in a hazy fog like someone had picked it clean.

"I'm surprised you didn't lie about being a prince too. We both know you have trouble telling the truth."

His mouth twisted, but he didn't respond. *Good.*

With stealth and precision, the aircraft turned in a counterclockwise direction as it rose into the sky. The segments separated and took off in pure silence.

* * *

Autumn stared out the side window as the aircraft flew. She could sense Dante's amber gaze burning into her cheek, but she paid him no mind. She was still in a hazy state.

The field of cobalt faded as they soared toward the city. This was far more than a city though. It put the local cities she'd visited back on Earth to shame.

The buildings were packed tightly, and they grazed the sky. They zipped by in a shimmering whorl of butterscotch, amethyst, sapphire, and ruby-red steel.

Some structures were standard rectangles while others were conical. Their varying hues glimmered beneath the light of the twin suns.

"This is Giarldinia, the capital city I told you about."

Dante's soft-spoken voice caressed her in a way that made her uneasy. The fact that she found the sound appealing at all felt like a betrayal of herself.

Her muscles went taut before slackening.

At least she had *some* idea where she was.

Giarldinia was on the way to Sanguis, minutes past the cobalt field on the planet Surge. She carefully cataloged her surroundings. She had to plan her escape.

Taking everything in, she noticed another unusual feature of the metropolis—and it wasn't just the walkways that floated through thin air at various heights around the buildings.

The inhabitants who ambled along the endless paths wore

the same bland shade of heather gray. If she remembered correctly, the woman who came to assist her earlier that morning had worn the same hue as well.

Every one of them sported a human skin tone.

What a weird place.

When she glanced ahead, the reflection of the aircraft sprawled across a wall of shimmering silver mirrors. *They were headed straight for it.*

She shrieked, cupping her palms against her mouth. At the last possible moment, her body suctioned against the seat, and they shot up vertically. Her stomach flipped.

Dante snorted as they leveled out again. All the pilot could do was stare at her through the visor of his helmet. Her cheeks heated with embarrassment.

After stabilizing, they zipped toward a higher set of buildings gilded in gold.

Autumn cupped her hands over her mouth to prevent herself from screaming again as the ship whizzed up, up, up like a shooting star. Dante bit his cheeks, struggling to hold back a smile.

They were faced with a massive waterfall that poured out of the sky from nowhere and disappeared into its own mist as it fell. After reaching the peak, they traveled over a tremendous rectangular body of crystal-clear water. And there it was—

The palace.

THE PALACE WAS one of the ugliest structures Autumn had ever seen. It was at least ten miles long and oval shaped, resembling a stadium with its sides curved toward the sky. The exterior was coated with a thick layer of onyx crystal. Two angular white pillars connected by an overhead arch adorned the front of the monstrosity. A pair of obsidian doors sat in between the columns. Flawless sculpted emerald shrubberies surrounded the walkway. On either side was a bed of brilliant cobalt grass.

A shiver trickled down her spine as she beheld the gargantuan structure. It was both horrific and ominous.

"Welcome to your new home."

Prison is more like it, she thought as her stomach knotted.

The aircraft hovered before landing on top of the building where a white X marked the spot.

By then, the residual effects of the sedative had worn off and her mind was clear. She needed to keep her wits about her, being on an alien planet and all.

Dante unclicked her harness and they walked into the sunshine. The dual suns warmed her skin, hotter than any summer day she'd ever experienced. Sweat beaded on her brow.

She followed him through the rooftop entrance. They walked down several flights of crimson velvet steps, around and around again, until she almost lost her bearings.

When they finally stopped, they exited through a sliding steel door into a never-ending hallway lined with the same crimson shade of velvet flooring. The rich violet walls were adorned with gilded crown molding.

They stopped before a door, dead center in the hallway. Dante punched a few buttons into a keypad, removed his glove, and scanned his thumb print. The scanner flashed neon blue, and the door opened.

He led her inside. "Sweetheart, there's some business I need to attend to."

Her forehead pulsated. "First of all, don't call me that. What kind of business?"

He ignored her question. "These are your private quarters. I'll return to you as soon as I can."

When she blinked, he disappeared into thin air. A pair of guards appeared and stood on either side of her doorway.

What she really wanted to say was, *don't bother.*

Five

DANTE STOOD in the shadow of two ceiling-high gilded doors that came to points at their peaks. A sliver of golden light shone between them, illuminating the otherwise dark hallway.

Fingers laced behind his back, chin and chest held high, he waited to be announced to his father: the Emperor of Eight Hundred and Ninety Skies.

He sucked in a deep shuddering breath. He owed his father a thorough report but couldn't tell him everything. Nobody could ever find out what he'd done. *He'd be dead.*

When he heard his name announced, he exhaled. The doors slowly creaked open.

The throne room was the way he remembered it, the three or so years he'd last been home. Plush maroon carpeting spanned the entire floor. Four white pillars circled a central skylight, shaped like a twirling star with freefalling embers. At the far end of the room sat a three-stepped dais complete with four veined steel thrones. A frothy red liquid flowed through the pipes.

Dante's loathsome father watched him, amber eyes flickering with strange delight. His thick head of obsidian hair was slicked back, landing a finger's length above his shoulders. His black-gloved hand stroked his goatee with careful precision.

Beneath his outstretched legs, bearing knee-high onyx boots, crouched an unfortunate servant trembling on all fours being utilized as a footstool. His eyes bulged with terror.

His father had always been cruel.

Beside him sat his mother in all of her splendor. A golden sunburst tiara topped her umber, glitter-flecked waves as her blue skin gleamed in the light.

A flicker of pity flashed through her brown eyes as she beheld the servant on the floor. Slowly, she met Dante's gaze and smiled radiantly. She was sunshine in Elattion form.

She rose and ambled toward him before pulling him into a tender embrace. She kissed his cheek and said, "You look well. I prayed for your safe return."

"Thank you, Mother, as do you. Thank the gods for your good health."

She nodded, cheeks flushing pink. She was far too good for his father. The monster. His mind couldn't help but drift to his situation with Autumn. He didn't deserve her either.

The emperor cleared his throat and rose, crunching the servant's spine with the full weight of his body. He groaned in agony before the emperor kicked him in the gut with the tip of his pointed boot, silencing him.

His father strode over and joined him and the empress at the bottom step of the dais.

"Well, it certainly took you long enough," he placed a hand onto Dante's shoulder. "You and that band of hooligans. Perhaps next time I should assign a chaperone to make sure you get the job done efficiently."

One had assigned himself to us; Dante was tempted to say but thought better of it.

Dante's mouth flattened as his father surveyed him. He

squared his shoulders, having an inkling of what was coming next.

"What the hell happened to your tail?" his father demanded. "This is an absolute disgrace, an Elattion crown prince without a tail! I've never heard of such a thing! Not once throughout all of history!"

"Well, I suppose that makes me the first then now, doesn't it?" Dante's lips tugged toward a smile as the emperor's face remained bright red from his outburst. "I plan to be the first at many things."

"Don't get smart with me boy, *what happened?*"

Dante crossed his arms. "An unavoidable malfunction."

The emperor huffed and paced the room, his scarlet cape furiously rippling against his back.

He went silent before bursting into laughter.

"I guess it's no matter, your strength and stamina are quite unmatched regardless," his father said. "Remind me once more, it's been over a year since last we've conversed. What of our conquests and the Grand Supreme's territories?"

"The entirety of Universe 2 has been secured," Dante straightened his spine. The Empress swayed in her golden tulle gown beside him. "All forty-seven planets are being rebuilt as we speak."

"Excellent," his father rubbed his palms together. "The Grand Supreme will be most pleased. And what of Earth and Universe 1? I'm assuming it gave you no trouble even in your *unfortunate* state."

"I'm afraid that, because of an error on my part, Earth was marred beyond recognition and had to be destroyed," he lied through his teeth.

The emperor's features hardened.

Dante continued. "I'd be more than obliged to report this information to the Grand Supreme directly, sparing you the pain."

"As is your responsibility, *not* mine," the emperor snapped. "He's been quite changeable as of late and I'm sure this news won't improve his mood."

He nodded and his father opened his mouth again to speak. "Now, I know I promised you could keep your human concubine as a reward, but I'm afraid this changes everything."

Dante folded his arms. "She's no concubine, and I'm afraid you're out of luck because she's already here. And there isn't a damn thing you can do to stop me from making her my bride."

"Where do you get off—"

"Oh, that's wonderful," his mother grinned. "You should invite her to the banquet I've organized for this evening. I'd so love to meet her."

"Don't you dare interrupt me while I'm speaking," his father raised his hand to strike her in the face, but Dante moved in front of her and accepted the blow in her stead.

His jaw cracked but it wasn't anything he couldn't handle. His father was a weakling.

His mother trembled and remained behind him.

The emperor continued. "*You* take a lower life-form as a mate? Despicable. I never thought I'd see the day. What will the rest of the universes think of the Martynes when they hear of this? I'll tell you exactly what they'll think. We're weak and inferior, especially after she bears your useless half-blood whelps."

Dante gritted his teeth.

His father gestured toward the Empress. She hesitated for a moment before approaching him. The emperor wrapped his arm around her waist and pressed his lips to her eyelid. She shuddered.

"I'll tell you what," the emperor removed his arm and

cinched his tail around her waist instead. "On second thought, invite—"

"Autumn."

"—Autumn," the corners of his father's lips curled, "to the banquet. I think I'd like to meet her after all."

Dante bowed then turned on his heel to leave.

"Ah yes, and one more thing," his father stopped him dead in his tracks. "Valdez has requested an audience."

Dante's insides twisted but he remained straight-faced. "What does she want?"

"She didn't say, but it's urgent that we report to Gypsum Palace as soon as possible."

"Her wish is my command," Dante grumbled, before heading toward the door. He could only imagine what nonsensical task his superior would assign to him considering he'd just arrived home after a treacherous year of space travel.

AUTUMN COULDN'T DECIDE whether she'd landed in heaven or hell. Her room was as exquisite as a dream.

Eggshell-white tiles lined the floor and warmed beneath the bare soles of her feet. In the center of the room sat a round bed as soft as a cloud, three times the size of the one she left back home. It was draped with fresh powdered linens and stationed atop a snow-white fur rug as soft as a rabbit's pelt.

A kitchen area lined the wall complete with stainless steel appliances and a tall round table with four futuristic clear bubble chairs. In the center of the table sat her precious snow globes: the *Alice in Wonderland* gift from her late mom and the silver-spired castle from Armienti who she'd yet to see on this planet.

A vase sat between the globes, spilling with oversized, multi-colored wildflowers. A note in Dante's distinctive handwriting said, *Welcome home*. Her forehead twitched with annoyance.

She discovered a bathroom with a jetted tub the size of an above ground swimming pool and a digital crackling fireplace.

A balcony with two crisp French doors overlooked an exotic garden area. The massive metropolis sparkled and buzzed with life in the not so far off distance.

Autumn was in the lap of luxury while her dad was twelve universes away back on Earth. Her chest hollowed, and her guilt amplified tenfold.

Her worst fear had been realized. *Her dad was all alone and there was nothing she could do about it.*

Four hundred and five days, she inhaled. It'd been four hundred and five days since they'd last been together.

She hoped he'd discovered her note, which explained everything with what little time she'd been given to write it.

Autumn gritted her teeth and balled her fists at her sides. *No,* she couldn't allow herself to be dazzled by her new accommodations. She had to find a way to escape and get back home. *She had to get back to Earth.*

Dante stole her and ruined her life. Her eyes burned with bitter tears. She'd never forgive him for this.

She trembled with fury and grabbed the vase filled with flowers and hurled it over the edge of the balcony. A clang and a piercing scream followed from the garden below.

She ducked below the railing, muttering curses before a knock rattled against the door. "Come in," she fidgeted her hands.

Dante strode through the doorway with a sickening grin on his face. "Do you allow just anyone into your bed chamber before asking for identification?"

She glowered at him. "Go away."

"You're on a foreign planet, you need to remain alert," he winked and sauntered over to her. "What are you doing on the ground?"

Dante stared at her with a strange expression before stretching his neck over the balcony.

"It's his Imperial Highness," a disembodied voice said, followed by whispers and gasps.

She continued to crouch down.

"I see you received my gift, and it went to excellent use."

"What do you want?" She rose and stumbled over her own feet.

Dante chuckled. "First, to check on you and make sure your new living arrangement is up to par."

"You mean it's really mine this time and you won't be weaseling your way into my bed again?" she said sarcastically.

He blinked then smiled. "That can always be arranged."

Her muscles went taut, and she folded her arms.

"Second, there's a banquet this evening I want you to attend with me."

"I'm busy," she brushed past him and took a seat on the bed.

She leaned over and dug through her bag for a paperback and started reading. She hoped he'd get the hint and see himself out of her room.

Dante strode over and snatched the book from her hands. She sighed as he took a seat at the edge of the bed. The foam sank beneath his weight.

"I'm afraid it's non-negotiable."

"I have nothing to wear," she narrowed her eyes at him. "I packed jeans, t-shirts, and sneakers. Maybe if you'd mentioned you lived in some fancy palace, I would've thought to bring my prom dress. But then again, it's hard to think straight when you're being kidnapped by a monster."

His amber eyes glinted. "I'm sending maids to prepare you for the festivities. You'll be meeting my parents so it's important that you make an excellent first impression."

"The emperor and the empress?" Autumn's mouth fell open.

Dante's lips curved. "The two and the same. I remember a time when you wanted nothing more than to meet them, so here's your chance."

With that he turned on his heel and exited the room, leaving Autumn with her now racing, panicked thoughts.

Seven

AUTUMN WAS unsure of how many hours had passed or even how time was kept on Surge.

She sat on her bed staring out the window. Darkness had fallen and the twin moons shone along the horizon like two crescent lanterns. Lavender wafted through the air from the gardens below. She sighed as she was overcome with nostalgia and reminded once more of her family and everything she could never have again on Earth.

"Oh Caleb," she murmured. She wondered how he was doing and if he'd recovered from Dante hurting him. She hoped he was thinking of her.

Since landing on Surge, she'd vomited four times. It was the combination of the sedative wearing off and the pressure of meeting his parents. She liked the idea more when she thought they were human.

Instead, they were the two most important people on the planet and rulers of multiple universes. It was just her luck.

She recalled foolishly *demanding* to meet them back on Earth.

How could she have known Dante was royalty? The joke was on her as usual. He was a liar and worst of all a *murderer*.

Although she was desperate for a friend, how could she ever trust him again after what he put her through?

A single crisp knock cracked against the steel door, distracting her from her wandering thoughts.

"Come in." She assumed it was the maids Dante told her would be coming to prepare her for the banquet.

The door slid open, and a silver cart rolled inside with a black satin garment bag hanging from a single bar. On the bottom sat a bin piled high with cosmetics.

Two doe-eyed women controlled the cart. Identical twins.

Their hair was so blonde it was white, and their eyes were the rich shade of summer clover. She guesstimated their ages to be somewhere in their mid-thirties, but she couldn't be sure. They were aliens who, for all she knew, aged differently than humans.

They curtseyed, keeping their eyes on the floor. They were clothed in familiar heather-gray bodysuits.

"Lady Autumn," the woman on the left spoke. "Master Dante sent us to prepare you for the banquet."

"Lady Autumn?" she snorted, and the two women tensed. *What the heck?*

"Just call me Autumn," she stifled a laugh with her hand. "Lady sounds weird."

"As you wish," the woman on the right replied. They gestured for her to follow them to the bathroom. A warm bubble bath was drawn, and she was stripped of her clothes and dumped inside. It was like being five all over again.

"I can take it from here," she said as she lathered soap and water all over herself.

The two women glanced at each other before bringing their gazes back to her. They trembled.

"Master Dante ordered us to prepare you. *Nobody* disobeys his command."

Autumn rolled her eyes. They were deathly serious, so she allowed them to continue.

She sighed as they scrubbed her from head to toe.

After what seemed like *forever*, they dried her off with a white fluffy towel and led her back into the bedroom.

They laced her into a satin obsidian corset and a silky undergarment was slipped over her thighs. She struggled to catch her breath with her waist halved.

Holy crap, she couldn't breathe in the bizarre getup.

Her hair was combed and styled half-up. Her curls draped past her shoulders, having grown a considerable amount in her sleep. A swatch of pink lipstick swiped against her lips and an iridescent eyeshadow brush fluttered over her lids.

Finally, came a brisk clicking sound. A pair of fingers cinched her nose, and she slammed her eyes shut as she was sprayed thoroughly. Puffs of glitter wisped through the air.

She exhaled as a three-tiered obsidian lace dress was passed over her head. Plum satin crisscross strings were fastened in the front, and her feet were socked and buckled into satin boots.

A mirror was flung in front of her, and she struggled to hide her shock. She wore a strange alien fashion, her hair iced with silver glitter resembling stardust.

"Thank you, I think," she stammered. "Sorry, I forgot to ask, what are your names?"

The women stared at each other wide-eyed as the bedroom door slid open, then averted their eyes to the floor without uttering a single word in response.

Dante, of course.

The two women curtseyed and rolled the cart from the room, disappearing through the door.

Dante strode over with his fingers laced behind his back,

his royal-purple cape dusting the floor. His mouth curved as he circled and inspected her.

"Stop it," she crossed her arms. "You're making me dizzy."

"Very, *very* nice."

She tried to walk away, but he took her hand and pulled her toward him. He grazed his vile blue lips against her knuckles.

He held her close for a moment before he fell to one knee. He dug a porous rock out of his pocket, the shade of moonstone, and presented it to her.

"What's this?" Autumn rolled the rough sphere in her palms, tempted to throw it in his face. She had a clear shot. But there was a sincerity about him as she inspected it.

"I want us to be *official* as you humans would say."

Autumn ran her fingers along a crease in its center. When she popped it open, she discovered a raw amethyst ring the shape of a snowflake, set in rose gold. She admired its magnificence.

"This ring belonged to my grandmother and has been in my family for generations. I'd like for you to wear it as my mate," he shook his head. "I mean wife, sorry." He corrected himself.

"But I—" She opened her mouth to protest but decided against it. She needed to pick her battles.

He slid the ring over her unwilling finger. It sparkled over her otherwise barren hand. She brushed him away. She didn't want any of this. Autumn wanted to get as far away from him as possible.

"You'd better be on your best behavior, or I promise there will be consequences," he winked.

Autumn pushed past him, her feet stomping against the floor. The door sealed behind them.

Eight

AUTUMN STOOD with Dante atop a winding split staircase. She sucked in a deep shuddering breath as they descended. The train of her dress slid over the steps.

A harp strummed accompanied by laughter and merriment. The scent of delicious food wafted through her nostrils, followed by a silent gag. Bile rose in her gut as she recalled the disgusting snakes Dante had tried to feed her on the way to Surge, hours after he'd threatened to conquer Earth and kidnapped her.

Something else had happened but her mind struggled to connect. Memories scattered and faded. Fine details were lost. She refocused on her current situation.

Her stomach grumbled as she snapped out of her thoughts. Her body trembled with hunger as her blood sugar plummeted. She hadn't eaten in over a year.

They walked through a spacious banquet hall decorated with golden spun tapestries, adorned with fiery sunsets and stars. A crystal chandelier twinkled prisms of light that played off the flecks of the gilded walls.

Relief seeped through her when she spied tables piled high

with sweet smelling fruits, fresh vegetables, pungent cheeses, and sizzling meats, although meat had always grossed her out.

Everything appeared surprisingly human, minus the eight-legged roast skinned-beast with a neon-pink hairy fruit stuck between its teeth, rotating on a spit over an open flame.

"Absolutely disgusting," she scrunched her nose. "Yuck."

Wine poured and champagne flutes clanked, while servers hustled wearing their light-gray bodysuits.

Every server in the room sported a human skin tone. She'd be fooled into thinking they were human if it weren't for their lengthy pointed ears. All the patrons, however, had complexions in varying shades of blue and were clothed in exquisite hues. Cerulean, mauve, garnet, magenta, and a shade of midnight.

When she looked closer at the crowd, there was an even stranger detail. More than half of the at least two hundred aliens in attendance were beautiful women. Some were topless; others were stark naked. Their hips swayed and breasts bounced with bizarre gold chains linking from a ring finger to a nostril.

She fiddled with her hands. *What the heck kind of planet is this?* She turned a full circle and searched the room.

"What do you need?" Dante placed a hand on her shoulder. Her anxiety spiked to an unimaginable level.

"Would it be possible for me to get a glass of wine? I know I'm only twenty but—"

Dante snapped his fingers before she could get her words out and several servers darted over. He handed her a silver goblet, spilling with crimson liquid, and took one for himself.

Although she knew much, *much* better, especially on a year-long empty stomach, she chugged the wine. *HUGE* mistake.

Holy crap. The contents of her stomach rose for the sixth time that day. Eyes widened, she cupped her hands over her mouth and gulped it down. It had a thick consistency and the salty, metallic taste of blood.

She stared at Dante as he swirled a goblet in his hand and took a lingering sip. He was cold and sophisticated. Mild amusement crept across his blue, scarlet-stained lips.

"How can you drink that stuff?" She wiped her palm against her mouth. Red liquid stained her hand. "Your food and drinks are *disgusting*. I'm never going to be able to keep anything down."

He chuckled and snatched the cup from her hand, placing it on a table. He grabbed a flute of golden bubbly liquid and passed it to her.

"I see you're not going to be able to handle any of our traditional foods and beverages. Try this instead. I promise it'll be to your liking."

Staring at the glass, desperate to unwind, she sniffed in its fruity scent before taking a languorous sip. The fizzy liquid was reminiscent of champagne, which she'd only ever tasted at weddings. Delicious. *Finally.*

As she enjoyed the beverage, she sidestepped just in time. A girl with silver, wavy, glitter-encrusted tresses sprinted toward Dante, almost knocking her over as she leapt into his arms.

He spun her around in a circle before planting her back onto her feet. She stood a few inches taller than Autumn with pronounced cheekbones and devastating blue features. Her eyes were a deep brown, and her lips were plush pink.

Her violet tulle dress brushed against Autumn's boots, and she leaned over and kissed Dante's cheek.

"I missed you," she jumped up and down, clapping her hands. She reminded her for a split second of her best friend, Lauren Gardner with her peppy enthusiasm.

"I missed you more," Dante placed his hand against the girl's cheek. "You were a babe when last I saw you."

Autumn carefully watched their interaction as she sipped her drink. The girl didn't seem like an ex. There was no hand holding or lip kissing. No chemistry whatsoever. She *had* to be family. She and Dante had the same facial structure down to the clefts on their chins. And their eyes were lively, full of secrets.

"There's someone I'd like you to meet," Dante gestured. "This is Autumn, my future mate."

She extended a hand to the girl if only to be polite, but her eyes thinned to slits.

"*What* is she?" The girl asked, treating Autumn as if she was invisible. "She resembles a hybrid, but she's different somehow."

Dante's mouth fell into a flat line. "Come now Leyla, don't be rude."

"I'm human," Autumn crossed her arms and scowled. "Not some hybrid."

Leyla's face contorted, distorting her lovely features.

"I need to speak with you," Leyla grabbed Dante's arm and yanked him toward her. "*Alone.*"

Leyla dragged him to the opposite end of the banquet hall, far out of earshot. Her cheeks heated like two fiery coals. She wished she could hear what they were talking about.

Aliens whispered and snickered all around her. The celebration seemed to go silent. Everyone was in on some sort of private joke that was far over her head.

Leyla shoved him against the wall and threw an all-out tantrum, arms flailing. Dante guided her back through the crowd as she huffed and puffed, blue face shifting to red.

"Pleasure to meet you," Leyla said curtly, before wandering off to wherever she came from.

Autumn's eyes widened. "What was that all about?"

"My younger sister often forgets her manners, like somebody else I know," he winked.

Sister. That was Dante's *sister.* Somehow, she wasn't surprised.

What a snob. Forget Lauren, she reminded her more of Misty Beckett, her high school bully and arch nemesis in both demeanor and rudeness.

"I don't think she likes me very much."

"Nonsense," Dante smiled and placed a hand on the small of her back. He guided her to the front of the room.

She hesitated. "I'm hungry." It was the only excuse she could think of on such short notice to delay the inevitable.

She grabbed a plate and filled it with food and ate. She needed some energy in her system; her arms and legs trembled slightly.

She hadn't forgotten the purpose of this meeting.

Dante's parents. *The emperor and empress.*

After stuffing her face with everything she could find, Dante ushered her to the front of the gathering. Her head grew so light she feared she might faint.

Dante leaned over and whispered into her ear. "When you speak to them, speak as if Earth no longer exists."

"What—why? Did something happen?"

"Just do as I say," he insisted.

Autumn nodded mechanically, literally on pins and needles as they approached. *What the heck was he talking about? He was always up to no good.*

Nine

DANTE SHARED an unmistakable resemblance to his father. They both had the same rich amber eyes and ink black hair. However, Dante wore his tresses loose about his head, while the emperor slicked his behind his elongated, pointed ears.

The empress who sat beside him was clothed in a flowing electric-blue gown with multi-hued floral appliques. Her light-brown hair sparkled with gold glitter and was styled in a pouf high above her head. Wispy tendrils fell gracefully around her youthful blue face, but a sadness lingered in her large childlike eyes, though Autumn couldn't pin down the source.

Dante fell into a deep, waist-bent bow. Not knowing what else to do, Autumn curtseyed.

The empress flashed her a welcoming smile, but the emperor's features remained solemn and drawn. She could've sworn a vein pulsated across his blue forehead.

Like father, like son.

Dante placed his hand on the small of her back. Her thoughts slowed to a crawl. "This is Autumn, the girl I told you about."

"How old are you, child?" The emperor's rich amber eyes roved over her body. "You're smaller and more youthful than I had anticipated."

"I'm twenty," she answered through numbed lips.

The emperor released a low chuckle and turned toward his son. "They get younger and younger every time, don't they? Soon you'll be stealing babies suckling from their mothers' breasts."

"Well, you would know better than anyone else," Dante crossed his defined arms.

Autumn stood there frozen as she identified all the exits she could see, desperate to escape this cringeworthy conversation. After all this time, she thought her dad had been mean to Dante.

"What she lacks in age she compensates for with charm and maturity. And in my opinion, her beauty is unmatched."

Autumn's face melted as Dante boasted of her beauty. Here, she was *no* beauty. Anyone with two eyes and half a brain could see that upon first glance around the room.

The emperor gestured a black-gloved hand to them to join him at the head table. He hissed at the empress to go find a new seat.

"No, Mother, you stay seated, and I'll stand," Dante offered.

The empress nodded. Her blue cheeks shifted pink.

Dante led Autumn around the table and pulled out a chair for her. She took a seat between his parents.

She would've preferred to be sitting in a universe or a dimension far away from such an intimidating pair. She crushed her palms with her legs to avoid fidgeting during this unwelcome situation.

The emperor turned toward her. "Where were you born?" His amber eyes flickered with curiosity.

"New York," her throat ran dry like desert sand. "It *was* a city on Earth." She recalled what Dante had told her. She wished she didn't have to lie on top of everything else.

"I've heard of it before," the emperor shrewdly stroked his goatee. "Its reputation preceded it, although I've never been there myself. If I had, I would've gladly leveled it to dust in my son's stead."

She blinked, then choked on her thoughts as a full-breasted servant bent over in front of Dante to distribute plates of food. He held Autumn's gaze.

She shook her head, trying her best to forget the words the emperor had said, mere moments ago. "It was an amazing place."

"Somehow, I doubt that," the emperor's scarlet-stained lips coiled.

Her stomach flipped in circles.

"What of your parents? How did they earn their place on your world before—"

"Oh, um, my dad was in the IT business and my mom—" she hesitated, eyes beginning to fog. She blinked away the tears. "My mom was an English teacher."

The emperor dragged his chair backwards, metal scraping against stone. A chill skittered down her spine. Everyone in the room stared.

"A word," the emperor said to Dante and pointed toward a door behind the table hidden beneath a glittering tapestry.

Everyone rose as the emperor led Dante behind the closed door. It slammed, echoing through the hall.

Her stomach churned into a tight knot, queasiness over-taking her. She had to get home, had to get away from this rotten miserable place. The empress stared at her dinner plate; eyes unmoving. The party paused for a deafening moment before continuing again.

"*Dante.*" His father's voice boomed from behind the wall,

while Autumn sat there wide-eyed. *"Get this filth out of my court. Not only is she a human, she resembles a hybrid."*

"She stays or you can find someone else to lead your endless conquests."

Silence. Autumn heard deafening silence, apart from her heart thundering at an impossible speed in her ears.

"You've damned us all, bringing back your human pet. You'll be the laughingstock of the realm. A tailless laughingstock."

Autumn glanced at the empress, who in turn met her stare. Autumn's eyes fell upon a bruise that bloomed black and blue beneath her sheer sleeve. The empress placed her palm over the mark.

"May I please be excused?" Autumn murmured.

"Of course," the empress whispered.

Autumn rose and curtseyed. The emperor and Dante continued to argue in the background, voices steadily escalating. She walked out of the banquet hall before hiking up her dress and breaking into a run.

Ten

AUTUMN RACED round and round up a swirl of crimson velvet steps, her three-tiered gown fluttering in the passing wind.

It was now or *never*.

She took her one and only chance, unsure of whether another opportunity would arise for her to escape this horrifying planet. She trembled as she pressed her sweaty thumb against the scanner of the rooftop door.

It didn't open. *Crap.*

"Come on. Come on, dammit." She slid her thumb against the scanner again and again, finally taking the toe of her boot and kicking the door once, twice, three times—

It opened.

She burst onto the rooftop, the warm night breeze blowing through the strands of her glitter-encrusted hair.

Her eyes darted around for a sign of anyone. But all was still and quiet.

Beyond the grounds of Sanguis, Giarldinia thrummed and sparkled with life. The stars zipped across the sky, amidst the glow of the twin crescent moons.

Hopefully she'd be flying soon enough, on her way home. *Whichever way home was.*

She needed to get back to Earth, her friends, her dad, and the life she'd left behind. Why was Dante lying about Earth being destroyed? She could only imagine.

After whipping around in a full circle, the obsidian gleam of the ship she traveled in on caught her attention. Autumn sprinted over and circled the aircraft, high-heeled feet scraping against the granulated rooftop. She exhaled a sigh of relief when she discovered one door had been left ajar. The aircraft was wholly unguarded.

"Hello," she called. No answer came.

Perfect.

Autumn boarded and headed straight for the control seat. She clicked her harness into place. In a fit of desperation, she tugged levers, pushed blinking buttons, and jerked handles. The door sealed vacuum tight. *Good, good.*

Another yank of a lever and the ship revved and vibrated, turning in a counterclockwise direction. It hovered over the rooftop.

Okay, she had to fly through Giarldinia and back to the field of vivid, cobalt grass that led to the space station.

And then what? She hoped she could take it from there.

As she hovered away from the palace grounds, a *BOOM* echoed from the top of the aircraft, followed by the scuffle of heavy boots.

Crap, crap, crap. She yanked another lever, and the aircraft doubled its speed and flew further into the city when—

It halted mid-flight and traveled in reverse.

Her heart exploded in her chest as she continued to tamper with controls, hitting them desperately. But it was no use.

Before she could blink, the ship was stationed back at the palace.

A hard lump fastened itself in her throat, and all she could hear was the sound of her own breathing. The smell of burning metal violated her senses.

The door ripped from its hinges and was tossed aside, scraping against the ground.

"Leaving me so soon?"

Goosebumps erupted over her skin. She opened her mouth to speak, but no words came out.

Eleven

"WHATEVER SHALL I DO WITH YOU?" Dante sauntered onto the ship; mouth twisted into a smirk.

Autumn unbuckled herself, heart speeding.

With her back against the wall, her eyes slammed shut. She could imagine the sheer magnitude of his power crushing her human frame.

Instead, Dante cocooned her within his royal-purple cape before sweeping her into his capable arms. She wasn't going down without a fight. An unfair fight but a fight, nonetheless. She tried to escape his grasp, kicking her high-heeled feet and wiggling her body, but her attempts were futile.

"Do you know how I punish deserters?"

"Punish?" she repeated, the blood freezing in her veins.

He nodded as he carried her through the door and back into the night. Warm winds gusted, bringing with them the scent of midnight flowers. The stars twinkled above, scattered around the pale glow of the twin moons.

"Life in the cells," Dante's mouth curved, his voice falling into a dead tone. "Unless—"

She gulped. *Cells. They have cells here too? Of course.*

"Unless what?" She was almost too afraid to ask.

"You give me what I want."

He planted her back onto her feet, gown swaying in the warm night breeze.

She folded her arms. "Why is it always what *you* want? What about what I want? What about what I need? I'm already your prisoner. You ruined my life, and I hate you for it," she paused. "And now you have me lying for you. Why?"

"You're not my prisoner," he shifted his weight. "You're free to do as you will, but it's not safe. You're not ready for what's out there."

"What exactly is out there?"

"Don't worry about it," he pulled her in close and tucked a glittered strand of hair behind her ear. "I saved your life and the lives of those you love, and this is the thanks I get?"

"Saved me? Don't make me laugh." She rerouted the conversation. "It's clear your family doesn't want me here. Why don't you just do us both a favor and send me back?"

He grew silent, features hardening. "I'm sorry you had to hear that."

She nodded. "How could I not? And how come I can suddenly understand your language anyway?"

He ignored her question. "I'm not your enemy, Autumn. I'm your friend," he kicked the gravel with the tip of his knee-high boot. "Our alliance created a viable reason for me to spare your planet."

"How can I believe a single word that comes out of your mouth?"

"You're just going to have to trust me on this one."

She pulled away, fists trembling at her sides. "You have to understand how lonely I feel. My only family is a hundred billion light years away."

Her dad. Who probably lost his mind after she'd disappeared.

"I regret how I handled this entire situation, but I couldn't afford to take any chances. I did everything for your protection," he paused. "I was terrified of losing you."

"Well, congratulations. I'm already gone," she brushed past him and leaned against the rooftop railing, propping her chin on a fist. She sighed, admiring the sparkling view of the metropolis and the aircraft whizzing around like shooting stars.

Dante glanced at the ground and then at her. He approached her tentatively. "You have every right to be displeased with me, but I swear I'll make it up to you somehow." He brushed his hand against hers, but her knuckles locked.

"I'll spend every second of every day trying to win you back. I can make you happy, if only you'll allow me the chance."

The idea of happiness was a foreign concept to her. She couldn't remember the last time she was happy. Being isolated on an alien planet with no friends, nobody to confide in, and her family universes away was the most miserable situation she could imagine.

"Come back to the banquet with me," he suggested.

She placed a hand on her hip and refused to move an inch. There was no way she was going back to that horrible place, filled with strange, naked, alien women and an emperor who loathed her.

She scrunched her nose. "I'd rather not."

"Please don't make me beg."

She snorted. Glitter fell from her hair and blew through the wind.

"You'd like that wouldn't you? To see me grovel."

She bit back a smile and nodded as he fell on his knees, his eyes imploring.

It nowhere near made up for the situation she was in, but it was a start. At least Earth was safe for now.

* * *

When they arrived back at the bustling banquet hall, they were greeted by whispers and snickers. All eyes fixated on her and Dante. She fidgeted her hands as sweat beaded on her upper lip. The attention was unsettling. But in this place, being human and standing next to the crown prince in a room filled with blue, ethereal aliens was a surefire attention-grabber.

With his usual swagger and grace, Dante ambled to the front table where his parents ate dinner. Autumn's blood frosted in her veins at the sight of his hateful father. His mother, the empress, didn't so much as look up from her plate while she consumed her lavish meal.

The empress seemed timid and broken. In some ways, Autumn could relate. Her life had crumbled before her eyes on many occasions.

A series of aggressive, inaudible whispers were exchanged between Dante and his father before he snatched a golden goblet out of his father's hand and took a long swig.

He rejoined her. She had no clue what he was up to.

Dante gulped his goblet dry then dinged it with a knife, grabbing everyone's attention. The room fell pitch silent. No one dared breathe.

"I'd like to propose a toast," Dante said in a voice that commanded attention and demanded the utmost respect.

He strode over to Autumn and took her by the hand. Her palms perspired in his grasp. The spotlight and hundreds of sets of inhuman eyes piercing into her were more than she could bear.

"The ravishing Autumn Ramon and I are pleased to

announce our intention to spend the rest of our lives together."

His words were punctuated by the crunching of steel beneath the emperor's slammed fist.

Dante's amber eyes glinted. "Autumn has added meaning to my previously trite life, which is now complete with her in it. Together we shall mold and shape the future of the Martyne Empire."

Autumn swayed in her gown as he continued, "I'd like to thank everyone who gathered here this evening to help us celebrate this momentous occasion." He turned toward his father and mother, raising his goblet. "And I'd like to give a special thanks to my parents for making our wildest hopes and dreams a reality. Long may they reign."

"*Long may they reign,*" echoed from the mouths of every alien being present at the gathering. Dante's parents remained deathly quiet. Neither of them raised a goblet in celebration.

Leyla's classically beautiful features contorted to that of disgust, rage, and hatred that could be felt from across the room. Autumn's face and neck flushed so hot she could barely breathe.

From now on, she was enemy number one, and she had to watch her back.

Twelve

LATER THAT NIGHT, Dante accompanied Autumn to her bedchamber. The evening had been successful, and he was grateful to re-open the lines of communication between himself and his future wife.

Hopefully, and he could only pray, *she despised him a little bit less because of it.*

Of course, there were no guarantees, and at that moment, he wasn't particularly fond of himself for what he'd put her through.

Still, he'd spoken the truth. He kept her planet safe like he'd promised, and he intended for it to stay that way.

They rounded a few flights of vermillion steps to the second floor. Autumn was quieter than usual, seemingly lost in deep thought. It was a plus that no hateful remarks were spewed his way. Although, he knew he deserved them.

What he'd done was *unforgivable.* Not only did he pilfer her from her world, but he gave her an ultimatum. Marry him or be conquered.

Who was he kidding? He'd never be worthy of her, not in

a million years. He was confident that if she loved him once, she could love him again though.

At least, that's what he kept reassuring himself.

Back on Earth she'd seen him for who he was and *not* for the crown he had to offer. That was the girl he wanted to spend the rest of his life with.

She'd smiled at him earlier, *actually* smiled and taken delight in his groveling. A clear sign, he supposed, that they were on their way to mending their shattered relationship.

It was so much better than watching her brood and attempt to escape. Thank the gods he'd found her when he did. She could've easily fallen into the hands of one of his enemies.

He'd never forgive himself.

When they arrived at her bedchamber door, she stared at him with those moon-colored eyes. Her full pink lips parted as if she meant to tell him something.

A secret perhaps, meant for his ears alone.

He leaned in closer and accidentally brushed her dress. His face warmed as his pants tightened. His need around her was unbearable.

"Yes," he met her gaze. He wished she'd invite him inside to bed her, but he also reminded himself of the promise he made and his intention to wait.

If she still wasn't ready for him by then, he would wait as long as he needed to. Even if it meant forever. She was worth it.

"I can't figure out how to get into my room," she folded her arms.

"Oh, sorry," he shook his head and keyed in the code to her door. He removed his glove and scanned his thumbprint over the reader. It slid open.

"If you need anything, I'm three doors down."

She started to go inside but then stopped in her tracks.

She turned around. "I have a question. I know I'm not supposed to care or anything but I'm just curious."

His brows rose. "Yes?"

"What was with all of those naked women at the party?"

"Why, are you jealous?" He chuckled.

Her expression remained straight. She blinked, her lashes grazing her rosy cheeks.

Dammit, she noticed. His face and neck burned. There was no getting out of this.

He swallowed hard. "Well, you see, years ago before we met, I used to pursue meaningless relationships that resulted in instant gratification."

"Why?" her mouth twisted to the side. "I thought it was just your cousins. You never mentioned you were a player too."

"I suppose I was lonely," he leaned a black-gloved hand against the doorframe. She swayed in her gown, staring at him with her tell-tale eyes. "My life is stressful, and I was seeking comfort, comfort I could never quite find."

Maeve, his prior love interest, had passed away unexpectedly, but he remained silent on the matter.

"Everything changed when I met you. You're different from any other girl," he shook his head. "I mean, all the women *I've* ever known. You're special, with your high morals, unmatched empathy, and sweet little interests. I find your inner beauty as mesmerizing as your outer beauty, Autumn Ramon."

Her cheeks shifted to the color of freshly fallen rose petals.

"To answer your question, I had relations with many of the women at the banquet. My father invited them as a means to humiliate me, and as usual, he was successful."

He leaned over and grazed his lips against her cheek. "I swear to you I'll never behave that way again. You have nothing to worry—"

She pulled away abruptly. "Good night."

The door slid shut in his face.

* * *

He arrived at his own chamber door feeling nothing short of foolish.

Perhaps he'd said too much.

It seemed he couldn't do anything right. There was no way of getting through to her. No way to make her understand.

She *hated* him.

He was one of the four, now *three*, most despised individuals in the 24 Universes. *Keyserike*, he spat into the carpet. So, it made perfect sense that his mate would loathe him as well.

Upon entering his permanent lodgings, he had immediate plans to immerse himself in a freezing cold shower, when he discovered—

He *wasn't* alone.

The dining area was still cast in shadow, but the doors of his balcony had been left ajar. A warm breeze wafted in, carrying with it a floral scent reminiscent of Autumn.

However, the door of his bedroom remained shut. A light shined beneath the crack.

What on Earth.

Opening the door slowly, carefully, he discovered two exquisite women lounging on the edge of the bed. They were naked.

The first had emerald skin and hair so blonde it appeared white beneath the hanging ceiling lamp. It cascaded down her back in loose ringlets. The second had warm brown skin and obsidian hair tossed over her shoulder.

His chest went so taut he couldn't breathe. His teeth ground inside of his mouth as he said, "I did *not* order an escort to service me."

The burnished-skinned girl twirled a finger around a loose strand of hair, exposing her pointed ears. "We're a gift to your Imperial Highness."

"Yes," the emerald girl bit her bottom lip and tugged her fingers at the spandex band around his pants. "We were instructed to satisfy your *every* need."

He ground his molars together, remembering the conversation he'd had with Autumn minutes earlier.

"Keep your hands off me," he snapped. Both women froze and trembled.

"But we—"

"Don't talk back," he folded his arms. "Just leave."

Knock, knock, knock. "Dante?"

His heart leapt to his throat upon hearing Autumn's voice.

Knock, knock, knock.

"Get out of my room," he hissed.

The two escorts sprang to their feet and sprinted toward the main entrance.

"Not that way you imbeciles, my mate is outside. If she discovers you here, I swear you'll be on the first ship to planet Varz tomorrow morning."

A fate he only wished on his mortal enemies.

"No, no please," they fell to their knees, palms pressed together.

"Find another way out," he ushered them aside.

He sucked in a deep breath and counted to five. A slow, even count.

He opened the door slowly and peeked his head outside. "Autumn, what a pleasant surprise," he smiled. "Can I help you with something?"

"Did I catch you at a bad time?" She tilted her head to the side, trying to peek inside of his room.

"No, not at all," he opened the door and gestured for her

to enter. "Please, come in."

She brushed past him, arms folded over her chest. "Are you alone? I could've sworn I heard voices in here."

"Yes, um—I'm perfectly alone," he crossed his arms. "What you heard was my broadcaster playing a local channel."

He flipped on a control panel and a green 3D holo-image flickered and rotated before them like a neon ghost. He prayed to whatever gods would listen that she bought his excuse.

She walked around the room, searching for something. "Can you turn on a light? It's kind of dark."

He flipped the switch at her request, palms sweating.

"The reason I'm here is to thank you for being honest with me about the women at the banquet. And—" she paused, fiddling her fingers together.

"And?"

"I need to ask you for a favor."

He waited patiently to hear what was on her mind, breath catching in his throat as the seconds passed.

"I know we made a deal that you would spare Earth in exchange for me marrying you, but I really, *really* need to see my dad. He needs me," desperation cracked through her voice. "And I still don't understand why you made me lie about Earth."

He paced the floor weighing his options. Unfortunately, he couldn't grant her request, as much as he wanted to. It wasn't safe.

"Under the present political climate, that's impossible."

As soon as he spoke, her eyes began sparkling with tears.

He crossed his arms. "But it doesn't mean an opportunity won't present itself in the future. I promise that as soon as I'm able to, I'll reunite you with him on two conditions."

"Okay?" She sniffed.

"You at least *try* to be happy here and maybe—spend time with me on occasion," he said. "Can we agree on that at least?"

"I'm not making any promises, but I'll try."

His lips tugged toward a smile then collapsed when he heard an unwelcome sound.

Crack.

She stretched her neck to peek behind him. "What was that noise?"

"I have an infestation of insects, and it seems they're gnawing away at my furniture."

She scrunched her nose in disgust.

"Have a good night and the most pleasant of dreams," he said, after accompanying her back to her chambers.

When he returned, he stormed into his bedchamber to discover his armoire severed in half. The two women trembled inside of the wreckage. Apparently, they'd been hiding inside and hadn't made their way out of his room like he had ordered them to.

He flung one escort over his shoulder and grabbed the other by her cascading hair. He sauntered over to the balcony and tossed them both over the railing.

They screamed as they collided with a bush, demolishing trees and flower beds from the garden upon impact. In a final fit of frustration, he took his mattress and tossed it over the edge as well. A series of pathetic groans followed.

Utterly exhausted, he collapsed onto the carpet next to his fireplace and drifted into a dreamless sleep. His first day back home after a three-year absence had been overwhelming, ridiculous, and infuriating all at once.

Thirteen

THE FOLLOWING MORNING, Autumn awoke to light streaming through the French doors of her balcony. Gold, marmalade, and amethyst rays glimmered into her weary eyes.

For a single moment, she could've sworn she was back on Earth lying in her own bed. For a moment she heard the phantom sound of her dad making sizzling chocolate chip pancakes on the griddle and brewing pumpkin spiced coffee for them to share.

What she would give to see him again. Instead, he was a distant memory.

She climbed out of bed and ambled over to the balcony, inhaling the scent of fresh lavender. When she closed her eyes, she could almost recollect her parents' faces.

Almost.

She kicked herself for not thinking enough to bring actual pictures of them. Her phone had long since died.

A warm salty tear rolled down her cheek, as she wondered what horrors awaited her on the day's agenda.

What was a princess-in-training expected to do with her spare time? She sighed.

She turned a full circle and surveyed her room. The extravagant gown she'd worn to the banquet the night before was tossed on the ground, a heap of satin corset, undergarments, and lace. Remnants of silver glitter were smeared across her sheets, and the contents of her bags had been emptied all over the floor.

She didn't want to be known as the messiest person in the palace. She'd attracted more than enough attention the night before, based solely on being a human.

On top of everything, Dante's family didn't seem particularly fond of her. Especially Leyla. *The snot.*

But where are Ronan and Armienti? She hadn't seen either of them. Her mind drifted to Armienti as she admired the beautiful, spired snow globe he'd crafted for her birthday. She was still surprised he remembered.

She withdrew from thoughts of him and raced around the room making the bed, re-stuffing her bags, and folding the dress she'd worn.

She drew a bath for herself and soaked her bones. Her eyes fell upon the strange twisting scar that littered her left wrist. For the life of her, she couldn't remember where it came from. She ran her fingers over the coarse healed skin.

After her bath she tossed on a gray t-shirt, light-wash jeans, and her Converse. She rifled through her cosmic backpack and discovered a watermelon lip gloss in the front pocket. To her delight, it hadn't dried out.

With one swipe, she was ready to face the day.

A loud, precise knock came to the door. Bright and early. It could only be one person.

She sighed. "Come in."

Dante sauntered through the doorway, *looking disastrous.*

Deep-purple bags sank beneath his amber eyes. His inky hair was frazzled and wrecked.

She wondered if he'd had another run in with the full moon, recalling his monstrous transformation. But as far as she could remember, the moons had been in crescent form the night before. Then it occurred to her. His tail was absent. *When had it gone?*

"What happened to you?" A smile tugged at her lips. She enjoyed the rare sight of him sans arrogant smirk and swagger. He deserved to be as miserable as she was, and this time, she didn't have to try. "And where's your tail?"

His eyes widened for a moment. "I trust you slept well." He ignored her question.

She nodded as his eyes darted around the bedroom; face etched with irritation. He huffed, balling his fists at his sides and stormed back through the doorway. His royal purple cape rippled over his shoulders. A series of gasps followed. Autumn tensed as footsteps approached, and Dante reentered the room with the twin maids who'd dressed her the night before in tow.

The maids lined up and stood before Dante trembling. Their emerald eyes averted to his feet.

"Answer me this," he linked his fingers behind his back. "Why is it that this room is untouched, and my lady has been left to tend to herself?"

One of the maids opened her mouth and spoke. "You—your Imperial Highness, we're understaffed, and we were going to get to it next we swear," her voice cracked.

His mouth fell into a tight, flat line.

"Stop it, Dante," Autumn placed a hand on her hip. "This is ridiculous. I don't need to be coddled. I can take care of myself."

Dante blinked, then narrowed his eyes at the twin maids. "Every morning, at first light, I want both of you in this room on your hands and knees scrubbing like slaves. Afterwards, I'll come to inspect, and if everything isn't to my liking, you'll answer for it."

The twins stiffened.

"Better yet," his lips twitched. "I'm assigning you to Autumn as her personal maids. In addition to your other household duties, you're to bathe her, clothe her, and wipe her rear if she dictates. So, you'd better get to it. The clock on my patience is ticking."

He snapped his fingers and they scurried to their assigned station.

"This is *completely* unnecessary," Autumn watched as the women ripped up her sheets and undid everything she'd done in a frenzy.

"A word," he gestured toward the door.

She was tempted to smack him in the face, but instead she followed. She reminded herself that he determined whether she'd be able to return to Earth.

They stood in the hallway.

"Sweetheart, I don't want you to think me cruel, but you have to understand there are regulated palace standards and traditions we abide by here on Surge," he said. "And I refuse to see you disrespected. I know you're a full-grown woman and you can take care of yourself, but here, that's not how things work. We're no longer on Earth."

Boy, did she realize they weren't on Earth—she wanted nothing more than to leave.

Her forehead twitched.

"In my home, *our home*, everyone knows their place, and everything exists on a schedule," they passed servants in the hallway who bowed and curtseyed. "While I'm here I take my meals at a certain time, attend council meetings, sentence prisoners, and so on and so forth."

"When do you have time to just relax and be yourself?"

"Never."

She rolled her eyes. "Why were you so different on Earth?"

"That was a one in a million scenario," he changed the subject. "By the way, I don't care for that color on you. We're having breakfast with my family, and I suggest you wear something a little more becoming."

"I don't care what you like. Stop being ridiculous," she brushed past him and made her way through the hallway. He lingered behind her.

* * *

They arrived at the banquet hall, clear of all decorations. Its metal rafters were bare, and the room was lit by floating votives of opaque glass.

Autumn hoped Dante's family wouldn't show up for breakfast so she could eat in peace. They rounded the corner and stood before a gilded door that grazed the ceiling. Her breath caught in her throat.

Crap, crap, crap, her hands fidgeted in her jeans pocket.

The door slid open and on the other side was a spacious room with walls the rich hue of sapphire. At first glance, they were reminiscent of Caleb's eyes.

Caleb, her ex-boyfriend, who as it turned out, only cheated on her to help his family. He was selfless, putting his family's needs before his own. Just like she did. She blinked away a tear.

The family she was unfortunate enough to marry into was awful. They sat together along one side of a long table covered with fruit, vegetables, and steaming cakes in unusual shades of golden yellow and neon pink.

The emperor wore his obsidian ensemble, scarlet cape draped over the back of his seat. The empress and Leyla were clothed in bodysuits of mustard and dusty rose, each with an angled glittered stripe.

Their hair was secured in high ponytails. Leyla's was flecked with lilac sparkle, and her mother's hair was adorned with gold.

No one spoke or acknowledged their arrival.

This freaking sucks. Autumn was tempted to turn around and run away but Dante's palm rested on the small of her back, urging her onward.

The royal family finally glanced up from their meals. The empress's face softened, and she flashed a small smile.

It surprised her that Ronan and Armienti were nowhere to be found. This was the second family function they'd been absent from.

"What is she doing here?" The emperor sipped his golden goblet. Traces of scarlet liquid coated his pale blue lips and obsidian goatee. "She should dine out back with the beasts."

Leyla snorted and the empress averted her eyes to her plate.

Dante glowered at his father who shrugged, tail thrashing, and continued to eat his meal as if nothing had happened.

"She'll dine with us whether you like it or not," Dante's mouth straightened.

Her heart thundered, and her breath ripped from her lungs as they ambled around the table where there were four chairs, *not* five. Again. She froze. Dante slid out of the seat and gestured for her to take it.

She sat down, not daring to survey her surroundings. He then proceeded to serve her himself, piling fruits and cakes atop her plate, and pouring orange fluid into her goblet.

Even after his spiel about knowing her place in the palace. Whatever.

Seconds later another chair arrived for him, and he sat

closest to his father. *Thank goodness.* Autumn sensed Leyla assessing her every move on the opposite side of the table.

"Why are you dressed like that?" Leyla's well-groomed brows rose. "You look like a filthy peasant."

Autumn took a quick glance at her outfit. American Eagle jeans, a t-shirt, and Converse. There was *nothing* peasant-like about it. Her outfit looked stylish. Leyla was the one sitting there in a body length leotard. If they were on Earth, people would have laughed in her face, or asked where the gymnastics competition was. She snorted softly.

"Enough," Dante hissed at his sister as he filled his own plate. Leyla rolled her eyes.

"Autumn, I'll have clothing constructed for you by the day's end. After breakfast, I'll send someone to your chamber to get your measurements."

"Thanks," she murmured.

Great, now she'd look as ridiculous as his mom and sister.

As she picked at her food, her appetite suddenly vanished. What the heck was she eating anyway? All the food was bright and off-color.

"Don't worry, it's been tested." Dante squeezed her shoulder and she brushed away his hand, cringing every time she was forced to touch him. He plopped a forkful of food into his mouth and winked.

The emperor cleared his throat, causing the hairs on her neck to stand on end. A wide grin flashed across his face.

"How did you find your welcome home present, Dante?"

Dante almost choked mid-swallow, eyes widening before narrowing at his father.

"That's not fair," Leyla slapped her palms against her thighs. "Why does Dante get a gift for doing his job and I get *nothing* for being stuck here all the time?"

"Don't worry darling," the emperor's lips tugged toward a smile. "I have something for you as well."

Leyla flashed a grin. *Spoiled brat.* Dante gulped down the remainder of his food, before turning toward his father.

"Although I do appreciate the thought behind your gift," the words rolled smoothly from his tongue, and he took a sip from his silver goblet, "I found it to be in poor taste. In the past I would have graciously accepted it, but as I've recently indicated, I've changed. I chose to return it unopened. I feel that it would be more useful in the hands of those who are far needier than myself."

Autumn blinked and Dante put down the goblet. He took his fork and speared another piece of fruit before placing it into his mouth.

"I see," the emperor said. "That explains the little redecorating project you did in the garden. All those plants were imported from Universe 16."

"Precisely, and if you *ever* send me a gift like that again, perhaps I'll redecorate an entire wing of the palace. It's in dire need of natural lighting."

The emperor's face shifted a deep scarlet, and he murmured something incomprehensible beneath his breath.

The empress cleared her throat. "Have you perchance started making plans for your mating ceremony?" She glanced between Autumn and Dante.

Before Autumn could blink again, the emperor ripped the table off the ground and smashed it into the wall with a *BOOM.*

The empress and her daughter screamed. Servants huddled, covering their heads as food and drink sprayed everywhere, dripping in splotches all over the floor and walls.

Dante's father sprang to his feet and lunged toward the empress when Dante caught his hands and jerked them behind his back. He held them steady.

"Leave," Dante said. "Quit embarrassing yourself more than you already have." The emperor spat on the floor and stormed toward the exit, cape rippling in a crimson wave behind him.

The emperor suddenly halted and turned around. "We don't have time for this nonsense. Valdez has summoned us."

And just like that, before breakfast had even started, it was over.

Fourteen

"WHAT WAS THAT ABOUT?" Autumn scurried beside Dante through the hallway, as he strode onward in silence. It took her legs four steps to match a single one of his strides. "And who's Valdez?"

"It's a story for another time," he stopped for a moment and rested his black-gloved palm on her shoulder. She promptly shrugged it off.

"I'm sorry you had to bear witness to that. I can only imagine what you think of my family. I must admit, I'm rather embarrassed by my father's behavior."

The sudden outburst, oddly enough, *didn't* have an impact on her perception of the royal family. It confirmed it.

His father was insensitive and cruel, his sister was a snot, and the empress she somehow pitied. It seemed the empress couldn't do *anything* right. The bruises on her arm were infuriating.

But Dante—she despised him more than any of them. He pretended to love her, pretended to care. Meanwhile, he was a monster holding her against her will, preventing her from going back home and seeing her family.

* * *

They arrived back at her bedroom door. Her short taste of freedom had concluded. On either side of the frame stood four towering guards cloaked in obsidian armor. They held metallic rocket launchers in their hands, with their faces helmeted.

She exhaled. "Why are they here?"

"For your protection," Dante keyed in the code to her room. The scanner beeped as he pressed his thumb to the glass, and they were permitted access.

"When do I get the code to my own room?"

"In due time." The door slid open, and he guided her inside. "I'll come to collect you in a few hours after my council meeting is over. If you like, I can give you a personal tour of the palace and the grounds so you can become acquainted," he paused. "Under no circumstances are you to leave your room without me. It's not safe."

He reiterated his orders to the guards.

She folded her arms. "This sounds a lot like prison to me."

"You're as free as can be but you don't even realize it," his lips flickered. "If you want to see what a real prison looks like I'll take you to Joule, one of our prison planets."

A shudder trickled down her spine. "No thanks, I'll pass."

He shrugged then grinned. "Try not to miss me too much," he turned on his heel and left. The purple cape attached to his fine-tuned body disappeared through the sliding doorway.

She was alone again, completely and utterly alone.

Her vision clouded as she ran and threw herself onto the bed. She buried her face in a pillow. She sobbed and sobbed until her eyes burned and the muscles of her abdomen ached. Vomit flowed all over the floor in a puddle of lumps and undigested fruit. So much for breakfast.

* * *

More than an hour had passed, and she lay sprawled across her comforter, cheeks streaked wet with salty tears.

She glanced through the window. It was beautiful outside. Beyond beautiful. The twin suns blazed and not a cloud could be seen in the clear blue sky.

She ambled to the balcony and admired the massive cityscape of Giarldinia.

If only she could have some time to herself. She needed time away from Dante. Time to think, time to breathe, and time to learn the layout of the palace solo and plan her escape.

Autumn wanted to wander the gardens below. They smelled of lavender and reminded her of the life she lost on Earth.

The gardens beckoned to her, unlike the cold beautiful room of her prison cell.

Although the bedroom door was heavily guarded, Dante had failed to consider the balcony. It hung a mere two stories from the ground. For all the superior intelligence he boasted, this sure was an easy mistake to prevent.

Tiptoeing on the balls of her feet, she quietly made her way to the bed and ripped up the sheets the twin maids had neatly tucked and folded for her.

She crawled on her hands and knees and knotted the smooth cloth creating a rope. She tugged, pulled, and bit down with her teeth to tighten it, then tested its sturdiness and threw it over the side of the balcony.

It dangled a few feet from the ground. She fastened one end to the rail and tugged it taut. *Good enough.* At this point she was willing to try any means of escape, and the drop wasn't much higher than her bedroom window back on Earth.

Before she left, she grabbed a paperback and tucked it into

her back jeans pocket. *A little reading might make me feel better*. Reading was the cure for everything.

She hopped over the wall of the balcony, doing her best not to look at the ground. She shimmied down the makeshift rope, bit by bit, careful not to look.

Relief flooded through her limbs when her sneakers finally connected with the cool, cobalt grass.

Up close, the garden was more magnificent than what she'd seen from the balcony. Oversized butterflies glided gracefully on the warm breeze. Dragonflies buzzed through the air while fist-sized lady bugs crawled around her feet.

The flowers stood a foot taller than her with thick, bristled stalks.

In the center of the trees, through the wildflowers and shrubs, sat an opalescent fountain decorated with swirls, waves, and stars. Beside it was the bed of flowers Dante had "redecorated." For what reason, she could only imagine.

She ambled over. took a seat, and read. The steady trickling of the water soothed her anxious mind and transported her into the pages of her story.

* * *

She wished she had her smartphone so she knew how much time had passed. Judging by the high placement of the burning twin suns in the sky, it looked to be early afternoon.

A pair of footsteps approached, followed by laughter. She was so immersed in the pages of her book; she didn't bother to glance up. Two warm bodies sat beside her on the fountain. The hairs on the back of her next stood at perfect attention. She could scarcely breathe.

When she finally mustered the courage to look, she saw two handsome well-built guys about her age. Maybe a little bit older. It didn't surprise her. Most everyone on Surge had been pleasing to look at. It was kind of weird.

The men wore navy bodysuits. The first had skin hued a dark shade of blue with umber-brown plaits affixed to his scalp, while the second had pale-blue skin with silver hair and hazel eyes.

They spoke among themselves, when suddenly they stopped. She held her breath and continued to read, heart pounding so hard she was dizzy.

"Who gave you permission to sit here idling?" The silver-haired man traced his thumb around her lips.

She shuddered and moved away. "Keep your disgusting hands off me."

"Don't get fresh with me girl, unless you'd like for me to get fresh back," he winked and ran his hand up her thigh.

"Don't touch me," she smacked his arm as hard as she could with her book and the two guys chuckled.

"Do you know what the punishment is for laying your filthy hybrid hands on an upperclassman?" the dark-skinned man interjected. "Death, unless—"

"You can persuade us not to," the other man licked his blue lips. "I know where I'd like for you to begin."

"Excuse me," she came to a shaking stand and placed a hand on her hip. The men snickered. "First of all, I'm not a hybrid or whatever you aliens call it. I'm a human. Second, I'm engaged to be married to Dante Martyne. That means I outrank you both by a thousand."

The men busted out laughing, slapping their thighs.

"The tailless wonder, you mean," silver hair chewed his lip. "You sure have a sense of humor on you, girl. What would the crown prince possibly want with the likes of you?"

Her eyes widened.

"I'm willing to bet you're a liar," silver hair came to a stand. "There's nothing I despise more than liars."

In a flash, her vision went dark in her right eye as a fist slammed into her face. Stars and shooting pain rattled through her skull. Her molars clamped onto her cheek, and she tasted thick, salty blood.

She cupped her pulsating eye with her palm and a second blow came to her nose. A crack thundered through her ears and a sharp sensation pierced her skull. More warm blood trickled down her lips and into her mouth. Vision narrowing, she wheezed.

"Get back to work, or better yet, run and tell your crown prince," the silver-haired man cracked his knuckles and his friend snorted.

Autumn turned and sprinted as fast as she could, traveling on pure adrenaline. Her heart pounded in her ringing ears.

Neither of the two men bothered to pursue her. They shrugged and carried on with their conversation as if nothing had happened.

Breath hissed through her nostrils, causing warm, thick blood to pool over the collar of her shirt. Blinding pain ripped through her face, crashing against her skull.

She passed men and women strolling the expansive palace grounds. *No one was phased, and no one bothered to ask if she needed help.* They were isolated in their own pretentious worlds.

Her vision blurred as she ran toward the main entrance of the palace. On her way inside, she stumbled upon the twin maids. They lugged heavy metal baskets of laundry, but when they looked her way, the containers fell to the ground, bodysuits and gowns spilling everywhere.

"Oh gods, what happened to you, Lady Autumn?" One of the maids ran her long fingers over her busted nose, it sang in pain. She flinched but didn't respond.

"Come on, we'll get you cleaned up."

They led her inside and everyone glanced before looking

away. *What kind of place is this where nobody cares for anyone else's wellbeing?* This *never* would've happened back on Earth.

She followed them into a bathroom with marble flooring and golden sinks. She finally caught a glimpse of her horrifying state. Her right eye was black and blue, sealed shut like a golf ball. Her nose sat askew on her face. She wasn't sure she'd broken it before, but now she was certain.

Exercising great care, the maids took damp cloths and cleaned her face and shirt. Autumn made every effort not to strain her muscles as they applied ice to ease the swelling. But still, something wasn't right.

"Thank you," she coughed, another dizzy spell creeping through her head. "What are your names? I feel weird calling you maid all the time."

"The two women glanced at each other. "Nobody from the palace has ever bothered to ask us what our names are before. Here we're known as 562 and 563," they paused. "But since you did, I'm Emblem and she's Allegoria."

"Nice to meet you," Autumn winced and extended a hand. They reluctantly shook it, appearing confused by the gesture. "Thank you again for helping me."

They nodded.

"You should get back to your chambers and rest." Allegoria ushered her to the door. She couldn't walk a straight line. A headache roared through her temples.

As they exited the washroom, she heard a familiar cocky laugh.

Crap. Her entire body went rigid.

Dante stood at the foot of the main split stairwell speaking to a group of onyx-clothed associates.

It was at that moment she put two and two together. The blue-skinned Elattions who wore varying colors occupied the upper class, while everyone else who appeared human or hybrid, and dressed in light gray, were the lower.

Her eyes fell upon her heather-gray shirt. That's why the men assumed she was a servant. That's why Dante asked her to change. She thought he was just being rude.

She stared for a moment too long and met Dante's amber gaze, then whirled around, concealing herself.

It was too late, he'd spotted her. Emblem and Allegoria tensed and fell into deep curtsies as he approached. Their white-blonde hair shifted against their necks as they stood up again.

Dante glanced at Emblem and Allegoria. Like frightened mice, they trembled and stared at his feet.

"Why didn't you wait in your room? I told you I would come get you when I was done," he said. "How did you get past the guards?"

"Autumn?" he repeated when she didn't respond. "Autumn?"

Her thoughts slowed to a crawl as she struggled to breathe. He placed his hand onto her shoulder, turning her around while she kept the ice pack pressed against her face.

His eyes flickered with burning hot rage as he removed the pack from her skin.

"You're injured," he gently brushed his fingertips over her swollen eye and crushed nose. She winced, sleep setting in. "How did this happen?"

She proceeded to tell him how she hated being confined to her room and how she knotted her bed sheets together and climbed from the balcony to explore the garden and palace grounds below. Then she was attacked.

As he listened to her claims, a sharp incline of energy zapped through the air.

The marble floor beneath their feet quaked and a cold sweat beaded against her brow. Her wheezing breaths grew shallow.

Smack dead in the middle of their conversation, Leyla

leisurely sauntered by. Her knee-high go-go boots clicked against the floor and a white feather fan fluttered against her face.

"What happened to you?" The fan partially concealed her lips. "You look even more hideous than usual; I didn't think it was possible."

"She was attacked. *Leave*," Dante warned.

"How unfortunate," Leyla pouted her full pink lips.

Dante's hand rested against Autumn's back as he led her toward the entrance. She was too nauseous and lightheaded to protest.

"Show me who did this to you. I'd look through your memories, but I don't want to risk hurting you in this condition."

"Oh, this is going to be good," Leyla brushed a stray lash from her cheek.

"Wait, no, I can't," Autumn looked away. "I can't let you hurt anyone else because of me."

"Don't worry, I'm just going to give them a good *talking* to."

She nodded reluctantly.

As he led her back to the garden, a frenzy began. Drones of courtiers followed them including his annoying younger sister. Autumn could barely walk. Her steps were shaky at best, and her vision narrowed and blurred at the corners.

Fifteen

AUTUMN STOPPED a hundred feet or so from the fountain with Dante. Although she had vision in only one eye, she was able to point out the two guys in moments.

She could never forget the douchebag faces of the men who threatened and hurt her.

She pressed the pack of ice against her skin. "That's them."

They sat smiling and joking amongst themselves without a care in the world.

"You're certain?"

"Yes," she flinched from that pain that zapped through her skull. "If I remember correctly, they mentioned something else too, about your tail—"

She couldn't help but wonder again *where* his tail went and for *how long* it'd been missing.

Without word or warning, Dante strode over as swift and nimble as the night. His royal-purple cape rippled with fury in the hot afternoon breeze.

The deep-blue-skinned man's jaw dropped as he laid his eyes on him. Before his friend could turn, Dante latched a hand onto the back of his silver hair and shoved him face-first into the fountain. His limbs kicked and splayed as Dante held him underwater for almost a minute.

Autumn gasped as Dante yanked him out, silver hair drenched and matted against his face. Water spewed from his vile mouth, and he fell to his knees and gagged. Dante then dragged him across the gravel by his collar and threw him at her feet, knelt and ripped him up by his hair.

"Is this your handiwork, Bryce?" Dante gestured at her face.

Bryce trembled as he beheld Autumn. She maintained her composure.

"Your Imperial Highness, please, have mercy. I didn't realize this lower—" he stopped himself. "Girl was of such great importance to you. I mistook her for a hybrid servant."

"You're a liar," she said coolly. "I told you Dante and I are together."

For a moment, she could've sworn Dante's cheeks flushed before his expression straightened again. He dragged Bryce kicking and screaming back over to the fountain.

Everyone gasped, and onlookers peeked their heads outside of the tinted crystal windows of the palace.

Dante wrenched Bryce's jaw open to capacity and positioned his mouth over the lip of the opalescent fountain. With one swift kick he rammed his boot into the back of his head.

Bryce shrieked as his teeth crunched and popped out of his mouth. Ruby blood splattered all over his navy uniform.

"Pretty good for a tailless wonder, huh?" Dante chuckled then folded his arms. "Your move. Fight me."

When Bryce whimpered and refused to stand, he grabbed him by his gloved hand and threw him into the air. A crackling ball of fire ripped from his palm and engulfed Bryce whole. He screamed as his charred body disintegrated before it hit the ground. Black dust blew through the breeze.

The second guy sputtered backwards and fled into the air with his superhuman abilities.

"Leaving me so soon, Farrow?" Dante shouted.

He soared after Farrow and elbowed him in the gut mid-air. Farrow tumbled into the opalescent fountain. Water and debris sprayed everywhere, soaking the crowd, including Autumn.

Dante knelt into the fountain and fished him out by his sopping wet plaits.

"Please, your Imperial Highness, please! I didn't do anything," Farrow shook violently.

"Well, that's just the point now, isn't it? You *didn't* do anything. You sat back and let her suffer."

He lit a massive flame in his hand and Farrow screamed as he suffered the same fate as his friend.

Autumn trembled from head to toe. She fell to her knees and vomited up her guts. The world spun uncontrollably.

Spectators ambled away, satisfied with the conclusion of the fight. The show was over, and they were off to find a different source of amusement.

He approached her and bent down to help. "Sorry I couldn't keep my promise."

Autumn tried to come to a stand, but she was too weak. Her body screamed in silent agony. With heavy eyelids, she collapsed on the ground, and everything went dark.

Sixteen

WHAT DOES *Dante need from me?*

Armienti exhaled as he laid in bed checking the messages on his communicator. Temporary comfort slumbered in his arms in the form of an emerald-green skinned escort. The winding strands of her red hair tickled his cheek. The bright light from the twin suns illuminated his darkened chambers through the open balcony doors.

His cousin had no problem pestering him, and he was *expected* to be at his beck and call.

However, he'd *failed* to send him and his brother invitations to the welcome home banquet organized by their stepmother.

It figured.

The curse of being a lesser prince. If only he'd been next in line for the crown instead of his cousin, then he'd have gotten the respect he deserved.

He sighed, rolling over in bed. As he sat up, he brushed a hand through his gilded locks.

Over a year had passed since they'd last spoken. Since Keyserike's demise. He'd been extra careful to avoid him for the entirety of the trip home. Not that Dante noticed, he was too preoccupied with the love of his life.

Dante always had a *unique* way of handling himself, but to extinguish half the crew and endanger everyone in the realm over a girl? Unfathomable. Armienti swallowed hard.

But still, he couldn't help but agree that Autumn was special. Maybe even more than special.

Dante, on the other hand, was a reckless maniac.

His communicator continued to buzz. Dante. He sighed. He'd make him wait just a little bit longer. *He deserves to wait for once.*

* * *

Dante paced the floor of the medical ward as Autumn was lowered into a rejuvenation tank, filled with blue, bubbling liquid. Medics strapped an oxygen mask to her face.

The rosiness drained from her cheeks. Her skin was cold and clammy and gray.

She remained conscious but barely.

Her skull had been cracked. Loose remnants of bone slid beneath her hair as her brain hemorrhaged.

What a fool he was for not noticing earlier. All he saw was her broken nose, blackened eye, and *red*. He'd let his anger and desire for revenge get the best of him.

Again.

Poor delicate human. It was all his fault for bringing her here in the first place. He deserved to die, not her.

Not a day had passed on Surge, and he'd failed to protect her.

Dante slammed his fist into the floor, the metallic tiles shifting beneath his might. Where was Armienti? An hour was far too long. He should've been there already. He messaged him again, finger sliding over the glass of his communicator. His forehead pulsated. Armienti wasn't off planet.

He struggled to maintain his composure as servants swarmed around the room, bringing fresh pillows and linens to make her more comfortable in case—

No, he couldn't allow himself to think that way.

The two useless maids he assigned to Autumn were present. He couldn't pinpoint why he hated them but deep in his gut, he did.

A hole hollowed in his chest. Why couldn't she have waited for him to get back from his council meeting? He would've gladly taken her to see the garden, the palace, and then some.

A curious brown eye peered from beyond the doorway, followed by full pink pouting lips.

Leyla strode into the medical ward, fanning her face with her obnoxious feather fan. Her long lashes grazed her prominent cheekbones.

"Will she die?" Leyla's eyes flickered to the rejuvenation tank then met his.

"Leave," he crossed his arms.

"I'm sure if the time comes, Father will give her a proper burial. Her body will be cast into space—"

"I said leave," he roared.

The entire room went pitch silent. Leyla stumbled backwards, heels scraping, eyes wide.

"Sorry."

Her cheeks turned red as she fled the room.

He shook his head, in no mood for Leyla's nonsense. *Why did she hate Autumn so much? Almost as much as his father did?*

When he looked at the door again, he beheld Armienti. He ambled into the room; golden hair tousled to perfection. A lazy smile crept across his pretty face. He reeked of a nameless female.

"How goes it cousin?" He grinned.

"What took you so long?" Dante hissed. "I summoned you over an hour ago."

"I was busy, if you know what I mean," Armienti winked, a lip-shaped bruise blooming along his throat. His cousin traipsed over and stopped dead when he beheld Autumn in the rejuvenation tank. Her eyes were closed, breathing and heart rate slowing.

"Holy shit," Armienti's cocky grin faded.

"Her brain is hemorrhaging."

"Good gods, how did this happen?"

"There's no time to answer questions. She's too weak and hasn't much longer to live. Everyone, get out." He waved a hand, dismissing the servants and medical attendants.

Everyone made their leave, and Dante shut the air-tight door.

"I knew this was a terrible idea," Armienti shook his head. "Humans are not equipped for deep space."

"If I didn't take her, her planet would've been compromised."

Armienti nodded, arms folded.

"Heal her." As the words left his mouth, he experienced a deep-rooted pang of jealousy that his cousin possessed such a gift.

"I—"

"Heal her," Dante tried his best to conceal the growing panic in his voice, but it seeped out regardless.

"I can try, but I've never healed a human before."

"Just heal her, please. She'll never recover at this rate."

Please, a word he used on the rarest of occasions. It was the closest his cousin would get to hearing him begging. Although, at that moment, he would've begged.

Armienti stopped the rejuvenation tank and the door opened. He reached his hands into the blue liquid and massaged his fingertips against her temples. They glowed as he transferred his life energy to her.

Dante watched in silence and awe as Armienti used one of his natural-born gifts. Once again, envy burned him to the core. Envy that his cousin could use his abilities to heal others, when he'd been cursed with the ability to destroy.

PART TWO

Diode

Seventeen

THE HUM of the central air conditioning made for the most relaxing sleep. Autumn rolled in the cool crispness of her sheets and stretched her weary limbs. Gold, purple, and orange rays of morning sunlight peeked through her blinds. She smelled chocolate chip pancakes sizzling on the griddle.

She stretched and sat up in bed. Her black metal Eiffel Tower lamp graced her night table. Her eighteen snow globes swirled on the shelf beside her closet, an arrangement of beautiful watery scenes.

Voices echoed from downstairs. Not just her dad's but the lyrical voice of her mom.

She sprinted downstairs, almost tripping and missing a step. Excitement warmed her chest.

Mom—Mom's here.

Autumn's mom sat at the kitchen table, cross-legged, sipping coffee with her dad. Her highlighted curls topped her head in a bun. Her chestnut eyes sparkled.

Autumn's heart skidded—

Her mom wore a hoodie and leggings in preparation for her morning run.

"Mom," she jumped into her arms, almost knocking her off the seat.

"Mija, what's gotten into you?" Her mom embraced her. Autumn held onto her for dear life and squeezed her with all her might.

"I don't want you to go. Please stay—please stay with me." A violent burst of tears streamed down her cheeks.

Her mom took a deep sip of her beverage. "Unfortunately, that isn't how this works."

"But it's dangerous, please don't go," she pleaded.

"I'll be back in twenty minutes. I'm only jogging up Lakes Road," her mom reassured her.

Her parents kissed and her mom walked to the front door, ignoring her warning.

"Mom, listen to me."

As Autumn reached the door, it closed and locked in her face. She grabbed the knob and tugged and pulled with all her might, but it was no use.

She slid onto the hardwood floor, and bitter tears ran down her cheeks.

A smoke alarm screeched. Thick black smoke flowed overhead. She choked,

feet twisting, as she jumped up and sprinted to the kitchen to help her dad.

He flipped pancakes on the stove at a furious rate, silver spatula in hand. Orange and purple flames crackled and blazed.

"Dad," she grabbed his arm. "Dad, we have to go right now."

When he turned around, his tongue flicked from his mouth and wrapped around her left wrist, singing through flesh and bone. Blood-red slits crossed his eight eyes. Brianna's severed head fried in the pan, sinew sizzling. Autumn's doppelganger who went missing. Her black vacant eyes shot open, and her mouth moved, jaw cracking.

"I know there's something going on between you and Caleb."

* * *

Autumn woke in the dead of night. Her tank top and satin cloud shorts were drenched with sweat. When she rolled, she collided with a gently heaving body.

Dante.

Why is he in my bed? Her forehead pulsated.

A nightmare. Her insides wracked and twisted. Her stomach bubbled over with anxiety. She was still on Surge. A loud gasp escaped her lips and he blinked. His amber eyes glowed, watching her.

She backed up. *Wow, he's close.* It was like her vision was magnified.

"How are you feeling?" He placed his palm over her forehead. He grazed his fingers against her temples with the lightest touch.

Her bones no longer screeched in agony.

She ignored his questions, climbed out of bed, and walked to the bathroom. She squinted as the lights came on. When she glanced into the mirror, the deep black and blue swelling around her eye had vanished. Her nose sat straight rather than twisted.

"How did I—what happened? How long have I been asleep?"

"Seven days," he ran a hand through his midnight hair, pale-blue muscles shimmering. "I stayed with you the entire time. I apologize. I wanted to make sure you were all right."

Seven days, her jaw dropped. An entire week. *Unfreaking-believable.*

She hugged her stomach as it gurgled.

"Is there anything to eat around here?" She set aside her annoyance over the fact that she was speaking to him *inside* of her room. His shirt was off, he was barefoot, and he wore nothing but a pair of black spandex shorts. He was way too comfortable.

He slid his communicator out of his back pocket. After tapping the screen, in a matter of moments, Emblem and Allegoria materialized.

Their hair was tucked in kerchiefs, and they carried steaming silver trays.

"Thank you," Autumn said as they placed the food on the table, curtsied, and vanished into the night.

Her mouth salivated. She flung open the tray and gobbled entire mouthfuls of vegetables, cheeses, fruit, and warm bread. She grabbed a glass of water and chugged it.

After she consumed the first platter, she reached for the second.

Her fingers trembled. "Are you going to eat that?"

Dante shook his head and gestured for her to continue. By the time she finished, her stomach was filled to maximum capacity.

"Curious," he muttered, before she collapsed on the bed in a food coma.

* * *

The following morning, Dante had gone. *Thank goodness.* To think he'd been watching her for the last week or so.

She blinked hard as the vibrant colors spilling through the French doors of her balcony stung her pupils.

Two shadows swayed in the corner of her room. Emblem and Allegoria.

Autumn rushed over and gave them each a hug. Their muscles tightened beneath her embrace.

"Thank you again for helping me."

Emblem pulled away. "You're very welcome, Lady Autumn."

"No, seriously," she paused. "Nobody else batted an eye."

"Lady—"

"You don't have to call me that, really. Autumn is fine," she reassured them again.

They nodded and led her to the bathroom where a steaming-hot bubble bath awaited. She was stripped, tossed in, and bathed. She sat there; mouth twisted to the side. Her fists balled as she grew more and more agitated by the minute. Once again, she was not permitted to bathe alone in the privacy of her own room.

She bit her cheeks, flicking the water with her finger, unable to *deal*. If she had a working smartphone, she would've texted Lauren and Ellie to complain. How she missed them.

After *bath time,* which was now a group event, she'd come to find her backpack was missing and her belongings had been raided. *Dammit.* Everything was gone, including her paperbacks.

"Where the heck is my stuff?" She crawled on all fours searching frantically under her bed.

Fortunately, her snow globes were on the table. But where were her clothes and books?

Emblem pointed to a door in the corner of the room. A door she'd never bothered to look behind. Inside hung countless tulle gowns of bone, teal, rosewood, and magenta, as well as diamond encrusted and bejeweled bodices. A row of full-body space leotards in various hues with angular glitter stripes hung beside them.

Oh no, no, no, no. This was *all* wrong. Crap, she was going to look as ridiculous as Leyla and the empress.

She reached for a dress.

"The ladies of the court wear bodysuits by day, and dresses are reserved for feasts and special events," Allegoria said.

"The empress, however, wears whatever she likes," Emblem added.

This could *not* be happening. She wanted her jeans and t-shirts, not a parade of strange alien costumes.

Left with no other choice, she picked the least offensive outfit. An obsidian bodysuit with a silver stripe.

After being strapped inside, she was pleasantly surprised at how light and breathable the material was against her skin. She stepped into a pair of knee-high go-go boots and her hair was sprayed with silver glitter.

She raced out of her bedroom, ready to *strangle* Dante. He had to be responsible.

She gasped as she was greeted by a dozen faceless onyx-clothed guards. They mingled along the crimson carpet like shadows.

"Where's Dante?" Her throat tightened, hands fidgeting behind her back.

"Which one, my lady?"

Crap, there was more than one? "Dante Martyne."

"The first or the second?"

His father's name must be Dante as well. "Um, the second, I think."

"He's in a council meeting."

She had no clue where that was but figured she could locate it with a little wandering. This time around, she planned to be more careful.

The sudden sharp shuffle of footsteps stormed behind her. When she stopped, they stopped. When she started walking again, they started again.

She whipped around with dizzying speed. "Are you following me?"

"We've been assigned to you as your personal guard. We're permitted to accompany you everywhere except for your chambers and the powder room."

She huffed. The lack of freedom in this place was suffocating. Dante had some major explaining to do, and she was sure he wouldn't like what she had to say.

Eighteen

THE ROYAL-PURPLE HALLS were crowded with well-dressed aliens. Women wore bodysuits in rich vibrant hues, hair spackled with bronze glitter. They curtsied, noticing her this time around. A complete one-eighty from last time.

Posers.

It reminded her of being around the popular crowd back at school, only she was the cool girl now. She bit back a smile at the refreshing change.

Not that she should care or anything.

She and her entourage arrived in an empty room on the first floor. It was vast and coated from wall to wall with crimson velvet carpeting.

Four steel thrones adorned with veins of bubbling red liquid sat atop a three-stepped dais. Her stomach twisted. Somehow the liquid reminded her of *blood*.

To the left of the monstrous seating arrangement was a door with neon green light streaming underneath.

The council room. From what she could detect, based on the shouting and table banging inside, a meeting was ongoing.

She raised a fist and pounded it against the door as hard as she could. She was going to make Dante pay.

When she raised her fist again, the door slid open. She was met face to face with thirty sets of vibrant eyes. Some gawked. Others were hungry with intent.

She opened her mouth to speak, when the light fizzled. Waves of electricity crackled from the ceiling. The emperor stood at the head of the room; eyes narrowed at her. His anger and hatred for her was apparent.

Dante strode out, cape billowing. The guards fell into waist-bent bows.

"You have some nerve," she hissed.

A lone cough echoed from inside the room. Dante glowered over his shoulder and led her away.

"You're displeased with me again. It seems I can do nothing right in your eyes. What have I done to offend you?"

She rolled her eyes. "Besides the obvious? What did you do with my clothes?"

"Oh, that," his lips twisted into a smile. "I treated you to a new wardrobe, one more in line with your rank. We'll be going off-planet soon. I've never heard a girl complain—"

"That wasn't your call to make," she crossed her arms. "You went through my things without my permission. The stuff I brought with me is irreplaceable. What do you mean we're going off-planet?"

He turned around and addressed the guards. "You're relieved for the time being." They bowed and walked away.

"Listen," he held her hands in his and she went rigid. "I want us to find a way to start over. I'm trying my hardest to be patient and understanding with you—"

"Well, you're selfish. You created this entire mess." She folded her arms and ambled through a door leading outside to a sunlit courtyard. It was empty, except for some stone benches between four white pillars. Servants silently swept the tiled floor, which displayed a mosaic of golden stars and swirls in a moonless sky.

She sat down and he took a seat beside her.

"How are you feeling, other than what I may or may not have done with your clothes?" He tucked a stray strand of hair behind her ear. "I was afraid I might lose you after what transpired."

"Fine, I guess," she glanced at her hand and the substantial amethyst snowflake-ring adorning her finger. "As good as I can be under the circumstances."

"I'm glad," he said. "I swear if anybody ever touches you again, I'll kill them."

It wasn't a lie. "Is that all you do, kill? And steal other people's planets?"

A soft chuckle reverberated from behind one of the columns. Leyla strode out wearing a grape and silver bodysuit. Her violet spackled hair glinted in the sunlight.

"You look well," Leyla's long lashes fanned her cheeks.

"Thanks," Autumn struggled not to roll her eyes.

"Foolish human, you really don't know anything do you?"

"Leyla," Dante warned.

"He hasn't been dubbed *Dante the Great Conqueror* for nothing," Leyla's lips coiled. "For him to arrive on a planet is the kiss of death."

Dante the Great Conqueror, Autumn silently mouthed. Her stomach churned with disgust.

Dante's amber eyes thinned to slits. "You'll answer for this later," he turned toward his sister. "Don't think this will go unpunished."

Leyla flinched and strutted off without another word, heels scraping against the tiles.

Autumn shot up from the bench, heels sliding across the freshly mopped mosaic. She was desperate to get away from him. Before she reached the center of the courtyard, Dante caught up with her, like he always did.

"Let me go," she screamed, flailing a heeled go-go boot at him.

The servants ceased their duties and watched the commotion.

"No, please, let me explain."

"I said, let me go!"

A loud crackling sound ripped across the sky. All four pillars crumbled to the ground. White dust and rubble sprayed. Dante leapt and shielded her from the debris, but the servants weren't so lucky.

Their bodies were crushed, limbs flailing. Oozing blood stained the white stone, seeping between the cracks.

"Why did you do that?" Autumn shrieked and pushed him away.

"I didn't do anything, I swear."

She ran over, trying to pull the servants from beneath the ruins, but they laid still.

She stared at him, trembling. "Who did this then, Keyserike?"

His eyes widened. "How do you know that name?"

"I—" her mind tripped and tumbled over itself. She wasn't sure why she blurted it out. The name had been whispered through her mind since the accident.

He smoothed a hand through his midnight hair. "You're delirious, my dear. Let's get you back inside. You need to rest. Your injuries have altered your mind."

He continued. "I promise, I'll get to the bottom of this."

Nineteen

AUTUMN SECLUDED herself in her room for the remainder of the day and night. For extra security, she barricaded the door with a table and chairs. She didn't want Emblem and Allegoria to bother her with baths and dresses and other *nonsense* she wanted no part of. Deaths had occurred.

She hoped Dante would get the hint as well.

Dante *the murderer, the liar*, and now, *the Great Conqueror*. Her gut twisted.

Deep down she knew she wasn't crazy. She'd heard that name somewhere before. Dante's reaction proved it. *Keyserike*.

Her mind drifted back to earlier that afternoon—those poor innocent servants. *Who would do such a terrible thing?* Tears violently streamed down her cheeks and adrenaline ripped through her body.

She needed somebody to confide in. She was lonelier than she'd ever been in her life.

The cushion beside her sank with the full weight of a body. Dante had teleported inside. She crossed her arms. "My door is locked for a reason."

"I need to talk to you. Hear me out."

"Did you find out what kind of monster killed those servants, *Dante the Great Conqueror?*" the words fired from her mouth.

"I had a feeling that was still bothering you," he ran a black-gloved hand through his raven hair. "And honestly, I don't blame you."

She walked toward the balcony, and he lingered close behind. The twin crescent moons cast a pale glow through the open doors. Giarldinia thrummed with life.

Fist-sized lightning bugs flitted through the garden. She rested her elbows against the balcony railing.

"I should've been the one to tell you, Leyla shouldn't have seized the opportunity from me."

"So, what stopped you?"

Deafening silence followed. *He's keeping more secrets. What else is new?*

She stared at him blankly; he was always hiding something. Back on Earth he lied to her about being an alien murderer, and in outer space his reputation preceded him.

"I'm involved in a business that I was hoping to have a discussion with you about after we were married, but as usual, my plans have been spoiled," he said finally.

Her eyes widened. "Why? Did you want to trick me into thinking you were somehow a good person? Because believe me, it didn't work," she paused. "What kind of business?"

"Um, well," he stuttered. "Along with my duties as crown prince, I'm expected to yield a certain number of planets per annum. It's a paid opportunity I've been involved in my entire life."

Her insides twisted to the point of inducing nausea. She could only imagine what happened to these planets and their poor inhabitants. What had almost happened to Earth.

"There are two types of planets that are widely sought

after," his voice fell into a dead tone. "Type Ones have something to offer us, whether it's a fleet of soldiers, riches, or natural resources. In this case, the inhabitants are permitted to occupy their worlds under a new jurisdiction. Their lives are generally unchanged. Type Twos however, or those planets that are perceived to be inferior, are enslaved and redeveloped to meet our needs."

Earth was a Type Two planet. All this time she was under the impression that it was a one-time deal. Like the aliens in the movies, always trying to conquer Earth for one reason or another. The bile rose in her gut.

"How many planets have you stolen?"

"A little over four thousand," his amber eyes glistened beneath the starlit sky. "But I'm set to inherit—*we're* set to inherit nine hundred and eighty of them," he corrected.

She slid to the ground, burying her hands in her palms, ready to bawl her eyes out for all the suffering he'd caused.

"Tell me what you're thinking," he knelt before her. "Unfortunately, I don't have the ability to read minds, only memories."

"Earth is safe right?" she finally asked. Although it was somewhat selfish, Earth was the only planet she truly cared about. Her friends. Her family. Her home world.

She tensed as he sat beside her. "I swear to you, on everything I hold sacred in this life, that your planet is safe. Like I told you before, think of it in human terms as a wedding gift from me to you."

She sucked in a deep shuddering breath, terrified and overwhelmed all at once.

"Thank you," was all she could think to say. She paused after doing a quick tally in her head. "What happens to the remainder of the planets if you're only keeping nine hundred and eighty of them?"

"You'll find out soon enough."

Twenty

THE FOLLOWING MORNING, all Autumn could think about were the planets that Dante had amassed over the years.

Four thousand planets. The insane figure made her head spin off its axis. The suffering he caused was unfathomable.

On the other hand, as horrible as it was, she was grateful that Earth was in the clear. Her friends and family were safe because of her sacrifice.

As she sat up in bed, smoothing the silken sheets beneath her palms, Emblem and Allegoria rustled in the corner of her room, furiously stuffing her dresses and bodysuits into a trunk.

"Wonderful, you're awake," Emblem stood up and smiled. "We've drawn a bath for you. After that, we need to be on our way."

"Where are we going?"

"Universe 16, the master has a surprise for you."

Surprise? A vein twitched against her forehead. Not *another* surprise. If she never lived to see a surprise again, it would be too soon. Crap.

She nodded reluctantly. After being bathed and clothed in a bodysuit the ripe shade of eggplant with a silver stripe, she was ready for the trip.

"Aren't you beautiful, a vision and a dream."

Autumn whipped around and Dante stood there, arms crossed. No warning or anything. He admired her, eyes gently grazing over her body. As much as she didn't want to admit, she couldn't help but stare back. He was handsome in his uniform.

Emblem and Allegoria averted their eyes to the floor.

"Where are we going?" She placed a hand on her hip.

"It's a surprise."

Dante offered her his arm and she rolled her eyes, reluctantly taking it. Emblem and Allegoria struggled to lug her trunk, tugging on their hands and knees. They passed her personal legion of guards, lingering in the hallway like shadows, and Autumn turned, repulsed by everyone's complete and total lack of concern for the hybrids.

"Can somebody please help them?"

The guards stared at her, unmoving, and looked to Dante for direction.

"Do as she says," Dante flicked his wrist at the maids wrestling with her belongings on the floor. "Don't let me catch you questioning her judgment again."

The guards tensed and hauled the trunk over their shoulders. Autumn huffed, as she could only imagine what Dante had in store for her that would require such an extensive change of clothing.

* * *

When they arrived on the rooftop, the early morning sky glittered with hundreds of jewel-toned aircrafts. Cubes, triangles, and saucers shimmered in the sunlight.

In the center was a circular spacecraft that was monstrous in size compared to all the others.

Out front, Princess Leyla cooled her devastatingly beautiful face with a magenta feather fan tipped with diamond encrusted swirls. Silver shimmered through the strands of her hair like galaxy dust. Her eyes rolled as she beheld Autumn, and she turned around, greeting her with her backside.

A greeting fit for a rude spoiled princess.

The empress flashed a small smile. She wore a burgundy bodysuit with a gold stripe that matched the gilded beehive atop her delicate head. Thankfully, the emperor was absent—the evil, rude, despicable man who loathed her without reason and who she despised in return.

Like father, like son, she supposed.

She did a double take. Ronan and Armienti lingered on the side lines. Boredom graced their faces. Armienti twirled a golden strand of hair around his finger and Ronan stared off into the distance. *How typical.*

She approached and pulled Armienti in for a hug. His back shifted beneath her embrace. When she pulled away, Dante placed his palm on her shoulder, making his presence known.

"To what do I owe this strange human greeting?" Armienti's golden lashes brushed the peaks of his cheekbones.

She pressed a glittered coil behind her ear. "Thank you for healing me. If it wasn't for you, I don't know where I'd be."

"Not a problem," Armienti muttered. "I'm glad I could be of service to you."

Dante huffed a breath. "All right, we should get going. We're going to be late."

Autumn waved goodbye as Dante ushered her away, mumbling something under his breath.

"What's wrong?"

"Nothing."

"Tell me," she insisted.

"I assure you, everything is okay," he squeezed out an unconvincing smile.

She rolled her eyes. *Sure.*

The interior of the ship was immaculate. Not a single soldier brawled in the hallway as they had done on Dante's ship that was stranded back on Earth. Instead, a sugary scent permeated the air. Autumn's stomach grumbled. She hadn't eaten yet. Her hunger had been insatiable since the accident.

Black carpets covered the floor, decorated with silver whirls resembling the cosmos. The walls were opalescent, creating a rainbow effect.

As she examined her new surroundings, Leyla strutted by, clipping Autumn's shin with the heel of her boot.

Ouch, she winced. Leyla's aim had been true. Again, she reminded her of Misty Beckett. Her bitchiness was unmatched.

"What's her deal?" She rubbed her palm against her skin, easing the sting. "I don't understand why she hates me so much."

Dante snorted. "She doesn't hate you. She needs to get to know you better. I'm positive that when she does, she'll love you as I love you."

Love. How could he claim to love her? Sure, she loved him back on Earth, but that was before she knew what he was capable of. How could she reconcile herself to love a monster, even if he was handsome to a fault *and* a crown prince? No, she could never forgive him.

When they entered the cockpit, there he was. The emperor harnessed into his seat. He glowered at her; steely amber eyes ripe with rage. A shiver trickled through her limbs.

Leyla fiddled with her sleek magenta communicator. A crooked smile swept across her full pink lips. "I smell something, Father. Do you smell it too?"

The empress glided in gracefully and took a seat beside her daughter.

"What's that?" The emperor tore his eyes away from Autumn.

Leyla peeked up from her device. "I smell the foul scent of lower life-form. Sure, you can pretty one up in dresses and finery, but underneath it all, she's no different. Little more than a beast. You might as well mate yourself to an animal, brother."

Leyla's wide grin faded as her communicator melted in her hands all over her gloves and lap. She gasped. Dante raised a palm and swept her into the air.

"This time you've gone too far, sister. This is two strikes now."

Leyla trembled wide-eyed, unable to move. "No wait, Dante, I was joking around."

He folded his arms, stretching his feet up onto the seat. "It didn't sound like you were joking to me. Apologize."

"I'm sorry."

"Not to me, to her."

"I'm sorry, Autumn."

"Good." He set her down and Leyla scrambled back to her seat, cheeks shifting red. Liquid metal clung to her clothes.

"In addition, upon our arrival you owe me five hundred pushups."

Leyla's mouth fell open. "Five hundred? That's not fair. I haven't been training recently."

"I can tell, you're getting out of practice," he winked.

Autumn took a seat, biting her cheeks. It took every ounce of energy she could muster not to grin.

Twenty-One

LEYLA DIDN'T SO MUCH as offer Dante a passing glance. She silently picked at her gloves where he'd melted her communicator.

He shook his head. He'd done just enough to shut her up. A warning, which served its purpose. But still, he had snapped.

The way she spoke to Autumn made his blood boil with rage. Although, he couldn't blame her. Leyla was a victim of her surroundings, as was he. It was common knowledge that lower life-forms faced discrimination not only in their world but throughout the 24 Universes.

With Autumn's human features, she bore a striking resemblance to the hybrids on his planet. It was an easy mistake to make, but he no longer had the tolerance for anyone disrespecting her.

He wasn't his father by any stretch of the imagination. He never snapped without cause. His stomach knotted at the comparison. He'd never be like his father, the coward.

Dante drifted from his thoughts and suddenly grew weary of the silent hum of space travel. She stared out the window daydreaming. *What could she possibly be thinking?* Her silent hatred for him impaled his heart like a spike.

After the ship stilled and gravity stabilized, he unbuckled her harness. He offered her his hand, pulse quickening as she took it.

He stared into her moonlit eyes, tempted to crush her lips with his. But here was neither the time nor the place.

The emperor strode from the cabin, head held high, and chest puffed out. His crimson cape flowed over his shoulders in a blood-soaked wave.

Leyla followed in silence, her arms crossed. His mother trailed her, gilded beehive sparkling.

"Are you okay?" He finally broke the deafening silence. "Leyla often speaks before she thinks. I'm sorry for what she said. She has no clue what she's talking about."

Autumn nodded slowly. "Where are we, and what's this all about?"

"We're on planet Diode located in the first sector of Universe 16," he paused. "And it's come to my attention that your name day has passed twice with no recognition."

Her features softened. "You knew?"

"I did," he stared at his boots before meeting her gaze. "And I plan to make it up to you tenfold."

Her cheeks blossomed. That was the first reason for their visit. He dreaded the second reason more than anything in the universes.

* * *

The smooth sand of Diode was the whitest she'd ever seen. It extended for miles and miles in every direction, rolling and rising in porcelain hills.

The sky was the shade of misty amethyst. So purple, she couldn't comprehend, couldn't believe it was real. She'd never seen anything like it before. Such brilliance and clarity. Such utter magnificence.

Three fiery suns beamed down from overhead with such intensity that she lifted her arm to smear the beading sweat from her brow. The soles of her boots cooked.

Jewel-tone spaceships landed, followed by the cyclical swirl of sand. The entire court accompanied them.

"Don't think for one second I'm here to celebrate the birth of your filthy whore." The emperor's mouth fell into a tight flat line. "I'm only here because I must be. This was not by choice."

"I believe the word you're searching for is crown princess." Dante flashed a taunting smile. "You should practice using it more."

The emperor growled and balled his fists at his sides.

Dante continued. "And you know what, Father? There isn't a damn thing you can do about it. Go ahead and tell me I'm wrong—"

The empress remained quiet; eyes averted to the ground. Leyla stood there silently, still picking bits of metal off her gloves.

As Autumn blinked, the emperor leapt into the sky, flying in the direction of their destination, until he was nothing more than a microscopic speck, glinting in the sun.

Autumn's kneecaps knocked together. She smoothed her palms over her face and sucked in a deep shuddering breath. Dante swept her into his arms and flew up, up, *up*, high into the sky. Strands of her glittered hair collided with the wind. Tears streaked her cheeks from the speed he traveled.

Her gut wrenched. She hated it. *All of it.* Being the center of attention and the catalyst of confrontation. For the life of her, she couldn't understand why Dante would ruin his relationship with his family to keep her here.

They soon approached a city floating in the sky. It wasn't

high-tech like Surge, but ancient. Crystal pillars and arches graced the front of every building. Gardens spilled with flowers and vines. Pink sparkling water flowed through fountains.

In the distance sat a palace, or at least Autumn assumed it was a palace based on its sheer magnitude and the company she kept. It was shaped like a giant white cube and filled with hundreds of tiny archways.

They landed in a garden lined with rich cobalt grass, surrounded by trellises and alabaster statues of monsters and gargoyles with ragged, vampire bat wings. Their almond-shaped eyes were black as death and stared at her in the most penetrating way.

Then, one blinked.

Twenty-Two

AUTUMN'S HEART came to a standstill as one of the statues approached her. The figure was tall and lean with chalk-white skin. Jagged vampire bat wings sprouted from its muscular back and dragged against the gravel. The creature blinked its slanted black eyes and sent her grabbing for Dante's hand. *Holy crap.* The statues were alive.

With inhuman grace, it fell to one knee. The surrounding alien creatures followed suit, bowing their hairless heads in silence. A sign of submission.

Dante muttered something in yet another strange language, filled with clicks and drags of his tongue. This time she didn't understand a word he said. She still had no clue how she was able to speak fluent Ivarkian.

The creatures rose and gestured for them to follow. She held onto Dante so tight her knuckles paled.

They handed her bouquet after bouquet of multi-hued wildflowers. From what she could tell, they were female, based on the curves of their hips and the roundness of their breasts.

She thanked them in English, and they smiled at her.

"What are they saying?" Autumn shifted the richly hued flowers in her hands.

"They're graciously welcoming their master and mistress."

"Mistress?" She scowled.

Dante winked. "You'll get used to it."

"No, I won't," she swore underneath her breath. She was *nobody's* mistress.

She squinted as her eyes adjusted to the impossibly bright light of the Palace. Column after column opened out into the ancient city. A subtle warm breeze flowed from one end to the next, and the floor was tiled with milky blue, green, and white crystal.

Oversized seashells filled with white linen cushions were scattered around the rooms, occupied by inhabitants who dined and lounged.

"Sweetheart," Dante's mouth fell flat. "I have a bit of business to attend to before the festivities commence. I'm leaving you in the care of my mother and sister. I trust that you'll be all right in my absence."

No, she wasn't okay, but what choice did she have? Autumn folded her arms tightly across her chest.

"Leyla," he redirected his attention to his younger sister. "Behave yourself. I don't wish to hear reports indicating otherwise. I'm under enough stress."

Leyla nodded mechanically, but as soon as Dante strode off, her brown eyes thinned into cat-like slits.

"Do yourself a favor, human, and stay out of my way. If you're fortunate enough, you may survive your pathetic name day celebration."

Autumn rolled her eyes. A promise this would be a miserable stay.

Twenty-Three

THE BLOOD BOILED within Dante's veins as he made his way through the bright open halls of Gypsum Palace. He'd been summoned to report to his superior, Valdez Aventura, Dark-Star General and reigning empress of Universes 14, 15, 16, and 17. Second in command to the *Grand Supreme.*

"This shrew, making me come all the way out here," he grumbled as he strode. His hair brushed against the back of his neck. His mind was haunted by long forgotten memories.

To think *he* had to report to anyone at all—a future emperor in his own right—like he hadn't been on tour for the last three or so years, while she lounged and polished her manicured talons, benefiting from his hard work. *Just like the late General Keyserike.*

He clenched his fists at his sides, quivering with bottomless rage. A crown prince acting as an errand boy. He hocked a ball of warm saliva in his mouth and spit it on the ground as he rounded the corner and made his way outside to the back gardens. His cape swayed over his shoulders in the warm breeze.

His father had beaten him to her. *Drat.*

Dante chose to tread lightly, unable to imagine what'd been discussed in his absence. Hopefully not the state of Universe 1, as he'd much prefer to speak for himself on that matter, lest it get back to their master in undue time.

Valdez stood on the edge of a stone bench in shooting stance. She held a flexed golden bow and arrow. Her toned jade muscles went taut then slackened as she nocked a gilded arrow and sent it whizzing through the garden at lightning speed, and straight through the heart of a sprinting servant.

Snagged, mid-flight, the Zexian screamed and fell to her knees, scraping desperately, trying to remove the arrowhead from her alabaster chest cavity. It oozed with black blood.

Valdez laughed and sent another arrow straight through her cheek. She fell to the ground, drowning on her own fluids. A final arrow ripped through her tattered wing. She spun around on the balls of toes and jumped up and down, grinning.

"Your turn, Dante," she whipped around and tossed him the bow and arrow. Her long, seafoam braid dangled straight along her back between her jagged wings.

He could scarcely believe she heard him approaching. Valdez was no Elattion, but had the cold, calculating ears of a viper.

Dante grinned; the precise expression Valdez expected of him. Deep down his heart raced. He worried what Autumn would think if she could see him, killing someone for no reason.

He nocked an arrow and aimed it at a gardener weeding flowers. At the last second, he sent the arrow speeding by the gardener's ear, narrowly missing his presumed target.

"Forgive me, it's been a while."

"Somebody's out of practice, I see," Valdez chuckled. She came up behind him and aimed the weapon. Her long, polished fingers slid over his black-gloved hands. She rested her chin on his shoulder. She smelled of expensive bath oils. "Here, allow me."

She sent an arrow straight through the servant's throat. The man fell to his knees gurgling. A second one lodged in his ribcage.

"Nice shot," was all Dante could think to say as the light faded from the servant's eyes.

"Thanks, now let's get down to business."

Dante felt no sorrow. No remorse. Only anger and rage. Only the pain of being controlled.

* * *

Autumn's eyes rolled to the back of her head, a pleasant shiver trickling down her spine. For frightening alien creatures, they gave the most relaxing massages. Elbows and dexterous fingers dug out the knots in the tight muscles of her back. Years of teenage stress instantly vanished.

If it wasn't for the Empress and Leyla flanking her, she would've drifted off. But she refused to leave herself vulnerable, *especially* in front of Leyla. Who knew what she was capable of?

White steam engulfed them from the bath house the Empress had recommended. A magnificent view overlooked the white ancient city. The violet sky glittered brighter than a million shining stars.

Lying face down, she stifled potentially embarrassing noises, in a state of ultimate relaxation.

"Have you put any thought into your mating ceremony?" The Empress turned her head, brown eyes assessing.

She sighed, as her relaxation came to a screeching halt.

"No, your Imperial—"

"Please, my dear, call me Isidora. We're practically family." The Empress's delicate mouth curled.

"No, Isidora, I haven't," she admitted as a small crack in her spine relieved tension. But it was futile, as the pressure built back up.

Leyla snorted. "Well don't you think that's something you ought to do, human? Considering the ceremony is happening whether you want it or not. I'm wagering though, that you want it more than anything. Who would be stupid enough to decline a prince? Especially one who is as wealthy as Dante and next in line for the throne?"

Her anger spiked, vision blurring for a moment. The woman massaging her back jumped before continuing.

"Dearest, please," Isidora pushed her head up. The snow-white alien woman removed her elongated fingers from her back. "You're making matters more difficult than they have to be."

"Is that why you hate me so much?" Autumn hissed at Leyla. "You really think this is what I want? To be a stupid princess? Well, for your information—"

"Ladies," Isidora shot them each a warning look. "The walls have ears. Enough."

Autumn fell silent, not because she gave an actual crap if anyone heard, but because she was tired of fighting. She was supposed to be using this time to unwind before her birthday extravaganza. It was surprising Dante remembered. She wasn't sure why she cared.

She laid back down and closed her eyes. Servants continued to knead her tight muscles.

"Good," Isidora lowered her face and returned to her own massage. "Tell me, my dear, what would you have the theme of the ceremony be?"

Autumn's eyes widened; she couldn't believe they were having this conversation. Seriously? She was twenty for good-ness' sake and thinking about her *wedding*. Under normal circumstances, she would've been talking about college or what guy she found hottest in class.

Or maybe, she and Caleb would've reconciled. Her mind drifted to his cute ebony curls and sapphire eyes. *Did he miss her? Had he recovered from the injuries Dante had inflicted on him before she was kidnapped?* She'd never know.

Her stomach knotted. The Empress was still waiting for her answer. Dante owed her the world for *ruining* her life.

She cleared her throat. "I want a fairytale themed wedding, with a gown so glorious it brings tears to the eyes of my husband. And a crown so bright it's blinding to all who behold. I want wings, and to walk the grounds of an enchanted forest."

A tall order, but they asked so she told.

"I knew it," Leyla glowered.

"Hush," Isidora raised her hand. "I'll see what I can do."

Not the answer she anticipated. *Good luck putting all of that together*, Autumn thought as she closed her eyes. *That is, if she didn't escape first.*

Twenty-Four

DANTE FELL into a bow before his superior.

"My lady," he took Valdez's hand and brought it to his lips. "To what do we owe the tremendous pleasure of being summoned to your glorious court?"

Servants ambled, carrying silver buckets filled with pink water. They set them on the ground with a splash as they went to clean up the bloody mess Valdez had left. Valdez chewed her bottom lip into a smile. "My, my Dante, you always were a charming one," she withdrew, taking the bow and arrow from his hand and passing it to a trembling servant. She leaned in close, tongue flicking against his ear. "I've always been curious to discover what your other charms are like."

"How deliciously naughty you are," he winked. "Somebody should wash your filthy mouth out with soap."

Valdez chuckled and turned away, long braid swishing against her back.

"Enough, out with it already." The emperor swirled his goblet before taking a sip. "I don't understand what all the secrecy is about."

Valdez's features straightened. "Well, somebody is impatient, isn't he? I suppose I'll get right to it then. I've summoned you here because rumor has it our favorite general has gone missing."

Dante's stomach twisted, but he maintained perfect composure. "How curious."

She nodded. "My sources tell me he was last spotted in the lower universes late last year."

Her sources? He cracked his knuckles. "What sources?"

"That scoundrel," the emperor snapped. "What would he possibly be doing all the way down there?"

"I suspect he may be organizing a rebel faction," Valdez replied. "The Red Cloaks have proved to be difficult in recent years with their idealizations and desire for change. Keyserike has voiced his frustrations with the hierarchy."

"I wouldn't put it past him," Dante concurred. "He's always been a slippery one."

Valdez's lips flickered. "The Grand Supreme wants us to deliver him alive so he can answer to him personally."

Dante crossed his arms. "His wish is my command."

"I've captured a Zexian traveler who is rumored to have seen him last," Valdez cocked her head to the side. "You shall question him, Dante. Find out what you can. The Grand Supreme won't allow us a moment's rest until we deliver him Keyserike."

* * *

Dante was greeted by all too familiar screams. There was no escaping them. Wherever he went in life, screams were sure to follow.

"I have no idea what you're talking about. Please, have mercy. I beg of you, please."

He'd heard it a million times. It was the truth. How could he know? Dante was sure he'd disposed of everyone who'd seen what took place with Keyserike. There were no Zexians on board that flight.

He paced the stone floor of the cell with slow, calculated strides. His boots scraped against the grain; black-gloved fingers laced behind his back.

"You lie," he made a fist and rammed it into the prisoner's frail gut. Bones crunched and cracked. Chunks of vomit poured out of his mouth as Dante struck him again and again. Desperate, he needed to make his performance convincing, lest both his superior and his father suspect his treachery.

It was for the good of the realm. Keyserike had to die sooner or later.

The emperor sat cross-legged in a chair and swirled a goblet filled with room temperature red wine. He took a languorous sip, allowing Dante to bloody his gloves.

Valdez stood in the doorway with her arms crossed, jagged wings twitching after every blow. A smile crept across her wicked, seductive mouth.

Dante didn't cease the beating until the prisoner's eyes were blackened and his wings were shredded to shards. Black blood trickled over his temples and onto his pearlescent skin.

"I'm not going to ask you again," he grabbed the captive's neck and jerked his face toward his. "What information do you have in connection with the disappearance of General Keyserike?"

The prisoner averted his eyes. Beating him bloody resulted in no confession. He'd have to resort to other means to get the captive to speak.

Dante yanked him by the head and placed his thumb and forefinger at the base of his skull and massaged them cyclically. He shut his eyes and scanned the dark corridors of his mind, navigating through the thick web of his memories. How he wished he could read thoughts in real time like his younger cousin Ronan did.

There it was: the confirmation he'd been so desperately searching for. He *had* been in Universe 1 at the time of Keyserike's arrival and had witnessed bits and pieces of the blood-soaked battle that ensued between them. He'd witnessed Dante transform but then his memories halted, and everything faded.

Dammit. He'd seen too much.

The prisoner had been alone at the time of the battle. Dante withdrew from his mind, his vision clearing.

His memories stopped abruptly. What did it mean? His left temple twitched.

The man had seen enough to be considered a threat. A witness to both the fight and the resistance.

He couldn't afford to take any chances.

Arms folded, he turned around and faced Valdez and his father.

"What does he know?" Valdez asked.

His father took a lingering sip of wine. "Yes, son, please do indulge us. Where is our favorite general?"

"He knows nothing," Dante smoothed a black-gloved hand through his tresses. "It seems he's a defector with no valuable information. A complete and utter waste of our time."

An outright lie. How he hoped the prisoner hadn't opened his mouth to anyone else. But there was no way to check. His memories ceased without a trace.

Valdez glanced at Dante. "I hope you're not too out of practice this time. I can't have you going soft on me."

"No, of course not." A command had been given.

"Any last words defector?"

The prisoner stared at the ground.

"What's the matter? No pleas or desperate prayers to the gods? Although, I doubt they're listening. They would never waste their valuable time on a nothing like you."

A warm, wet sensation collided with Dante's cheek as the prisoner spit in his face. Dante wiped it with his finger. He deserved it. If not for this, for everything else he'd done.

With a single wave of his hand, screams reverberated throughout the chamber. Fire engulfed the prisoner whole, and his flesh and bones charred to dust.

* * *

Autumn couldn't bear to talk about her mating ceremony a moment longer. Her insides were wracked with anxiety. The empress went into never-ending detail about her dress and the extensive list of guests that were to be invited. Three thousand. A total of *three thousand* guests. All of alien high society would be present.

The empress informed her it would be viewable via projection, which to her understanding was the Elattion form of live streaming. *Who knew how many alien beings would be watching them? No pressure.*

As her head spun off her shoulders, she asked to be excused and shown to her room. She rolled her eyes as ten onyx-clad guards accompanied her from the bathing house, up several flights of crystal steps, and through brightly lit winding corridors.

Her lodgings were located at the end of a gilded hallway with rows and rows of closed terracotta doors. Rich amethyst shined through the angular skylit windows.

Behind one of the doors, she heard growls and groans that were animalistic in nature. She kept on moving, though the hair prickled up on the back of her neck.

She grabbed her stomach as she sprinted inside her room, positive she would be sick.

Emblem and Allegoria unpacked her stuff as she raced through to the bathroom, feet pounding against the warmed tiled floor. She caught a glimpse of the ancient city as she opened the bathroom door and thrust her head into the gilded toilet.

After she vomited up her guts, she wiped her mouth on her arm and sat on the floor.

"Deep breaths," she muttered to herself. "Deep breaths." The pressure was unbelievable.

Emblem sprinted in after her. "My goodness, are you all right?"

"Yeah, I'm fine, thanks. The stress is just getting to me."

Emblem knelt beside her and rubbed her hand over her back. Her emerald eyes bled with sympathy. "Yes, I can imagine. It must be difficult for you to be so far away from home."

"Yeah." That about summed it up, along with the marriage she was about to enter against her will.

"My lady," Allegoria poked her head through the doorway. "Master Dante wishes to see you."

Master, she rolled her eyes. "Please don't tell me he's here."

Allegoria shook her head. "No, he's outside by the hot springs and requests that you bring a swimsuit."

"No, tell him I forgot it."

"Actually—"

Autumn crossed her arms and sighed. "Don't worry about it. I'll tell him myself."

She wiped her mouth and brushed her teeth. She left her hair unbound and un-glittered, for once, and left the room to see what Dante wanted. *He is so ridiculous.*

Twenty-Five

THE HOT SPRINGS were a sight to behold. They sat at the edge of a cliff overlooking the ancient city. Steam bubbled along the watermelon hued water in a gray haze. The violet sky glittered with a hint of twinkling stars.

Autumn fanned herself with her hand. She approached Dante while he lounged against a stone wall, his eyes closed. His powerful blue muscles gleamed in the water.

She subconsciously chewed her bottom lip. He looked handsome with his strong jaw and slicked obsidian hair.

Even still—his good looks won't make me forget what he's done.

She cleared her throat. "What do you want?"

The stationed guards marched off as soon as she spoke, metallic guns scraping against the stone ground.

Dante opened his eyes and cast a lazy glimpse. His mouth curled, then fell flat.

"I thought I told your useless maids to fetch your swimsuit," he folded his arms. "Perhaps I should order their ears suctioned out."

"I'm not swimming with you," she placed a hand on her

hip. "They brought it, but I decided to leave it behind. Stop being so rude to them. They didn't do anything to you."

"You're right, I'm in a foul mood," he shrugged then grinned. "Unfortunately for you, it's not a request. It's a command."

She threw her hands in the air in protest. "I don't have time for this."

Autumn stomped away, then froze as a cool tingling sensation trickled through her limbs. She floated in the air and found herself standing face-to-face with him again.

"You don't have time for me?" He blinked, long lashes grazing his cheeks. "Preposterous. Either you remove your clothes and join me for a swim, or I'll do it for you. You have thirty seconds."

He stepped out of the water, completely naked from the waist down. Autumn's cheeks heated to a boil. It'd been so long since she'd seen so much of him. It was a sight she no longer knew how to process.

"Fine," she groaned and climbed out of her bodysuit, wearing a corset and panties.

"That's all I get?" He smiled.

She rolled her eyes and submerged herself in the water.

"Are you happy now?" She took a seat on a stone lip, opposite him.

"Very. I trust you had an enjoyable afternoon, and my sister was well behaved."

She nodded. "Yeah, I guess so." *For a brat,* she was tempted to add. "Where were you all afternoon?" She closed her eyes. Trickling water numbed her to relaxation. A scent like Palo Santo drifted through the air.

"Why do you have a sudden interest in my whereabouts again?" He swam over and dipped himself into the water before rising to his feet. "Are you trying to tell me you care?"

"If I'm going to be your wife, shouldn't you tell me these

things?" She opened her eyes slowly. "On Earth, husbands tell their wives everything. Unless, of course, you're hiding something from me *again*."

Dante maintained a neutral expression. "I was in a meeting."

"Planning to steal more worlds?" She closed her eyes again and rested her head against the stone wall. The ripple of waves followed. He was so close their knees grazed.

"Do you think that's all I do, plan destruction and world domination?" he muttered. "And more importantly, do you think I've chosen this life?"

She swallowed hard, as he leaned over. His lips brushed against her jaw.

"I—"

"What if I was to tell you I was busy ensuring, not only our family's safety, but the safety of your planet and the rest of the realm?" He leaned over, whispering in her ear. "Don't underestimate the lengths I would go to keep you safe. I've killed for you before and I'd do it again."

"Well, that doesn't make it okay," she said. "All lives are precious."

"Not all, but I like how you think. You see the best in everyone, even if they don't deserve it. I remember how back on Earth you saw the best in me."

She glanced away before meeting his gaze. "I did until I found out you were a murderer, and how you hurt Caleb—"

Dante ran a hand through his damp tousled tresses. "It was well deserved after what he put you through. I'd do it again in a heartbeat."

A cool trickle rolled down her spine. "How could you say that? He cheated on me to help his family. They'd be out on the street if it wasn't for him. He loves me, and I love him."

His mouth twisted to the side. "That's not love. He should've tried harder, Autumn. Found another way. Taken up a second job. I wouldn't have put you through that for any amount of money. I would have worked my hands raw for you. That's what separates a child from a man. A child is easily purchased, and a man earns his own way."

Autumn sat there speechless, trembling. Dante was so close she could hear his heartbeat. "Men don't steal—"

"They spare," he corrected her. "Earth would be no more if it wasn't for me."

<h1 style="text-align:center">Twenty-Six</h1>

AUTUMN'S MAIDS strapped her into a fresh, satin, obsidian corset. She stared into the mirror, thoughts returning to Dante. How he claimed he would've found another way for them to stay together. The way Caleb had *failed* to. How he wouldn't have been so weak.

"Turn," Allegoria said, distracting her from her thoughts.

"Oh sorry," she muttered.

"You certainly are different from the other mistresses we've served." Emblem fluffed a black tulle dress, with a plum satin bodice. Silver buttons trailed down the front in a sparkling display.

"How am I different?" Autumn wrinkled her nose. "Do you mean, because I'm human?"

Emblem shook her head. "No, because you say please and thank you—"

"And because you asked us our names," Allegoria added.

Autumn's face contorted. "What kind of place is this?" *How ridiculous. What a rude bunch of aliens to not be considerate of those who serve them.*

"My dear," Emblem unbuttoned the bodice and Autumn

stepped inside the mess of tulle fabric. "You have no idea how difficult it is for people like us."

"People like you?" her brows rose.

"Commoners."

Autumn stretched her arms into the air. "Of course, I do. I used to be a waitress who served people food and drinks. I cleaned up their messes after they ate and dealt with their nonsense."

The twins gasped. "*You* were a servant?"

"Yes."

"Well, this is news to us," Allegoria combed Autumn's damp coils into a loose half-up style, while Emblem secured her dress. "You've certainly managed to make an impression on his Imperial Highness. He's been dramatically altered since your arrival."

She scrunched her nose. "What do you mean *altered*?"

Allegoria's clover eyes went wide. "Forgive me, my lady, I spoke out of turn."

"No, tell me, please. I won't say anything, I promise."

"He's much tamer," Emblem smoothed the dress with her palms. She sprayed silver glitter over Autumn's damp curls.

Tamer? What the heck was he, a wild animal? In a distant jumble of memories, she recalled Dante transforming into a ferocious beast. At this point, she could no longer differentiate her imagination from reality. Deep in her gut, she had a feeling that wasn't what Emblem meant.

Knock, knock, knock.

"Come in," Autumn yelled, immediately regretting her decision.

The door creaked open, and Princess Leyla strode inside. She wore a spectacular dress of dark-magenta tulle, a satin heart bodice, and a black velvet choker around her slender blue throat. Her brown eyes narrowed to slits, and glittering waves swept over a barren shoulder.

"Oh, it's you," Leyla's jaw clenched. "I thought this was my brother's room."

Autumn folded her arms. "No, I have no idea where he's staying."

"Figures," Leyla rolled her eyes. "Foolish human, you should at least keep an eye on your prize. There's no telling what he might be up to."

Foolish human.

Leyla flashed a wicked grin.

Autumn balled her trembling fists. "What the *heck* is that supposed to mean?"

Leyla shrugged and turned on her heel. She stopped suddenly and peered over her shoulder. "You look hideous, by the way. Like an animal in heat. What a waste of a trip. It would've been better if you hadn't spawned at all. Like the universes needed more of your weak pathetic kind—"

Autumn's fists trembled. "Get out."

Leyla's upper lip curled. "With pleasure."

The princess went to leave when the door cracked and flew from the hinges. Autumn ducked down to the floor as it tumbled through the air just missing her head and catapulted between the open columns.

CRASH.

Leyla stumbled backwards, eyes widening, as she sauntered from the room.

Autumn pressed her palms to her cheeks.

"Are you okay?" Emblem and Allegoria asked concurrently.

Autumn nodded, her blood simmering to a rage. That little brat *attacked* her.

"I hate her," she hissed. It was unfathomable she could despise someone more than *Misty Beckett*. Leyla was like Misty on steroids. "I wish she would stay away from me."

"The princess is her own person," Emblem frowned.

What an understatement.

"She's spoiled rotten," Allegoria added. "A true Martyne princess who always gets her way. But I have a feeling she's hiding something."

"Like what?"

Allegoria shook her head. "It's just a feeling."

"Believe it or not, I knew someone like her back on Earth."

She could only imagine who Misty was terrorizing now.

* * *

Not long after Leyla's departure, Dante strode in, chest held high, onyx hair still damp from the spring. He examined the door frame. Emblem and Allegoria stared at his feet.

"What transpired here?"

When Autumn didn't answer his question, he asked the guards. They offered him a detailed account of her confrontation with his sister. By the time they finished the tale, his blue face hinted at deep crimson.

She sighed. Great. Why did Leyla have it out for her anyway? It made no sense. She hadn't been anything but kind.

"My sister attacked you again?"

"Yes."

"Huge mistake."

Dante led her through the hallway. The suns shined in triplicate rays, glittering off the gilded walls. From what she could gather, it was night on Diode, although darkness never set in.

Her heart thrummed in her ears with anticipation.

"By the way, you look lovelier than dawn," his amber eyes flickered in the light.

Her cheeks heated. "Thanks," was all she managed to say, when a familiar whining and growl came from behind a closed door. The hairs on the back of her neck prickled. "What's behind that door?"

He shrugged. "I'm sure it's nothing to worry about."

As they ambled through a series of never-ending hallways, the sound of jeers was followed by crackling roars. She whipped her head around and attempted to catch a glimpse, but to no avail. Someone, or *something*, sounded like it was in pain. Her stomach churned.

They arrived in a hall with sapphire, magenta, emerald, and gold floating lanterns. Banquet tables were piled high with golden trays of exotic fruits, vegetables, and fish. She marveled at the pastries and miniature cakes.

Champagne flutes clanked and disgusting red bubbling wine poured into most every goblet.

The room was filled to the brim with a mixture of Elattions and Zexians. Jagged wings sprang from backs and women wore dresses that paled in comparison to her own, while the men all dressed in onyx bodysuits.

The Empress sat at the central dais. However—

There was no sign of the emperor, or Leyla.

"Where is she?" Dante scoured the room for any sign of his sister. She was nowhere to be found.

While they waded through the crowd searching, a jade-winged alien waved Dante down. Her waist-length braid shimmered in the light.

"Pardon me. I'll be but a moment," he whispered into her ear.

He walked off and stood in the doorway with the strange alien woman. As far as she was concerned, everyone was strange here.

She fiddled with her hands. *A drink would be awesome right now.*

Reaching, she grabbed a bubbling flute from a passing tray

and gulped it down whole. Relaxation set in, followed by a painful grumble. She hadn't eaten anything since their arrival.

Autumn grabbed two green gelatin cubes from a tray. She poked them with her finger. *What the heck are these?* She sniffed them, they smelled sweet enough. They tasted like pure sugarcane.

"Didn't anyone ever teach you not to play with your food?"

The air was knocked from Autumn's lungs as she was shoved chest-first over a table. White-hot pain radiated through her stomach, and food and drink stained her gown as she pushed herself to a shaking stand.

Leyla turned and smiled as she made her way through the dense gathering.

Something deep and furious and latent inside of Autumn shattered. Leyla wouldn't get away with this.

Molars grinding in her mouth, Autumn raced after her. Her vision was blood-red.

Leyla stopped to grab a drink from a servant, while out of control rage swelled through Autumn. Upon reaching the bratty princess, she shoved her, and Leyla gasped before toppling down face-first. This got everyone's attention.

"You," Leyla pushed herself to her feet and charged at Autumn with her inhuman speed. Autumn was able to trace her like she was moving in slow motion. For a moment, Leyla seemed slow and clumsy.

Autumn ducked under her swinging arms and Leyla crashed into a table, breaking it in half. Servants went flying and food and drink splashed all over the walls.

The entire room was silent. Autumn's face and neck burned as dozens of inhuman eyes pierced into her, but Leyla didn't relent.

Leyla rose to her feet, gown shredded to rags and the silver strands of her hair in mass disarray. She bared her fists, and her mouth curled into a pretty snarl.

Without hesitation, Autumn ran and tackled her.

Leyla screamed as she went airborne and crashed through a stone column. Stone crumbled in a spray of white dust. Autumn inhaled, choking on the particles.

The emperor walked through the doorway; eyes hot like two burning amber coals. "What the hell is going on here?"

Leyla climbed from beneath the rubble, eyes flickering with rage. "She attacked me."

Dante strode in and yanked a groaning Leyla to her feet. "I've had just about enough of your antics."

He grabbed Autumn by the hand and led them both away. "We'll take this outside."

The emperor glowered and stormed out of the room. Dante's face was as hard as stone.

Twenty-Seven

BLOOD POUNDED in Autumn's ears as Dante marched her and Leyla through the hallway. Their feet dragged against the marble floor, and her stomach toppled. *Where were they headed?* She frowned. At this rate, she'd never see her friends and family again.

Leyla followed, the pale blue drained from her face, leaving her almost colorless. Leyla stared at the ground, not so much as offering her brother a passing glance.

They arrived at a ceiling-high set of terracotta doors and entered a small room with lush green vines hanging from a ceiling trellis.

Open columns allowed a view of the outside of the palace. Crackled gilded vases with tall, dried grass lined the walls. At the center of it all was a velvet mustard carpet leading up a ten-step stone dais.

The emperor and the alien woman who Dante disappeared with earlier were seated on top. The woman looked different from the Zexians she'd encountered up until this point. Her eyes were blue like sea glass, and her skin was jade with a long braid that fell midway between a pair of ragged, vampire bat wings.

Although she possessed an inhuman beauty that was almost painful to behold, her mouth was twisted and cruel like a jackal.

Dante teleported to the top of the dais and took a seat next to his father and the woman whose eyes shredded into her soul.

Dante smoothed a black-gloved hand through his midnight hair. "Does anyone care to explain what just happened?" His voice was as chilly as a winter's morning. His amber eyes were wild and unsteady.

The woman snapped to her feet. "They destroyed my beautiful banquet hall. No explanation needed. The hybrid dies." She reached from behind her throne, grabbed a golden bow, and aimed it at Autumn.

"I'm inclined to agree," the emperor concurred.

Dante's eyes narrowed at his father. "Are you, now? Pity nobody asked your opinion." The emperor went rigid before swirling his goblet of wine in his black-gloved palm.

Leyla grabbed Autumn's hand for a moment, but Autumn brushed her away.

"I don't believe I've introduced you, Valdez." Dante said. "The human is Autumn, my soon-to-be wife."

A flicker of surprise flashed through Valdez's features before they hardened. "She's a human?" Valdez nocked her bow back and released it. It whizzed between Autumn and Leyla, shattering through the door. She took her seat, legs crossed.

Dante looked at Leyla. "I'm waiting, sister."

Autumn's heart thrummed in her ears. Her throat went dry. The arrow came so close to them, she felt the wind blow past her ear.

When Leyla didn't speak, he said, "Well, at the very least

you can tell us what happened, considering you embarrassed our house on a foreign planet."

Autumn stared at Dante's unsettling coolness.

"Autumn attacked me first," Leyla folded her arms. "She shoved me over a table for no apparent reason."

"I did not," Autumn's forehead pulsated.

"Somehow, I'm not inclined to believe that sister. I have eyewitnesses who say you attacked Autumn in her bedchamber earlier this evening. And as we both know, humans have no abilities."

"She provoked me," Leyla shuttered.

"How so?"

"She, um, she—" Leyla stumbled on her words.

"Just as I suspected."

"It's true," Leyla insisted.

"Is it?" Dante cocked his head to the side.

"She provoked me by breathing. By existing. By being here to begin with. It's not right and it's not fair, Dante. I hate her. *I hate her.*"

The emperor snorted. Valdez stared at Autumn, assessing.

Autumn's breath caught in her throat as she watched and waited. It was obviously *all* Leyla's fault.

After a short while, Dante oozed with his usual self-satisfaction. "Perhaps I'll take a look for myself."

"No," Leyla picked up her tattered gown and sprinted for the door, but Dante was on top of her faster than Autumn could blink. He grabbed his sister kicking and flailing. He knelt and pressed his forefinger and thumb to the back of her skull. Her eyes fluttered closed and she fell out cold. *What was he doing?*

After a few minutes, he stood up, leaving his sister still seated on the ground in a dazed state.

He crossed his arms.

"Well, what did you see?" Valdez hissed.

Dante straightened his spine. "They'll both be punished."

Autumn's mouth fell open. "What are you talking about? She—"

Dante smiled. "It will be enacted upon our arrival home."

Silence, absolute silence, engulfed the room whole.

"Any objections? Good, that's what I thought. We've wasted quite enough time on this nonsense. We should get back to the party. Or what little you left of it."

Twenty-Eight

DANTE SAUNTERED beside Autumn through the hallways of Gypsum Palace feeling like complete and utter garbage. It wasn't the witness's life he wasted earlier that day, or the never-ending collection of planets he'd conquered at his master's whim. Or seeing Valdez again.

He couldn't stand to look at his mate, her exquisite dress in tatters. Black and blue bruises tainted her delicate skin. Her bottom lip was split wide open. And once again, her name day celebration was spoiled.

Leyla loathed her. He'd never seen the true extent of her hatred until *this*.

A few years prior he would've sided with her, as it had been ingrained in him since birth. Lower life forms were vermin, and they needed to be conquered to make room for higher life forms like himself. They were a waste of life, breath, and resources. The universes were built on their sweat and blood.

That was before he was tasked with going to Earth, fell in love, and what was done was done. The irony of it all.

They turned a corner and Autumn dragged her leg, limping. He offered her an arm.

She rolled her moonlit eyes. "You *never* fail to surprise me."

He sighed. *What now?* He mentally prepared himself. Although, he had an inkling what was troubling her.

"What's wrong?"

"Seriously?" Annoyance seeped into her voice. She scowled. "Two seconds ago, I was attacked by your sister, and an arrow flew by my head. Now, somehow, I'm in trouble in all this?"

Dante sucked in a breath. Perhaps he crossed a line. He only meant to scare them into telling him what happened. He didn't mean to start a war, especially since Autumn was finally starting to come around.

"Forgive me, I would never do anything to hurt you. You must understand, I have two roles to play in this. I'm the crown prince but I'm also your future ma—"

"I don't care. Don't ever scare me like that again."

Autumn pushed him aside. *Just when they were starting to make some progress.*

Such anger. Such a red-hot rage she had brewing deep inside of her. Dante wasn't ashamed to admit he found her disposition rather exciting, in all the *wrong* ways.

When they arrived at her bedchamber, Autumn squeezed between the guards, opened the door, and slammed it without so much as a goodnight. Or a goodnight kiss, which he was secretly hoping for, but would have been too much to initiate under the present climate.

The door hit so hard a crack formed next to the ceiling. *Great.* Another sum he would owe to Valdez once the trip was through.

The guards watched him through their shielded helmets. His eyes narrowed. He dared one of them to say something.

To laugh. To make a noise. To so much as *breathe*. He'd tear them apart limb from limb, starting with their skulls.

* * *

Autumn never returned to the party. Her birthday was ruined again, two years in a row. She waited patiently until Dante left. He lingered by the door for a few moments before making his exit. She supposed he hoped she would invite him inside so he could finish what he had started earlier at the springs. That would never happen, especially after he behaved like such a jerk.

Punish her? For what?

Instead, she would try to get some sleep in this impossibly bright world.

As she dug through her trunk, a wide grin spread across her lips when she discovered a thick book with at least eight hundred pages. It *hadn't* been there prior.

Nestling herself in bed, she read until her eyes grew heavy, then yawned.

The triple suns shone at full radiant force. Autumn laid in bed tossing and turning, eventually burying her weary head beneath a pillow. She groaned and uttered a curse. She'd never sleep a wink at this rate.

Why did it have to be so bright?

Then—

The crying began again. A series of high-pitched screeches echoed through the hallway. Hair rising on her neck yet again, Autumn stumbled to her feet and tiptoed to the door. She cracked it open, and the guards remained still, unphased by the violent screeches. Someone, or *something*, was in pain.

She made her way through the guards.

"M'lady, where are you going?" one of the guards muttered.

Autumn ignored him and followed the sound of the commotion. The guards flanked her as she walked down the hall. *The door.* The screeching came from behind the door she and Dante had passed to and from the doomed ball.

Her heart thundered in her ears as she turned the knob. A warm, faint glow bloomed between the cracks.

Every single pore inside of her body screamed for her to stop as the door opened.

Twenty-Nine

EMBERS FROM A FIREPLACE flickered and danced before her eyes. She was slammed with a wall of pure heat. Her satin cloud pajamas clung to her skin, and her jaw dropped. *No, no, no, this couldn't be right.*

Aliens both Zexian and Elattion stood in a circle jeering. They jabbed red-hot pokers into a cage while two tiger-like creatures wrestled.

Bared claws shredded through fur and flesh. Snarls ripped through the air as the beasts rolled against the grid of iron bars.

One beast snapped its jaw around the other's neck, drawing first blood, then ripped out his opponent's throat. The injured beast slumped into a lifeless heap; eyes closed.

"Meow."

Beside her feet sat a baby creature, contained in a miniature prison. Its watermelon-pink fur, striped faintly with black, was as soft as a feather. It blinked its large innocent sapphire eyes.

An agonizing tightening formed in Autumn's chest. She had a suspicion the animal had seen one of its parents die. Eyes blurring with tears, she blinked to clear her vision.

He was all alone in the world, the same way she was alone here since being snatched from Earth.

"Take me to see Dante," she said to the guards.

* * *

They arrived at a door in a neighboring hallway. She raised her fist and pounded against it as hard as she could.

Dante emerged, black spandex shorts hanging low on his hips. His sculpted abs and muscles shifted in the golden sunlight.

"Can I help you?" He leaned against the doorframe. The strands of his ink-black hair fell over his eye.

She opened her mouth. "I—"

"Please, come in," he invited her into his room and closed the door behind them.

The room was extravagant. Columns lined the furthest wall overlooking the sun-cast city. Green vines hung in tangled bunches from a ceiling trellis. Hot air drifted in a gentle breeze.

"I've been praying to the gods for the last two years for a second chance with you. Can I offer you something to drink? I can order champagne." His fingers tapped against the glass of his communicator.

"No, thanks. I'm okay," she wrung her hands behind her back. "I need—"

"Are you sure? It'll help us both relax."

He pressed his lips to hers, fingertips running through the strands of her hair. He held her in his strong arms, and she melted into his touch. *Oh gosh, he thought she was here to sleep with him.*

"Actually—" she interrupted as he laid her on his bed.

He knelt and brushed her navel with his calloused palm.

"There's no sense in being shy about the nature of your visit. I can sense your excitement." His mouth curled.

She gasped as he brought his lips to her skin and kissed her, teasing and running his fingers against her thighs. "Afterwards, I need to discuss something with you, something very important. What happened earlier—"

"There are these tigers," her insides tightened from his caress as she started to lose herself. *She shouldn't be enjoying this so much.*

Dante stopped. "A what?"

She sat up. "It's horrible, they're torturing and killing them."

"Oh, I thought you came here to—never mind then. My mistake," he glanced away.

"Follow me," she tugged him by the hand. She had to get back, had to put an end to the abuse. The animals were helpless.

As they left the room, she could've sworn Valdez's clear blue eyes blinked and then vanished into thin air.

* * *

Dante kicked the door in. It crashed and splintered against the wall, rubble crumbling everywhere.

A snarl ripped through his throat. A convincing one. It was so convincing that in his tired state, he managed to startle himself. Grown men and women trembled in their heavy boots as they fell into low respectful bows.

"What the *hell* is going on in here?" Dante said in the nastiest voice he could muster. He did his best to feign concern for Autumn's sake. In reality, the men and women assembled were engaged in a standard practice. A fighting ring, with wagered bets. A legal activity in Universe 16, planet Diode, Sector 1.

Somehow, their actions managed to upset his mate, so he humored her—the sweet, sensitive, delicate creature that she was. A true child of Earth, unable to grasp a simple concept such as gambling.

Her discomfort left him unsettled to say the least, especially after they suffered yet another misunderstanding. An especially humiliating one for him, but by now he was used to being humiliated by her.

"Sire, we're engaged in a bet," one Zexian Lord stepped forth. His pitch-black eyes met Dante's. A pair of alabaster wings sat high on his back.

"I'm afraid I don't care for your insolent tone, my lord." Dante folded his arms as he concocted an excuse to end the ongoing match.

A hot breeze drifted by. *Drat, he should've thrown on some clothes. It would've been more intimidating than standing in his undergarments.*

"But, sire—"

"Enough. Speak again and I'll have your tongue."

He continued. "For the inconvenience you've caused, I'm seizing your assets."

He snapped his fingers, and the guards swarmed the room. They kicked over tables and chairs and snatched bags spilling with rubies.

Autumn's eyes widened and she grabbed hold of his hand. Dante bit back a smile.

The guards slung the sacks over their broad shoulders.

"Let this be a lesson to all who defy me."

His statement was accompanied by groans and grumbling. Dante stifled a laugh.

When he went to leave, Autumn stopped and tugged against his arm.

"Wait," she pointed to the ground.

He saw a small makeshift container housing a baby ling.

Its tail thrashed and it blinked at him with its large sapphire eyes.

"We can't leave him."

Dante sighed and reached into the cage. What Autumn planned to do with the beast was beyond him. As he went to pick it up, it hissed, bearing a sharp set of teeth. He held it by the scruff of its neck and handed the insolent animal to her. It purred in her arms.

"Please, sire," he heard from across the room. "That ling is purebred and costs almost as much as a destroyer."

"What part of that is my problem? My lady has staked her claim."

As they left the room, grumbling ensued in the background. Grumbling and *rage*.

Thirty

AUTUMN SAT on the white linen comforter of her bed as the baby ling purred in her arms. Vines swayed in the warm breeze while midnight sun glinted through the columns. She ran her fingers through his fur with a feather-like touch. The lightweight creature stared at her, blinking his brilliant blue eyes.

"What are you going to do with that beast?" Dante sat on her bed and scowled.

She rolled her eyes. "I'm keeping him as a pet."

"A pet?" His brows rose. "Lings are vicious creatures used exclusively for fighting. They'll sooner rip your throat out in your sleep than be the tame pet you're hoping for."

Hmmm, sounds like someone else I know.

Autumn stroked the ling's head with her finger, and he purred and closed his eyes. When Dante reached to do the same, he hissed. His tail puffed and claws bared.

She chuckled "He doesn't like you. I wonder *why*?"

"Good, I don't care for it either."

She laid back and placed the ling on her stomach, he snuggled his head against her breast. "He needs a name."

"How about *useless animal?*" Dante crossed his arms. "Or *animal that I'll throw into a fighting ring and make a great deal of money from?* Or, perhaps, *purchase another destroyer for my fleet?*"

The ling hissed at him as if he could understand Dante. The creature was far more intelligent than Dante gave him credit for.

"I think I'll call him Mr. Hiss."

Dante made a face. "What an absurd name."

"Well, I like it."

Dante sighed. "Mr. Hiss it is."

He stood up from her bed, stretched, and yawned.

"My dearest Autumn, it's getting terribly late," he blinked away the sleep in his eyes. "I'm afraid I must retire to bed. It's been a delight as always."

She hated to admit but she didn't want him to go and leave her alone again on this weird planet. Even if he pissed her off with his mock trial. Even if he tried to sleep with her earlier. Even if he conquered as many planets as he claimed. If only to thank him for rescuing Mr. Hiss.

Maybe she was just plain tired of being lonely.

"Stay." She was in disbelief as the word slipped through her lips. "But only if you want to," she added.

Dante turned around, stray strands of midnight framing his face. "Are you sure?"

"Yes."

He walked over and climbed beside her in bed. She placed her new pet between them. Boundaries were established.

"Good night," she watched him before closing her eyes.

"Good night."

Autumn dreamt of Earth, the planet she called home fourteen universes away. Try as she might to prevent them, visions of the slumbering blue prince crept in. His slow even breaths.

His blue shifting muscles. The way he whispered her name while he slept.

Thirty-One

MEANWHILE, *back in Monroe, New York...*

Guillermo Ramon sat at the kitchen table. His trembling finger traced the mouth of a steaming hot cup of coffee. Light shone through the backyard window, in glimmering rays of gold and orange. It was a typical summer morning.

It'd been well over a year since his daughter's disappearance. He'd spoken endlessly with the Monroe town cops and troopers, as well as the best investigators New York State had to offer, but no one was able to help him. Everyone thought he was crazy. At this point, he probably was. He certainly looked the part.

His once well-groomed beard was haggard and long, hanging over his neck in stringy strands. The right eye of his glasses was cracked through the center from a fit of rage he had in the living room a few weeks prior. Dirt etched itself beneath his fingernails from searching the forest time and time again for Autumn, well after the cops had given up.

At this point, he had nothing left to live for. His wife was dead, and his only daughter was abducted by an alien.

Dante was an alien.

Dammit! He took his cup of coffee and smashed it against the wall. Pieces of white glass shattered and fell to the ground, leaving a dark brown splotch over the paint. He threw his laptop on the hardwood floor, cracking in two, wires hanging.

What's the point?

He rose to his feet to throw the chair as well, when the doorbell rang. *Ding-dong.*

Mr. Ramon inhaled a deep shuddering breath and smoothed his hands through his hair. He made his way over to the front door barefoot. He didn't care who saw him like this. Or smelled him; he hadn't bathed in days.

He flung open the door and growled. "What do you want?"

He regretted it when he saw who was standing there.

Lauren's long golden hair was tucked behind her ears, cascading down the middle of her back. Winged liner decorated her eyelids. Ellie's freckled cheeks pinkened and her hair sat bone straight over her shoulders, framing her heart-shaped features.

They plastered smiles on their faces. Lauren held a white box of Italian cookies tied with a string and Ellie clutched an apple pie. Home-baked. His face softened.

"We just wanted to check in with you and let you know we're thinking about you," Lauren's voice was unsteady.

"We brought you baked goods," Ellie added.

"Thank you," he replied. "Do you want to come in?"

"Actually, we have to—" Ellie stuttered.

"Sure," Lauren nodded politely.

The girls followed him inside and he closed the door behind them. Although the lights were dimmed, a tinge of embarrassment shuddered through him.

"Can I get either of you girls some coffee?" He walked to the sink, where dishes were piled so high that they spilled onto the counter.

Lauren's crystal blue eyes widened. "Sure, that sounds great."

"Lauren," Ellie whispered, but her quiet plea was ignored.

He turned and added more water to the coffee pot, as well as a filter and some fresh grinds.

Lauren's brow furrowed. "How are you holding up, Mr. Ramon?"

"As good as can be expected under the circumstances."

"We heard about the note," Ellie blurted but then covered her mouth.

He sighed. *At this point, who hadn't? It was all over the news.*

Ellie continued, "you know that can't be true, right? There's no such thing as aliens."

"I know how crazy it sounds, but my daughter doesn't lie." Autumn had always been truthful to a fault, or so he'd thought before Dante came along.

"Of course not," Lauren's voice cracked.

He could tell right away she was skeptical like all the others.

"It's just that, um, she told us something different."

He sighed. She'd told them she was studying abroad, but even all of Europe had been scoured and there was still no sign of her.

"I know," he said quietly.

"Do you think that maybe she wrote that letter because she didn't know how to explain that she wanted to be with Dante?" Ellie played with the ends of her stick-straight, umber-brown hair. "Nobody liked him, and we all kind of gave him a hard time when he was here."

The words drifted through the air like a death sentence.

He always knew there was something wrong with that boy. He murdered not one but *two* people. *Brutally*.

His teeth ground within his mouth. If only she'd waited in the car at Farrah Falls, none of this would have ever happened. He wished he'd been firmer. He shouldn't have brought her at all. That's what a good father would've done. He should've protected his daughter, but it was too late; she was gone.

"Are you all ri—"

"I'm sorry, girls. I'm going to have to cut this visit short," his voice jumped, and his vision blurred with erupting tears.

The girls watched as his resolve melted. He slid down to the floor, buried his hands in his palms, and released deep dragging sobs.

Lauren knelt and rubbed a hand on his back. "Mr. Ramon, please don't cry. It's going to be okay."

"I'm sure this is all a big misunderstanding. Don't lose hope. I haven't. I'm sure they'll find her," Ellie added.

Somehow, through his tears, he managed to smile. If only at the sound of her name and her memory. It'd been so long that his daughter's face had begun to fade.

* * *

The next morning, Mr. Hiss purred and rubbed his head against Autumn's ribs. As she rolled over, she was greeted by a puddle of wetness. She sat up. His pink, black, and white fur was matted against his soft underbelly.

"Gross," she moved her palm out of the wet spot. "Bad," she held her finger against his snout. "Bad."

Mr. Hiss licked her finger with his rough tongue and rolled onto his back purring, soft belly exposed.

"I told you, that animal is useless and now you've come to find he's untrained."

Her eyes darted across the room to Dante, who pulled on

his onyx knee-high boots. A royal-purple cape was affixed to his shoulders.

"Where are you going?" she asked, not that she cared or anything. Curiosity got the best of her, or at least, that's what she told herself.

"Why?" He grinned. "Afraid you'll miss me?"

"Never."

He snorted. "Never is a long time. How about I tell you in exchange for a kiss?" He batted his eyes. She rolled hers in return.

When he stepped toward her, his nose crinkled. "After you bathe, of course. You reek of that filthy beast."

Mr. Hiss growled and sprang to his feet, hissing at Dante with his tail puffed.

"I think he understands you, so shut up. You might hurt his feelings."

Dante's mouth curved before he turned on his heel. "Council meeting." He slipped out of the door as quiet and graceful as a passing shadow.

Now she owed him a kiss. She bit the insides of her cheeks. What an idiot she was for being so excited.

Thirty-Two

IT WAS ONLY a matter of time before Dante was required to check in with his master, the reigning Grand Supreme Emperor of Universe 24, commonly referred to as *the Master of the Universes.*

The Grand Supreme would only have two questions on his mind: *what was the state of Earth, and where was the missing General Keyserike?*

For the life of him, Dante couldn't understand his master's fixation with Earth. Sure, it was a beautiful planet, his mate's home world, but as she pleaded in his arms for him to spare her world and tried to persuade him with logic, wouldn't Jupiter or Mars have served the same purpose?

An involuntary shudder rattled through his spine. The Grand Supreme could never find out what Dante had done. Everyone he knew and loved would die. He thought back on their most recent conversation.

"My dearest Dante, do you know why I've summoned you here today?"

"No, Lord Izzo."

"I'm dispatching you on a voyage to the farthest end of the

universes where intelligent life has never ventured. Yield Universe 2 as usual. But in Universe 1 thrives a tiny blue planet called Earth. After it's rebuilt, leave not one of the inhabitants alive."

"Yes, Lord Izzo."

Why was there so much emphasis placed on Earth?

Sure, it was a pretty planet that'd since grown on him for obvious reasons, but what was all the fuss for? The humans were a helpless species who posed no threat. Did they really have to be extinguished?

His muscles tensed as he arrived at the throne room. Servants hauled in a large steel projector unit. Thank the gods his master wasn't here in the flesh. The last thing he needed to see right now were his beady little eyes and self-satisfied smirk, permanently plastered to his face.

Valdez sat on the throne, picking at her manicured nails and bouncing her crossed legs— even she was on edge.

The servants plopped the projector atop the dais. They turned it on, unable to darken the room. Excessive sunlight beamed through the pillars and danced against the heated breeze. A faint green-and-white light crackled then flickered into a ghost-like hologram, revealing the most fearsome creature in the 24 Universes for the last four centuries.

Thirty-Three

UPON FIRST GLANCE, no man, woman, or child would think much of Grand Supreme Emperor Izzo. He stood at a total of 147 centimeters and weighed approximately 63 kilograms. Although Dante had never picked him up himself, that was his closest guesstimation.

He often dreamed of slamming Izzo's skull against the wall and crunching it between his fingers into bubbling mush. He didn't dare seize the opportunity.

No one did. To date, he had remained unchallenged.

Izzo's skin was rough and scaled, the deep color of toxic waste. His eyes were thin black slits, and his head was horned in the shape of a crown.

A true freak of nature, but he possessed unfathomable power.

Izzo topped his throne, swirling a goblet of red wine in his hand. His tail thrashed and talons scraped against the metal. He grinned, saliva dribbling from his mouth, revealing jagged yellow teeth. He was cold, calculating, and disgusting all at once.

Nausea coursed through Dante as he forced himself down on one knee. His father and Valdez followed suit. A crowned prince, emperor, and empress, showing submission to this *beast*.

"Dante, my boy, how well you look," Izzo's forked tongue flicked through his cracked lips.

"Thank you, Master Izzo," a forced smile crept across his mouth.

Dante's father stood beside him; arms crossed. "Let's get down to business. We don't have all day."

"Temper," Izzo waved a taloned finger. "Temper. I'm here to speak with your precious son, lest you forget why I allowed you to keep your kingdom and territories."

The emperor's mouth tightened. "Apologies, my lord."

Valdez snorted and crossed her legs.

"I've heard wonderful tidings of your work throughout Universe 2," Izzo said. "It's in the process of being rebuilt as we speak. In accordance with our agreement, I shall keep 70 percent of the planets, and you and yours shall acquire 30 percent, along with your usual stipend."

"Thank you. You're most gracious," Dante said.

"I'm perplexed, however, as to what happened with Earth. Surely someone with your tremendous ability and intelligence shouldn't have suffered any difficulty at all."

Dante laced his fingers behind his back, resting them over his severed tail stump. A phantom pain radiated through his legs.

"Yes, Dante, please do tell. It's most unlike you to make such a novice mistake," Valdez's mouth twisted into a smile.

Dante inhaled a deep breath. He dreaded this exact conversation for over a year. Answering to his master was stressful and often unpredictable. His father watched and waited.

"As I'm sure you've heard, my lord, I suffered a crystal liquid fuel leak."

Izzo nodded. "I'm well aware, thanks to your father, and no thanks to you. But I'm curious as to why you didn't bother to reach out to me yourself."

"I assumed—"

"Well, you assumed incorrectly."

Dante nodded. "Apologies, my lord."

"What of Earth?" Izzo flicked his sharp tongue, changing the subject.

Dante's heart slammed against his chest, but he made no outward indication. "There was a complication."

"How so?" Izzo's expression turned deathly serious. "I gave you fairly specific instructions, and as you very well know I don't tolerate failure."

"Earth was maimed beyond recognition and had to be destroyed," he lied. The room went so silent as he anticipated the ceiling crashing in on them. It was the first time he'd ever disappointed his master. His father inhaled a breath.

"And the humans?"

"Met their end in the process. I regret that I won't be able to erect a city in your godly name."

"It's no matter, we'll utilize a nearby planet. The humans are more trouble than they're worth."

Dante remained silent. He didn't understand any of it. *Why did he send him there in the first place?*

"Also," Dante hated to discuss the matter, but there was no other way. "I took for myself a spoil of war. A mate from Earth." The room fell pitch silent, and the temperature of the room seemed to rise. A single drop of sweat rolled down his back, and his hands slid against the fabric of his gloves.

Izzo placed his goblet on the ground and crossed his legs.

"You can't be serious. That's where your little doe-eyed fawn is from?" Valdez snorted.

Izzo cleared his throat and grinned, bearing a set of jagged yellow teeth.

"Well, she must be quite the girl." Izzo paused. "Although I do wish you ran this match by me initially, I cannot see a reason to deny you. You've been both diligent and productive throughout the years. An obedient subject and a true supporter of my cause, even if she is *human*."

"Thank you," Dante leaned into a bow.

"It's just, I worry," the room stilled again and swirled in heated silence, "about your offspring and whether they'll bear your extraordinary abilities. Abilities I find most advantageous."

Dante's stomach churned. Izzo was making plans for his *unborn* children. The idea made him want to vomit.

"But I suppose we'll cross that avenue when it comes."

Dante nodded. "Thank you, my lord."

"My pleasure," Izzo smiled. "And just to confirm, she's the last of her kind?"

"Yes," his hands fidgeted beneath his cape. "She's the very last human."

"Excellent, I don't want any more humans running around than necessary. Oh, and one last matter before I make my leave."

"Yes," Dante straightened his spine, desperate to exit the room.

"What of Keyserike? Have you located my missing general?"

"No, sire. We received a lead and conducted an investigation, but the prisoner had no information," Dante said.

"You must use whatever means necessary to locate him. I want that deserter's head on a platter. Nobody plays me for a fool and lives to tell the tale," Izzo pounded his fist against the arm of his chair.

"Agreed," Valdez interjected. "And I have a fabulous idea. I'd like to accompany Dante back to Surge so we can continue our investigation. I swear, we won't rest until we find him."

"Splendid."

Valdez's lips crept into a smile. It was official. He was in a world of trouble if anyone found out what he'd done to his master's third in command. Even more so if he discovered Earth had been spared and the humans were alive and well.

DANTE HATED to have this conversation, *utterly dreaded it*, but there was no other way.

"My sweet darling Autumn, may I have a word with you?"

She sat on the bed, stroking the head of the beast he confiscated for her. She blinked her large innocent gray eyes, stripping him bare with her moonlight gaze.

"About?"

"Earth."

"What about Earth? Did something happen? Is Earth in trouble? You promised me, Dante, you promised me."

Yes, he'd promised her. But now, they were all in great danger.

He sat down, folding his hands in his lap. Autumn huffed and puffed while her new pet buried his head against her chest.

"It's just, you have to understand—"

"No, no, no, you can't do this. Please, you can't."

"Did I actually say—" he started and then stopped.

A deep, latent, furious energy consumed the room, possibly rivaling his own, causing a flash of white light. A pillar smoked and then exploded, sending rubble and dust flying through the air. Dante was knocked against a wall but caught himself before smashing through it while uncontrollable tears streamed down Autumn's cheeks.

He stared at her, wide-eyed. "I knew you had abilities, but I had to see for myself."

* * *

Autumn stumbled backwards, almost falling off the bed.

"Abilities, what are you talking about?" Her eyes widened. "I'm human, just human, remember? Stop being weird and trying to change the subject. What's going on with Earth?"

She crawled on the ground and pulled Mr. Hiss out from underneath the bed. His talons bared before vanishing into his soft pink fur. She cradled him in her arms, tears streaming down her cheeks.

"I may be a lot of things but I'm not a fool," Dante cocked his head to the side. "I saw what you did to my sister, smashing her clear through stone. But I refused to believe it until I saw for myself."

Somehow, she doubted it. Leyla had a theatrical flair to her, bratty and dramatic.

"No, you're wrong. Leyla did that to herself."

"There's no sense in denying it. I'm *never* wrong."

"Stop being a cocky jerk. It's the truth."

His mouth curled. "Be careful what you wish for. Put that ling down and lay a hit on me, mate."

Her eyes widened. "Don't be ridiculous. I'm not going to hit you. Get out of my room!"

He loosened his royal-purple cape and it rippled to the ground. "I said hit me."

"Not until you tell me what you were going to say about Earth."

"It can wait."

Autumn stared at him, baffled. *What the heck?* He couldn't be serious. Dante wanted her to hit him? She'd never been in a fight in her life. Sure, she smacked stupid guys in the face here or there for being fresh but never a full-on fight. And never with someone with Dante's bloody track record.

A cold chill trickled down the length of her spine at the recollection of what he did to Caleb. How he broke him like a savage and tortured him with his mind.

Suddenly, she remembered something.

Memories flooded back of Keyserike. The pink blob monster who ate whole soldiers and Brianna. Poor Brianna whose eyes he plucked from her skull.

Dante had annihilated him to fine space dust. His strength and power were unimaginable, and he wanted to fight her.

No freaking way.

She took a stumbling step backwards. Dante snatched Mr. Hiss from her arms before she could protest. Mr. Hiss wiggled and turned before leaping to the ground and scampering underneath the bed. His sapphire eyes glistened in the shadows.

"I remember."

His amber eyes widened. "What do you remember?"

"*Everything.*"

"Impossible."

"Then who's *Keyserike*? Stop avoiding the question."

Dante crouched down and resumed a fighting stance. Her heart pounded in her ears.

"Don't you *ever* mention that name again. It's for your own safety," he said. "Stop procrastinating. Come at me with everything you have."

How ridiculous.

It was clear he was convinced she had some sort of ability. But how? None of it made any sense. Unless—*Armienti.*

"If you miss, there will be consequences," he winked.

All out of options and desperate to prove he was wrong, she charged at him with her eyes closed and arms swinging, a shrill scream piercing her lungs.

Right before they collided, he stepped to the side with the grace of a cat, causing Autumn to stumble face first toward a wall. Deftly, Dante grabbed her hand and flipped her around before her brain could even register what had happened. She gasped as he pulled her in close. Cloud satin slid against solid onyx spandex. His midnight hair swayed in the heated afternoon breeze.

"Look at your face," he chuckled, tracing her lips with his black-gloved fingertip. Her nose crinkled with frustration as she bared her teeth in a snarl. "Don't you think for one moment I would allow harm to befall *my property*."

"Your property!?" She balled her fists and gritted her teeth.

He grabbed her wrists and pulled her toward him in response. "Yes, *my property*. Make no mistake, Autumn Ramon, you belong to me."

"I do not!" She twisted and turned trying to escape, but he leaned down claiming her mouth with his fiery lips and smooth tongue. She shoved him away and he laughed, crossing his arms.

"The clothing you wear. The air that fills your lungs. The food and drink you consume. That useless animal under the bed and your home world planet Earth, are mine, that I allow you to enjoy. Perhaps you should call me master like everyone else," he grinned.

Autumn lunged at his knees like a football player tackling an opponent, but he stepped aside like fluid lightning. Her mouth agape, she was about to eat the corner of the bed when a cool tingling sensation flushed through her limbs. She struggled with all her might, straining her fingers, arms, and legs, but she was frozen.

Dante whisked her into the air and circled her, fingers

twined behind his back. A taunting smile crept across his lips. "Surely you can do better than that."

"Let me down, dammit! Let me down!" she roared, twisting, drenched with sweat, as he held her steadfast with his mind.

"I know what you have deep down inside. That anger. That rage. I've felt it for myself. It's a permanent part of you, utterly Elattion."

Autumn screamed and screamed, until her throat went raw. She fought with all her might, but Dante was too strong. She was like a fly entwined in a spider's web and he was ready to sink his fangs into her. Her mind raced a million miles per minute.

"What if I were to tell you, I know who killed your mom?"

Her eyes bulged from their sockets. "I'd call you a liar. You're a fucking liar!"

"I'm quite serious actually."

Her heart imploded deep inside her chest. Dread and agony consumed her before her emotions turned to pure unadulterated rage. "You're a liar!"

Blue light. Hot and cold. Love and hatred. Pain and pleasure from deep inside of her sprayed the ceiling in a violent explosion. Rubble fell to the ground in a torrential swirl. Breaking free of his hold, she rammed Dante in the shin, causing him to stumble two steps backwards.

Autumn trembled when she realized what she'd done, what she'd felt, and what Dante had claimed. Dante knelt, rocks and pebbles crumbling all around them. Placing his thumb and forefinger beneath her chin, he propped her head up to meet his gaze.

"Our great work begins upon our return to Surge."

"Tell me who killed my mom," she glowered at him.

"In due time. Until then, this stays between you and me."

Too little too late, her personal guard marched through the door, surrounding them with guns cocked.

"At ease gentleman," Dante raised a palm. "This was nothing more than a lover's quarrel."

PART THREE

Sanguis

Thirty-Five

LEYLA COULDN'T BELIEVE her eyes. Her brother had stooped to a new level of cruelty. She wanted to run, wanted to scream, wanted to pluck the winding strands of hair from her scalp. But she refused, and she wouldn't give her maids the satisfaction of watching her freak out.

"Princesses do *not* freak out," she silently mouthed to herself.

That morning, she received a white package secured by a magenta satin bow. She hoped it was a peace offering of some sort from her brother, considering she'd been on her best behavior the last week of their family trip to Diode.

She'd hoped in vain. Dante never forgot *any* of the wrongs against him. Instead of a peace offering, the package contained what she feared most.

"Tell him I refuse," she snapped at a maid, shoving the package away. "Or better yet, I'll tell him myself; you're too much of a coward."

Leyla headed toward the door but then fell to her knees and sobbed her eyes out. The maids surrounded her and rubbed her back.

"It'll be okay, my lady, it isn't the end of the world. We're—"

"But it is. People will never look at me the same again," she choked through bitter tears, cheeks slicked wet. If only she'd kept her mouth shut, kept her opinions of Autumn to herself. But Dante had probed her memories. *Who knew how far back he had gone?*

She hoped upon hope he hadn't scanned back to the night before his arrival home, or she risked him discovering everything she hoped he wouldn't.

Thirty-Six

AUTUMN COULDN'T STAND to look at herself.

She stared into the bathroom mirror with a vacant expression. Her gray eyes were listless, golden olive features drawn. Emblem and Allegoria toweled her dry with fluffy white towels. Although it was unnecessary, she didn't bother to protest this time.

As far as she was concerned, she didn't deserve to breathe. She was a murderer, no better than Dante and the person who murdered her mom in *cold blood*.

"Are you okay, my lady?" Emblem's clover eyes sparkled with concern.

"Just call me Autumn already," she walked into her lavish suite. *What's wrong with these maids? My lady this and my lady that.* She wanted to scream, but her throat was still too raw.

The dual suns sparkled with rays of gold and orange through the open balcony doors. Warm lavender drifted and aircraft hummed through the buzzing metropolis. A nostalgic scent from home couldn't calm her now.

"Okay, Autumn," Emblem trotted after her. "I'm sorry."

"It's okay."

When Autumn met her gaze, she was reminded of the servants crushed beneath the rubble in the courtyard. Their innocent bulging eyes, shattered bones, and ruby-red blood staining the swirled star mosaic floor.

All thanks to the abilities she never asked for.

"I'm fine," Autumn's eyes clouded with tears. She blinked away the fog. How could she go back home? What would her dad think? What if she accidentally killed one of her friends? No, she could never let that happen. And Caleb...her lips trembled. She risked hurting him as well.

Autumn took a seat on her bed and stared at her palms, unable to breathe. For a moment they dripped with red blood. She blinked hard.

"Well, you don't look fine to me," Emblem said. "What's bothering you? Is it your upcoming wedding? Are you getting cold fee—"

Two heavy boots hit the floor, distracting her from her thoughts. Autumn hugged herself.

"Leave us," Dante waved a hand. Emblem and Allegoria exited the room like scurrying mice.

The door slid shut and Autumn sat there in silence.

"I thought you'd be dressed by now so we could have breakfast together before—"

"Well, I'm not hungry."

Mr. Hiss stretched and yawned on the far end of the bed. Another wet spot drenched his soft pink underbelly. Dante frowned.

"You're awfully gaunt as of late. Have you been eating? Or have those lazy twin maids of yours been forgetting to serve your meals? When I get my hands on them—"

"Don't you *dare* comment about my weight," she hissed. "Of course they're feeding me. I haven't been hungry. It's kind of hard to eat and sleep when you've killed somebody, although you don't seem to have a problem."

He smoothed a black-gloved hand through his midnight tresses and changed the subject. "Our wedding will take place early next month. There will be *many* in attendance."

"Great," she sighed. *Like she cared.*

"I want nothing more than to make you happy."

"Then send me back to Earth."

"In due time, after things settle down," he paused. "Let me apologize in advance for what I must do. Valdez demands retribution for her damaged banquet hall. She'd rather your head, but I'd never allow that to happen."

"Why not bother Leyla?"

His white teeth sparkled with deviance. "She's been dealt with, don't you worry."

He turned around and handed her a small white box. "Here, put this on."

She opened it and made a face.

He snorted softly. "Just put it on and meet me outside. Do your best to seem upset about this punishment. Lest Valdez gets a better idea. Believe me, she can be creative."

"Fine," she agreed, although she didn't see what the big deal was all about.

* * *

Dante waited in the hallway for Autumn to dress when he heard heeled footsteps scraping against the crimson carpeted floor.

"Dante, please, please, you can't make me do this," Leyla's brown eyes were red-rimmed, tears spilled down her cheeks.

He folded his arms. "I'm afraid you brought this on yourself, sister."

"But, but what will people think when they see me?"

"Perhaps you should've taken that into consideration before—"

Autumn stepped out of her room wearing the heather-gray bodysuit he presented her with earlier. She looked as radiant as glowing moonstone despite being clothed in the color of the lower classes. Her eyes sparkled in the rising sunlight.

Leyla's bottom lip trembled. "It suits her better. Make her wear this, not me. I'm a pureblood princess."

"And soon, Autumn will outrank you. So, suck it up. It's only for a week," he turned toward Autumn. "You, however, will remain in my service until our wedding. And thereafter as needed."

"But why?" Autumn protested. "She's the one—"

"Enough," he raised a hand. "We're going to be late, and you both have lots of orders to take."

Thirty-Seven

NEON BLUE LIGHT shone beneath the conference room door. It slid open to darkness. Autumn counted at least thirty high ranking Elattion officials clothed in obsidian, their prominent features illuminated through the shadows.

An oval table sat in the center of the room, cloaked with a replica of all twenty-four universes. Scattered throughout the map were brilliant spheres covered with glowing ice, fire, sand, and tangled vines.

On the far end was a tiny blue and green planet marked by an X, resembling Earth. She gulped. *Why was Earth crossed out?* She grew dizzy for a moment then sucked in a breath.

While she tried to decipher the hieroglyphic-like characters surrounding the planets, her eyes connected with Valdez's, her mouth twisted like a viper, wings settling against the back of her chair.

Ronan and Armienti sat watching her, arms folded and muscles shifting, and at the head of the room stood the emperor, his legs as firm as two mighty tree trunks.

Dante left them at the door and took the seat closest to his father. Leyla hugged herself and stood by the wall.

This can't be happening.

The emperor shot Dante with a side-eyed look. "Now that we're *all* in attendance, let's begin. Least pressing business first. Kintuck, I'm assigning you to oversee production of our newest crystal mine on Varz. You and your family will leave tomorrow at first light."

"Of course, Your Imperial Majesty, thank you. I won't disappoint you," a man answered through the shadows.

"You're very welcome," the emperor smiled through his midnight goatee.

Clank...Valdez slammed the base of her silver goblet against the table interrupting the meeting. *Clank, clank, clank*... "Servants, my thirst grows greater with each passing second and my patience is wearing."

Crap. Autumn scanned the room, and Leyla stood there, arms folded. Defiant.

"You're more qualified to do this than me," Leyla hissed. "You better get to it."

"You're up first. This is all your fault," Autumn whispered.

"I'm waiting," Valdez licked her lips.

When neither Autumn or Leyla moved, Valdez whipped a familiar golden bow and arrow from behind her chair, nocked the arrow back and shot it between them. It sank deep into the wall, tail vibrating until it exploded. Leyla stumbled backwards and Autumn bit back a startled scream.

"Valdez, stop it right now," Dante said.

"I was only—"

He snapped his fingers in the air. "Leyla, today."

Leyla groaned, dragging her feet over to a nearby metal vase of water on a stand. She carried it, splashing liquid over the floor, and haphazardly poured it into Valdez's goblet. Valdez took a sip, flashing a wicked smile.

"As I was saying," the emperor's eyes widened. "Varz will

provide us with infinite wealth. It's a major asset to The Empire."

A flash of silver caught Autumn's attention. Armienti raised his goblet in the darkness. She supposed it was her turn now. She grabbed the vase from Leyla and carefully poured the water into his goblet.

Armienti's lips moved as if he wanted to speak.

"What," Autumn whispered. "Do you want to laugh at me too? Your poor cousin's kidnapped future mate is a servant again."

"You were a waitress back on Earth which, to my present understanding, is different from a servant. Have you forgotten your human terminology already?" His crystal blue eyes smiled.

She glowered.

"Actually," he pressed his gilded hair behind his blue pointed ear, "I want to apologize to you."

"For what?"

"Dante came to me. About—for making you different."

"Oh," she took the vase and hugged it tight. "That."

"This wasn't my intention," Armienti said. "I only meant to heal you. Not to give you—"

"Well thank you. There's nothing I can do about it now." Although she still wanted to cry her eyes out for the people she'd killed. Her bottom lip trembled.

And now she was afraid to go back to Earth and the havoc she could wreak there.

A whisper of a voice penetrated the depths of her mind. *Be careful what you think; we're not alone.*

Autumn met Ronan's emerald eyes. She nodded slowly and returned to her post.

"What was that all about?" Leyla whispered.

"Mind your own business."

Leyla groaned, turning away.

"As I was saying," the emperor's voice boomed, distracting them. "We must stop at nothing until we locate General Keyserike. Lord Izzo demands retribution. He wants him returned to Universe 24 alive."

For a split second her eyes connected with Dante's, but she couldn't allow herself to think too much. She was afraid someone else might hear.

* * *

After three hours of indescribable boredom, Dante's father finally concluded the council meeting. His ears rang with statistics, coordinates, and possible planets where Keyserike could be seeking refuge. There was even fear of a coup.

They'd be better off searching the deepest depths of space for the remnants of his charred body and bones. As well as the bodies of his unfortunate crew.

His father was one of the first to leave the room. High ranking lords and officials followed.

"Wait for me outside," Dante said when Autumn and Leyla went to leave.

They rolled their eyes. Autumn looked especially pretty when she was cross. He couldn't help but bite back a smile that deflated as soon as he beheld Valdez.

"A word," he said.

"Certainly," Valdez nodded and tucked wisps of hair behind her pointed ears.

When the room finally emptied, she sat back in her chair picking her red manicured talons. The cruel yet beautiful features of her face sat straight.

"What you pulled earlier was unacceptable," Dante folded his arms, shoulders squared.

"I'm your superior," she chewed her bottom lip into a mischievous smile. "You don't have permission to instruct me.

Those girls owe me a new banquet hall. The decor was ancient and irreplaceable."

"Don't pull that rank bullshit on me; you're a guest in *my* home. You could've killed them." *Especially Autumn*, the more vulnerable of the two. After what happened, she needed his protection now more than ever.

She chuckled. "Oh Dante, like I didn't hear what you did in my home. My officials have yet to cease their whining about the ling you stole."

"I'll gladly compensate you," Dante offered.

"There's no need. I think it's rather pathetic on their part. They deserved to lose it," she paused. "As for the girls, I only miss when I intend to."

"Well don't let it happen again."

"You used to be so much fun," she grinned. "Now you're boring and considerate. I never thought I'd see the day Dante the Great Conqueror—"

"My family is off limits. Now if you'll please excuse me, I have other business to attend to."

He turned on a heel, anger brewing deep inside. Valdez swiveled her seat, grinning in the shadows.

Autumn and Leyla stood on either side of the doorway; arms crossed.

"Leyla, you're free to go about the rest of your day, until tomorrow morning, of course. I'll have a fresh set of grays delivered to your room," Dante winked.

"Oh, thank the heavens," Leyla threw her arms up in the air. "Pouring water is such a wretched chore. I'm not sure how the hybrids do it all day." She strode away, heels scraping against the crimson carpeted floor.

Dante chuckled softly. *It's the first chore she's ever done in her life.*

"And as for you, Autumn my dear, you shall come with me."

"Why do I have to stay? She started this whole thing," she protested.

"It matters not to me. Go change into something a little more *comfortable*. We have training to do."

"Training?" Her eyes widened.

"Yes, *training*." His lips curved.

Thirty-Eight

THIS COULD *NOT* BE HAPPENING. *Training.* What the heck did she have to train for? A marathon? To be some kind of perfect alien wife? With all the rules and regulations instilled in her so far, she didn't want to find out.

Her stomach churned. All she wanted was to get far away from Surge, go back to her friends and dad on Earth, and for this whole ordeal to be nothing more than a nightmare. Yet, there she was in Universe 13, separated from everyone she loved and prepping to marry *Dante the Great Conqueror* in a few short weeks. It took everything she had not to scream at the thought.

She wanted to see Caleb again. *Oh, Caleb.* Every time she tried to imagine him, his face faded, just as the faces of everyone else she loved back on Earth faded. Instead, the images that remained plastered to her mind were the crushed and mangled bodies of the servants she'd murdered—severed limbs drenched in a pool of blood, while still more blood smeared into a mosaic of swirls and stars.

* * *

Autumn was led by her guards to a wing of the palace she'd never been to before, separated by two steel ceiling-high sliding doors. She dressed comfortably, as Dante requested, in a pitch-black bodysuit with a pair of knee-high boots. *Alien fashion,* she sighed. *It totally sucks.*

As she walked through the doors, they vacuum sealed behind her.

It wasn't her imagination. Her feet weighed a million pounds. Sweat beaded across her brow. She knelt, scarcely able to catch her breath, scarcely able to stand. When she went to rise, she fell to her knees again.

At that instant, she heard footsteps and chuckling approaching. She caught a flash of too-white teeth. Dante strode through the hallway shirtless, blue muscles flexed. His spandex shorts hugged his thighs in all the right places. She blinked; she'd stared too long. Her cheeks burned.

"Kill the gravity," said Dante, and the gripping sensation against her body stopped.

Autumn laid in a fetal position, exhausted. She shakily rose to her feet and brushed herself off. "Are you trying to kill me or something?"

"This is your first lesson. When entering an alien planet, always expect the unexpected. Not all gravity levels are like here, Diode, and Earth. This was only five times higher; some planets can exceed a hundred."

Her jaw dropped. "A hundred times normal gravity? What kind of training is this anyway? I thought you wanted me to learn how to be a better cook for you or something."

Dante winked. "Now there's an idea I'll have to keep in mind. Although, the pizza you made for me back on Earth was excellent."

Her forehead pulsated. "When? How did you— Did you sneak back into my house after you left?"

He brushed past her and never answered. She hobbled behind him, muscles screaming in pain.

They entered a gymnasium with a central skylight. Silver metallic tiles coated the floor. In the far corner was a stack of black mats, piled high.

A flash sparkled along the ceiling. She spotted a shirtless Ronan and Armienti wrestling mid-air. They slammed one another into the walls before Ronan landed face first into the tiles, leaving behind a crater.

"I win," Armienti flew down, landing on the floor. He pulled his brother to his feet, patting him on the back.

She took two steps in retreat, trembling. "I hope you don't expect me to fight," she said to Dante.

"Not at first, but you'll learn how to control your abilities. It's a necessity, or you risk hurting others and yourself. I know you don't want either; I know how much you worry."

"How?"

"You often cry out in your sleep."

"How would you know that? Have you been spying on me again?"

He chuckled and walked away. *Creep.*

"Nice to see you," Dante reached to embrace his cousins, but they stiffened like something was bothering them.

I wonder what's with them.

"Good luck, Autumn. You'll do great," Armienti said. Ronan and Armienti exited the room, grabbing steaming towels from a table in the hallway.

"What's going on with them?"

"Never mind, you should be more concerned with the task at hand. We're not leaving this room until you land a hit on me."

"I'm not hitting you until you tell me what the deal is with Keyserike and who Emperor Izzo is." She placed a hand on her hip. "You also promised me information about my mom's killer."

"In due time," he crossed his arms. "I'll give you what you want."

Dante sauntered to a far wall of the room and pressed a bright red button. Sliding metal panels bricked over the skylight.

"Oh, and I failed to mention, I'm placing the gravity three levels higher than what you were accustomed to on Earth."

The topic of Keyserike and Lord Izzo was bound to arise in conversation. It was unavoidable now that Autumn regained her memories because of her change. Dante planned to work her to the bone for any information he had to offer though. The less she knew, the better. It was for her own safety.

It was in her best interest to learn how to control her abilities, not that he would dare risk her in a battle or an invasion. She was far too precious and needed his protection. He made that mistake once—he hadn't forgiven himself for that—and didn't dare to make it again.

Dante folded his arms, unphased by the increased pull of gravity against his body. For all he cared, it could be raised to a thousand.

Droplets of sweat beaded Autumn's hairline. A smile crept across his lips as she fell to her knees, body shaking. He watched and waited for her first move.

Thirty-Nine

AUTUMN'S HEAD swam with a dizzying heaviness as she struggled to stand. Her limbs dropped, and she inhaled deep, heavy breaths.

"What's the matter, my sweet? Are you giving up so soon?"

The sound of his smooth, arrogant voice made her blood boil in her veins. How he enjoyed maintaining the upper hand, asserting dominance over others, and being an arrogant jerk. He glided effortlessly through the air chuckling.

She rose and moved her legs one shaky step at a time. "Tell me about Keyserike."

His mouth fell into a tight, flat line. "Quit distracting yourself and focus on the task at hand. You're wasting your energy, and we have a long, grueling training session ahead of us."

He floated higher, mid-way to the ceiling. Autumn groaned, walking with slow calculated steps. "That's not fair, I can't fly. I'll never—"

"Sure you can," he crossed his arms. "Don't focus on limiting beliefs. Anything and everything is possible. Imagine a ball of light and pull it toward your core. Hold it there, then release it."

She fell to her knees and squeezed her eyes shut. When she came back up to a trembling stand, she brushed against his solid form.

"Over here," his breath caressed her neck.

She raised her fist to punch him, but he disappeared. A pair of boots tapped against her head. Her eyes bulged, teeth gritted as she jumped to grab hold of them, out of breath. Her body was heavy like it was weighed down by wet sand.

As she closed her eyes, she visualized the light he'd spoken of, and soon felt its golden rays and burning hot embers flush against her skin. She held it at her center then released it into the air. When her eyes opened, she was floating. Despite her predicament, she couldn't help but smile.

"Look Dante, I'm flying."

"That you are," he applauded.

She swam and twirled through the air, weightless. As he glided closer, she took her boot and rammed him in the shin with all her might. He sputtered backwards and caught himself.

"Don't you ever put your filthy shoes on me again."

He chuckled. She'd tricked him.

* * *

The Emperor sat in the empty council chamber signing a never-ending stack of virtual death warrants. His temples throbbed.

There were so many fine details about his son's latest mission that didn't add up. For one, he returned maimed after his yearlong stay on Earth, and General Keyserike was *coincidentally* last spotted in the lower universes.

He wondered if the two had met and under what circumstances. *I can only imagine what's happened during his absence,* he thought with a sigh.

Although that blob of filth deserved to meet his untimely end, he wished his son would've been more subtle about it. Together, they could've made it look like an accident.

How will we explain this mishap to the Grand Supreme? Our loyalty could come into question.

The emperor ground his teeth. How he despised his son's human whore. She was nothing but a distraction. The weak, useless, half-blood whelps the girl was sure to bear for his son would be most counterproductive to their goals. It ensured future generations of his family would remain in servitude forever.

A throat cleared, distracting him from his tortured thoughts and he glanced up from his work.

"Lady Valdez, I didn't hear you come in."

"I've been here the entire time, my lord," her full jade lips bowed.

The emperor ceased his signing. "How can I be of service to you?"

Valdez took a long red nail and traced it along the black, blinking replica of Universe 13. "I don't feel we're being quite aggressive enough in our search for our favorite missing general," her lips curved in a cruel smile that he appreciated from across the table.

Why couldn't Dante have selected a mate of her *caliber? A union like theirs would be incredible.*

"What do you have in mind?" He stroked his goatee.

"I say we demonstrate a brute display of force. Then any party with knowledge of Keyserike's whereabouts will be forced to come forth out of fear, lest they meet a similar fate by association."

"Excellent, I always enjoy a good show," the emperor grinned.

"We'll have Dante host and invite Lord Izzo and the rest of the universes to tune in. Make no mistake, Keyserike and his supporters will see how we handle those who defy us."

As will Autumn. She'd see firsthand the monster his son was. It was the perfect plan.

Forty

WHEN AUTUMN RETURNED to her room, her legs trembled beneath her weight. The dual suns lowered in the sky, casting a magenta and marmalade glow along the horizon. Aircraft zipped through the mighty metropolis.

She fell face-first on her bed, sore muscles screaming in pain. Three times the regular gravity was excruciating, but the expression on Dante's face when she kicked him and defeated him at his own game was *priceless*.

It sucked to be him.

She'd have to remember to do that more often. He could use a good kick occasionally.

While she laid there, her bedroom door opened—Emblem and Allegoria entered. Emblem carried a small bottle of golden oil and placed it on the table.

Mr. Hiss slunk out from beneath the bed. He stretched and yawned before climbing onto the mattress and nuzzling his soft pink nose into Autumn's side. She reached, barely able to pet him.

"Rough day?" said Allegoria, helping her out of her bodysuit.

"Yeah, it was the worst."

They stripped Autumn down to her panties and draped a warm towel over her thighs. She rested her head, closing her eyes.

Two heavy boots hit the floor beside her and her relaxation came to a screeching halt. *Crap.* Dante teleported into her room again.

"Go away," she groaned.

Mr. Hiss froze, eyes wide and tail puffed. He sprang underneath the bed.

"Why are you here? Why can't you just leave me alone?" Autumn closed her eyes.

"I wanted to make sure you're okay."

Her forehead twitched as Emblem and Allegoria took their leave.

He took a step closer. "I wanted to say I'm sorry for the way I behaved."

Autumn pushed herself up, covering her breasts. "Sorry isn't going to cut it. What you did was rude and unacceptable. Not to mention—"

"I know," he glanced at his black-gloved palms. "Sometimes I tend to get carried away, which I'm not proud of. I'm here to fulfill my end of the bargain."

She flinched in pain, then fell face-first into the pillow once again.

"You must be sore. Let me help you."

He removed his gloves and sat beside her on the bed. With Autumn too weak to protest, he slathered golden oil over his hands. He rubbed them together, gently kneading them into her shoulders and the tender muscles of her back and arms.

She bit her lip, desperate not to make a sound as he worked her knots out, calluses scraping against her skin.

"Thanks," she wrapped the warm fuzzy towel around her body, fastening it.

"Not a problem," he paused. "You asked me about Keyserike."

"Yeah, what's the deal with him? Why is everyone looking for him?"

"What happened between us was a long time coming," he cracked his oiled knuckles. "I've known him since my formative years."

"How?"

"My father sent me away at the tender age of eight to reside in Universe 24, the most remote of all the universes."

"Why would he do something so cruel?" Her heart ached from being separated from her own family.

Dante sighed. "He's a coward and a weakling who abandoned me when I needed him the most. Rather than challenge Lord Izzo for his claims, he offered me up as tribute in the form of a collaboration. Lord Izzo was especially receptive when he learned of my unmatched abilities. He decided I'd be useful to his cause."

"Which is?"

"Conquering the universes, a vision my father shares as well. We have a planet-split in place in exchange for his protection."

He stood and stretched, ambling toward the balcony door. A warm breeze blew against the white gossamer curtains. "Childhood was miserable for me, and my training lasted many years. I worked directly under Keyserike. Or rather, I did everything, and he reaped all the rewards. Sometimes I was punished for his errors."

"Is that how you got the scar on your chest?" She recalled the deep jagged gashes over his chest and rib cage.

"No, that was something else but—never mind," he folded his arms, glancing away. "I'm sure you're wondering if I regret killing him. The answer is no. I'd do it again in a heartbeat if I had the chance. In fact, I wish I'd done it sooner. It enrages me to no end every time I think about the way he wanted to hurt you and take you away from me," his fists trembled at his sides with unseen fury. Moonlight shimmered through his hair.

She quivered, recalling Keyserike's bumpy acidic tongue and the burns it left over her skin that took forever to heal. And Brianna, poor Brianna, had it worst of all.

"Thank you again. I'm not sure what I would have done if you weren't there."

"What you witnessed must be our secret, or we're all in very real danger. Like you said, we should share everything with each other."

Bzzzzz, Dante's sleek black communicator buzzed as he removed it from his back pocket. "Dinner is served."

"I'd rather eat here. I'm in too much pain." Which was partially true. In reality, she didn't want to encounter his miserable family. They were too much to bear.

"Then I'll carry you the entire way. You deserve to feast after a job well done. Not many could lay a hit like you did on your first try. I'm curious to see what else you're capable of."

* * *

Dante could only fathom what his father wanted from him.

Messaging him for dinner. *Please.*

It was highly unusual, sinister. Deep in his gut he suspected Valdez was responsible. If only he could keep her at bay. If only she wasn't so nosey, insisting on accompanying him back to Surge for an issue she could've solved from her home planet. He hoped upon hope they hadn't discovered his secrets.

Forty-One

AUTUMN'S CHEEKS heated as Dante carried her down two flights of winding steps. The tulle train of her dress glided across the crimson velvet rug, strands of her silver hair sparkling like glowing starlight.

Normally, she'd walk and would drop dead before letting him carry her, let alone touch her, but she was sore and *starving*. Since developing her abilities, her stomach was emptier than ever, like she hadn't eaten in centuries.

When they arrived at the banquet hall, all conversation ceased.

They approached Valdez, who sat at the head table. The emperor, his wife, and Leyla all wore their garish finery. A pair of gilded, spindly antlers graced Valdez's brow. Her long body and limbs were draped in a too-short obsidian toga with gilded bracelets and stacked armbands.

"What's the matter Dante, is there a malfunction with her feet that she can't carry her own weight? Or are humans truly that weak?" Valdez's soft lips played into a wicked smile, bracelets jingling along her arm.

"Her feet are functioning quite well, actually." He winked.

The emperor grumbled and rolled his eyes.

Dante placed Autumn on her feet. Her sore muscles quaked. "You'd be surprised how strong we humans are. Don't for a second underestimate us."

Leyla's eyes widened and Valdez crossed her arms, shifting her long slender legs.

"She speaks."

Autumn rolled her eyes. "Of course I speak. Don't be an idiot."

Valdez chuckled softly. "You talk a tough game for the last of your kind."

"The last of my kind?" Her heart stopped. *What is she talking about?* "I thought—"

"We'll have this discussion later, my sweet," Dante whispered in her ear. Her heart thundered so fast she could barely see straight.

"No, we need to have this conversation *right* now."

Valdez crossed her legs. "Watch your tongue, human. Just because Dante let you off easy, doesn't mean I will. One more word out of your filthy human mouth—"

The rage inside of her spiked for a split second and a votive shattered across the room. Dante wrapped an arm around her waist, which she attempted to pry off.

"Forgive her; she knows not her place. She's still new to our world and our customs," Dante addressed Valdez.

Valdez's mouth tightened like a viper. "I'll gladly school her."

"I'd like to see you try," Autumn countered and then glowered at Dante. "And you."

Leyla gasped, taking in a deep sip of wine, blue dimples protruding against the rim.

"On second thought, you're not worth my time," Valdez picked at her perfectly manicured talons before she turned to Dante. "Keep your pet human on her leash."

Autumn bit her cheeks, prepared to scream at both of them. Her heart violently slammed against her chest bringing with it a blinding wall of pain.

My dad and friends are dead. My dad and friends are dead. Dante is a liar!

"Enough of this nonsense," the emperor slammed his goblet against the table. "We have business to discuss."

"It can wait," Dante rubbed his palm over the small of her heaving back. "First I owe my beautiful fiancé a dance."

Dante swept her into his solid arms and carried her toward the center of the room. She snapped out of her daze.

"I can't believe you. I can't believe—" Autumn breathed as Dante pressed his mouth to hers, black-gloved hand tangling in the back of her unbound hair. Her anger faded for a moment while she was overwhelmed by the flavor of cinnamon. Another votive shattered mid-air.

Dante placed her back onto her feet and pulled away. "Sorry, I know how I disgust you, but I had to shut you up somehow. You're making a scene. You really must get your emotions in check. We'll have to work on that, but more importantly, you need to watch what you say and *think* around Valdez."

Autumn rolled her eyes. "You're a fine one to talk. You punch everything that gets in your way like a savage beast."

"I know, fire rages through my blood," he mused. "But I assure you, I'm much better than I used to be."

He bowed and laced his fingers in hers, resting his other hand on the small of her back. Autumn reached, brushing it upward. The gentle strum of a harp swelled.

He spun her around before pulling her in close. "I swear on everything I hold dear in this life your planet is alive and well."

"Then what was Valdez talking about?"

"You're just going to have to trust me, but we can't have

this conversation here," he murmured into her ear. "And certainly not now."

Holy crap, her eyes widened. "Are you trying to tell me nobody else knows? How can you possibly expect me to trust you after everything you put me through?"

"Everything I've done and everything I will continue to do is because I love you. I made a promise that no harm would befall your planet and I intend to keep it. Your planet is safe."

Autumn noted the sincerity in his eyes. The sincerity of a monster, sure, but she had no other choice than to take his word for it. They were twelve universes away from Earth and as much as she'd like to escape and go back home, it was proving to be difficult.

They ceased their dance, and everyone clapped as he kissed her knuckles with his vile yet handsome blue lips. She crossed her arms. *How can I still find him handsome? What is wrong with me?*

Then, came the whooshing of a gilded arrow followed by gurgling. An arrow pierced the neck of a servant. Dark blood seeped and faded into the plush crimson velvet carpet. He drowned in a pool of his own fluid.

"Impressive," the emperor sipped his wine unphased.

Shock and horror were apparent on both Leyla and the Empress's faces. Their deep brown eyes bulged. Autumn's stomach knotted. *What's wrong with Valdez?* She thought as she inadvertently wrapped her arms around Dante's waist.

"Wonderful. I have both of your attention now," Valdez ripped the arrow from the throat of the dying servant. His eyes closed, never to open again.

Dante glanced between them, eerily calm. "What is it you need from me? I know you haven't messaged me for naught."

"I'm reopening the Chamber of Horrors. You're going to be the host," the emperor's lips curled.

"Very well then. Is that all?" Dante laced his fingers behind his back.

"The first round we'll clean out the cells. Some of those prisoners have been sitting for quite a while."

Dante nodded. "Good idea."

The emperor continued, "From there on out, we'll import until that traitor Keyserike is brought to justice. Nobody makes a fool out of us."

The emperor turned to the empress, his daughter, and Autumn. "You're expected to attend as well. You're not going to want to miss the greatest show in all the 24 Universes."

The color faded from the Empress and Leyla's blue faces. Autumn didn't like the sound of this at all. *The Chamber of Horrors.* The nightmares never ended.

Forty-Two

DANTE DID *NOT* WANT Autumn to attend. He dreaded it. What was he supposed to do? A formal invitation had been extended by his father and Valdez, and from time to time, the Grand Supreme tuned in as well. *Nosy bastard.* Dante understood what was expected of him.

He admired Autumn in the dark-lit conference room. She was fierce, strong-willed, and downright *distracting* as she poured water into goblets clothed in her skin-tight, heather-gray bodysuit.

His face warmed as he stared at the slope of her thighs, glancing away when she looked at him. Her punishment was really a secret way for him to spend more time with her, but he'd never admit it aloud. Otherwise, she wouldn't be bothered with him. Autumn hated him, and she'd hate him even more after this afternoon. Hopefully not for everything though.

By the end of the meeting, all he could recall was that planet Varz was thriving under his father's reign. Somehow, Lord Izzo was involved and Keyserike was still at bay.

Huge surprise. He'd be at bay forever.

As everyone filed out of the room, including Valdez, who stared at him for a moment too long, spiky wings twitching, Autumn approached him with her rosy cheeks and eyes too large for her heart-shaped face.

She folded her arms. "I'm not coming to your stupid event."

"You have to," Dante said. "I have something for you. I hope you'll be pleased."

"Another gift? If you really want to make me happy, teach me how to control my abilities and send me home," she muttered.

"In due time. When everything settles down." Panic overtook him. His heart clenched at the notion. If she left, he feared she'd never return to him.

* * *

Guillermo Ramon walked, boots crunching through the crisp fall leaves at Farrah Falls. Another Thanksgiving had come and gone. Another holiday he was forced to spend at home alone. Autumn was gone and his late wife Margaret. Her name hadn't crossed his mind in years—he never let it, but now the name echoed in his mind like a song stuck in his head.

Margaret Ramon.

Close behind, Lauren and Ellie bickered amongst themselves. He thought it was nice but unnecessary that they offered to help him search for his missing daughter over Thanksgiving break.

His daughter, their best friend. It was understandable when he thought of it that way.

"Mr. Ramon, what makes you think she'd be all the way out here?" Ellie's teeth chattered.

"Ellie," Lauren hissed, white breath flowing. "We're here for you, Mr. Ramon, whatever you need."

"Thank you, girls."

In reality, Guillermo came to what little was left of the forest after the massive fire *every* week in hopes of finding Dante's home. The home Autumn had mentioned when the cops came to his door to arrest him. If only he'd gone, he wouldn't be in this predicament right now.

Guillermo planned to strangle Dante and demand to be brought to his daughter. Little punk. When he got his hands on him, he'd be sorry.

But every time he searched he'd found nothing. Only trees, leaves, and painful memories.

They walked past the frozen falls, bitter wind whistling off the ice and all around them. Guillermo stopped and turned around, pulling his warm knit cap over his frozen ears. "Have either of you ever been to Dante's house?"

"Is that where we're going?" Lauren's blue eyes widened. "I had no idea he lived in the middle of the woods. Is that even legal?"

"Why would he live all the way out here?" Ellie made a face. "And why would Autumn—"

"She's right," Lauren said. "She really could be in Europe. Why would she lie?"

Guillermo shot them each a look.

Lauren jumped. "Sorry, or we can help you look like we said we would."

Ellie nodded. "Who knows, maybe we'll run into—"

Lauren shook her head, covering her mouth.

"Never mind, I shouldn't have said anything."

Guillermo's brow furrowed. "Who?"

Ellie stuttered. "No one, just some people that we used to know."

Forty-Three

AUTUMN DUG through her canvas crossbody bag for what little was left of her belongings from Earth.

"Finally," she muttered, hands sliding over a paperback she'd "forgotten" to return to the library. Only, the page wasn't creased where she remembered leaving off. In fact, there was no crease at all. She grumbled to herself. What she really wanted to read was *Dracula,* but it was nowhere to be found.

Autumn stood up and stretched, biding her time. Dante disappeared and promised to return for the event that she dreaded more than anything later that afternoon.

The Chamber of Horrors. The name sounded terrifying.

Autumn needed a distraction. She was one book away from having nothing but reality to face. Cold, cruel, painful reality. Her life was in shambles.

She left her room, a book in hand, flanked by her personal guard. They trailed her, their metallic guns clanging through the never-ending stretches of hallway, down a flight of winding steps through the dark barren banquet hall.

When she rounded the corner to pass through the throne

room to where the quiet enclosed courtyard was, a chill rippled down her spine. She was met face to face with Princess Leyla Martyne.

Autumn stumbled backwards, accidentally colliding with a guard. He fell to one knee, head bowed, and apologized profusely. She assured him it was okay, her gaze focused on the princess.

Leyla cooled her beautiful face with a white feathered fan, dripping with sparkling diamonds. Her pink lips twisted to the side.

"I've been meaning to tell you something," Leyla crossed her arms.

Autumn rolled her eyes, pushing her aside, but Leyla grabbed her arm. Autumn ripped it away in response, her book falling on the floor.

When she bent to collect her book, Leyla snatched it up instead and thumbed through the pages, making a face.

"What's this nonsense?" Leyla asked. "It looks terrifically boring."

Autumn reached and ripped it from her hands. "Mind your own business. How do you know it's boring if you've never read it?"

Leyla blinked. "Wait—" she said as Autumn ambled away.

She turned and stopped. "What do you want?"

"I've been meaning to tell you something."

"Okay?" Autumn watched her, shifting her weight.

"The way you handled Valdez yesterday was pretty impressive." Leyla's lengthy lashes brushed the peaks of her high cheekbones. "Nobody I know would dare tangle with her and *especially* not a human."

"Stop mocking me."

"I'm being serious," Leyla quirked a brow. "Someone needs to put that murderess in her place."

"Someone needs to put you in your place too," Autumn

paused and rerouted the conversation. "Why do they call it the Chamber of Horrors?"

Leyla went deathly serious. "You'll find out soon enough. Let's just say the palace isn't carpeted wall to wall with red for nothing."

Leyla turned on her heel and strode away, fanning herself. Autumn stood there in silence, heart pounding in her ears.

* * *

Dante sat in a swiveling chair, feet outstretched over a table as a trembling manservant slathered shaving cream over his throat. A razor gently pulled across his skin as he prepared for the upcoming event.

He had to look his best considering the festivities would be streamed throughout every universe, through the homes of commoners and elites alike. His master was sure to tune in. He was prepared to uphold his reputation. And more importantly, the sanctity of the realm.

Whilst he was being groomed, his eyes were drawn to a prisoner in the corner of the room with his hands and feet bound tight and a black sack secured over his head. Fortunately, he'd gotten to the prisoner before Valdez and his father had.

Blood boiled through his veins. He found this prisoner particularly offensive. A sharp prick nicked Dante's throat followed by a droplet of blood. The servant tending to his shave trembled, holding up the razor sheepishly. Dante rolled his eyes and waved him off. There had been quite enough bloodshed in the palace as of late, especially with Valdez slithering around with her own selfish agenda.

An agenda he'd yet to figure out.

Licking his fingertip, he smeared the droplet against his skin. He cracked his knuckles and walked over to the corner of the room. Day glow seeped through the window with a golden tangerine hue as Dante grabbed the prisoner by his collar and tore off the simple cotton sack. A pair of unfocused eyes watched him.

"Look, for this is the last stream of light you shall ever behold," he pointed toward the window. "You've created so much trouble. Where I'm sending you, even the scavengers won't find you."

The prisoner moved his mouth, tongue scraping, but no words escaped. Only the flow of weak dry breath. All thanks to the bit lodged between his teeth. He was a shell of his former self, finally broken.

"Excellent, that's what I thought, no objections," Dante chuckled softly. "You used to be full of them."

Dante snapped his fingers, and the guards marched in and hauled him off on the next flight off planet.

Forty-Four

AUTUMN REACHED THE CENTRAL COURTYARD, the bones of her fists aching from clenching them so hard.

"Annoying Leyla," she grumbled, but she was still nowhere near as annoying as the guards following her everywhere. "Wait here." The guards halted at the doorway at her request. Finally, she could have some room to breathe, some room to think. Some freaking peace and quiet.

The dual suns shone high in the sky, casting long, lingering shadows through the columns that'd since been repaired. It was like nobody had died and no blood had ever been spilled. She ambled over to a white stone bench. Oversized butterflies and dragonflies flitted through the warm summer breeze without a care in the world.

She thumbed to the first page of her book and read. All was silent, until the columns whispered and then screamed like thousands of people all at once. She whipped her head up, adrenaline seeping through her limbs. A dripping body dragged itself across the ground face down with bizarre movements, leaving behind a long black puddle.

She dropped her book and sprinted over, kneeling to see if the person was all right. It stopped, wet gargling breaths seeping through its lungs. The pale gray dying face of her mom stared back at her, eyes bulging.

"Autumn? Autumn?"

She woke with a start and was met with Dante's amber gaze. He blinked. Autumn stretched and yawned; suns lowered in the sky. Her hair stood on end as she stared at the mosaic floor. It was empty and sparkling.

"How long was I asleep?"

"A few hours. The guards tell me you were crying out."

"Oh," she grumbled, cheeks heating. She sat up, running her palms through her glittered hair.

Dante sat beside her and smoothed his cape beneath his thighs. "Something about how you didn't mean to kill anyone. You know what happened was an accident. You didn't kill anyone on purpose, and there was nothing you could've done to prevent it."

"I know, but it still doesn't make it right."

"You're a good person, Autumn. You're sweet and kind. You're so much better than I could ever be." He reached, handing the paperback to her. "The books you read probably aren't helping either."

She snatched it, crossing her arms. "Well, I didn't have that many choices considering I was being kidnapped. Wait—how do you know what helps?"

His lips flickered. "I still remember the first kill I made. It haunts me to this day. Sometimes I can still see his face when I close my eyes. His draining life force. I know what you're going through, how you feel."

"No, I think our situations are a little bit different."

"Perhaps," he mused. "Anyway, I have something for you. Another present to celebrate our upcoming wedding."

"No thanks," she flipped back to the creased page she left off on.

Dante ran a black-gloved fingertip against the spine of the book. "Trust me, you'll want this."

She stared at him; curiosity piqued. "I don't know…"

"There are no strings attached. I just want you to be happy."

"You and I both know there's only one thing you could do to make me happy."

He glanced away, picking at his gloves, and then rose. Autumn reluctantly followed, mortified she'd been crying in her sleep. Now everyone knew about the horrible dreams she'd been suffering.

* * *

Dante led her to a ceiling-high gilded door at the far end of the third floor. He removed his glove and pressed a bare thumb against a scanner. A neon blue light flashed as they were granted access.

Autumn's heart thrummed as they entered a dark, musty room. Black robed figures scratched quills against parchment, while others clicked data into tablets. The room was shaped like a tunnel. It carried vertically through many floors to a source of natural sunlight.

"What is this place?" She folded her arms and surveyed the shelves filled with scrolls.

"The information in this room is highly protected. It contains stories of old and the deepest secrets of the universes. In short, this is my personal library," his lips twitched.

She bit back a grin and spun around on the heel of her shoe, losing her balance. She could only imagine what stories lay before them.

Autumn jumped into the air and floated up, up, up, to the

highest shelf. She unfastened a random scroll, but her smile faded when she saw a strange hieroglyphic language.

"What language is this?" Her nose scrunched. "I can't read any of it."

"Ivarkian and a mixture of Tribault and Flue."

"Why would you bring me to a library with stories I can't even read?" She refastened the scroll and placed it back on the shelf.

He crossed his arms and floated beside her. "Well, if you'd let me finish, I'd explain that my team of scribes are in the process of translating and hologramming. These texts have needed an update for a long while," he paused. "When they're finished, I'm giving them to you."

This hardly made up for anything. Kidnapping her from her planet, giving her alien abilities, forcing her to marry him, but she couldn't help but say, "Thank you."

"You're very welcome," he said. "I bet you didn't know I enjoy reading as much as you do." Dante slid his sleek communicator out of his pocket and checked the time. "I'm glad you find my gift pleasing, but we must make haste. Our presence is expected in the throne room."

Autumn nodded mechanically.

PART FOUR
The Chamber of Horrors

<h1 style="text-align:center">Forty-Five</h1>

WHAT MADE the Chamber of Horrors so horrible?

Was it the delicacies being served? Or the exquisite clothing the courtiers wore? Or was it the bubbling champagne and wine pouring? If anything, it looked more like a celebration than something *horrible*.

Autumn blinked as black dots buzzed through the air. *Drones.* Her eyes followed them as they zipped around in circles again and again, until she met Valdez's bloodthirsty glare. Her blue eyes simmered in her skull. A shiver rattled through Autumn as they held each other's stare.

The emperor sat atop the dais swirling a golden goblet filled with red wine. His blue lips hinted at vermillion. The Empress stared off into space with her brown doe-like eyes.

Leyla on the other hand texted on her brand new, hot pink communicator. When she saw Autumn, she looked away.

"Why don't I have a communicator?" Autumn whispered to Dante, suddenly envious she no longer had a phone, and no friends to talk to.

"Why do you need one? So you can send messages to

everyone about how much you hate me?" He winked. She rolled her eyes.

"Believe it or not, I have better things to do." *Like plan my escape.*

He placed his hand on her shoulder. "You'll have one in due time."

"That's what you always say. I'm tired of waiting for everything. Stop treating me like a child. I'm twenty years old for heaven's sake—"

"You know, only children remind others of their age."

She crossed her arms, cheeks burning. Her temples pulsated. She experienced a brief rush of adrenaline when she counted the seats. There was one for the emperor, the empress, Leyla, Dante, and Valdez whose lips twisted in a scowl.

There was no seat for her, yet again.

Dante snapped his fingers and servants came sprinting over with a chair, apologizing profusely. After the seats were rearranged, she broke into a cold sweat as every last pair of inhuman eyes in the room fixated on them. It was like speech class all over again. She wished she could run, wished she could disappear.

Or at least hide in the back of the room, like Ronan and Armienti who lounged against the wall. They crossed their strong arms staring out into space. *Why were they never seated in a place of prominence as Dante's cousins?*

Without a second thought she rose to her feet and made her way over to them.

"We're about to start," Dante said.

"Just a sec," she approached his cousins, making her way through the dense crowd. "Why are you always lurking around?" she asked when she reached them.

Armienti chuckled, pushing a golden strand behind his ear. "If it isn't apparent, we're hardly welcome at court."

"The emperor deems our presence necessary *only* when it's advantageous to him," Ronan added.

"But why? I thought you were family, and family sticks together."

"Don't worry about it, Autumn," Armienti's mouth curved. "Things are the way they've always been. If I were you, I'd be more concerned about this event. There's something you ought to know—"

"And if I haven't told her, it's not your place to do so," Dante rested a black-gloved hand on her shoulder. The *nerve* of him.

"Cousin—"

"Tell me what?" Her fists trembled at her sides. "You're always hiding stuff from me. You promised."

A trumpet sounded. The emperor rose and took one last swig of his wine. "Greetings, ladies and gentlemen. I have an announcement to make," the room fell silent. "Henceforth, our event shall be hosted by my eldest and only son Dante, your *future* emperor."

Clapping and whistling erupted throughout the room.

"Additionally, we have two guests of honor in attendance. Lady Valdez Aventura and our very own Grand Supreme, reigning god-emperor of Universe 24."

The Grand Supreme. Autumn's eyes darted around the room, hoping to catch a glimpse of him, but to no avail. The hairs on the back of her neck stood at perfect attention. A microscopic dot buzzed through her line of vision. *He must be watching from the drones.*

She locked eyes with Armienti. What did he have to tell her before Dante had silenced him, and why did the Grand Supreme choose to tune in? The *Master* of the Universes.

"Let the event commence."

Forty-Six

DOZENS OF PRISONERS were ushered into the room by obsidian-cloaked guards. Long poled tasers buzzed against their limbs. Members of the upper class strode behind them, arms folded, eyes averted to the ground.

Autumn shoved her thumb into her mouth, chewing the nail down to the nub. A drop of metallic blood rolled against her tongue. Everyone stared at her and Dante, seated atop the dais.

If only she could join the crowd and not be the center of attention. If only she could escape. *Dammit*, her heart raced. She wanted to be home away from all this. In bed with a book, her dad downstairs tinkering on his computer, her mom still alive.

Home, she released a deep aching sigh. But at this rate, she'd never get there.

The procession halted.

Dante straightened his spine and drank from a goblet of red wine. *Like father, like son.*

Valdez chuckled softly, her red-glazed talons gliding

against the arms of her seat. The fabric of her jewel-toned blue dress slithered up her long thigh. The room fell silent.

"Who amongst you wishes to go first?"

Nobody answered.

"Very well then, I shall choose." Dante gestured toward an alien with salt and pepper hair and wide brown eyes. His golden skin was smudged with blue.

"You sir, approach me."

The man glanced around, realizing he'd been summoned first. He obediently walked over, legs swaying with each step. His head hung low.

The man fell to his knees, staring at Dante's boots. His large hands quaked.

"What's your crime?"

"I-I-I—"

"You, you, you," Dante laughed into his goblet as he took a sip. Autumn's stomach knotted as she stared at the man, terror apparent on his face, and Dante who was expressly unsympathetic. "Either tell me what you've been accused of, or I'll pick a crime at random. Although, I already suspect what you've done."

The man gulped. "I was caught impersonating an upper-classman. It was only for a few suns and moons. I wanted to gain access to the palace. To know how the super elite live."

Gasps erupted all around the room and Valdez slapped her knee. "I swear Dante, they never learn."

Dante placed his goblet on the edge of his seat. "Is that all?"

"No, sire. I transmitted the data I obtained to the Red Cloaks."

"I see," Dante said, appearing to think deeply on the matter. "As I'm sure you're aware, the punishment for treason is death—"

The man stood up and sprinted through the crowd, arms flailing. Dante raised his palm, but a golden arrow whizzed through the air connecting with the prisoner's knee, snagging bone and flesh.

Autumn and Leyla covered their mouths. Leyla's legs trembled together, her communicator bouncing in her lap. *She had to find a way out of here. An escape from this craziness,* Autumn thought.

"Pity. For a moment, I thought of commuting your sentence."

Dante raised a hand and looked at Autumn for a moment too long. His amber eyes burned into her with guilt.

Valdez shot to her feet and a beam zapped from her eyes. The man screamed. Gray smoke poured from his mouth and tears rolled down his cheeks from his bulging bloodshot eyes. His bones shattered with a single crack.

Autumn closed her eyes, inhaling the smell of burning flesh. She shuddered.

The man twitched and flexed as the soldiers grabbed him and dumped his body into the hallway. A round of whistling and applause erupted.

Dante finally tore his eyes away from her. "Apologies, my lady. I'll get the next one."

"It's quite all right," Valdez said. "It's not fair you get to have all of the fun."

Autumn's stomach knotted, inducing vomit. There were thirty more prisoners she had to sit through, thirty more rounds of this torture. *No, no, no.* As she went to stand, Dante placed his hand on hers, and she fell to her seat. Everyone stared at her before focusing back on the condemned.

The next prisoner reeked of arrogance, almost as much as Dante regularly displayed. His muscles bulged through his onyx bodysuit. He brushed his purple silver hair behind his blue pointed ears. He was a beautiful specimen of a man. Beautiful but cruel, like all the rest.

The prisoner rolled his eyes. "This is a complete and utter waste of time, your Imperial Highness. Why don't we both agree to disagree, and you let me go. Your time is better spent sentencing lower life-forms. They're a waste of oxygen and space."

"Did I grant you permission to speak, my lord?"

"No, I speak on my own free accord," the young man crossed his bulging, muscular arms.

"Speak out of turn again and you die."

The man's jaw tightened then slackened. "That's fair, I suppose. Forgive me, sire."

"Now tell me, what do you claim is a waste of my time? I know you're of my father's court, but I don't recognize you."

"That shrew, she lies," he pointed into the crowd. A young woman appeared. Her left eye was sealed shut, as swollen as a golf ball, and her hands were littered with fresh purple bruises.

"Step forth, my lady."

Her heeled boots glided over the crimson velvet floor. Trembling slightly, her eyes roved through the crowd. Dante placed his goblet on the floor and descended the steps. Autumn's eyes drifted over to the Empress who clutched her own wrist. She gulped.

"Did he do this to you?" Dante ran his fingers over her eye.

She nodded slowly.

"Don't lie," the man screeched. "You've always been a liar."

The woman's muscles tensed then relaxed as Dante placed his thumb and forefinger at the base of the woman's skull and massaged them cyclically into her flesh, probing her memories.

The woman trembled as she closed her eyes, legs giving out from beneath her. After a period, Dante pulled away leaving her laying on the floor, breast rising and falling in a peaceful slumber.

"What did you see?" the man's jaw quaked.

Dante folded his arms, shifting his weight. He mumbled something incomprehensible underneath his breath before turning toward him. "Enough."

The man's face shifted a furious purple as he dug his gloved fingers into the fibers of the carpet. "What? What is that supposed to mean?" The prisoner's hands balled into fists.

"Outside of training, under no circumstance is it acceptable to lay a hand on your mate."

"You're a fine one to talk," the man bared his teeth at Dante, strands of silver-purple hair falling over his eyes. "You, your wretched father, and Maeve. Where is she now—"

Dante blinked and the man flew into the air suspended. He tried to move, eyes bulging. The entire room remained quiet. Everyone stared. His right arm outstretched as he whimpered, trying to move it. "Please, please."

"Don't bother begging, you're wasting your breath," Dante said before the man's right arm ripped, severing from his torso and slammed against the wall. The man stared at Dante, mouth hanging open.

"Let this serve as a reminder to keep your hands, or hand rather, to yourself. Although, I'm positive it won't be an issue where I'm sending you."

Dante's face was purple. The air sweltered in the room. A team of guards grabbed the armless man and disappeared into thin air.

* * *

The trials continued all afternoon, and it came to a point where Autumn could bear no more. Her chest loosened when the prisoners were finally whittled down to three, each with a black sack over their heads, hands bound.

She shuddered to think of what crimes they'd committed. Whatever they'd done, they sure *stank*. She gagged. They smelled like cheese mixed with rotten eggs. *Yuck.*

"What do we have here?" Dante crossed his arms, making a face of disgust.

"They saved the best for last," Valdez coughed, a bejeweled hand over her mouth.

"Get on with it, Dante," the emperor's face shifted to a pale nauseous gray. "The stench is unbearable. End them, or I shall."

Autumn held her breath momentarily.

"Approach," Dante gestured to the first of the three.

"How can he do that if he can't see? That's not fair." Autumn shot to her feet. Everyone stared at her but this time around she didn't care. "Stop this right now."

"Silence," Valdez hissed, eyes narrowing to razor-thin slits. "Don't you dare interfere, human."

"Thank you, m'lady, but I don't need your pity or your concern," the hooded figure walked toward them with slow, shaky steps. He was barefoot, with long twisted brown toenails. A guard cut the sack from his head with a knife.

"If anything, I pity you for being betrothed to this monster and having anything to do with his house."

"Mind your tongue," Dante cracked his knuckles.

The elderly Elattion hybrid stared at the dais. He wore a tattered heather-gray robe, and his blue eyes shifted.

"I do apologize to your Imperial Highness. With my frail bones I'm unable to occupy a kneeling position."

Guards swarmed behind him pointing their metallic guns. "This prisoner openly disrespects you, sire. Shall we blast his knees?"

"No," Dante folded his arms. "Tell me what you've been accused of, old-timer."

"I've merely spoken the truth in public forums about your realm and the wretched way you and your father rule it, along with the atrocities you've committed with that witch beside you. There's no hope for any of you elites. You're all the same. Selfish, cruel, and power hungry. And the Grand Supreme is the worst of all."

Gasps erupted throughout the room. "You speak of treason, sir, and the punishment for treason is—"

"Death, I'm sure, but I'd rather die than be in your presence a moment longer. You're like a black cloud poisoning the universes, rotting them to the core."

Autumn sensed the shift of energy in the room, but Dante continued to listen.

"With your gleaming arrogance and complete lack of empathy, the Martyne dynasty will fade to dust. And to be quite frank, I'll be glad to see it go."

The man turned toward Autumn, their eyes locking. "You, my dear, should run far away from here and never look back before it's too late for you too. *That boy is no good for you.*"

The warning echoed in Autumn's head like a nostalgic gong. "You're way out of your league."

"How dare you speak to her in such a manner, you babbling fool." Dante cracked his knuckles.

"Remain together, and you'll be each other's undoing," the man stopped and addressed Dante. "Perhaps I'm not as foolish as I appear. I know all about Key—"

"Enough of this nonsense," Dante shot to his feet, fire crackling in his palm. He raised his hand to throw the ball of fire, but the man vanished into thin air. The buzzing drones popped and exploded, raining black powder and soot from the ceiling.

Autumn stumbled to a stand and dashed through the crowd. She was desperate to get out of there when her eyes fell on a chipped hot-pink gel set. She stopped dead in her tracks. Her heart sputtered.

Only one person she knew sported that blinding shade of pink.

Forty-Seven

AUTUMN'S HANDS trembled as she reached for the black hood covering the prisoner's head.

"Wha—what are you doing?" Dante asked as he strode after her.

A gasp exploded through her mouth as she stared at Misty Beckett's glassy cerulean eyes. Wet tears and bleeding mascara streamed down her cheeks. And the smell—Autumn covered her mouth and gagged.

"Well, well, well, what do we have here?" Amusement played across Dante's blue lips.

Autumn stared in horror at Dante. "What did you do?"

"Are you not pleased, Autumn? Is this not what you've always wanted? To make her suffer the way she made you suffer. Every time I think of how she hurt you it enrages me to no end."

Misty's red-rimmed eyes widened with terror.

Dante unfastened her gag and Misty dropped to her knees, breath rasping. "I don't understand what's going on. Where are we? One minute I was at the wedding of the century, and the next, it was dark and cold and empty for what seemed like forever, and now I'm here."

Her eyes gravitated to Dante's, and she shrieked. "Get away from me! Get away from me! You weird alien freak!" Her eyes darted around the room. "You're freaks, all of you!" Misty hugged her tattered golden sequin gown. Her fabulous Bermuda tan faded. She looked normal and mousey for once.

Misty stumbled to a stand, examining Autumn from head to toe. "Why are you dressed like that with weird glitter hair and a leotard?" she practically screamed. "Why aren't you scared? We have to get out of here." Misty sprang up and grabbed Autumn's hand, but all she could do was stare.

This seriously can't be happening. What was Dante thinking?

"I'm afraid she isn't going anywhere with the likes of you." Dante folded his arms, muscles shifting beneath his uniform. "You, on the other hand, are stinking up my court."

Misty scrunched her nose. "What's he talking about? Why are we here? We have to get back to our families. I'm sure they're worried about us. Autumn, you gotta snap out of it. You have to get me out of here."

Another guard approached Misty from behind and dumped a bucket of ice water over her head. Misty screamed as the water ran down her back.

Autumn hated to admit it and tried her best to ignore the thought. No, she shouldn't be happy. *This is wrong.*

She recalled Misty's smug expression during their last exchange at the wedding. The way she talked down to her like she was somehow superior. How the tables had turned.

Dante folded his arms. "Good, now that you're silent—"

Misty balled her fists at her sides. "Screw you, I didn't do anything wrong. You kidnapped us and hurt all those innocent people. Wait until the police find out. They'll toss your sorry ass in jail for life. Autumn, please, we have to go now."

"Oh, but you did do something wrong," Dante paused. "My wife tells me everything. That's why I'm sending you to a place where you can put your charms to good use. A place where your skill set is in high demand."

"Your wife? What are you talking about?" Misty's jaw dropped. "Autumn did you marry this creep? Seriously? Even *you* deserve better."

A black sack fastened over Misty's head. "Please, please, I can pay you. My parents will give you whatever you want. No amount is too much. Please, I want to go home. Please, I don't want to go wherever you're sending me."

"I'm afraid money will only get you so far," Dante chuckled.

Misty was hauled off screaming and crying through the room and into the sunlit hallway.

Autumn could barely breathe. As soon as Misty left, shame consumed her. She *never* tried to stop Dante. She was just as bad as he was. Worst of all, she enjoyed it.

A round of applause sounded. Servants sprayed perfume, relieving everyone of Misty's foul stench. The funk of a hot summer wedding and a full year of unbathed space travel was thick in the air.

"Disgusting," Dante plugged his nose with his black-gloved fingertips.

Autumn threw a hand over her lips to keep her guts from spilling through her mouth. Her knees knocked together as she turned toward the final prisoner, the smell coming from them nostalgic.

Guards tugged at the obsidian cloth hood that concealed the prisoner's face.

Dante's face paled. "Holy shit. He's not supposed to be here."

Autumn stared, knees buckling. Her vision blurred to

black. A pair of sapphire eyes watched her before she succumbed to the darkness.

Caleb.

Forty-Eight

DANTE PACED the floor of Autumn's bedchamber. It was too much to expect a miracle after what'd transpired. His cape whipped over his shoulders as the twin suns lowered over Giarldinia. Droplets of sweat slicked his furrowed brow.

He messed up again, royally. He couldn't begin to imagine what Autumn thought of him now, between the obligatory show he was forced to put on at the Chamber of Horrors and her discovering he'd abducted her foes.

She was supposed to witness Misty's punishment, *not* Caleb's. Caleb was scheduled to be dispatched to Varz. For the life of him, he couldn't figure out how he missed the flight.

"What's wrong son? Trouble in paradise?" The emperor teleported into the room. A smile crept over his crimson stained lips.

His blood pressure spiked, but he relaxed upon seeing Autumn still slumbering on her bed. She'd been out for several hours.

"How dare you come here with that smug look on your face and inquire about my personal life," Dante cracked his knuckles.

"Whatever do you mean?" His father swirled his goblet, taking a lingering sip.

"Don't pretend you're not somehow responsible."

"Believe it or not, I have better things to do than sabotage your doomed relationship."

"Father, leave."

"This is pathetic. I wish you would come to your senses. You're brilliant, and she's such a nothing," the emperor said.

"Leave."

"Okay, I'll go. I've merely come to congratulate you on an excellent show. They're raving about it throughout the universes, and the Grand Supreme was most pleased. Although, he can't understand why you omitted the existence of two more humans when you told him you destroyed them all."

"My apologies to him. It slipped my mind. But rest assured, they've been dealt with and will not pose a problem to any of his plans."

"Dante, you cannot screw this up. Tread carefully." The emperor disappeared into thin air. When Dante looked again, Autumn sat on her bed, arms folded.

* * *

Autumn balled her fists taking deep controlled breaths. "You have some nerve. How could you do this? What were you thinking? What part of bringing Misty and Caleb to Surge did you think was a good idea?"

She huffed and puffed, chest tightening. Red clouded her vision. Caleb's liquid blue eyes flashed through her mind. There was so much she needed to tell him. So much she didn't get a chance to say last time. She *had* to see him.

"I brought Misty with us to punish her for how she treated you. Believe it or not, I care for you more than anything. I won't for a second tolerate anyone disrespecting you. It will never happen again on my watch."

"You have an interesting way of showing you care. So far, I've only seen you think about yourself. You don't care about how I feel." Autumn folded her arms. Although the look on Misty's face was *priceless*, she didn't dare admit it aloud. But Caleb—her stomach twisted. He deserved better.

"Why did you bring Caleb after we patched things up? He apologized and everything was good between us," she glowered.

Silent. Dante was always silent with no reasonable explanation for any of his ridiculous behavior.

She continued. "Well?"

Dante shifted his weight. She threw her hands into the air, exasperated. She ambled to her closet and selected a pure obsidian bodysuit. Carefully, she combed her glitter flecked hair into a high ponytail, fastening it with a tie.

"What are you doing?" he asked as she finished pulling on her boots. "Are you going somewhere?"

"Do I need your permission for everything? Can't I just have some peace and quiet? I know we made a deal, and I'm holding up my end of the bargain as best I can, but I feel like a prisoner all the time in my own home. Or at least I thought this was my home."

"Of course it's your home. By all means, you can walk around if you like. Explore to your heart's content."

She ambled toward the door. "Good. It annoys me that you keep tabs on me all the time. I feel like you don't trust me or something. I don't even have the code to my own room."

"It's not that, it's just—"

She walked through the door, and it slid closed behind her, never giving him a chance to respond. Trailed by too many guards, she made her way through the hallway and headed to the gravity room to get some much-needed training in, but not before bumping into Leyla. The princess was clothed in heather-gray, although her punishment ended weeks ago.

Forty-Nine

LEYLA'S HEART stilled when she encountered Autumn. She folded her arms, shifting her weight from side to side.

"Where are you going?" Leyla inquired.

Autumn sighed. "All of you Martynes are so freaking nosey. Mind your own business." She attempted to walk by, but Leyla blocked the hallway.

"I'm sorry for what happened to your friends, that they wound up in such a terrible situation. It's humiliating to be put on trial and sentenced," Leyla muttered.

Autumn blinked. "Stop pretending that you care about what happens to them or about my feelings," she paused for a moment. "And by the way, they're not my friends and *neither* are you. I'd never be your friend. You're rude, self-centered, and selfish, just like your brother."

It must be nice to have friends, Leyla omitted. She could count on one hand the number of people who cared about her.

Autumn pushed up against her arm, this time with twice the force as the altercation they had at the banquet hall. An inhuman force Leyla picked up on long before her brother did. Autumn's rage was sharp and bottomless. Mixed with Elattion blood, it was deadly even if she'd yet to realize it.

"Why are you still dressed like a hybrid? You made such a big deal before," Autumn asked.

Leyla's cheeks burned with shame. "I forgot I was still wearing grays. It's an easy mistake to make when you're a busy princess." *Not wasting her time reading and training all day,* it tempted Leyla to say. "Now if you'll excuse me, I have more important matters to attend to."

"Excuse me? Excuse you. You're the one holding me up. I have places to be too," Autumn snapped.

Leyla groaned as she slipped inside her room. She fell to the floor trembling, throwing a nail in her mouth. She'd rather Autumn hadn't noticed she was still wearing grays. Leyla didn't want her brother to find out.

* * *

Autumn rolled her eyes as she walked down the hall. The clinking of guns and armor accompanied her steps.

"Annoying Leyla," she grumbled. *Why can't anyone here just be normal?* Why was everyone always out to get her?

She reached the bottom floor, still pondering her frustrating circumstances, and passed an ongoing banquet.

There was a party every night, complete with fabulous food and dancing. Her eyes rolled. *The aliens and their vanity.* But as she rounded the corner, a dark shadow engulfed her. Cool particles seeped through her flesh, causing the hairs on her arms to rise. Her eyes slammed shut as she succumbed to the darkness.

A moment later she was surrounded by pure amethyst night. Twisted blades of cobalt grass were cool beneath her soles. Twin moons shone high in the sky like two paper lanterns, surrounded by glittering stars. Fog escaped her lips after each trembling breath.

"If I'm honest, I'm not sure what I'm going to do with you, little girl."

Autumn turned and was met with Valdez's scalding eyes.

"Little girl?" She placed a hand on her hip. "I may be short, but I'm hardly *little*."

Valdez's mouth twisted into a cruel scowl. "Well, I'm far more experienced than you in *every* way."

Valdez stroked the length of her jade braid. "I can't figure out what Dante sees in you. You're a distraction and a liability. Not to mention, lower life-form filth. You deserve to die like the rest of your inferior species."

"Stay the heck away from me," Autumn folded her arms, straightening her spine. Her blood came to a rapid boil.

"I could kill you right now and make it look like an accident," Valdez whipped out her golden bow, nocked it, and held it square between her eyes. A smile played across her full lips. The smile of a cold-blooded murderer. "Nobody would ever find your remains where I'd send them. No, that would be far too easy," she lowered her weapon. "You deserve so much worse. I'm going to make you suffer. I'm going to make you wish you'd never been born."

"I'd like to see you try. There's nothing you can do to me that hasn't already been done."

"I'm positive I'll think of something," Valdez's lips flickered. "I saw your little friends. Perhaps they deserve worse as well. Dante went far too easy on them. The crystal mines of Varz and the pleasure planet of Halvana? Please. I would have sent them straight to Universe 24 to answer directly to the Grand Supreme."

Her stomach knotted. *That's where they went—Varz and Halvana.* She shuddered at the mention of the Grand Supreme.

"Mark my words, it's only a matter of time. And the best part is, you won't remember a word of our conversation. Stupid human." Valdez snorted.

Valdez snapped her lengthy red talons and Autumn woke at the entrance of the banquet hall. Her limbs were heavy as she emerged from her daze. A shiver rattled through her core. She had to escape. Had to rescue Caleb. Had to get the heck off this planet and back to Earth. Back to her dad. She had to tell him she was still alive.

What Valdez didn't count on was her remembering their entire conversation. She couldn't be easily manipulated anymore, all thanks to the Elattion blood pulsing through her veins. No matter the risk, she would get off this planet.

Fifty

AUTUMN STOOD in the training room, gravity cranked ten times higher than Earth's normal gravity pull. She was able to bear it this time, fueled solely by her anger. Her knuckles burned as they collided with a floating punching bag. Wincing from the pain, she swung again and again and again. Her eyes clouded with rage. She had to get stronger, had to be able to defend herself.

Two heavy boots landed on the ground. She whirled around, gaze connecting with Dante's twinkling amber eyes. A cocky smile crept across his beautiful mouth. She knew she shouldn't be admiring it.

"This is the absolute last place I expected to find you."

She stared for a moment too long. He was *shirtless* too. His strong blue muscles and scars gleamed in the light. Her face warmed and she turned back around, beating on the punching bag with all her might.

Dante released a breathy chuckle and she stopped. "What? What's so funny?"

He shrugged. "It's nothing."

"It's obviously something. Tell me." She stomped her foot in protest. He folded his arms, muscles shifting.

"It's just—never mind." He stretched his legs from side to side, knuckles cracking.

"Spill it, Dante."

"Very well," he ran a hand through his tousled hair. "It's just that your technique is well—strange."

Strange? She stared at him, her nose scrunched. "Mind your own business." She continued throwing her fists at the bag.

"You'll never hit anyone at this rate. I'm assuming you want to hit me," his mouth curved. "You want to hit me more than anything."

"I have better things to do," she lied, but really, she wouldn't mind connecting her balled first with his arrogant chiseled face after everything he put her through and the suffering he inflicted on others. He was more than deserving. She wanted to throttle him.

"Here, let me show you," he appeared behind her, calloused palms sliding against her arms. He balled her hands into fists and repositioned her legs with his knee.

"When you swing, you need to work on your posture and footing. Keep your core taut. Be more precise with your movements unless—"

She turned and looked at him. "Unless?"

"You intend to fight dirty," he winked.

Her heart sputtered. Fight dirty, like he crushed Caleb's arm, breaking bones and tendons with his boot? His phantom screams assaulted her ears as she and Dante hit the punching bag together, his fists guiding hers.

His warm hard abs pressed against her back. She could still see Caleb's teary sapphire eyes and the expression of horror on his face when he was hauled off to Varz. Autumn turned and swung her fist in Dante's face. He caught it before her next breath.

"I'm going to make you pay for everything you put me through," Autumn trembled, teeth grinding in her mouth. His mouth tilted.

"I don't doubt it," he placed his thumb and fingers under her chin propping up her head. He moved his face close, the scent of spicy cinnamon overwhelming her. "You'd better train hard then, Autumn Ramon, and tirelessly if you want to stand a chance against me. I'm undefeated for good reason. And not just in this universe; in all of them."

She pulled away, fists balled at her sides. "One day you'll get what's coming to you. Karma always catches up. Mark my words.."

"Perhaps," he chuckled, crossing his arms. "But until that day, a more significant day is approaching. Our wedding. I just thought I'd remind you in case you've forgotten."

The breath caught in her throat.

"Don't remind me," she muttered. Nothing terrified her more than marrying this monster, and the time had almost arrived.

"I promise it won't be all that bad. Who knows, you might even enjoy it."

She pulled away, but Dante snatched her knuckles and kissed them. His vile blue lips were smooth against her skin. Before she could ball her fist and smash it into his arrogant face, he was gone in a flash.

This was the man she was being forced to marry.

* * *

She spent the final weeks before the royal wedding of the century, or so it was called, training. She trained all day and all night, neglecting her new collection of stories until the midnight hours.

She had to admit, they were interesting, and she was grateful to Dante for giving her access to his library. Especially interesting were the stories about ancient humans and Elattions breaking tradition by falling in love and saving empires.

PART FIVE

Wedding Royale

Fifty-One

THE EVE of her wedding day had finally arrived. Autumn had been dreading it since she was back home on Earth and made a deal with the devil. As she sat on her balcony, the twin suns blazed hot against her golden-olive skin. Not a cloud could be seen in the clear blue sky. In her hands, she clutched a hologram note from the Empress. Her stomach churned as it read to her aloud:

Dear Autumn of Earth,

Or should I say daughter? It's high time that we make a greater effort to get to know each other. We'll be family soon enough. You're formally invited to tea in the back palace garden at lunchtime. I so look forward to you joining me. And dearest, I shan't take no for an answer.

Love,

Isidora, your future mother

The sign-off burned Autumn's heart like acid, although she was sure it wasn't the empress's intention.

She had one mom, and she was buried back on Earth. Her mom's life halved in the blink of an eye over someone else's carelessness. Dante had lied. He promised her information leading to her mom's murderer and *never* followed through. She sighed a deep aching sigh. She needed to find Misty and Caleb and get out of here.

"If you don't come inside, you're going to be late," Emblem chirped as she held a satin robin's egg blue dress in hand. Black buttons trailed the front in a vertical line. The white collar was starched and pressed.

She dragged her bare feet back into the bedroom and groaned, flopping on her bed. "I don't care. I don't want to be here."

"We know," Allegoria pulled a box from her closet containing a pair of patent leather Mary Jane shoes. "But you need to try and make the best of a bad situation, and the empress has pure intentions. It's the other ones—"

Emblem sped over and placed a hand over sister's mouth. "Shush, the walls have ears."

Allegoria nodded mechanically.

"Don't worry," Autumn twirled a stray coil around her finger. "I don't like them either."

Emblem and Allegoria removed her satin cloud shorts and white camisole top, the only pieces of clothing she still had from Earth thanks to Dante's raid. They pulled on the knee-length dress and white knee-high gossamer stockings. A black velvet headband was pressed through her coils and silver glitter was sprayed through her hair, like stars floating through the galaxy.

She glanced as she passed a mirror leaving her room. She looked like Alice lost in Wonderland.

* * *

Autumn had never been to the back of the palace before, and she had to admit, it was one of the most spectacular sights she'd ever seen. On the right was a rectangular cobalt maze that extended for miles to the edge of a cliff. A long reflection pool sat in the center. Rows of trees sparkled through its gentle waves. And to the far left was a sleek black dome surrounded by guards. Giarldinia buzzed with futuristic excitement beyond the landscape.

The empress sat with her entourage beneath a draped linen tent, which fluttered in the warm breeze. Two servants fanned her with giant white feathers while guards surrounded her with metallic guns.

"Oh Autumn, dearest, over here," the empress waved, a bright smile flashing across her face.

She wished she didn't have to go through with this. Tea with the Empress of *nine hundred and eighty planets*. She gulped. The guards allowed her entrance and she fell into a deep curtsy.

"Thanks for inviting me, your Imperial Maj—"

The empress chuckled. "Please, my dear, call me Isidora. Or better yet, Mother." Autumn's stomach flip flopped as she sat beside her in a garden chair, unable to utter the word *mother* without coming to tears. "You wanted to see me?"

"Indeed, I did," Isidora straightened her arms, revealing a purple bruise along her slender blue wrist. Autumn tried her best not to stare.

"I trust you're overjoyed about your upcoming ceremony. I can't believe the eve of this historic event is finally upon us. I never thought I'd see the day."

Autumn smiled warmly but secretly wanted to scream, "*No way.*"

"Yes, I'm thrilled," she agreed, if only to be polite.

"I know you're lying. I can hear your innermost thoughts," the empress smoothed her hands against her golden dress.

Great, she can read minds too. Autumn stumbled up slowly to leave. She hadn't anticipated an attack.

"Have a seat. Don't worry, I promise I won't pry again," the empress reassured her.

Autumn sat back down, face and neck burning, totally embarrassed.

"I do apologize," the empress continued. "It was never my intention to make you uncomfortable. Sometimes I peek out of curiosity and to understand the kind of personality I'm dealing with. No need to be embarrassed. We're family."

The arrival of the tea interrupted their conversation. A female servant glided over and placed a golden leaf tea set on the table. A dried pink lotus flower sat inside her cup. As the servant poured steaming water, it opened slowly, coming to life. A brief smile crept across Autumn's lips, which she stifled.

"As I'm sure you know, my son is a little rough around the edges. That, however, doesn't make his feelings for you any less real," the empress placed her cup on the table. "I know what he did. I know he risked *everything* to be with you. And I know your capabilities."

Autumn's body went taut then slackened. "You know about Earth and Key—" Autumn went to speak but no words came out. Her tongue knotted in her mouth.

The empress came to a graceful stand, tulle gown gliding against the cobalt grass. "Come daughter, shall we?" She offered her a hand. Autumn rose, still unable to form words.

She followed the empress, and they walked through the colorful gardens around the reflection pool. The guards remained at a respectful distance.

Isidora loosened the mental grip on her tongue. "What's going on?"

"The walls have ears. You must be careful what you say at all times. Someone is always watching and listening. It's clear to me you're unfamiliar with this concept."

Autumn nodded slowly. "How do you know about Keyserike and Earth?"

Isidora laced her fingers behind her back. "I know my own son, and I know what he's capable of, especially when his judgment is clouded."

Autumn swallowed hard.

"We'll keep this information to ourselves. It's too dangerous if it falls into the wrong hands. I hope I can count on your discretion," Isidora said. "But that's not why I've summoned you here."

She finally put two and two together. "Do you want my opinion on my dress, or the cake, or flower arrangements or something?"

"No, not exactly," Isidora waved the servants and guards away.

She smoothed her hands against her golden gown. "Are you still a maiden?"

Autumn's eyes widened. *The nerve of her. What was this, the eighteenth century?*

"Never mind, I don't mean to pry. You don't have to answer."

Autumn remained quiet, her stomach knotting. For all she knew Isidora was sifting through the layers of her mind, digging up as much information as she could.

"I need you to understand something Earth daughter. After your ceremony tomorrow, your duty will be solely to my son."

"Okay," Autumn stuttered. *What the heck was that supposed to mean?* She wondered.

"You must honor and obey my son and trust his good judgment in all things. Always be submissive to his will."

Her blood pressure skyrocketed. *His will? No way.*

"You must be willing and sweet when he comes to visit you in your bedchamber, starting with the bedding ceremony after the wedding tomorrow night. The emperor and I are most eager for you to provide us with an heir, and I'm confident that, with the way my son looks at you, we'll have one in no time at all."

Autumn stood there frozen and horrified as the empress lectured her about the birds and the bees and unrealistic expectations she wasn't going to follow. She had some *nerve. But wait,* her mind backtracked.

"What's the bedding ceremony?" Autumn was almost afraid to ask but had no other choice.

Isidora chuckled softly. "It's a long-standing ritual here on Surge practiced among the elite classes in which wedding guests and members of the court witness the first act of intimacy."

Autumn's jaw dropped. *That jerk.*

"And please don't fret. Although it's a broadcasted event, it will only be witnessable in the nearby universes."

The contents of her stomach prepared to empty.

"You suddenly look pale, my dear. Are you feeling unwell?" Isidora's voice seeped with concern.

"I'm fine, thanks." But really, she wanted to *murder* Dante.

"You'll make a wonderful addition to our family. Make sure you get a full night of sleep. You need to be well rested for tomorrow's events."

"Thank you, I will," Autumn curtseyed before marching back to the palace to find Dante. Blood-red clouded her vision.

Fifty-Two

DANTE HOVERED in the air in a deep state of meditation. He focused on the sound of his breath and the pull of gravity against his bare chest from the chamber he occupied.

As of late, it was easier to concentrate because Ronan and Armienti steered clear of him after he endangered everyone over a human. *Or so he figured.* To everyone else, she was just a human, but to him she meant everything.

Autumn, he sighed, dreaming of his future wife. The gentle slope of her hips and her soft pink mouth pressed against his. Their naked bodies entwined.

His stomach knotted when she admitted she still loved Caleb. A twinge of jealousy simmered him to the core. How he despised that Earth boy, who finally got what he deserved.

His revenge fantasy was short-lived as the steel door ripped off the chamber and smashed against the wall behind him. Autumn stormed in, fists balled at her sides and a murderous expression on her face. He bit his cheeks to stop himself from grinning.

How adorable she was when she was angry. He could *never* get enough of her.

"Autumn, what a surprise. How can I help you?"

It really was a surprise considering they hadn't spoken in weeks. Not since she found out about Caleb and Misty. But Dante didn't regret his decision, and he refused to tolerate any mistreatment of his mate to be.

"You," she floated in the air.

He was impressed by the control she displayed after such a short while on twenty times Earth's gravity. Maybe one day she'd kick his ass after all. How he looked forward to it.

"You have some nerve," her aura radiated with red-hot rage. "I agreed to marry you, but I never said I'd sleep with you. Your mom—"

"Had a wonderful time with you," he smoothed a hand through his hair. "She's done nothing but sing your praises. Daughter, she calls you."

"I had a good time with her too, but you're getting off topic," her cheeks shifted to pink.

"She told me all about the crazy bedding ritual and how you think I'm going to have your kids and listen to everything you tell me to do. Don't count on it."

"Did she now?" A smile playing across his lips. "Well, it's not too far off."

"What?"

"Everyone obeys me," he winked.

"Well, I won't. I can think for myself. I don't need you ordering me around."

He landed feet-first on the steel tiled floor. He ambled over to a pile of steaming towels on a table, took one, and wiped it over his sweat-soaked face.

"Dante, you can't make me do this. It wasn't part of our deal. I agreed to marry you and nothing else."

"I'm afraid tradition is tradition," he said matter-of-factly. "It's been around for thousands of years."

"Well, your traditions here suck. None of this would've ever happened if you hadn't come to Earth. I'd still be at home. I'd still have my family and I'd be in college. I could've made a difference in people's lives and made the world a better place," she paused. "And who knows, maybe Caleb and I would still be together. He was always kind to me and cared about my feelings and what I thought, unlike you. You're the most selfish person I've ever known. You ruined my future. I hate you, and I don't care what you've been through."

The last sentence stung like acid. "You should freshen up. A banquet is being prepared in our honor," was all he could think to say, caught completely off guard.

When he glanced at the doorway again, she'd already gone.

* * *

Autumn returned to her room, chest aching from crying so hard through the long empty crimson halls. She threw herself on her bed and sobbed. Mr. Hiss stretched and yawned, nuzzling his warm pink nose into her side. Her hands grazed his fur, feather-soft to the touch. She was unable to believe she was really going through with this.

Tomorrow she'd be Lady Martyne, whether she wanted to or not.

She grabbed her phone from her crossbody bag. If only she could charge it and call home to let her friends and family know she was still alive.

Everything she'd done so far was to keep them and the rest of the planet safe. She never would've left if she had a choice. She was completely and utterly isolated.

However, in all her misery, she couldn't deny she was

starving...again. Her stomach twisted and growled from a stressful day.

Not bothering to change, she wiped her eyes and headed downstairs to the banquet. After all, she was the honorary guest.

Fifty-Three

THE BANQUET HALL buzzed with its usual evening excitement. Alien nobility pranced around in their finery, heads held high. Autumn was tempted to roll her eyes. What she would've given for a slice of pizza, chocolate chip pancakes, or a pumpkin spiced latte right now.

Something normal and human.

Her heart sank. This was another painful reminder she was no longer on Earth and would never return.

Servants clothed in heather-gray hustled around carrying trays piled high with food. The entrees were different for once. There were no cheeses, fruits, or breads but brown sliced meat. She gagged. *Gross.*

She hadn't consumed meat for as long as she could remember and didn't plan to start, even to be polite. Then there were vegetables and what resembled rice. A meal more her speed.

Autumn scanned the room. *Where the heck was everybody?*

She rolled her eyes. What a waste of time. Dante wasn't here to greet her, and this was all his idea. *Typical.* As she turned to go back to her room, her stomach disobeyed. *Grumble.*

She walked to the head table. All inhuman eyes watched her, causing the hairs on the back of her neck to stand at perfect attention. Everyone stood up, out of respect, before taking their seats again.

Autumn groaned at the gross meat platter set before her. She switched it with a neighboring plate. *Nobody would notice, when and if they decided to join her. And if they did, it was their problem.*

"Do you not care for your meal, m'lady?" Horizontal lines crept across a servant's youthful brow.

"No, it's fine. Thanks—" She lied, fidgeting her hands.

"Are you sure? I can easily bring you something else to eat."

"No thank you," Autumn said again.

Autumn forced a smile out as a member of the court approached her, interrupting their conversation. The alien woman adorned from head to toe in finery opened her mouth to speak but then stopped, eyes bulging from her skull. Her bejeweled hands grasped her throat as she fell chest first into the table rasping for air. Food and dishes spilled in a heap all over the floor.

Violent wet coughs ricocheted around the room. Half of the guests grabbed their necks, knees buckling to the ground. Their faces shifted deep purple. The other half stared on in horror, mouths ajar. Screams erupted throughout the hall. The air caught in Autumn's throat as she chewed and swallowed a vegetable.

She waited, eyes closed, certain that she would meet the same fate—but death never arrived.

"What the hell is going on here?" The emperor roared as he entered the room flanked by Dante, his wife, Leyla, and Valdez. A shudder exploded down Autumn's spine.

Everyone fell silent, dead bodies piled across tables and crumpled in chairs.

Dante raced her way. "Are you okay? What happened?"

She quivered uncontrollably. The full magnitude of the situation finally registered. "I'm not sure. I was eating dinner when everyone started choking."

Worry invaded his eyes. "How do you feel?"

Adrenaline pumped through her limbs. "Fine, I think."

Dante scanned the room. "Which plate did you eat from?"

"This one," she pointed at the vegetables and rice.

His concern simmered to rage. "Guards, round up the taste testers and chefs on duty." They did as he commanded.

She followed Dante and his family over to the throne room, trailed by the remaining courtiers. Everyone trembled, staring at the floor. Death had mildly escaped them.

She and the royal family took their seats. Guards dragged fifteen chefs through the doors. Their eyes bulged. Terror ripped across their faces. Five taste testers followed who were shoved to the ground at gunpoint.

Drones buzzed overhead. *The empress was right, someone was always watching.*

Dante crossed his legs and cracked his black-gloved knuckles. "Who cares to explain why a mass poisoning has taken place on the eve of my wedding?"

The room remained silent.

Valdez snorted. "Of course nobody is going to answer. You should up the stakes a little. How about every time you ask a question and don't receive an acceptable answer, everyone loses a body part?" A smile played across her venomous lips.

Autumn's eyes widened. *Sadistic bitch.*

"I shall ask you again, and you know I never ask for anything twice. Who is responsible for the poisoning?" Dante demanded, fists clenched.

"Enough of this. Enough," Autumn shot to her feet.

Everyone stared as she opened her mouth. "You don't have to do this. There's no way they're all responsible."

Dante cocked his head to the side. "Do you have a better suggestion, sweetheart?"

"Oh, spare me," the emperor cracked his black-gloved knuckles. "I can't believe you're entertaining her suggestion. She's a soft, useless human. Cut them up."

Her blood boiled and her fists clenched. *Soft, useless human.*

"I'm not talking to you, Father," Dante snapped. "Do continue."

"Instead of killing them, you can send them to the mines. You've already suffered a loss, rather than add to the body count, you can have twenty new workers. And slaves to help prepare the food to keep the others alive."

Dante folded his arms, contemplating. "Very well then, that sounds like a plan to me. Now that we're in agreement, you're all sentenced to life on Varz."

"You can't be serious," the emperor shot to his feet. "Don't you dare let them off easy. They poisoned over half my court."

Dante rolled his eyes.

"I'm inclined to agree," a nobleman shouted from the crowd. "The punishment doesn't fit the crime. Many of my friends and people of great prominence have been murdered in cold blood, and you let *that* filthy human decide their fate? Pathetic. What's wrong with you, your Imperial Highness? Use your head."

Dante glowered at the upperclassmen. "Pity no one asked your opinion, Lex," he cracked his knuckles. "I can still lose my temper if pushed the wrong way. You'll accompany them along with anyone else who dares open their mouth."

* * *

Servants spent the rest of the night cleaning up dead bodies and bringing the banquet hall to its pre-massacre state. Autumn was still in disbelief about how close she was to being poisoned and reunited with her mom. Although she still missed her mom terribly, she didn't want to see her this way. She planned to live her life to the fullest and escape this horrible place. Still,something didn't add up. Why was she the only royal at the banquet hall?

Fifty-Four

AUTUMN DREADED the next morning more than any morning in her life. More than the morning of her mom's burial. More than the morning of the day of her abduction. Even more than the morning Caleb told her he no longer loved her and was taking Misty to prom. This was the worst morning of her entire life.

It was the morning she'd be married off against her will to a *monstrous* alien prince.

She'd barely slept a wink after the poisonings and the trial that'd taken place. So many people were murdered, and others made to be slaves. Their freedom was lost in the blink of an eye. All because somebody wanted her dead. She shuddered.

Valdez.

But she had no proof, only a single threat.

Upon first glance in the mirror, she appeared more exhausted than she'd ever been. Her silver-gray eyes were adorned with deep purple bags. *Great.* She sighed.

After taking a long luxurious shower, she heard a commotion beyond the door.

She threw on a fluffy white towel and went outside, horrified to find a team of maids along with Emblem and Allegoria.

A woman with burnished skin approached, face as pretty as a doll.

"We're here to accompany you to the Empress's private suite to prepare you for your wedding."

She nodded mechanically as her stomach bubbled over. She followed the entourage, hair dripping wet from her shower. They walked up several flights of winding steps to the eighth floor of the palace.

In all the rooms she'd seen, it was the first time the crimson carpet transformed into royal purple. The gilded walls shimmered as the sun played off its flecks.

She was ushered to the end of the hallway, to a white ceiling-high door with a crystal knob. Inside was a series of well-lit suites separated by white silk screens. Taupe seashell shaped couches occupied the center of the room. The bright wooden floors sparkled in the sunlight.

A balcony sat on the left with two open French doors. A warm breeze drifted, smelling of lavender. The nostalgic scent reminded her of her predicament and how she'd never see Earth again.

The air traffic was dense. Hundreds of thousands of microscopic aircraft hovered toward the palace. They were here for the wedding.

"I hope you slept well." Autumn turned and was met face-to-face with Isidora, who grinned, brown eyes smiling. She wore a golden satin bathrobe.

"I wish I'd slept better," Autumn admitted. "I can't stop thinking about yesterday."

Isidora smoothed her hands through her hair. "I understand. That's all anyone is talking about. Please be rest assured, a tragedy of that magnitude will never happen again. The offenders were punished, but right now we have a wedding to prepare for."

I doubt I could ever forget this.

Isidora examined her face. "You look scattered. We should start with your makeup."

Princess Leyla stood behind her mother with a hand on the fullest part of her hip.

She recalled their last encounter where she was dressed like a hybrid, although her sentence had been up for weeks. Now she wore a plum satin bathrobe. Her light-brown hair cascaded with a deep side part.

"You look positively atrocious." Leyla's usual attitude was alive and well. Autumn was tempted to counter, but there was too much on her mind. Mainly, the marriage she was about to enter against her will.

"Thanks, Leyla. I know how bad I look."

Leyla's lips flickered with amusement. "The same goes for every morning, I'm sure. It must be a human condition."

"Ladies," the empress hissed before gesturing to Autumn. "Come have a seat. You need to be on point. You're the star of the show."

Autumn sat down at the empress's request. A maid presented her with a magenta satin bathrobe.

Emblem and Allegoria disappeared behind a screen and reemerged with flutes of bubbling champagne, as well as berries powdered with sugar and dipped in chocolate. Autumn stared at the platter of food reluctantly, as did Leyla. The empress didn't bat an eye.

"Please ladies, there's no need to be wary. This food has been triply tested. The same goes for all the food and drink scheduled to be served during today's festivities."

Dante had told her the exact same thing when she arrived on this planet and look what happened.

Stomach grumbling with fury, Autumn took the

empress's word for it and ate, ignoring memories of the mass poisoning that'd taken place. The champagne eased her nerves as her eyelids were powdered with a soft bristled brush.

Simultaneously her hair was combed, styled, and clipped half-up. As per usual, the strands were iced with glitter.

Isidora gasped, waving her hands in the air. "Absolutely beautiful. I have the perfect accessory." She rose to a graceful stand, left the room, and reemerged with a mirrored box and presented it to Autumn.

Autumn opened it slowly. Inside sat a raw crystal tiara banded with silver satin. Emblem secured it to Autumn's head.

"Thank you," Autumn muttered, if only to be polite.

This was the first time she'd worn a crown besides Halloween when she played a princess. Now she was a real one, not that she wanted to be.

"It's no trouble at all," the empress chirped. "Really. I wore this very same tiara on my wedding day."

"That's not fair," Leyla interrupted. "I thought you were saving that crown for me. I didn't realize you planned to use it to adorn her unfit head."

"Leyla, please, not now. Your day will come."

Autumn's forehead twitched.

A cart was rolled out carrying a white satin garment bag containing her wedding gown. The bodice was short-sleeved and diamond-encrusted, while the poofy skirt was adorned with white applique flowers. On the back hung two iridescent floor-length fairy wings.

If her friends could see her, they would've laughed. *Autumn the fairy princess.* She'd gotten her wish.

"Aren't you magnificent my dear," the empress said after she was dressed.

"Even I have to admit, you do clean up rather well."

"Leyla," Isidora hissed. "Enough, we're going to be late."

* * *

After racing down eight flights of winding steps to the ground floor of the palace, Autumn was breathless. The dress was heavy, and for the first time, she was thankful for all the gravity training she'd done in the hopes of kicking Dante's ass for everything he'd put her through. If not, it would've been impossible to move.

She made her way to the Great Hall and couldn't help but stare. All sorts of frightening creatures lingered in the hallway, some more frightening than others with pink skin and long elephant trunks.

Some were covered entirely with matted fur. Some had slime dripping from their skin. Some were giants, while others were far shorter than her.

However, what they all had in common was that they were dressed elegantly for the event. She tried her best not to stare.

The Great Hall existed in the back of the palace where she'd never ventured. Drones buzzed through the air broadcasting the event to the farthest areas of the universes. Reporters held microphones and desperately tried to speak with her, but the guards kept them at bay.

She stood in pitch darkness before two broad doors with golden handles. Isidora and Leyla slipped away. The empress reemerged with a sizable bouquet wrapped with silver satin.

"I was told this is part of your custom," she handed her the bouquet. "You'll do wonderful, daughter."

She left Autumn alone with her heart thrumming in her chest.

This wasn't what she wanted, and she never imagined getting married without her dad walking her down the aisle. Dads were supposed to be there to offer a shoulder to lean on, and advice that she desperately needed right now. She closed her eyes and held her breath as the doors slowly creaked open, aware of every drop of beaded sweat on her body.

Dad.

* * *

Guillermo Ramon shot up from his bed in the dead of night. *A dream.* He smoothed his hands over his weary eyes, his vision blurred. He could've sworn he heard his daughter's voice desperately calling out for him through the drifting shadows.

Despair consumed him as he grabbed his glasses and ambled over to the window to gaze at the pale full moon.

He'd stop at nothing until he found her.

No man, woman, or *alien* would stand in his way. When he got his hands on Dante, he planned to strangle him. He planned to make him pay.

Fifty-Five

AUTUMN'S HEART hammered out of her chest as she was greeted by a deep blue spotlight, followed by a sea of black. As she walked between the doors, her lips parted a touch.

She didn't expect this at all.

Stars flickered through the sky and a brook babbled beneath the wooden bridge she walked over. It creaked beneath her weight.

A landscape of evergreen trees sprayed for as far as her eyes could see. Fireflies flitted through the air and crickets chirped. For a split second she could've sworn she was home again at Farrah Falls on a warm summer evening.

Shrubs adorned with white roses matched the bouquet she held.

Beyond the bushes laid hundreds of seats filled with guests who watched her make her way through the room. Two blue alien girls, wearing fairy wings, skipped along a trail of silver satin, tossing rose petals from their baskets.

Autumn followed them up a flight of steps covered by cool gray mist. Microscopic drones raced through the darkness.

Hologram projectors sat at various points in the room, broadcasting the live event.

She walked behind the skipping children for what seemed like a solid mile. Eventually, she reached the home stretch.

At the end of the aisle was an arch composed of lavender, roses, and vibrant lilacs. Golden lanterns drifted and Dante, who she barely recognized in his all-white uniform, stood underneath. His shining raven hair was pulled into a low sleek ponytail. A waterfall poured in gentle waves behind him, water splashing against the rocks.

He'd never looked so neat before, but even worse, he was too handsome for words.

She gulped, her brow erupting in sweat, unable to believe she was going through with this. She trembled with each approaching step. The room simmered like a sauna.

He smiled and whispered into her ear. "Glad you could make it."

"Well, I didn't exactly have a choice," her voice dripped with sarcasm.

He leaned over again. "Sure you did. You have a choice in everything."

Autumn's cheeks heated as Leyla strode over and snatched the bouquet from her hands. She stood behind them, a hand affixed to her hip.

In the crowd, the emperor watched them with a less than thrilled expression on his face. The Empress on the other hand grinned like a fool. Ronan and Armienti lounged against a sidewall in the shadows.

When she spotted Valdez, her eyes pierced her like an ice pick. It was unsurprising, considering her threats.

Autumn was positive that she was responsible for the poisonings. She scrunched her fingers into fists.

A short, wrinkled Elattion man approached them, clothed in a scarlet cloak. Everyone took their seats.

Dante leaned over and whispered into her ear. "The first half of the ritual should seem familiar to you; I've done my research." He winked.

He pulled away and she held her breath.

"Honored guests, I wish to thank you for joining us on this most historic of days to celebrate the union of Prince Dante Martyne II and Autumn Ramon of Earth. If anyone can think of a reason why these two shouldn't be joined, speak now or forever hold your peace."

There was nothing but stifling silence. She expected someone to say something, *anything,* but no objection came no matter how hard she hoped.

"Do you, Prince Dante, take Autumn to be your wife?"

"I do, and I promise to love her until my dying breath."

She stared at him, noting the sincerity in his voice.

"And do you, Autumn, take Dante as your husband?"

"I do," the words left her mouth in slow motion. She couldn't believe she was really going through with this.

"Most excellent. Now, if I may have the rings." One of the little blue girls skipped to the altar carrying a white satin pillow with a rose gold and a silver banded ring tied to the top.

"Let this ring represent your eternal love for one another as it has no beginning and no end. Let it bind you together forever."

Dante took the rose gold ring and slid it onto Autumn's reluctant finger. Trembling, she slid the silver ring onto his finger.

He leaned forward and flattened his palms against hers before joining their foreheads. Her heart sped. "What are you doing?"

An icy hot tingling sensation consumed her body. Her eyes drifted closed as it overpowered her. After they held the position for a few moments, it stopped, and she could see again.

"Now we're bound together. Heart, mind, and body. Two halves of one soul."

Bound together? The breath caught in her throat.

"I now pronounce you husband and wife. You may kiss your bride."

Dante leaned over and pressed his lips to hers. He pulled away after a moment, blue cheeks flushed.

Sweetheart, we have to take care of some business before we can enjoy our feast.

Autumn rolled her eyes until she realized those words didn't come out of his mouth, they flowed through her mind.

Her jaw agape, she spoke, "What did you do to me?"

Fifty-Six

"I-I-I, DON'T UNDERSTAND," Autumn said as Dante led her out of the Great Hall. Everyone stood and applauded. Rose petals fluttered from the ceiling. Dante waved and smiled as drones buzzed.

Her blood pressure rose, and her face heated with anger. When they exited the Great Hall, she was practically ready to explode. "What the heck did you do to me? I don't want you creeping through my head."

"It's part of our agreement. When two mates are bound, they're granted the ability to communicate telepathically with each other," he leisurely replied.

Great, just great. Another vital detail he omitted.

"Is there any way to undo this?" she pleaded desperately.

"Not that I'm aware of," his lips flickered with amusement.

They entered a room with a stack of tablets. Dante grabbed one and scrolled. Autumn peeked, scrunching her nose at the strange hieroglyphic language.

"What is this?"

"Our marriage contract."

She squinted. "I don't understand any of this." She knew better than to sign a document before reading it.

"I'll read it to you," he said. "By signing this document, my family hereby agrees to waive your substantial dowry."

"My dowry?" she growled. "You kidnapped me. I don't owe you a penny."

He continued. "You're bound to serve the Empire, as am I—"

His face shifted from content to rage. "If you fail to provide me with a fit heir our marriage will be deemed null and void, and I shall be forced to take a wife of the emperor's choosing."

"You didn't really think I'd let you get off that easy did you, Dante?"

They whirled around. The emperor rested his hip against the doorway. "Do you like that little clause I added at the end?"

"Just so you're aware, neither of us are signing anything until this document is revised to our liking."

"We'll see about that."

Autumn stared at the document, fed up with everyone's hatred, fighting, and nonsense. With a swipe of her fingertip, she signed her name on the dotted line.

Dante's eyes bulged in disbelief. "Why did you do that?"

She folded her arms, ignoring his question.

The emperor flashed a cocky smile. "That's the most intelligent decision I've ever seen you make. Perhaps I was wrong about you. Perhaps you do have a brain."

She exited the room nonchalantly. His insults no longer phased her.

Dante followed her through the door and back into the Great Hall. It'd since cleared out. When they entered a neighboring room where the feast was scheduled to take place, a spotlight flashed on them, and everyone applauded.

Dante took her by the hand and whisked her onto the dance floor at the center of the tables. Candles flickered in the dull blue light. Iridescent tinsel twinkled from the ceiling and shimmering chandeliers. Four barren winding tree stalks surrounded the stage. He bowed and she curtseyed. They swayed to the gentle strum of a harp.

"Am I really so horrible that you can't conceive of a life with me?"

"Stop. If you want to talk to me, just talk," she groaned.

"Sorry," he whispered into her ear. "Am I really so horrible that you signed our future away?"

The guests surrounding them blurred as they danced. "You already ruined my future, so I figured I'd repay the favor."

"So that's what this is about. Just for the record, I would love our children regardless of their abilities. Nothing could stop me," sincerity twinkled in his brilliant amber eyes.

"I don't want to think about having children," she glanced away.

"I've been ready only recently, but I respect your decision to wait. Never mind, forget I mentioned anything," he muttered.

They finished their dance and met with an echoing round of applause. Dante took her by the hand and walked her to the front table. He pulled out her chair and she sat, and he grabbed a silver goblet of red wine.

She glowered, hating how handsome he looked. It was criminal. *Children*—not if she had anything to do with it. She'd escape from this planet, rescue Caleb and Misty, and they could all go back to Earth and resume their lives. He lied about the state of Earth, and she planned to use it to her advantage.

Dante raised his goblet. "I'd like to propose a toast to my dazzling wife who I knew I loved since the moment I first saw her. Autumn, there are no words, ballads, or poems I can think of to rival your loveliness and your pure heart. Thank you for agreeing to spend your life with me."

She applauded politely, knowing it was expected of her. After all, the event was being broadcast to every planet in the universes. Her eyes drifted to the emperor's table. He sat there glowering while Valdez picked at her red polished talons. *Murderess.*

Dante returned to his seat, and like a flash, another figure approached—Armienti, with his golden tousled hair and piercing blue eyes.

"This is complete and utter nonsense. I can't believe you're actually going through with this charade."

Dante's mouth fell into a tight flat line. "Come again?"

"She doesn't want you and she doesn't want to be here. Your selfishness is unmatched," Armienti spat.

Dante snapped his fingers. "Escort him back to his chambers. He's obviously had too much to drink."

Guards lined up and ushered Armienti out the door. "Congratulations—" He fell into a mocking bow as he faded from view.

Autumn's cheeks flushed with heat as all eyes in the room fixated on them. Dante rested a hand on her shoulder.

"Let the feast begin."

Dinner was served, and for the first time since she'd been altered, her appetite was non-existent. Dante, on the other hand, inhaled those disgusting miniature serpents he tried to poison her with on the voyage to Surge. Her nose scrunched. *Gross.*

"Sweetheart, I assure you all the food has been triply tested. I even had them prepare your favorite."

She stared at the chocolate chip pancakes on the table, complete with syrup. She almost wanted to smile, but anger simmered through her about how he extracted this information.

Their thoughts were bound together forever.

"I bet you didn't know we had chocolate here," he grinned, wiping his mouth with a cloth napkin.

"This is my second favorite actually," she lied, sushi being a close tie.

Autumn crossed her legs and bounced her knee remembering that, after all the festivities, there was an age-old ceremony scheduled to take place. She was not taking part in any of it if she could help it.

When Dante turned to talk to another guest, she grabbed a knife and pressed it into her diamond encrusted bodice.

She refused to go down without a fight.

* * *

Dinner was followed by more drinking and dancing. Golden sparkling bottles of champagne popped, and guests laughed and waltzed across the floor.

Simultaneously, a line formed of esteemed guests that wrapped around the room, who wished to present them with spectacular gifts. They received everything from gold, weapons, elaborate armor, a fleet, and fabrics to create the finest clothing.

On top of it all, Autumn had no clue what anyone was saying. Sure, she could speak Ivarkian, although she had no idea how she learned it in the first place. The rest of the languages were a mystery.

Dante, on the other hand, fluently spoke in many tongues. He used his wit and charm, laughing and engaging everyone. People seemed to enjoy his company. She fidgeted with her hands.

At the back of the line stood two well-built lizard-like creatures, dressed in plated onyx armor. Their forest-green-and-purple scales shimmered in the light. Their caramel eyes blinked revealing cat-like slits.

They appeared out of place as they approached holding a sealed golden chest with the crest of a headless man propped up against a tree.

Dante folded his arms, muscles shifting beneath his white uniform as they placed the chest on the floor with a heavy thud.

"The Grand Supreme expresses his deepest regrets that he was unable to attend your wedding ceremony. He's instructed us to present you with this gift on his behalf."

They popped open the top and the container spilled with glittering rubies.

"Tell Master Izzo thank you. His gift is most gracious and most appreciated."

They bowed at the waist, leaving the chest behind. The other gifts paled in comparison.

"What's with all the rubies?" Autumn asked.

"Out here in deep space we don't deal in dollars and coins like you're accustomed to, rather ruby and credit," he said. "And as you know, our most valuable mineral is crystal."

She nodded, recalling everyone fussing over Varz.

Their conversation was interrupted by the arrival of a sixteen-tiered cake topped with icing, multi-hued roses, and other assorted foliage.

For a moment she was reminded of the wedding she'd served at back on Earth.

Oh Caleb, she thought as her heart clenched. Dante's eyes flickered to her then looked away. She had to rescue him and Misty and figure out a way to get back to Earth.

Her hands trembled with ire as the cake was sliced and served. Suddenly, Dante dropped his fork and snatched her hand. Everyone stopped eating. Her heart slammed against her rib cage. He held her in his arms and made his way toward the door.

Autumn clawed against his shoulder with all her might. "Whe—where are we going?"

He kissed her lobe. "Relax."

"Dante, I'm not going through with this."

He chuckled softly as he carried her. The entire court followed.

"I'm serious, I didn't agree to this—"

Dante raised a palm, halting the procession before the winding crimson steps. "I want to thank everyone for coming to celebrate with us. This is as far as I'm permitting the procession to go. My wife and I wish to maintain our privacy during the final part of the ceremony."

Whistles and groans followed, but a loud round of applause erupted as they ascended the stairs. She sat still in his arms, goosebumps prickling over her skin. Valdez's eyes narrowed as she turned on a heel and stormed away, gossamer toga flowing.

"She doesn't like you," Dante quirked an onyx brow.

"I don't care," Autumn's eyes darted around the hall as she tried desperately to plot her escape. She had to get away from him.

His mouth tilted to a smile. "I wouldn't worry about it. She doesn't like anyone, including me."

He carried her to the end of the hall where her bedroom was located. He placed her on her feet and punched the code into the keypad beside her door.

Autumn rustled searching desperately for the knife she'd hidden in her bodice earlier. The door slid open.

"Looking for something?" he leaned against the door frame, sliding his face toward hers.

She shuddered. "No, I—"

"I want to thank you for a lovely evening, Autumn

Martyne. You certainly stole the show," he pressed his lips against her forehead. She stood there, mouth ajar as he strode to his own room a few doors down. "I hope you sleep well."

He stopped and turned before entering the code into his own side door panel. He slipped the knife from his sleeve, twiddling it between his fingers like a prize. "Pity you won't have the pleasure of sliding this blade through my throat tonight. Perhaps another time."

He smirked, leaving her alone in the hallway. She stood there in silence.

Fifty-Seven

AS AUTUMN ATE chocolate chip pancakes for breakfast the next morning, she pondered her situation. Why the heck was she here if Dante didn't plan to sleep with her?

Not that she cared or anything.

He was a vicious monster who conquered worlds. But why put her through this nightmare and force her to marry him?

A knock came to the door, breaking her chain of thought.

"Come in," she wiped her hands on a cloth napkin.

A guard ambled through the door and fell into a bow. "Your Imperial Highness, Master Dante requests your presence in the throne room at your earliest convenience." *Your Imperial Highness*, she was officially a princess now.

She crossed her arms. "Tell him I'm busy."

The guard trembled.

She sighed. Everyone was so terrified of him. It was ridiculous.

"Never mind, I'll be right down."

* * *

After purposely taking a long hot bath to make him wait, she made her way downstairs clothed in an obsidian bodysuit with an asymmetrical royal purple stripe. Her hair was bound in a high glittered ponytail.

Dante stood by the pulsating steel thrones and spoke with his parents. Lights twinkled against his raven hair from the skylight.

He turned toward her. "Wonderful, you're here."

The emperor regarded her shrewdly while the empress flashed a bright smile. Sunlight played off the strands of her gilded hair.

"So how was she, Dante?" The emperor's mouth flickered with amusement. "Was she worth all the trouble?"

Bile rose in Autumn's gut. Dante didn't dignify his father with a response. *Pig.*

"We'll be stepping out for a few hours," Dante finally responded.

The emperor rolled his eyes. "Enjoy, and remember our little agreement."

Dante huffed and led Autumn from the room. "I'm so sorry about him. He's such an imbecile. Sometimes I hate him so much that all I see is red." A vein twitched furiously across his forehead. He smoothed a hand through his raven hair, tousling it.

They arrived at the far end of the palace before a pair of sleek knob-less doors. They were at least twenty feet high.

Light glimmered through the central crack. Guards stood on either side of the exit, metallic guns in hand.

Dante placed his black-gloved hands on her shoulders. "Close your eyes," he said.

Her eyes widened. "Why?" *Maybe he planned to pay her back for last night,* a shiver rattled her core. "No, I don't trust you."

"And I don't trust you not to peek," he chuckled.

When she still didn't budge, he went on, "Fine, I'll close them for you," he cupped his hands over her eyes, obscuring her vision.

A rush of warm breeze erupted against her skin, carrying with it the scent of lavender. Light appeared through the cracks of his hands.

He urged her forward, his solid body brushing against her back. "I'll let you know when you can stop."

The floor grew slick beneath her heeled go-go boots. Aircrafts whooshed amidst the bustling metropolis.

"Okay, here's good," he removed his palms from her eyes.

Light filled her vision and cleared as she opened her eyes. Excitement and delight brimmed through her.

Fifty-Eight

A WHITE CAR bearing a striking resemblance to the Ferrari Dante had stolen back home sat before her with tinted windows, rainbow chromatic wheels, and humming butterfly doors.

The crappy college commuter car she'd owned back on Earth paled in comparison.

She cupped her mouth and jumped up and down in disbelief and excitement. Then suddenly she stopped.

Her demeanor became serious. "Is this—"

"Stolen? Not this time. I had this craft created for you. It's one of a kind."

She exhaled a deep sigh of relief and walked over, pressing her hands against the glass window.

"Do you want to take it out?"

"Yes," she replied, beyond elated. Perhaps now she could plan her escape for real.

The doors flew open swiftly and silently like a falcon preparing to take flight. They climbed inside. The interior was supple oxblood leather. The doors were sealed vacuum tight.

"I love my new car, thank you," she reached, fingers

grazing over the buttons and gadgets all resembling cars back home on Earth. "What's the catch?"

She waited, heart thundering in her ears. He had to have some kind of angle. Something he wanted from her.

"There is no catch. I want nothing more than for you to be happy in your new home," he ran a hand through his midnight hair. "I know that can never happen if you're cooped up in the boring palace all day. I do apologize if I've been somewhat overbearing. Your safety is my top priority. I couldn't live with myself if something happened to you again. You've been through enough."

She exhaled a deep sigh of relief and nodded slowly.

Thousands of tightly spaced gem-hued buildings surrounded them. They glimmered in the early afternoon sunlight. Her car sat at the edge of a tiled walkway surrounded by other crafts. Beyond them was a cliff thousands of feet to the shadowy ground below.

Her brows furrowed. "Where am I supposed to drive this car?"

"This isn't a car. It's an aircraft. We'll take it onto the skyway. It's the primary mode of transportation around the city."

"Why does it have wheels then?"

"For decoration," he winked.

She peered and there were crafts whizzing around the airway faster than any car or airplane she'd ever seen. The only reason she was able to follow their movement was because of her change. But still, she was overwhelmed.

Nine lanes, nine lanes of color and dust, she counted then gulped.

"Those aircraft are moving faster than the speed of light. Don't I need a license or something?"

"No," he crossed his arms. "It's not like Earth. All you

need is my permission which I've whole heartedly granted you."

He paused for a moment. "Hold on, I'll deal with those pesky aircraft," he lowered the window. "Guards, I'm imposing a temporary travel ban on the skyway. Sound the alarm."

A siren roared in a female voice in a series of languages she didn't understand—aside from Ivarkian.

"How do I know Ivarkian again?" she asked him, unable to recollect exactly when she learned the dialect. But he ignored her question as usual.

"Problem solved."

She couldn't get over how similar her aircraft was to the cars back home. There was a backup camera, a rearview mirror, side mirrors, and even three-point seat belts installed. Two floor pedals sat beneath her feet. Her heart skipped when Dante handed her a full-faced helmet with an opaque visor, along with leather driving gloves.

"Put these on," he said. "Although this craft resembles a car it has a bit more *kick* to it."

He grabbed a helmet, placing it over her head. She caught a glimpse of his simple silver wedding band, still in disbelief they'd gotten married the night before.

He tugged on her seatbelt, *unsurprising*, and handed her a key. She twisted the key beside the wheel and the engine revved before going silent. The aircraft levitated above the ground.

"This is so cool," she grinned.

"Is it now? Try pushing the right pedal and giving it the tiniest bit of crystal liquid fuel."

When she pushed the pedal, she accidentally applied too much force. They flew into the city at such a speed that the skin of her cheeks rippled and flapped against the oncoming wind.

"Stop!"

She slammed on the brakes, and they were choked forward before knocking against their seats, narrowly avoiding whiplash.

"Okay, sweetheart, this time try applying half the amount of pressure. Remember, all you have to do is tap it."

"Sorry, I didn't realize it would have that kind of reaction. It feels almost like a rocket ship." Or so she imagined the sensation of blastoff.

She hit the pedal and the aircraft accelerated from zero to eighty in the blink of an eye.

"Much better. Remember, less is more," he reiterated. "Now turn right so we can enter the skyway."

When she cut the wheel, the aircraft whizzed in a 360-degree circle. Dante grabbed it. "Remember *less* is more."

She halved the pressure, and to her delight, they successfully entered the skyway. She maneuvered the aircraft into the center lane. There were nine lanes in total separated by clear glittering tubed lights. She cruised with control, pleased with her accomplishment.

"Wonderful, I knew you'd get the hang of it."

"How fast does this thing go anyway?" she asked.

"Its maximum speed is five thousand kilometers per hour. You need a little more practice, in my honest opinion, before you travel at that rate."

She nodded. It probably wasn't a bad idea considering she hadn't driven in over a year.

And under no circumstances are you to enter outer space with this vehicle. It's designed for interplanetary travel only, his thought boomed through her mind.

She glowered at Dante, and he shrugged innocently.

"Sorry, I know you don't like when I communicate this way, but I was just taking a peek in that head of yours to make sure that everything that happened yesterday wasn't a dream."

Fifty-Nine

DANTE STARED at Autumn as she grinned beneath her helmet visor, cheeks shifting to the color of freshly picked roses. Try as he might, he was unable to prevent his own cheeks from warming. How beautiful and innocent she was. While he, on the other hand, was so very undeserving of her and terrified she could never love him again now that she knew what he was truly capable of.

A monster, she continuously called him.

That, in fact, was why he forced her to marry him, to keep an eye on her and ensure her safety. *Among other reasons he'd yet to admit.*

Despite their many obstacles and the mountain of hopelessness that stood before him, he remained determined to win her back. No matter the cost.

The faint sound of buzzing in his side pocket distracted his tormented thoughts. He slipped his sleek black communicator out and peered at the caller.

"Dammit, no, no, no," he murmured, sliding the screen up. "Hello?" he said in a disgruntled tone.

Words were exchanged and he hung up, burying his

helmeted face frustratedly in his palms. The aircraft grew pitch silent.

"What was that all about?" Autumn asked, cutting the aircraft too close to a divider for his taste. She nearly knocked the lights off the track.

"I need you to pull over at the nearest exit. I have to get back to the palace immediately for an emergency council meeting." Which he knew would only result in one thing. There was only so long he could avoid the inevitable.

For the first time ever, she didn't protest and did as he requested. A grave expression consumed her previously elated face. He hated seeing her upset. His heart sank deep within his chest. They switched seats and he navigated the aircraft back to Sanguis.

"It's not Earth, is it?" she asked, her voice tremulous as she wrung her hands in her lap.

"No, I promise you Earth is fine. Everything is taken care of," he reassured her.

"You always say that, but how? How is it safe if we're not even in the same universe?"

"It's safer that you don't know the details for now. I swear on everything I hold dear in this life you have nothing to worry about."

She paused. "Is Surge under attack?"

He snorted but then went serious. "Good heavens, no. Nobody would have the gall to attack my planet. We Martynes are feared across the universes. Our reputation has preceded us for centuries."

She nodded and stared out the window in silence. Although he was tempted to comb through the winding corridors of her mind and reassure her, he refrained.

When they arrived at Sanguis, Dante parked the aircraft at the docks, and they left their helmets and gloves on the seats. They made their way toward the palace entrance.

"I trust you'll be all right in my absence."

"Sure," she said quietly, and he teleported to the council meeting. His stomach twisted and turned with uncertain dread.

* * *

Dante arrived late to the council meeting, which was an absolute first for him. Not only had his father started speaking, but the projector was running, and a ghost-like hologram slowly rotated above the table, displaying his plans.

The Grand Supreme listened in eerie silence. Thirty sets of eyes settled on him including the blue glassy pupils of his hungover cousin, Armienti, who he did his best to ignore. He still couldn't believe how he behaved at the wedding.

"How nice of you to finally join us," his father's voice dripped with cruel sarcasm. "I hope you were at least doing something of importance. Although, I can't imagine what could be more important than performing your duty."

"Please forgive me, Father. I came as soon as I heard. What has happened?" A single drop of sweat slid down his back upon the realization that his master was listening in on the entire conversation. One small slip up could have devastating consequences.

"We've received news of an open rebellion on Varz. Our representatives have been overthrown by a rebel faction. The Red Cloaks. It's rumored Keyserike has been spotted sniffing around our claim."

"That is so like him," Valdez crossed her toned arms, flashing a venomous smile. "He's always been one to come and pick at the bones."

"The Red Cloaks?" Dante made a face. "They're at it again? This news is most unfortunate."

"It's more than unfortunate, it's outrageous that a group

of lowly peasants dare to challenge our authority. That's precisely why you're all assembled here. You're the most elite of the elite warriors that we have to offer. I'm hereby dispatching you at first light to go subdue those filthy rebels and transport them back to Surge to be sentenced," the emperor slammed a black-gloved fist against the table. "Torture them, burn them, do whatever you like. Just make sure they're returned alive. I'm going to make a terrible example of them. Led by my brilliant son Dante and his extraordinary talents, hand in hand with Lady Valdez, I'm confident you will emerge victoriously."

"How long do you estimate this mission will take?" Dante rested his hands in his pockets.

"Why do you ask? Are you in some sort of hurry? I can't imagine what for."

A long awkward silence followed, and everyone gawked. Dante was tempted to roll his eyes.

"No, not at all," Dante straightened his spine. "I need to prepare rations and ensure that the destroyers have enough crystal liquid fuel to last the entirety of the journey."

"Excellent," his father grinned through his black goatee. "It seems you've learned from past errors. The length of this trip depends on you, my boy. I estimate at least ninety suns and moons."

His father flicked on the lights. "You're hereby dismissed. Go and make your final preparations. Except for you of course, Dante. I wish to have a word in private."

High level officials bowed and walked around him and his father. He ignored his pretty blond-haired cousin Armienti who regarded him for a moment too long. He caught the edge of Valdez's icy stare as she exited the room.

The door slid closed, and his father continued. "I know you must be beyond frustrated right now, so soon after your wedding, but I require your full cooperation in this matter.

Our claim, and more importantly, the Grand Supreme's claim, is at stake."

"Frustrated doesn't skim how I'm feeling right now." Dante didn't put it past himself not to rip someone's head clear from their shoulders. He couldn't stop imagining his own father's decapitation.

"Please spare me your feelings. You should focus your infamous fury on subduing those damn Red Cloaks led by our mutual enemy, Keyserike. They're the real threat here," the emperor paused. "Besides, you owe this to me for I've made an extraordinary exception allowing you to wed your Earth whore. If you value her life, you'll obey my command."

He saw a flash of red, his molars ground in his mouth. "And if you value your life, you'll cease your idle threats. Don't think I haven't realized it was you who shoddily orchestrated those poisonings and murdered half our court in cold blood."

"You're wrong. Those deaths are still under investigation, which we could've performed ourselves if you didn't go rogue and show mercy. You've become so soft and foolish around that girl, it makes me sick. I wonder what tricks she's spinning between her legs."

Dante snapped his jaw tight. "Watch it. Everyone knows I've surpassed you in strength and ability ages ago. You're nothing more than a weakling. A puppet in the Grand Supreme's master scheme."

In the blink of an eye, he wrapped his hand around his father's throat and slammed him against the wall. His father dangled, his expression somewhere between horror and surprise.

"Since we're exchanging threats, I have one of my own. If you touch a single hair on her delicate human head while I'm away, my face will be the last thing you shall ever see."

* * *

Autumn ducked as the steel conference room door flew from its hinges and shattered against the wall. She couldn't believe what she overheard. They were going to Varz. And she planned to make it her mission to come along and rescue Caleb. She couldn't wait to hold him in her arms again. She couldn't wait to go home. Back to her dad, back to her life. She didn't care what Dante wanted anymore.

Sixty

AUTUMN FRANTICALLY SEARCHED through her bedroom. She located her canvas crossbody bag and stuffed it full of bodysuits. She shook her head, groaning to herself. If only Dante hadn't purged her belongings, she'd have something normal and human to wear back to Earth.

A firm knock came to the door, and she stopped dead.

"Just a minute," she shoved her pre-packed bag into the bottom of her closet. Her heart pounded through her throat.

"Come in."

Dante strode through the door, feral and agitated. Strands of his midnight hair frazzled like static electricity. She hated how she could sense his emotions and thoughts now. His mind was a complex and confusing place to be trapped.

As he took a seat on the bed, Mr. Hiss sprang from the comforter and into the shadows beneath the mattress. His large, innocent sapphire eyes glistened. The neighboring fireplace crackled. The glow from its sparkling embers danced across the floor.

"I know you heard everything. I sensed your presence in the hallway."

"I—" she began and crossed her arms. "Okay, I was eavesdropping. Is that a crime?"

"No, of course not," he glanced at the floor. "So, you know I'll be gone for at least ninety suns and moons then."

She nodded slowly, tempted to smile, but it wasn't appropriate under the circumstances.

"I'm so sorry about this situation. This isn't how I imagined things would turn out. I wanted to make everything up to you—"

"Well, you can't," she blurted, placing a hand on the fullest part of her hip and then paused. "Unless you take me with you."

"Why on Earth would you want to go to Varz?" His mouth twitched. "Is there something of interest to you there, or rather, *someone*?"

Her heart sped. "I still can't believe what you did. Why couldn't you just leave my friends back home? They never did anything to you."

He rose to his feet, his royal purple cape slithering over his shoulders like a viper. "Friends? I recall the situation somewhat differently. They got what they deserved. I'd gladly suffer them again. I won't tolerate anyone hurting you, nor will I apologize for protecting you. I don't think that's truly what you find bothersome. I know you still love him."

How could she not? She and Caleb grew up together and were each other's first kiss. They went from best friends to boyfriend and girlfriend to—she didn't want to think about it — and then back to lovers again. *And somehow, in the interim, I became Dante's wife.*

Caleb was the best thing to ever happen to her. Minus his slight indiscretion which she forgave him for under the circumstances.

He changed the subject. "I would never in this lifetime take you on such a dangerous mission. It's beyond irresponsible. Terrible and unspeakable things happen to women in deep space every day, and I won't risk you."

"I could just stay on the ship and wait."

"No."

Her forehead pulsated. "What about Valdez? She's a woman and she's coming."

"Valdez is different. You're not like her and I'm glad for it," he paused. "You'll remain here with my mother and sister where I know you'll be safe." The light played off his amber eyes and the slopes of his cheeks in a spectacular sort of way. "I'd sleep better knowing you're safe."

He reached into his pocket, pulled out a teal communicator, and handed it to her. "This is long overdue. If you like I can provide you with regular updates of my whereabouts. If not, I won't. But I still think you should have one. I'm sure you'll be traveling around the city at some point."

She held her alien cell phone in the palm of her hand. "Thank you."

"Not a problem. You should get some sleep. The sendoff ceremony is at first light and if you want our relationship to be believable, you'd better be there on time," he bowed, took her hand and kissed it. "Goodnight, Lady Martyne."

He turned on his heel and left. She waited a few seconds, jumped to her feet, and continued to pack her bag. She had to get out of here one way or another.

Sixty-One

AUTUMN OPENED her eyes just as first light shone in the sky. She trembled, sitting up in bed, trying to figure out a way to sneak her belongings from her room undetected, especially after her maids arrived. They seemed quiet enough and never stepped out of line, but who knew if they could be *trustworthy*? Like the empress had warned her continuously, *the walls had ears, and someone was always watching.*

Emblem and Allegoria sprinted through the door, carrying a red-apple paper package secured by a golden bow. They stopped, catching their breath. Sweat dripped from their foreheads.

"Princess Autumn, we're here to prepare you for the sendoff ceremony. Departure is in under an hour," Emblem said through strained breaths. "Here's a gift from your husband."

Figures.

Allegoria placed the tidy package in Autumn's hands, and she tore it open. Inside was a floor-length celestial gown adorned with silver shooting stars and crescent moons. She sighed, and then grinned. If she tucked her bag underneath the extra fabric, just so, it would go undetected.

"Thanks, I love it. This is exactly what I needed."

I knew you would, Dante's voice rattled through her mind like a migraine.

She groaned. *I told you to stop doing that!*

A laugh followed before dead silence fell. Her communicator buzzed, causing her heart to skip beat. She went over to the table and checked it.

One new message from Dante. *Big surprise.*

You really do need to hurry. We're leaving shortly.

Autumn groaned, heading toward the bathroom, not wanting to get out of bed. After a full-blown tornado of suds and violet glitter, she was fully clothed. Emblem and Allegoria left.

Finally.

Heart hammering, she raced over to her closet and grabbed her crossbody bag, stealthily tucking it underneath her dress and securing the strap until it was out of sight.

When she reached for the door, she heard a *meow* as soft as a whisper.

Mr. Hiss sprinted over and rubbed his soft pink and black fur over her ankles, purring. He stopped, glancing at her with his crystal indigo eyes. His velvet button nose flushed.

As his tail gently thrashed over the floor, Autumn sighed and picked him up. She refused to leave him behind in this miserable place. Who knew what would happen to him if she wasn't here? Although she could only imagine what her dad and friends would think of him back home on Earth, it was a risk she was willing to take.

* * *

When Autumn arrived at the far end of the palace where the docks were located, a substantial gathering of lords and ladies flooded through the door.

"Excuse me." Everyone bowed and curtseyed, creating a path for her. Although she'd never admit it, she was finally getting used to being a celebrity.

As she made her way to the front of the crowd, the radiant morning suns sprayed a kaleidoscope of color over the jewel-toned city. The rays twinkled in her sleep-laden eyes.

She scanned for Dante but mistakenly held Valdez's stare. Her golden armor looked both fearsome and outlandish, with gilded gloves and ram horns twisting from her forehead. She looked every bit the murderess that she was.

Beside her, the emperor glowered, and the empress winked. A small smile played across her lips like an untold secret ready to be spilled.

A tap came to her shoulder and Autumn whirled around. Mr. Hiss puffed in her arms. Her heart almost burst from her ribcage from the terrifying sight. Dante stood before her wearing a full-face helmet with elongated horns. Two slits revealed his amber-and-green-flecked eyes. The pads of his shoulders were sprayed with spikes, and the shade of his armor resembled spilled blood.

He looked more horrifying than the devil himself.

She stared in silence as he brought her hand under his helmet and kissed it. Mr. Hiss growled and he chuckled.

"I don't know why you insist on bringing that animal with you everywhere. Dare I say, you've acclimated yourself to my court."

She rolled her eyes. "I have better things to do." *Like escape,* it tempted her to say.

"I know," a seductive smile played across his lips as he led her away from the crowd beneath a shadowy arch.

Her heart sped as they stood together. *Could he know what*

she was up to? He removed his helmet, placing it onto the stone lip of the wall behind her and leaned in close, hair tousled. She was overwhelmed with the scent of cinnamon. It was overpowering.

"You know, if you need anything from me, I'm only a call or message away," his long lashes grazed his cheekbones.

She crossed her arms, clutching Mr. Hiss. "I wouldn't count on hearing from me."

Well, just in case, Autumn heard him think loudly in her head. She stumbled backwards and he laughed, "Sorry, I couldn't resist."

She grumbled, cheeks heating. "Stop doing that, it's so annoying."

He shrugged innocently then smirked.

"Eww, you two are disgusting. Don't think for a second I don't know what you were doing beneath the shadows of that arch," came Leyla's voice.

Dante wrapped his arm around Autumn's shoulder, grazing his lips against her lobe.

"You've busted us."

She pulled away so he wouldn't brush against the bag beneath her dress. *What a close call, holy crap.*

Leyla folded her arms and a wave of heat settled in Autumn's cheeks. Although they hadn't been doing anything but talking, the shame remained.

"Well maybe you'll have a better understanding when you're in love someday, Leyla." Once again, Dante brushed her side only inches from her crossbody bag. She stood as stiff and rigid as a board. Mr. Hiss's tail thrashed.

"I seriously doubt it. I never would have married someone like *her.*"

Dante placed his arms around both Leyla's and Autumn's shoulders, pulling them in close as they walked. They made their way back to the crowd.

"I'm so glad I finally have my two favorite ladies here with me. I'd like to have a little chat with both of you."

"Okay?" Autumn and Leyla simultaneously replied.

"While I'm away I'd like for you two to play nicely. Especially *you*, Leyla."

Leyla folded her arms against her silver off-shoulder gown. "I don't think I can make any guarantees. I detest her too much." Leyla stopped and stared at Dante, her brown eyes wavering.

"You'd better treat my wife with the respect she's entitled to based upon her rank while I'm away, and I better not hear any reports indicating otherwise."

Leyla rolled her eyes. "How can I? She doesn't deserve this, nor does she deserve you. She's—"

"One day she'll be your empress, and you'll treat her as such."

Empress, Autumn's throat tightened with smoldering anxiety. She had to get out of here.

"You know, sister, I heard a nasty little rumor."

Leyla stopped dead, brows knitting. "What is it?"

"I hear Prince Brumha is desperate for a bride."

Her jaw lowered. "Is he the—"

"Yes, he's the absolutely hideous one who drools whilst he's speaking and belches for hours after every meal. I hear he eats his victims alive."

The blue color slowly drained from Leyla's face. She cupped her hand over her mouth.

"Disappoint me and he becomes my first choice for your husband. He has an excellent fleet and resources we can most certainly utilize."

"Please, he's an ogre. You wouldn't really do that to me, would you? *Would you?*"

"If you want to find out, test me and see. I assure you it would be a seamless transaction."

Dante kissed Leyla's cheek as she stood there frozen with fear. "I'm glad we understand each other, sister."

A drum thrummed in the distance.

"Greetings, lords and ladies. I wish to thank you all for joining us on such short notice. As you're aware, I'm sure, there's an open rebellion on Varz, one of our most valuable claims," the emperor cracked his black-gloved knuckles. The fabric of his crimson cape fluttered in the early morning breeze.

"At this point in time, I wish to call forth my elite warriors embarking on this treacherous mission so I can bestow my blessing upon them."

Dante, followed by Valdez and twenty other warriors, approached the podium, forming a sea of onyx armor and Viking-esque helmets.

"Kneel."

Everyone knelt in a horizontal line and removed their helmets, except for Dante and Valdez who stood with their arms folded, their spines straightened in an arrogant display of pride and might.

"May you all be successful on this most important of missions. May you reign carnage and hellfire onto our common enemy, quashing them mercilessly. Remember, failure is unacceptable. If you fail, don't bother coming back. You're no longer welcome in this realm."

"Hear, hear!"

"Now, be off with you. Make me proud."

Metal clanked as fists banged against steel armor in a rhythmic pattern. Soldiers rose and boarded their triangular space crafts. Autumn's heart sputtered. She needed to find a way onto a ship. She needed a way out of here.

"Sweetheart," Dante said as he rejoined her, "before I forget, here's access to my lines of credit so you can buy whatever you want while I'm gone," he handed her two square silver metal cards with alien symbols and carvings on them. She palmed them before slipping them into her dress pocket.

"Thanks. Are you sure there's no way I can come with you? I'd rather—"

"I'm sure," Dante smoothed her cheek with his hand. "This mission is treacherous and there's no place—"

"For someone as pathetic and human as you are," Valdez interjected. Autumn's blood boiled to a rage for a split second when she met Valdez's gaze. Valdez took a step back, seemingly sensing the change in energy, but she didn't address it.

"Enough," Dante said, eyes flickering to Valdez. "For someone I care about more than anyone," he corrected.

Valdez's mouth tightened into a bitter line. "Come on, Dante. We're going to be late."

"Wait—" Autumn grabbed his hand in a desperate attempt, twining her fingers in his. "I, um, uh, didn't get to say goodbye."

Valdez groaned and stormed away, golden metal boots scraping against the marble floor. Her jade ponytail flapped with an impatient fury.

"I'd like to see you off somewhere a little more private," she squeezed his hand and chewed her bottom lip. "Is there any way we can go to your ship before you depart?"

He removed his helmet, holding it in the crook of his arm. "Sure," the apples of his cheeks flushed.

"I'd like to see if it meets my standards."

They walked hand in hand as Autumn secretly surveyed the premises. She could barely breathe.

Sixty-Two

DANTE'S HEART rattled against his ribcage. Why was he so nervous, even more nervous than heading into a war zone?

Autumn's touch made his mission seem insignificant. *Was she finally ready? Did she finally want him? Or was she secretly trying to come along?*

Deep down, he knew there was only one human reason she'd want to. *Caleb.* If only he hadn't been so sloppy with his disposal. He'd be sure to take care of him this time around.

Heat settled in his cheeks as he carefully considered the last option. No, she wasn't the least bit cunning. She was sweet and kind and honest and everything he wasn't. She definitely wanted him.

The reassuring brush of her hand against his as they entered the cavity of his destroyer sent shivers crashing down his spine. Even Mr. Hiss, the soft, useless animal that he was, remained quiet purring in her arms.

Secretly, he wanted Mr. Hiss's approval as well.

He pushed a button and the door slid shut. All he could hear were the sounds of their beating hearts and the muted flow of breath.

"We don't have long," he placed his horned helmet on the floor. "But I'll gladly give you what little time I have left."

* * *

Autumn stared at Dante and the sincerity in his amber eyes. She broke his gaze to look around the ship. It was tiny, clearly meant for a few passengers. There were no sleep chambers, only upright control seats. The sides were lined with box-like cabinets.

"This is how you'll be traveling for the next three months?" Her jaw lowered. It wasn't the least bit luxurious, unlike his other ships. And certainly not fit for royalty. It was actually kind of cramped.

"Sadly, yes," he cocked his head to the side. "This is standard issue for this sort of mission. Why do you ask?"

She shrugged nonchalantly and walked across the small room, trailed by her gossamer starlit gown. There had to be some place she could hide.

She changed the subject. "And all the ships have the same layout?"

Why so many questions, Autumn? He caressed her thoughts and she tensed, annoyed that he was probing through her mind...again. She had to be more careful. "No reason. Just curious."

"Sure," he chuckled softly. "I think I know why you're really here."

"You do?" Her heart accelerated. *Oh no, oh no, oh no. Crap.*

He placed a hand on her cheek. "I think you're worried about me a little more than you like to let on. I think you might even be a bit curious about what we could be together if we gave our relationship another try. We're married and bound for life, after all."

"Don't remind me," she muttered. Mr. Hiss still purred in her arms.

He leaned over and kissed her cheek. "I promise, I'll return to you unharmed. You need not worry. And then maybe—we can finally give ourselves the second chance we deserve—but only if you decide it's something you want."

"And what if I refuse? What if you're just too much of a monster?" She crossed her arms, and a hollow knock came to the sealed door.

His lips flattened as he pushed a button on the arm of the control chair and the door slid open. A soldier fumbled inside and bowed.

"Please forgive the intrusion, my lord and lady, the emperor announced we're ready for departure."

"Thank you," Dante ran a hand through his silky midnight hair.

"Well, I suppose this is goodbye for now, but I hope you'll give my proposition some careful thought."

"I wouldn't count on it," she murmured as she left and disappeared with Mr. Hiss into the sunlight. She was glad she would never see him again.

She raced around frantically as the ships soared one by one into the purple-and-pink misty morning sky. Her heart hammered, she needed to find a departing ship, any ship. This was her one last chance to escape Surge.

At the far end of the docks sat a ship that looked in line with the ones that were soaring into space. Onyx black and triangular. A destroyer. *Why wasn't it with the rest?*

She raced onboard, Mr. Hiss in hand. Her heart pounded so hard against her ears, she feared she'd vomit. She spun on her toes within the ship, looking for somewhere to hide.

And then came the footsteps.

She sprinted and crawled into a side cabinet just in time. The door slid closed, and she clutched the bulky fabric of her dress. She held her breath and hoped Mr. Hiss wouldn't make a sound. His fuzzy soft tail gently thrashed against her bare arm, while he nuzzled his warm nose into her.

Seatbelts clicked into place, followed by silent revving. The sweet smell of cool, flowing mist wafted into her nostrils. She inhaled and suddenly became drowsy, head nodding. Autumn shuddered as her eyes closed, and she rested against the bottom of the cabinet, succumbing to the darkness.

PART SIX

Varz

Sixty-Three

"OH, NO, NO, NO, NO."

Autumn opened her eyes one by one. Her head was heavy, and the side of her mouth was wet with drool. Mr. Hiss snoozed against her side in his own little dreamworld.

How long was she out?

She silently yawned and stretched, peering through the crack of the cabinet.

"Unfreakingbelievable. I can't believe I forgot my communicator," came a voice.

"Well, you certainly can't use mine. I'm afraid I'll miss a call," said another.

"You and that guy?" the voice said insinuatingly. "You're almost as bad as Dante and—"

To Autumn's surprise and horror, her concealed bag emitted a long crisp beep followed by two violent buzzes. She rustled through the layers of her dress, desperate to stop it.

If you need anything at all, don't hesitate to contact me. I hope you'll consider my proposition. I'd like more than anything for us to be a family. Autumn rolled her eyes at Dante's desperate plea in text form.

When she looked through the crack again, a blue-and-green eye stared back at her. She covered her mouth, trembling, and Mr. Hiss puffed and yowled.

* * *

Dante sat in the control chair and sighed. His chest ached like someone had sucker-punched him. Stars twinkled in the never-ending vastness of space. It was cold and eerie dark, like an endless night.

Autumn read his message but refused to reply. Perhaps she really didn't want him. Perhaps he'd taken things too far and was a monster after all.

She couldn't forgive him for what he'd done. No matter how hard he tried.

He didn't blame her.

The worst thought in the world, though, was that everything he'd done thus far had been in vain. All he ever wanted was a family that actually wanted him around. A family worth fighting for.

"What a shame."

He whipped around and crossed his arms when someone spoke from the rear of the destroyer.

Valdez slinked from a dark corner, golden armor shimmering in the shooting starlight. How unsurprising.

"Were your own accommodations somehow not fitting for this voyage, Valdez?"

She chewed her bottom lip into a smile, reeking of cold-blooded mischief. "It's two to a destroyer, and I figured, why don't we two of the highest rank ride together for old times' sake."

"Is that so?" He checked his communicator again. *Still no reply.* He grumbled beneath the warmth of his breath.

Autumn probably thought he was pathetic, stealing her, then chasing her to the end of the universes.

"No matter how much you pretend, she's not Maeve. Nothing you do can ever bring her back," Valdez remarked.

Sixty-Four

AUTUMN'S FISTS shook with fury. She was prepared to fight. As the compartment door opened, she swung her fist and clipped her discoverer's nose, crushing cartilage and bone. Her other fist slammed into a rippled gut. A deep-rooted satisfaction consumed her. A primal urge she'd yet to satiate.

"Ouch. Why, you little," Armienti went to retaliate then stopped. "Autumn, what are you doing here?"

She jumped up, still wearing her long flowing celestial gown, and resumed a fighting stance. Mr. Hiss growled, his sapphire eyes glowing in the darkness.

When he opened his mouth, a swirling beam of crackling electricity shot out. She gasped, scooping him into her arms. He purred, nuzzling her and retracting his claws. *Holy crap. Mr. Hiss has abilities too.*

"I know exactly why she's here." Ronan ambled to a chair nonchalantly, placed his boots up on the dashboard, and proceeded to text an unknown party.

"When did you learn to hit like that?" Armienti plugged his nose, ruby-red blood dripping down his lip. "That was utterly Elattion."

"I'm so sorry. I've been training—I didn't mean to. Sometimes I don't know my own strength. Here, let me help you."

She ripped a piece of her gown and gently blotted Armienti's nose, although it was twisted and crooked.

Armienti groaned, popping it into place. It smoothed and straightened, and the bruise vanished. He possessed the ability to heal not just others, but himself as well.

"Why are you here?" Armienti crossed his arms, shifting his weight from side to side.

"I, umm, I—"

"She's run away," Ronan smoothed a hand through his hair and snapped an alien selfie.

"You're on the run. But why? Did something happen between you and Dante? I thought—"

"Well, you thought wrong," Autumn took a seat on the ledge of the side compartment, placing Mr. Hiss next to her. "I never wanted to come here, and I never asked for any of this. All I want to do is go home."

"With her fellow humans," Ronan added. Her forehead twitched. He was almost as bad as Dante, probing through her mind. "Caleb, especially. She's still in love with him."

"Interesting," Armienti crossed his arms, leaning against the wall. He went quiet, entering a deep state of thought. "I'm afraid that's not going to happen."

She stood up shuffling her feet, fists balled. "Then I'll take your ship by force."

Armienti chuckled, running a black-gloved hand through his gilded hair. He cocked his pretty head to the side. "Out of curiosity, what will you do once you've overpowered us and taken the ship?"

"I'll travel to Varz and Halvana, get Caleb and Misty, and we'll all go back home to Earth."

"How do you suppose you'll cross the sectors and borders

of each universe? You know you need prior clearance for that, don't you?"

She crossed her arms. She hadn't taken that detail into consideration. *Crap.*

Armienti continued. "And how do you suppose Dante will react to your disappearance? If you think he's a monster now, wait until you really get him going."

She ground her teeth at all the subtle details she'd neglected.

"If you think he'll just sit around idly, you're sorely mistaken. He'll destroy the universes to get you back, and he'll start with Earth. They don't call him the Great Conqueror for nothing. He lives up to his name in every sense of the word."

"I really don't think that's true."

"And why is that?"

"He already lied to the Grand Supreme, telling him Earth was destroyed. Also—I remember what happened with Keyserike, and I'm not afraid to spill the truth."

"Fascinating," Armienti stroked his cleft chin. "So, on the off chance I decide to help you, what's in it for me?"

She glowered as he winked at her. "Nothing. You can have the satisfaction of knowing you've done the right thing for once in your life."

Ronan interjected. "I'll take you. I just so happen to have some unfinished business on Earth. I've been hoping for an excuse to go back."

Armienti rolled his eyes. "Really, Ronan?"

Ronan nodded, the apples of his cheeks flushing pink. "You'll never understand. You're too busy thinking about yourself."

Armienti scowled, muttering something incomprehensible.

"Thank you," she bit back a smile. "I couldn't do this without you."

Her dad, her friends, she would soon have everything she'd ever wanted. She'd have her old life back, and *Caleb*.

She couldn't wait to hold him in her arms again. No matter the risk.

* * *

There was something Dante couldn't quite put his finger on. He'd known Valdez since he was a child. She was a few years his senior and practically raised him in the Palace of Despair, at the furthest end of Universe 24. She'd witnessed his ups and downs, his first kill. She was cunning, fiercely independent, and a murderer.

Only now, he couldn't get a moment's peace. She refused to leave his planet, even though she was an Empress in her own right with her own territories to rule.

They were stuck sharing a destroyer for at least thirty suns and moons. Could she know what he'd done to Keyserike and to Earth? He pondered quietly, staring into the depths of space. Sparkling stars zipped through the never-ending vastness.

Valdez sat in the chair beside him, combing her long jade hair and fastening it into a tidy braid.

"How is everything with you? After, you know—"

He snapped from his thoughts and stared at her. A playful smile crept across her lips. It was a strange sight to see her smiling. It was an expression she only used when she wanted something.

"I'm not sure what you're referring to."

"Maeve's death," the words played off her lips.

"I'm fine," he rested his head back, closing his eyes. Every time her name was mentioned, it was like a gut punch.

"That's it? That's all you have to say about your great love?"

"I—yes. I'm extraordinarily tired and I need to get some sleep," he yawned and stretched, eyes still shut. "I suggest you do the same. This will be a long, exhausting journey."

The room went pitch silent for a moment, then Valdez continued. "You know, Autumn *so* reminds me of her."

Dante's eyes shot open, and he cast her a lazy glimpse. Her long lashes grazed the length of her cheekbones.

"Autumn is a completely different person with her own goals and aspirations. She's nothing to do with her."

Valdez chuckled softly. "Well, you had me fooled. Between the pretty little way she carries herself, her hair, and those eyes. It's clear to me you have a type, or simply a placeholder for the time being."

"No, you have it all wrong. We love each other more than anything."

He secretly peeked at his communicator. The inbox was still empty. His chest sank. Perhaps he'd hear from her tomorrow.

"You being in love again is admittedly a strange thing. I'm not quite sure how to feel about it."

"Then do me a favor and don't feel anything at all."

"I'm your superior," she snapped. "How dare you speak to me in such a tone. I could—"

"The fact that I'm speaking to you right now is a hundred percent your own doing. There were a dozen ships to choose from, and for whatever reason, you settled on mine." He stared at her, biting back a smile and winked. Valdez's face flushed before her jade complexion returned. Her fists balled up in her lap.

"Fine, I'm going to sleep *far* away from you."

She shot up from her seat and strode to the back of the destroyer. She settled on a corner and rested her head against the wall, closing her eyes.

"Good, finally some peace and quiet," he muttered.

Valdez peeked. Clearly, she heard him.

Sixty-Five

CRAP. *Of all the rotten luck.* Autumn rustled through her bag. She had to have one here somewhere. Mr. Hiss nuzzled his head into her side. Her stomach twisted and cramped as Ronan and Armienti talked among themselves about sex and fast ships and other nonsense that single guys talked about.

Armienti stopped and folded his arms. "What are you searching for? Perhaps I can be of assistance. You're causing the worst raucous I've ever heard."

"Mind your own business," she grumbled. "You'd never understand anyway." Sweat beaded along her forehead. She was about to be in a world of trouble.

"Try me," he winked.

She rolled her eyes. "I don't have time for this."

Her stomach ached as she searched, and searched, and searched, desperately. *Ah, here they are.* She pulled out a box of tampons. She hadn't had her period since she arrived in space. Maybe her newfound abilities had something to do with it. Or more likely, the stress of being so far away from home and everyone and everything she knew and loved.

"I know you're menstruating. I can smell you from across

the room," Armienti announced, and her cheeks melted. "You should've just said you're having lady problems."

"Stop smelling me," she threw her hands into the air.

Tears welled up in the corners of her eyes, and she stormed to the far end of the ship for some privacy. She grumbled on the way back and sat on the floor by herself until Mr. Hiss trotted over and climbed in her lap.

She stroked his fur in silence while he purred. Her forehead pulsated. This was going to be the longest, most miserable trip ever, but it was worth it to hold Caleb in her arms again and travel back to Earth to finally be reunited with her friends and family.

Armienti rose and glided toward her, inhuman, beautiful, and precise with his movements.

"You know, I didn't mean anything about what I said before. I can smell everyone. Truly, I can. Sorry if I came off as rude or prying. I never meant to be so."

"I don't care," she crossed her arms and closed her eyes. "All I care about is getting Misty and Caleb and going home."

She opened her eyes after a few moments of awkward silence. She sensed she was being watched.

"What?"

"If you want, you don't have to sit all the way over there by yourself. We don't bite. We promise. You can even have my chair if it would be more comfortable—in your condition," Armienti offered.

She stared at him. *In her condition.* She folded her arms, considering his angle.

"Stop being such a princess, no pun intended." Armienti's mouth tilted.

She nodded; her back ached against the hard steel wall.

"Fine," she rose and walked over, Mr. Hiss in hand, and plopped into his seat. Even she had to admit it was comfortable. Both guys stared silently at her as the stars and endless space whizzed by the windows. This was going to be a long ride.

She sighed. *Now what?*

"I still can't believe you're really going through with this," Ronan said. "I can't believe you're backing out of being a princess. Granted, Dante is no prince charming, despite his many efforts."

"Maybe he was at one time, but not anymore," Armienti added. "He's just downright irresponsible and selfish. He put us all in very real danger by bringing you here. If Valdez or the Grand Supreme caught wind of what he's done with Earth and to Keyserike, I'm positive we'd all be extinguished."

"What did he do with Earth? Tell me. He told me it's safe, but that's all he'll say," Autumn pleaded.

"Fascinating," Armienti folded his arms, muscles shifting. "He hasn't even told his own mate what he's done. That's *so* like him."

Armienti stroked his chin then continued. "Well since you asked, he had the bright idea of emptying half of the crystal liquid fuel from the ship we used to travel home, which was a huge risk in and of itself, and filled the stranded one. He then harnessed its energy and maxed out the forcefield, hiding Earth from plain sight, rendering it invisible to space traffic."

Ronan finished texting on his communicator and added, "There were guards left behind to watch over it at all times who were never informed of the replacement ship's arrival. He plans to change them out every five or so years. It's a costly expenditure he's paying for out of his own pocket, kind of like your wedding. He nearly bankrupted himself in an attempt to make you happy. That's why he's personally overseeing this mission. Our missions are all paid opportunities. We don't have much say in how they're conducted, but we do have a choice in the ones we accept, unless the Grand Supreme states otherwise."

She stared at them, flabbergasted. Dante hadn't lied. Earth was safe.

"That's all fine and well, but I still don't think I can love him. Especially after what he put me through," she closed her eyes. Mr. Hiss yawned and stretched.

"That's very understandable. He's never had much luck with love. Bedding girls, sure, but he's only had one love prior to you," Armienti said.

She recalled back on Earth the nameless girl he mentioned during their trip to the Freedom Tower. The one who passed away and made Dante go quiet. She'd never seen him so quiet before.

Armienti crossed his arms. "Her name was Maeve."

"What happened to her?" Autumn dared ask, but she wasn't sure she wanted to know.

"Dante allowed her to accompany him on a mission and there was a complication, to say the least. Her body was discovered shortly before departure. He never forgave himself for putting her in harm's way. He changed after her death and has been spiraling ever since."

"How did she die?" Autumn asked.

"She was in the wrong place at the wrong time."

She stared at Armienti, quietly contemplating.

"He's not the easiest man to love," Ronan interjected. "But he loved her with all his heart, just as he loves you."

"And honestly, I can see why," Armienti's lips curved. "You're certainly worth fighting for. Although, I wholeheartedly disagree with the way he handled this situation. It was foolish and irresponsible. If I were him, I would have gone about it differently. I would have given up my title and everything if it meant being with a girl like you. But that's just me. I suppose love is a little different when you're a crown prince with so much expected of you."

She stared at Armienti, chewing her bottom lip. He was a

total operator who probably said that to all the girls he met. But it was strangely flattering to hear him admit it.

"Well, I've only ever wanted one guy."

Caleb. She loved him. She was supposed to love him. He was safe. They grew up together, went to all the same schools, dated, and had a little blip, but they got past it. They could work through anything if they put their minds to it. They shared an intimacy she'd never shared with anyone else.

"Dante will just have to learn to live without me."

Armienti sighed, smoothing a hand through his gilded tresses. "Well, we'll do the best we can for you, but one day I may call upon a favor from you in exchange for my help."

"What type of favor?" she scowled.

"Just be prepared," he chuckled. "Promise you'll be ready when the time comes."

She hesitated. This was a huge mistake. Her gut screamed.

"Okay, I promise." She was so desperate she agreed and had no clue what she'd gotten herself into.

* * *

Autumn was stuck on the ship with Ronan and Armienti for a little over a month. She pondered what Armienti wanted from her. The idea that she owed him some mysterious favor was unsettling. Her stomach twisted and churned with endless possibilities.

In the meantime, she trained hard, getting into the best shape of her life.

The destroyer had a built-in gravity chamber. She slammed her body around, day after day, night after night, withstanding the highest levels of gravity. She wanted to be ready for anything and everything that would come her way. They were headed into a dangerous warzone, and she needed to be able to defend Caleb.

* * *

Dante couldn't believe Autumn—

Hadn't.

Messaged.

Him.

Once.

It was utterly insane. She didn't message to say hi, or have a safe trip, or even to talk about herself.

Even his mother and Leyla had left him messages, despite what he promised to do to his sister if she failed to respect his wife, and he meant every word of it. As expected, his coward of a father avoided him. He meant what he said about killing him if he so much as touched a hair on Autumn's head.

He grumbled, his face warming with humiliation and defeat as his finger hovered over Autumn's number. He knew she was displeased with him, but this was absurd. He never dreamed marriage would be so lonely. It was like he was single again.

Could anyone love him?

On the other hand, thirty days with Valdez was driving him mad. He glanced as she changed in front him. She stripped herself bare before pulling on her gilded, bejeweled armor, fit for an Empress of multiple universes.

"For heaven's sake, show some decency," he fastened his harness as they approached Varz at lightning speed. They were scheduled to land in under an hour.

"What? Don't tell me this is the first time you've ever seen a naked woman before," she smoothed her hands down her hips.

He rolled his eyes, exhaling.

A vicious smile spread across her lips. "I mean, really, who haven't you been with? There were the maids, countless ladies, and Maeve, I'm sure."

"Enough," he placed his boots onto the floor with a heavy thud.

Valdez took the seat beside him, strapping herself in. She held her horned helmet in the crook of her arm.

"What's done is done, and I care not to call attention to my past indiscretions," he said. "Maeve and I were never together, not that it matters anymore, and not that it's any of your business."

They were interrupted by the hollow rattle of turbulence vibrating through the ship.

"*Arrival on Varz is scheduled in five minutes,*" the dashboard announced.

Finally. Dante couldn't wait to put an end to this nonsensical conversation. He couldn't believe his superior was drilling him on topics that had nothing to do with their mission.

His sordid love life.

It could've been worse though. At least she didn't discuss Keyserike, who oddly enough never came up in conversation over the course of their voyage. He supposed he should be grateful she found other things to focus on.

The ship clanged and descended through the rainbow atmosphere, smashing into the brown muddy earth below. *Excellent.* He cracked his maroon-gloved knuckles. He couldn't wait to punish the responsible parties for pulling him away from home when his and Autumn's relationship was still so fragile. He planned to make them pay for the distraction and most unwelcome setback. He prayed he and Autumn could somehow recover after all this.

Sixty-Six

AUTUMN FRANTICALLY CHANGED into a black bodysuit, along with gloves and a helmet. Thankfully, Ronan had plenty of spares packed away on the destroyer. It was far more battle-friendly than the wispy celestial dress she stowed away in.

Mr. Hiss purred on the control seat, rolling, soft underbelly exposed. He was adorable and helpless at the same time.

"He's certainly taken to you," Armienti pulled on and laced his heavy black boots. "Typically, lings aren't civil, especially as they get older. They'll rip each other's throats out."

She shrugged. "He seems tame enough to me. Hopefully he likes his new home on Earth."

She could only imagine what her neighbors would think when she brought a hot-pink baby tiger back home—let alone how her dad would react, but she'd worry about that later, along with how she'd explain her multiple-year absence to him. She could only hope he found her note describing her whereabouts.

As she pulled her helmet and visor over her face, she took deep controlled breaths.

I can do this. I have no choice anyway—no chickening out, Autumn.

"Make sure you keep your helmet on, or else this mission will be over before it starts," Ronan urged. "I'm really looking forward to our trip back to Earth, and I don't want anything to ruin it."

Armienti pulled his own helmet over his head. "We both know why you want to go back to Earth, Ronan. Stop fretting, it'll happen. Your precious Sean is waiting for you."

"Who's Sean?" she asked.

Ronan's cheeks flushed red like tomatoes. "You met him briefly at the rollerblading rink."

She recalled the strawberry-haired skate clerk Ronan made out with in the parking lot. The way they shoved their tongues down each other's throats in public. *It figured.*

She nodded, more than willing to comply with the request. However, what she couldn't hide was her height. She was one foot shorter than everyone around her. She'd never taken it into consideration.

She trembled as the door opened and they disembarked. The sky was the uncomfortable color of freshly spilled blood, and the ground was coated with a mucky clay, like wet cement. Sparse cobalt reeds blew in the arid wind, and caverns were visible in the distance, along with thick, churning black smoke.

The gravity was ten times that of Earth, but Autumn barely noticed because of her hard training sessions.

Elite soldiers congregated around Dante and Valdez, the sight of them sending a shudder down her spine. A golden bow and a quiver of arrows were slung over Valdez's shoulder. For a moment, Dante's and Autumn's eyes united beneath the full-face visors of their obsidian helmets, but Autumn glanced away.

Dante strode over but then stopped, folding his arms. He surveyed her from head to toe.

"My father has stooped to a new, all-time low, sending children on a mission like this. It makes me furious," he balled his fists at his sides.

Ronan and Armienti glanced at one another and shrugged.

Armienti cleared his throat. "Ah yes, the boy. He, um—"

"I volunteered," Autumn said in a low gruff voice. "I wanted to serve the emperor and the highest good of the realm the only way I know how."

"Impressive," Dante cocked his head to the side. "You have a true warrior's spirit."

Autumn nodded slowly, careful her helmet didn't slip from her face exposing her cover. It was slightly too large.

Dante continued. "I like your enthusiasm for this cause. Perhaps I was wrong. You're a man after all. Welcome aboard."

"Thank you," her mind raced, "Sire," was all she could think to say.

Dante lowered his voice to speak with his cousins. "Despite the orders that were previously issued, harm no women or children. They're innocent in all this. Make sure the soldiers abide by these rules as well. Anyone who disobeys my command will answer directly to me. I shall handle Valdez and her bloodthirsty streak."

Dante turned on his heel to leave but then stopped. "For future reference, soldier, you're to remove your helmet when addressing your superior. I wish to look upon the face of the man so brave enough to volunteer."

She froze, her heart pounding in her ears.

"That means now," Dante crossed his arms. She turned to make a run for it.

BOOM.

Rubble sprayed around them in a tornado of granules. Dante blocked the worst of it from hitting her, and she held her helmet in place for dear life. *Holy crap.* Aliens retreated on foot, holding what appeared to be homemade explosive devices considering the spindly, haphazard way they were assembled. They almost looked like they were made back on Earth.

"That was a fatal error."

Dante formed a fireball in his hand and scorched the clay ground, burning them all to a blackened crisp, mid-retreat. The rest of the team sprinted, and Dante soared through the air. Large balls of fire ripped across the muddy terrain. Valdez stared skeptically for a moment, before joining Dante and the rest of the crew.

Autumn's heart pounded in her ears, hoping Valdez wasn't on to them. She was a perceptive mind reader. .

"Have either of you ever been to this planet before?"

Ronan and Armienti shook their heads.

"No," Armienti admitted. "There's nothing here of interest to either of us. But I'm sure the mines can't be too far off. They're entirely underground, obviously, where the crystals are harvested."

Autumn flew ahead. "Come on, we need to hurry up and get out of here."

* * *

After searching for hours on end past obsidian tinted domes and burnt, smoking heaps of bodies, they came upon a cave sealed by two steel sliding doors. Rubble explosions ensued not too far off, casting smoke and dust through the air.

Autumn was sweat-slicked and exhausted from searching, figuring this place had to be the one, although there was no clear entrance inside. There were no keypads, or scanners, or anything the least bit high tech. *This couldn't be happening.*

She furiously pounded her fists on the door, trying to get someone's attention, when Ronan came over and kicked a hole, using the full force of his boot.

"What a flimsy design. It's no wonder the slaves escaped and are causing such a ruckus."

They climbed, pulling each other through the crevice. She grew nauseous with what she found.

Sixty-Seven

AUTUMN CUPPED her mouth from the thick, overpowering odor of sweat and despair. Bile rose in her gut. Dark trenches held countless toiling slaves swinging rusty pickaxes, clothed in heather-gray rags.

Looming figures oversaw them, cracking energized whips. Screams and cries echoed through the maze of caverns resembling a hornet's nest.

Thousands upon thousands of slaves toiled, chipping away crystal into metal baskets. Her blood froze in her veins. She'd never seen anything so terrible in her entire life.

She couldn't believe Caleb was here, forced to endure this miserable situation, all because of Dante's jealous nature.

She cleared her throat. Nobody paid her any mind.

"What did you expect, for everyone to stop and bow?" Ronan removed his helmet and ran a hand through his brown hair, tousling it. "You need to annunciate yourself, princess."

She trembled, not wanting any attention on her. She wanted to run away and hide, wanted to scream. But there was no escaping. She needed to find Caleb and get out of here.

She cleared her throat. "Um, excuse me."

But nobody stopped. Pickaxes scraped against stone.

"Ex—excuse me," she said a second time, her voice meeker than the last.

"Enough," Armienti whipped off his helmet and held it in the crook of his arm. "Everyone, *stop* what you're doing at once by order of the Martynes."

The entire operation ceased, and a gigantic green taskmaster with a dribbling chin ambled over, his crackling whip in hand. His eyes widened, and he fell on one knee.

"Your Imperial Highnesses, forgive me. We weren't expecting you. How can I be of service?"

Autumn glanced at Ronan and Armienti. "You're also princes?"

Armienti nodded. "We figured you knew."

She didn't. It was another detail never divulged to her.

Autumn continued. "We're here for the human."

The taskmaster stared at her strangely. "Which one, m'lady?"

"There's more than one?" Her heart thundered. "What are you talking about?" As far as she could recollect, Misty was on planet Halvana serving out her sentence. Caleb was the only one supposed to be here.

"The crown prince sentenced them," Ronan straightened his spine. "He ordered the harshest punishment in the book. Now we're here to collect them."

The emerald-skinned taskmaster stroked his wet chin. "I'll retrieve them at once."

Autumn's eyes widened. It didn't make any sense. Unless —Her knees knocked violently together, and she became faint. *Her mom's murderer, just as Dante had promised.*

The taskmaster shouted something in his slobbery, disgusting language, hocking saliva in his mouth. She gagged, heart slamming against her ribcage in anticipation.

Two green creatures dragged Caleb out, half-dressed and

unconscious. They threw him at her feet, dust settling. She cupped her mouth muffling a scream as she beheld five raw lacerations littering the smooth skin of his back.

She knelt, trembling, trying to wake him up, but he was out cold.

"Caleb…Caleb. Is he dead?" She shook him, but there was no response.

"No, he's fainted. He's certainly a fighter. But sooner or later, his spirit will be shattered."

Her breathing grew shallow when they left and returned with Marcela. She was wily and timid for the first time ever, a far cry from her days as a manager who ruled the Monroe Diner with an iron fist. Her greasy, matted hair hung in her round face.

Behind her stood a lanky tan boy who shared Marcela's dark eyes and wicked witch nose. She did a doubletake. She'd seen him somewhere before but couldn't recall where. Her glower hardened. The guy stared at the floor and refused to make eye contact. Her eyes wavered with tears.

"That seems to be all we came for," Armienti reached into his pocket and pulled out a gilded drawstring pouch. He handed it to the taskmaster. Bright red rubies spilled into his calloused palm.

"For your trouble. We were never here."

The taskmaster bowed before shoving the satchel into his pocket and ambled away. "Allright, everyone, what are you looking at? Get back to work." He cracked his electrified whip. Everyone stumbled, swinging their pickaxes.

Autumn stroked Caleb's hair. "We have to get him out of here. He needs help."

Caleb shuddered awake. His eyes bulged in his head when they met with hers.

"Oh, thank goodness you're okay," she held him close, mindful of his scars.

He remained silent as if traumatized.

She glared at the other guy. Marcela was all too silent. They were probably in shock. Nonetheless, she was tempted to punch him in the face for everything he put her family through. In fact, she wanted to repay the favor, but it wasn't right. She was *no* killer.

She struggled to bring Caleb to a wobbly stand, still in disbelief they were finally together again.

"We're going home," she squeezed his hand.

He stared at her in deafening silence, a glazed expression plastered over his face. She could only fathom the horrors he'd endured over the last year.

They climbed through the steel hole and back into the muddy wasteland, and then they soared into the blood-stained sky.

Armienti held Caleb while Ronan secured Marcela and her mom's murderer in his capable arms. They were far faster than her in the air, as she was still mastering the art of flight.

She flew behind them, hair flowing in the oncoming wind, until she caught a flash of light in the corner of her eye. A powerful presence.

"Hurry, take them ahead, you have to get them back to the ship so we can get out of here." Armienti soared, followed by Ronan, like whizzing specks of light before disintegrating into the blood-red sky.

When Autumn turned to follow, an elbow slammed between her shoulder blades accompanied by a sharp jutting pain. The world swirled around, and around, and around again, until she crashed headfirst into a cave, crumbling it to dust. She pushed herself to a shaky stand, eyes widening.

"I knew it was you, human."

Sixty-Eight

VALDEZ REMOVED HER BEJEWELED HELMET, her jagged wings twitched against her spine. An arrogant smile pressed its way across her lips. She was as beautiful as she was terrifying.

"Did you really think I'd miss you? Your stench is unmistakable."

"Screw you." Autumn quivered with rage, balling her fists.

Valdez cocked her head to the side. "I can't help but wonder what brings you to Varz. I know it's certainly not your mate, who you so selfishly never contacted since his departure. Now, I understand why. He's been waiting on you for many suns and moons. Too bad he'll never see you again."

Autumn went to fly away, but Valdez jumped into the air and punched her in the gut. Saliva poured from her mouth as she doubled over in pain, gasping for breath. Her hands grasped her back. She fell to her knees in blinding agony.

"I find something else perplexing. Where is it you developed abilities from? As far as I knew, humans had no abilities. They're as useless as muck."

Autumn came to a trembling stand and charged at Valdez,

who stood there, arms crossed. A cocky smile graced her full, jade lips. Autumn easily disarmed her, grabbing her wretched bow and arrow and sliding it over her wings.

She nocked an arrow on the bow, aiming it square between Valdez's eyes.

"Surrender now, or I'll do it," she quivered, gloves sliding against the arrow. "I'm serious. You're dead."

Valdez erupted into a boisterous fit of laughter. "My dear, you can't be serious. You truly think my only ability lies within that inanimate object? Well, you're wrong. I'm not number two to the Grand Supreme for nothing. I was raised in the Palace of Despair, and I've eaten sweet, innocent flies like you for lunch my entire life. And right now, you've thoroughly moistened my appetite."

Autumn released the bow and the arrow whizzed straight toward Valdez's inhumanly beautiful face.

"Freeze."

Suddenly, Autumn couldn't move any of her limbs no matter how hard she tried, and the arrow stopped mid-flight, falling to the ground. She struggled with all her might, but Valdez waltzed over and punched her in the nose, sending her sputtering into a nearby bed of reeds. Autumn kipped up to her feet, red clouding her vision, so furious that tears streamed down her cheeks, mingling with blood.

Valdez cackled. "What's wrong, human? Have you had enough?"

Autumn struggled to catch her breath, and something inside of her shattered into a million pieces. She charged Valdez, knocking her clear across the muddy scape. Valdez's eyes bulged as she slammed into the ground, wind ripping from her lungs. Her wings became tangled and crooked and misaligned.

Autumn grabbed an arrow, approaching Valdez, and slid it

between her fingers. Valdez coughed up blood, spitting it onto the muddy ground.

"Freeze."

Autumn was stuck in place, her mind scrambling like an egg.

"You really have some nerve challenging me. Too bad your bravery, or stupidity, rather, was in vain."

Valdez wrapped her long, sharp talons around Autumn's throat and tore them through her flesh, cutting off her circulation. Autumn gasped for air, struggling.

"I remember this expression all too well." Valdez grabbed an arrow and slid it between her fingertips, holding it to Autumn's face. She licked her lips. "Let's see how pretty you are without your eyes."

Her vision darkened as she squirmed in Valdez's grasp.

She'd never see Earth, her friends, Caleb, or her dad again if she couldn't escape. And she'd never hold her mom's killer accountable for his actions.

A squish and a scream followed as Autumn fell to the ground, gasping for breath. Valdez had an arrow lodged straight through her knee cap. Blood gushed from her spectacular gilded armor. She rolled on the ground, groaning, clutching her injured limb.

Autumn gasped a breath as Armienti aided her to her feet.

"We have to go now."

Autumn turned and shot Valdez a murderous glare before they leapt into the sky and soared away.

* * *

When Autumn and Armienti arrived at the ship, flecks of light glimmered from the vermilion sky, followed by dark flowing smoke and balls of blazing fire.

Dante and his crew were on their way back at top speed.

Autumn shuddered at the thought of Valdez telling Dante everything and the repercussions of what she'd done. Fingers trembling from her altercation, she pulled out the communicator Dante gifted her and texted him. She was desperate and needed to sound convincing.

"Hope you're safe :)" She wrote, smiley face included. Maybe then he wouldn't know she was on Varz. He'd assume she was back home and would be there when he arrived.

Only, she wouldn't be.

"Are you okay?" Arimienti took a seat, fastening his harness.

"Yeah, I'm fine," Autumn replied. She was more worried for Caleb, who'd yet to speak a word. He stared at her, his sapphire eyes wavering and glazed. Marcela and the other guy trembled in the corner, hugging each other, still in shock and horror over everything that'd taken place. She couldn't begin to imagine how much they suffered.

She took a seat with Armienti. Mr. Hiss climbed onto her lap and purred.

Ronan sat with Caleb and the others. The cruiser ascended into the sky and into outer space. Three down, one to go. Next and last was Misty, who Autumn admittedly didn't feel the need to rescue at all, but it was the right course of action. She had a family and a home to get back to, even if she despised her to the core.

Sixty-Nine

AUTUMN SHUDDERED at the thought of the pleasure planet of Halvana. It's all she could focus on during the return trip home. Anything to distract herself from watching Caleb day and night, leaning against the wall in the back of the destroyer, listless and unspeaking. Marcela and the other guy huddled in the opposite corner, trembling beside each other.

She couldn't bear to look at her mom's murderer. The sight of him made her physically ill.

She'd deal with him later. He owed her answers.

Instead, she approached Caleb feeling guilty as ever.

Dante made him suffer from day one because he was jealous of their relationship.

Mr. Hiss trotted over as well, fluffy tail swaying. Caleb flinched at the sight of them.

"Are you okay?" she asked quietly to no answer. Not that she expected one. "Please, I can help heal your wounds. If you let me see them, I—"

When she reached to touch him, he moved away, staring blankly into the corner of the destroyer.

"Please, I just want to help. I know you're in pain."

Before she could blink, a ball of warm saliva dripped down her cheek. She wiped her finger against the wetness, eyes widening. The breath hitched in her throat.

Caleb spat in her face.

"No shit, Sherlock. Stay away from me."

"What are you talking about?" She recalled their last kiss and his tender embrace. Four solid years of high school and then some. Her hands quivered, her anxiety piqued. He told her he loved her and always had. She risked everything to rescue him.

"Autumn, don't play stupid," he muttered, voice dry and cracked. His sapphire eyes sliced through her like daggers.

Her eyes wavered with oncoming tears. "What are you talking about? I don't understand."

"You don't understand?" he huffed. "Please."

She shook her head, still running her fingers against her cheek in disbelief. Nobody had ever treated her so horribly, but she tried to give him the benefit of the doubt. He was kidnapped just like she was. He wasn't in his right mind.

"You're one of *them*."

She stared at him. "No, I'm not. I'm human and we're going back home to our families where it's safe—"

"You're not human anymore, and you're not the same girl I grew up with. You're a freak with weird alien powers. Stay away from me. You're dangerous, just like Dante."

Her brows furrowed. "No, I'm not. Do you seriously think I wanted this? Do you think I asked Dante to kidnap you? Well, I didn't. Please, Caleb, you have to believe me."

Caleb crossed his soot-stained arms. "I don't know what to believe anymore, but I know you've changed. You're not the same Autumn I grew up with. At first, I had my doubts, until you refused to help us, and I watched your obnoxious wedding procession."

Autumn's jaw dropped, and Mr. Hiss growled, tail puffed. "I didn't have a choice."

He rolled his eyes. "That's not what it looked like to me. They forced us to watch it on repeat while we worked like it was some kind of sick treat. I saw the way you looked at Dante. The way you danced and kissed. You're not fooling anyone, Autumn. I'm sure he's screwed you too."

"I-I love you, Caleb. How could you—"

"Save it."

The bile rose from her gut, and she vomited all over the floor, splattering chunks on her armor and Caleb's tattered grays. He jumped back making a face of disgust.

Ronan and Armienti stopped their conversation and sauntered from the control seats. "What's going on here?" Stars whizzed by the windshield, dark as night. The destroyer bumped and rattled with turbulence.

All Autumn could do was stare in deafening silence as she wiped her glove against her mouth.

He didn't love her. He'd said so himself. She was dangerous.

"What did you do to her?" Armienti grabbed Caleb by the collar and yanked him to his feet with a single pull. Caleb's head whiplashed and he groaned.

"Answer me, human, or your dead body will belong to the stars," Armienti demanded, black-gloved fist clenched in his face.

Caleb twisted his mouth to the side and glowered. "I told her the truth."

Ronan crossed his arms. "Any remarks you may or may not have, keep them to yourself. If it wasn't for Autumn, you'd live out the remainder of your miserable existence chipping away crystal on Varz. We could still return you, if you'd prefer."

Caleb shuddered before his eyes thinned to slits. "Who are you, her side piece? I can't keep track anymore."

Armienti's face flushed, and he stuttered. "Shut your mouth."

Amidst the chaos and commotion, Autumn locked eyes with the quiet guy from across the room. He flinched and turned away. She shot to her feet and approached him.

"What are you staring at?" She struggled to control her temper. Her molars ground in her mouth. She was consumed by a fiery rage, burning her to the core. Her Elation urge to fight. "You're the worst one of all. Do you know who I am?"

The guy met her glare, teeth chattering. "Yes, I remember you, Autumn. You're Ellie's best friend."

She stared at him baffled. *How did he know Ellie?*

"Please don't hurt him, Ramon," Marcela said through cracked parched lips. "He's my son."

"Don't talk to me ever, ever again," she crossed her arms, addressing Marcela. "I have no use for you either." She recalled how cruelly she treated her during her days at the diner. She'd never forgive her.

"Stop acting like an entitled child," Marcela hissed. "You haven't learned anything, have you?"

Suddenly, she put two and two together, Marcela and *Tyler Sanchez*. He hosted the house party at Worley Heights. Her last party on Earth. Ellie hooked up with him.

"You killed my mom?"

"What?"

Marcela stared at him, wide-eyed. "What is she talking about, Tyler? I hope that's not true. Please tell me it's not true."

Tyler buried his face in his hands. Tears streamed down his cheeks. "I didn't know I hit your mom at the time. It was raining so hard out, I couldn't see, and I was out way past curfew with a brand new license. I saw a body tumble and I panicked and sped off. Then one day I woke up on a spaceship. I spent what felt like forever in the darkness. That's where I learned who I hit. I'm so sorry, Autumn."

"I can't believe you," Marcela gasped, cupping a hand over her mouth. "I'm absolutely disgusted and horrified."

Before Autumn could stop herself, her fist connected with Tyler's jaw sending him clear across the room. He hit the wall with a thud, echoing through the ship.

She lunged, ready to pummel him, when Armenti restrained her from behind. "Let me go." She struggled.

"You need to settle down. This isn't like you," Armienti held her still.

She gasped and snapped out of her trance, scarcely believing what she'd done. "I am so, so sorry." She apologized, although he should've been the one to do that.

Marcela pressed her hands together. "Please don't hurt him. He's my son and the only person I have in the world."

Her eyes roved between Marcela and Tyler sobbing uncontrollably on the floor. She was not a murderer and refused to stoop to that level. Unlike some people she knew. Temples pounding, she pushed Armienti away and walked to the control seat. She collapsed into it, engulfed by sorrow. Maybe she was a danger, after all.

* * *

When she woke up, the ship had settled. She rose, brushing up against Armienti who shared the tight control seat.

His eyes fluttered open. "How are you doing?"

"How do you think?"

She was tempted to say awful but didn't have time to dwell on her feelings. She needed to come up with a plan to rescue Misty.

She reached to check her communicator. No new

messages from Dante, not that she cared. She was relieved, or at least that's what she told herself.

She should be relieved, right? She sighed. Nobody gave a crap about her. She was a freak with dangerous abilities.

Ronan unbuckled his harness. "We must hurry. We're only a few days ahead of Dante and the others. They'll more than likely stop on Halvana to celebrate their victory."

"Agreed."

Seventy

ALTHOUGH THE PLANET was clean and regulated, the streets of Halvana were in shambles. Timid and haggard occupants cast their eyes on the ground as Autumn walked with Ronan and Armienti. She hugged herself.

Alien men and women danced in the windows of stacked high-rise buildings in various stages of undress. Futuristic aircraft whizzed through the sky, which was the rich, smoky shade of rose quartz, lit by three crescent moons and twinkling starlight.

"Let's hurry up. I want to get out of here," Autumn insisted. *This planet is so creepy.*

For the first time ever, she was worried about Misty and hoped for her safety. She wouldn't wish this bizarre place on her worst enemy. But at the same time—

Karma was a bitch.

Armienti winked. "We're moving as fast as we can. This is a planet that prioritizes pleasure."

Disgusting pig, she rolled her eyes.

"I agree," Ronan added. "The sooner we get out of here, the sooner we can get back to Earth."

Although Autumn missed her dad, the idea of returning to Earth now was dreadful. Her heart sank as she secretly worried he'd reject her the same way Caleb had. It was more than she could handle.

Armienti sighed, placing his hand on Ronan's shoulder. "You'll be reunited with your precious human, I promise."

Moments later, they arrived at a tall, mirrored building with a twisted spire. Inside was gleaming white, almost clinical, and bore the overwhelming scent of flowers.

They stopped at a front desk where two women stood wearing long black jackets glittering with brocades of golden buttons.

"Can I help you, my lord? Shall we retrieve your usuals?"

"Usuals?" Autumn made a face. "You mean you've been here more than once?" She was not surprised.

"Um, no thank you," Armienti's blue cheeks shifted burgundy. "We're here for a girl. She's human actually."

"Ah, I see. Let me check her availability." The woman's nails clicked against a scanner.

"No, forgive me, *not* in that way," Armienti smoothed a hand through his gilded hair. "We wish to buy out her contract."

"Okay, I do believe I found her," the woman pressed a fallen lock of pink hair behind her pointed ear. "However—"

"Yes?"

"It seems her contract has been locked by Prince Dante Martyne, future Emperor of Surge, and Lord of Universe 13."

"No, that's impossible, it was he who sent us," Ronan blurted. Autumn shot him a dirty look.

"Here, we'll sort this out right now. I'll give him a call," the woman's fingers clicked against her sleek black communicator.

"That's unnecessary," she placed a hand on her hip. "I'm

his wife, Autumn Ramon-Martyne, and I authorize her release."

"It'll just take a second, my lady."

Her stomach flopped, and her hands sweated within her gloves before she straightened her spine and mustered up the biggest threat she could think of.

"Excuse me, how dare you question my authority," she feigned. "When my husband hears how disrespectfully you treated me, he'll—"

"Forgive me, my lady, I was merely adhering to protocol," the woman lowered her head.

"Well now you know better, don't you? Release her, immediately," Autumn crossed her arms.

"Okay," the concierge clicked and scanned the profile. A 3D holographic image rotated. "Her buyout price is 100,000 rubies."

Say what?

Autumn's mouth practically hit the floor. *Holy crap.* She managed to keep her cool then chuckled. "Is that all?" She batted her eyes.

"She's our most expensive and in demand escort. Her beauty and skills are prized."

"Well, I can certainly afford such a small amount," Autumn slid Dante's credit chip from her pocket. This situation was all his fault, so she had no reservations about making him pay for Misty's freedom.

She stood there tapping her foot, breath caught in her throat, as she waited for the transaction to be approved. *Please let it go through, please let it go through, please let it go through.* Not long after, a beep sounded. The concierge smiled and handed the chip back to her. She pocketed it.

"Don't ever let me catch you questioning me again," she added for good measure, chewing her cheeks to disguise a threatening smile. *It was definitely something Dante would say.*

"No, of course not, my lady. Forgive me," the woman stuttered, her face going pale. Then she signaled with a wave of her hand.

Misty walked out, accompanied by two surly guards, carrying metallic rocket launchers. She held her head high. She wore a gray string bikini with a blinking metal collar around her neck like some kind of animal.

A shudder rattled down Autumn's spine. Misty flinched as her collar was disconnected. She ran her fingers against her slender throat.

"You're free to go, dear."

"Well, it's about time," Misty threw her hands into the air and ambled over barefoot.

Suddenly, Autumn stopped dead and her knees knocked together, almost buckling beneath her weight. She froze as Dante and his entourage approached the building.

Seventy-One

"HOW ARE we supposed to get out of here?" Autumn hissed at Ronan and Armienti, as she scrambled away from the door. Misty struggled in her grasp.

"I thought we were leaving. What are we waiting for?" Misty headed toward the door then gasped. "Oh no, he's here too," she practically shrieked.

"Worry not, we'll handle it," Armienti reassured her.

They walked ahead while Autumn pulled Misty behind a trickling fountain. She stood there holding her breath, hand cupped around Misty's mouth to prevent her from screaming again. Pink sunshine seeped through the windows, sparkling against the flowing droplets of water.

Dante strode through the door, palming his communicator. *It seemed he'd received her text message after all and chose to ignore it.* Her forehead pulsated.

A quick scan of the crowd indicated Valdez was nowhere to be found. Her stomach knotted. *What if she told him everything?*

"It figures neither of you could wait until our scheduled departure," Dante shook his head, then smirked. "I'm sure you've already spent a handsome chunk of your pay on escorts."

"Well, we just—" Armienti smoothed a hand through his gilded locks.

Dante reached into his pocket and pulled out two silver credit chips. He placed one into each of the cousin's palms. "Here's to a job well done and subduing those filthy Red Cloaks who dared to challenge our reign."

"Th-thank you," Ronan stuttered, before taking the credit chip.

"Much appreciated, cousin," Armienti added.

Autumn's grip tightened around Misty's mouth as she twisted in an attempt to break free. She held her still. One wrong move and they'd be discovered.

"What happened to that child you arrived with on Varz?" Dante cocked his head to the side.

"Unfortunately, he didn't make it. He was caught in the crossfire."

"That's a shame," Dante's eyes flickered to the floor. "I would've liked to meet him. His efforts weren't in vain. Because of him, we accomplished our mission."

Soldiers marched around Dante and entered the facility. He folded his arms then continued. "I've been meaning to discuss one other matter with both of you. It's about you know who," he lowered his voice to a whisper. "I did what I had to do, what anyone would've done in my situation. It was the safest and smartest course of action for everyone."

"We—we know," Armienti fumbled his words. "We don't blame you for your decision."

"Thank you. I thought all this time you were angry with me," Dante twisted his mouth to the side.

Armienti blinked. "Well, we're not. It was all one big misunderstanding," Armienti patted Dante on the shoulder awkwardly.

"Don't let us hold you up," Ronan interrupted. "We were just on our way home."

"I'm not going inside. I never planned to," Dante admitted as he stared at his communicator.

"Why not?" Armienti shifted his weight from side to side.

"If there's even the slightest chance I could mend my relationship with Autumn, I want to take it. She means everything to me, and that starts with rebuilding our trust. I'll admit our foundation is rocky, but that doesn't mean I can't fix things with a little effort on my part."

"Well, we wish you all the best," Ronan smiled as he and Armienti left Dante standing in the lobby.

Dante lingered for a while before pulling her paperback of *Dracula* out of his armor. Autumn almost gasped but somehow managed to stay quiet. He sat on a bench and read for hours before he fell asleep, chest gently heaving.

Autumn took Misty and left. Her heart ached with confusion. After everything they'd been through, he remained determined to fix their relationship, while Caleb treated her like she was different and the years they'd shared together meant nothing.

Seventy-Two

AUTUMN ARRIVED BACK at the destroyer with Misty to a far bigger nightmare than when she left. Caleb's hands were bound to Marcela's and Tyler's as they squirmed on the floor trying to free themselves. Mr. Hiss rolled on the control seat. His soft wet underbelly was exposed as he purred without a care in the world. *How she wished she had his problems.*

"What happened here?"

Armienti sighed. "An escape attempt."

"Don't you, for a second, think of trying to run away," Ronan snapped at Misty. "Or else you'll join them."

Misty's knees buckled and she fell to the steel tiled floor. "I don't know what I did to deserve this," tears streamed down her cheeks. "One minute I was at a wedding dressed in limited edition *Chanel,* and strutting around in my brand new *Louboutins,* which by the way are *ruined,* and the next I was abducted by aliens, spent forever on a spaceship, and then I was forced to—" she paused, snot rolling her nose, "entertain, and you did nothing to help me."

Autumn rolled her eyes. *Enough of the pity party.* "You

really can't think of anything, Misty? Why would something this horrible just happen to you out of nowhere? I'm sorry your perfect life was ruined. I'm sorry you didn't get to spend your never-ending bank account on shoes and fancy clothes and drive around in your brand-new forest-green Range Rover to frat parties. And summer—" Autumn emphasized, bending two fingers on each hand, "in the Bahamas."

Misty stared at her in silence.

Autumn continued. "Some of us have real problems to deal with. We don't all get to live in your fantasy world."

"I know why," Caleb's sapphire eyes thinned to slits as he interrupted their conversation. Autumn stiffened, and Misty glanced away. "Don't pretend you're any better. Don't you, for one second, pretend you're innocent in all this."

Autumn ignored Caleb. "You really can't think of anything, Misty? Something you said or did? The way you treated everyone for years? The way you betrayed me?"

Misty remained silent. It figured she had nothing to say. A simple apology would suffice, but apologies were beneath Queen Misty.

Autumn threw her hands into the air. "You know what, I'm tired of this. I'm tired of constantly fighting with everyone, always bending over backwards only to get shit on in the end."

"Tie her to the others," Autumn sat down and crossed her legs. Mr. Hiss climbed into her lap with his soaking wet fur and purred. Her temples throbbed with an oncoming migraine.

Ronan walked over and Misty shrieked, clawing against the floor. "We can do this the easy way or the hard way." Misty stood up and sprinted. Ronan caught her in the blink of an eye and dragged her to the back of the destroyer kicking and screaming and tied her to the others. A cloth gag was fastened around her mouth.

Good. Finally, some peace and quiet, she yawned and stretched.

"Are you okay?" Armienti asked.

After a long pause she admitted, "No."

Autumn couldn't take it anymore, constantly giving people what they wanted her entire life, only to have them walk all over her. What about what she wanted?

Rain

Seventy-Three

AFTER A MONTH of treacherous space travel, sparse rations, and no cordial interactions to speak of, Autumn arrived back on Surge. The destroyer wasn't equipped to handle a year-long journey and had to be changed out for a larger vessel.

The only one excited to embark on the voyage back to Earth was Ronan, for obvious reasons. Armienti opted out, stating he had better things to do, and at the very last minute, so did Autumn.

There was no place for her on Earth with her new abilities. She was *dangerous*. If the man she thought she loved couldn't accept her change, how could her dad? Or her friends? What would they say? The pain from their rejection would destroy her. Or even worse, they might get hurt because of her.

She shot Caleb a longing glance one last time. His sapphire eyes twinkled beneath the gray cloudy sky. Her chest hollowed with an unsettling void of childhood love long lost.

Droplets of rain coated her hair and face for the first time since she'd been in space. It was the same kind of rain as her last day on Earth and when she had to say goodbye to her mom forever. It was like Surge sensed her sadness.

* * *

Sanguis hadn't changed during her time away. As usual, a frivolous banquet ensued that she made sure she missed. Hopefully nobody had noticed her absence. Why would they? She wasn't memorable.

On the way back to her room, she spotted Leyla dressed in heather gray. She slinked through the hallway, her lips coated with dayglow pink lipstick. Autumn rolled her eyes. Leyla's skin paled like she'd seen a ghost.

"Ridiculous," Autumn mumbled, so not in the mood to deal with Leyla and her antics. Once again, she caught her wearing the forbidden hue when their punishment ended months ago.

* * *

The dark-gray sky shone through her pristine balcony window and drizzle pooled along the white concrete, skidding into the garden below. Autumn's faint reflection shone dimly through the glass as the dismal weather unfolded and turned torrential.

From now on, she'd be careful to remain in her room until Dante's return. He was only a week behind. She didn't need to answer anyone's annoying questions like: *How have you been holding up?* or *Where have you been for the last few months?* For which she didn't have an acceptable answer.

Her eyes burned after the marathon of crying she completed. Nobody wanted her. Not her friends, and despite what Dante had said about fixing their relationship, *she'd yet to hear from him.* She wiped her eyes, annoyed that he crossed her mind, yet again.

She sat quietly eating lunch in her room, mulling over her frustrating situation. She hoped she'd made the right decision to stay behind. Afterwards, she climbed into bed with one of her newly translated books. She read, wearing her favorite pajama set again; a white cotton camisole and a pair of satin cloud shorts.

As she flipped to a new screen, a thunderous knock rattled against the steel door.

Before she could answer, Leyla waltzed into her room. She wore a navy-blue bodysuit with an asymmetrical silver stripe. Her hair glittered like twinkling comet dust.

Leyla scoured the room with her brown eyes, too large for her heart-shaped face.

"It must be nice to be out doing who knows what for the last forty-five suns and moons," Leyla placed a hand on her hip. "But fear not, I covered for you."

"What's it to you?" She slid the screen of her book, not paying Leyla any mind. "Did you miss me or something?"

"No," Leyla glanced to the side. "Of course not."

"Are you worried I'll say something to Dante, and he'll marry you off to ugly prince whatever his name is?"

Leyla shook her head. Her glittered waves shimmered beneath the overcast sky light, streaming through the French balcony doors.

"Then are you just here to bother me? If that's the case, I'm not in the mood," Autumn said. "I promise I won't say anything to your brother if you leave me alone right now."

Leyla tensed then slackened. "I'm being serious, Autumn. I came to see you out of genuine concern."

"Well, your concern isn't needed. Go away."

Leyla folded her arms.

Autumn began reading again and Leyla didn't move an inch. She groaned. "I know how much you hate me, so why can't you just leave me alone? I don't want you here. I don't want anything to do with you."

Leyla straightened her spine, her voice faded to a whisper. "I don't hate you though, not really. You're just different and in many ways. I feel like a hypocrite for behaving the way I did, and for siding with my father."

"Well, you sure had me fooled," Autumn rolled her eyes. "What the heck are you talking about?"

Leyla twisted her mouth to the side. "It's not fair that Dante gets to break and make all the rules, and I'm forced to suffer in silence. I'm capable of so much more than people credit me for. I'm not just a spoiled princess. I can make my own decisions. I can take care of myself," she chuckled. "Well maybe a little, but still, I never stood a chance with the way I was raised and the society we're forced to live in. It's not a kind one, and I don't make the rules."

Autumn sat up and crossed her legs. "Well, I'm not sure what you expect me to do about it or why you're telling me any of this."

"Maybe I can help you understand. Tonight, if you're not doing anything and if you promise—"

"Promise what?"

"To keep a secret," Leyla's long lashes grazed her cheekbones. "I'd like to bring you somewhere."

"Okay?"

"Seriously, Autumn, think about it. And if you decide you'd like to join in. Meet me on the palace docks after first dark."

Seventy-Four

AUTUMN COULDN'T BELIEVE she was going through with this, but curiosity and loneliness got the best of her. After Emblem and Allegoria's hundredth check in for the day where thankfully she was able to convince them she was away on vacation for the last month and a half, she waited by the door for the hallway to still.

She relieved her guards for the night. Was it a smart decision? *Only time would tell.*

After the hallway grew quiet, she slid her door open and then tensed as Mr. Hiss purred, pressing up against her leg. He tried his hardest to stop her from leaving.

"You scared me," she stroked his feather soft fur. "Don't worry, I'll be back as soon as I can."

He stared at her innocently, his sapphire eyes blinking. Somehow, she knew he could understand her.

* * *

The dock was chilly and slick after a long day of torrential rain. It was quiet except for the sound of her heels scraping against the concrete-like ground. Giarldinia buzzed and hummed, full of nightlife.

Her admiration of the city was interrupted by the flicker of light coming from one of the aircraft.

When a hand touched her shoulder, she whirled around, and her jaw dropped. "Why are you dressed like that?" She scanned Leyla from head to toe. She was clothed in heather gray. Her complexion shifted to golden-olive and her long wavy light-brown hair was shaded black as midnight just like her brother's.

She reached into her crossbody satchel and handed Autumn a matching bodysuit. "Here, put this on."

Autumn scrunched her nose. "Why? I thought—"

"Would you stop asking so many questions?" Leyla rolled her eyes. "By the way, for tonight, you can call me Iris."

"Okay, Iris..." Autumn's brows furrowed. *Things were getting weirder by the second.*

Another body brushed up against her opposite side. Armienti stood there dressed in gray as well. His skin was tan, and his blonde hair was secured in a neat low ponytail.

"You can continue to call me Armienti. I care not who knows who I am," he winked.

"Boo, you're no fun," Leyla pushed him aside, making her way toward an aircraft.

"I'm not here for fun," Armienti chuckled. "I'm here to make sure you two don't do anything stupid or get yourselves into trouble."

Autumn sighed and crouched behind an aircraft for privacy. She changed, pulling off her black bodysuit and reemerged wearing heather gray.

"Not bad," Leyla grinned. "You should put a disguise in place as well. You're pretty memorable, especially your eyes."

"But—but how?" Autumn stuttered. Elattions had the ability to shapeshift, like Dante had on Earth, fooling her with his human disguise. But she was unsure of how the transformation took place.

"It's a feeling. A warming feeling that consumes your entire body," Leyla smoothed her palms against her stomach. "Hold it in your hands and visualize what you wish to change about yourself."

Another visualizing exercise. She sighed and closed her eyes. She started small, considering she already resembled a hybrid with her human features. When she opened her eyes, Leyla and Armienti applauded.

"Very good."

"What changed?"

"Your eyes."

She touched her eyes, and they felt no different than before, but when Leyla held a compact mirror from her bag to her face they had shifted to a deep brown. For a split second, she mistook herself for Brianna. A shiver rattled through her from the passing wind.

"All you need is a name now."

"How about—" Autumn thought for a moment before finally settling on her favorite month. A beautiful month, bridging spring to summer. "June."

Leyla shrugged. "That's an unusual name, but I suppose it will do."

"Well, I think it suits you," Armienti added. "It screams of Earth."

"Um, thanks, I think." Autumn tucked a curl behind her ear, unsure of what Armienti meant by his remark. The way he stared at her with his brilliant blue eyes made her suspect he had more on his mind than compliments and friendship.

"We should get going. We don't have much time."

* * *

Giarldinia was overpopulated. Virtually no part of the walkway was unoccupied.

The hybrid inhabitants scurried around bumping into her at every turn. It was like being in an amusement park with winding paths and whizzing aircraft zipping overhead. Her boots suctioned like magnets to the ground with every pass and turn. It explained why nobody fell to the ground, thousands of feet below.

"Where are we going?" Autumn asked, overwhelmed by the traffic.

Leyla and Armienti sauntered on, unphased by the activity.

"We're almost there, but we need to hurry," Leyla checked the time on her magenta communicator. "Curfew is approaching, and the streets will be swept for violators. Only those with my father's signed permission and appropriate identification are permitted to walk around late at night."

An alarm sounded, speaking in dozens of different languages. They ducked into a side alley way. Destroyers hummed overhead and heavy boots marched against the metal walkway at a furious pace. Guards cocked their guns. Autumn's heart pounded into her ribcage as they slipped through a dark door, and it sealed with a whoosh behind them.

Seventy-Five

AUTUMN WALKED DOWN many flights of stairs with Leyla and Armienti toward pulsating music and sparkling rainbow lights. It took her eyes a moment to adjust as they pressed through a cloud of smoke and into what appeared to be a club. Hybrids danced and hung out at tables and bars. Everyone seemed unphased by the alarm raging and the flashing lights outside.

From afar, they appeared almost human.

Leyla grabbed Autumn by the hand. "Come on, there's someone I want you to meet."

Leyla tugged her toward the back of the club to a group of laughing hybrids who appeared to be around Autumn's age.

"Iris, I'm so glad you could make it." A tall guy approached them with a moonglow mohawk, swirled tattoos running down the side of his throat. All Autumn could do was stare as he lowered his lips to Leyla's. *Holy crap.*

"I missed you so much."

"I missed you too," Leyla's face flushed. She turned toward Autumn. "Kyo, there's someone I'd like for you to meet."

"Oh, ummm, nice to meet you," Autumn stumbled on her words, still in disbelief. "I'm J-June."

"Excellent to meet you," Kyo pulled Leyla into his arms. "I haven't seen you around the city, but boy, do you look familiar."

Behind Kyo and Leyla, a projector streamed featuring exciting recaps from the year, including her wedding day. *Oh no.*

Autumn gulped. "Nope, you must be thinking of someone else."

She forced a smile as a lone bead of sweat dripped down her back. Her hands fidgeted.

An image of the emperor followed. It rotated with a ghost-like glow. *Boos* erupted around the room as hybrids threw their drinks against the likeness. Glass smashed and metal clanged against the wall while food dripped in heaps onto the floor. Leyla tensed, and Armienti rolled his eyes.

"Someone needs to get that murderous pig off the throne," Kyo clenched his fist. "I'd love to fight him, along with his son and that evil witch from Universe 16. The way they enslave entire planets and the way they use us to do their dirty work is infuriating."

Armienti snorted, "I'm sure that will go over well."

Kyo cocked his head to the side. His friends placed their drinks on the table in unison. "I'm not kidding. You have no idea what I'm capable of."

"That's my cousin," Leyla crossed her arms. "He thinks of himself as quite the jokester." She kicked him in the shin, and Armienti winced.

"I see, nice to meet you too." Kyo stared at him skeptically before extending a calloused hand.

"Pleasure," Armienti muttered. "Although what you speak of is treason."

"Square," Kyo chuckled. "You'll always exist under their

thumb if you think that way. Someone needs to put those Martynes in their place. And the Grand Supreme is the worst of them all. Constantly flexing his greedy hand and extending his empires—"

Leyla gulped and twined her fingers with Kyo's. "Surely they're not all bad."

"From what I've witnessed, they're all the same," Kyo countered.

Autumn cleared her throat, interrupting the conversation. It was getting way out of control. "So anyway, how did you two meet?"

Leyla batted her eyes. "Well as you know, June, I work in the kitchens of Sanguis. Late one night whilst I was retrieving a snack for the empress herself, I ran into Kyo while he was unloading one of the royal food supply ships."

"It was love at first sight," Kyo squeezed Leyla. "I took on extra shifts just so I could see her. I became kind of a stalker to say the least," he chuckled.

Leyla continued. "But we've been together ever since. It's been two going on three years."

"You sure have the prettiest eyes I've ever seen," one of Kyo's friend's interjected, speaking to Autumn. "You look just like the crown princess."

Leyla's eyes widened and Autumn glanced into the reflection of her communicator. *Crap, her disguise wore off.* She focused briefly and her eyes shifted from pale-gray back to brown. "Uhh, contacts."

"In any case, she's with me," Armienti wrapped his solid arm around her shoulders. "So, look to yourself."

"Geez, I was just paying her a compliment. No need to be defensive. You're lucky to have a girl who resembles Princess Autumn," he said. "I feel bad for her, mated to that monster. I dream of finding a girl like her someday."

"Dream on," Armienti took Autumn by the hand. "Why

would the crown princess have any interest in the likes of you?"

Armienti leaned in close to her and bit back a smile. "Come dance with me."

"Um, okay," she stuttered.

Armienti swept her across the floor beneath the smog and twirling rainbow neon lights. Her knees grazed against his.

"Can you believe this tough guy, talking down about our family? Leyla deserves so much better." Armienti rolled his eyes and slid his hand down the small of her back.

"I think he's trying to impress her," Autumn said as he twirled her by the hand. "And to be honest, he didn't say anything untrue." The Martynes were a family of murderers whether he would admit it or not.

"You always think the best of everyone," Armienti pulled her in so close she could smell the peppermint on his breath. His body was solid muscle against his delicate frame. "I admire you for that and the way you always put other people before yourself, like your father and your friends."

"I guess that makes me a sucker," Autumn snorted. "You saw the way they treated me before they left. They don't give a crap that we helped them. Part of me kind of regrets it."

"They were probably in shock," Armienti suggested. "Can you blame them? So you're aware, I was against bringing them, but Dante chose to avenge your honor. He can be petty like that sometimes—well, all the time."

"Yeah," Autumn caught a flash of Leyla making out with Kyo on the sideline.

"Speaking of Dante, have you heard from him?"

Autumn shook her head. "No."

"I'm sure you will. You're a very special young woman. A rare jewel in these chaotic universes. He would never ignore you."

"Hopefully Valdez won't say anything to him about what happened." She'd never be able to explain her way out of that one.

"We'll worry about her later."

The music stilled to silence followed by light applause.

"Where did you learn to dance so well?" Kyo approached them. "Those are upper class sequences."

Leyla cleared her throat. "I thought I told you, they're kitchen servants like I am. Occasionally, we get to attend banquets and dance moves become second nature after seeing them so often. Although, we've never been invited to participate."

Suddenly, Leyla reached into her purse and popped a bright pink pill into her mouth. She grabbed Kyo's drink out of his hand and swallowed it.

"Iris, seriously?" Armienti folded his arms. "Where did you get that from?"

Leyla chuckled. "They're harmless really, they just take the edge off. Do you want one?" She rustled through her purse and placed a blue pill into his hand.

"Maybe later," Armienti put the pill in his pocket.

"Well don't waste it," Leyla folded her arms. "These are difficult to come by. Do you want one, June?"

Autumn shook her head. "No thanks, I'll pass."

Leyla shrugged. "Suit yourself"

Kyo continued. "Interesting. I didn't realize you all worked in the palace. I'll come visit you all one day."

"Sure," Leyla tilted her head and grinned.

Autumn's stomach knotted and churned with dread.

* * *

"Isn't he adorable?" Leyla asked as they rode back to Sanguis minutes before sunrise. She hadn't stopped giggling since taking that pill. Autumn was glad her disguise passed.

"Ummm," Autumn picked at her short bare nails. "I wouldn't exactly call him adorable, but he seems nice enough and I think he really likes you."

A long breathy sigh erupted from Armienti's mouth as he flew the aircraft. "I didn't care for him. He's pompous, and he doesn't like our family—not that I can blame him, but still, to say such horrible things."

"Well, I think he's sweet," Leyla's complexion shifted back to pale blue. Her brown eyes sparkled in the rising sunlight. "And I lov—"

"Don't say it," Armienti waved a hand dismissively. "He doesn't know who you are. What's he going to do when he finds out you're Leyla Martyne?"

"I–I don't know but it doesn't make my feelings for him any less real," Leyla admitted.

"What's Dante going to say when he finds out? He *will* find out. He always does," Armienti maneuvered the aircraft through the skyway as gracefully as a bird. The early morning suns glimmered tangerine as they hovered over the docks and gently landed on the ground. Dust and gravel settled.

"I'm hoping he'll be glad for us. He has Autumn. What more could he want? Our relationship is none of his business," Leyla crossed her arms, mouth twisting.

"He doesn't have me," Autumn wrung her fingers in her lap. "I haven't heard from him since he left. He doesn't give a crap about me." As far as she was concerned, nobody did.

Leyla's mouth curved. "Sure he does. You're all he ever talks about—"

Autumn folded her arms, forehead pulsating "Well, he has a funny way of showing it."

She stumbled out of the aircraft wordlessly and bit back the tears coming from her eyes. She couldn't tell if Leyla's aphrodisiac was contagious or if she actually missed him. But how could she miss a guy who spent his entire life conquering planets and enslaving their inhabitants?

Seventy-Six

THE NIGHT before Dante's long awaited arrival home, Autumn couldn't sleep. She stared at the ceiling. Her limbs jittered at the thought of seeing him again.

"Why is this happening to me?" She held her palms against her smooth, warm cheeks.

What would he be like once he was back? Was it possible she made the wrong decision to stay behind? Maybe she should've risked traveling back home with the others.

No.

Her friends and family would never accept her. Caleb had said so himself. *She was dangerous.* She couldn't risk hurting or killing anyone else.

Dante loved her as she was. At least, that's what he said. But then again, maybe he'd changed his mind over the time they'd been separated. Despite what he'd claimed, she'd yet to hear from him.

Her text had been unanswered.

Autumn closed her eyes. Her face warmed, against her will, in the darkness. Why did she miss him? *Why?* She longed for him. Even if he was a monster.

* * *

As the sun rose, warm orange and gold rays streamed over the pristine white balcony that extended from the side of her room. The mega metropolis glowed and hustled with life.

Autumn sat at the edge of the bed, marveling at the beauty outside her window when a rap came to her bedroom door. Normally, she would've been annoyed, but she finally grew used to never having privacy.

The obligatory perks of being Dante's wife.

Ever since they'd been married, it felt like her life had morphed into a reality show. Everyone was always watching and seeking her attention. *It was so annoying.*

"Come in," she yelled as her head collided with her pillow. Leyla walked through the door.

Autumn was delighted that they'd grown closer. Leyla was like the sister she never had but always secretly wanted. It was difficult for her to believe they were once at odds with each other but now she knew her secret—one she hoped would never get out.

Leyla flopped beside her on the bed. She wore a bubblegum-pink satin bathrobe. Her wavy light-brown hair cascaded loosely over her shoulders and pointed blue ears.

"Rumor has it Dante should be arriving in time for tonight's feast," Leyla said jovially. "I was thinking maybe we could plan something special for his return."

"What do you have in mind?" Autumn pressed her coils behind her ears.

Leyla grinned. "Obviously, we should have a party, but we need a theme." She crossed her arms and entered a period of deep thought.

Suddenly, Autumn was struck with an interesting idea. She recalled her favorite holiday back home. Halloween. Now that she thought about it, she'd never celebrated a single holiday in outer space. "Why don't we have a masquerade ball?"

"What's that?" Leyla's nose crinkled. "I've never heard of a masquerade ball before. Is it some kind of Earth tradition?"

"Yes, they had them back on Earth. I've never been to one before. I've only seen them in movies. Basically, everyone gets dressed up and places masks over their faces to hide their true identities."

"That does sound like an amusing concept." Leyla twirled a long wave around her finger. "Let's tell my mother so we can begin planning."

Autumn didn't mind seeing the empress. She'd been nothing but kind since she arrived on Surge. It was the emperor she didn't care for. Hatred for her seethed from every pore in his body. One look from him made her feel queasy.

* * *

When she arrived with Leyla at the private breakfast nook adjacent to the banquet hall, her stomach knotted. Leyla's parents sat there eating together, clothed in their spectacular riches. The empress wore a gilded bodysuit with a red asymmetrical stripe. Her hair topped her head in a sparkling golden beehive with tendrils framing her youthful face. The emperor wore a bodysuit as black as midnight with his crimson cape rippling over the back of his chair. A servant knelt on the floor and polished the emperor's onyx knee-high boots.

The emperor's angular face hardened to stone as he beheld Autumn. She accepted the cold cruel fact that he hated her but was confident she was safe because he was terrified of his own son.

Dante promised to kill him if he so much as laid a finger on her.

Autumn averted her gaze and ignored him. The empress

on the other hand looked as charming as ever. Her dazzling brown eyes smiled at their unannounced visit.

"Is this how you choose to wander the halls of my palace now, in such a frivolous state of undress?" The emperor snipped as he looked at them. Autumn and Leyla stood there in matching satin bathrobes. Autumn's robe was the shade of ripe eggplant.

"Forgive us, Father, we have something we can't wait to tell Mother." Leyla said sweetly, batting her lashes.

The emperor rolled his amber eyes. "Very well then, out with it."

"Yes?" The empress wiped a napkin against her mouth as she chewed and swallowed her breakfast.

"We want to host a party to honor Dante's triumphant arrival." Leyla's eyes met Autumn's. "What was it called again?"

"A masquerade ball," she added as her bare feet slid against the heated tile.

Leyla continued. "It's an Earth tradition."

The empress flashed a pleasant smile as Autumn re-explained the concept for the second time.

The emperor folded his arms and kicked the servant who polished his boots in the gut. "What an idiotic idea, honoring your fallen planet. How would you be able to tell anyone apart?"

"That's kind of the point," Autumn said. She and Leyla looked to the empress for approval or some sort of indication.

"Well, I love it," Isidora added. "And I'm sure Dante will love it too. Preparations will commence immediately."

"Absolutely nonsensical and a complete and utter waste of time," The emperor hissed beneath his breath. "If it wasn't for my son, you know where you'd be."

Autumn rolled her eyes and left the room with Leyla. She bit her tongue so hard it bled a little.

Seventy-Seven

WHEN AUTUMN RETURNED with Leyla to the banquet hall, she could tell her sister-in-law had more tricks up her sleeve.

"We should tell Ronan and Armienti. I'm certain they'll want to be part of the festivities." Leyla rubbed her hands together.

"Um, sure," Autumn stuttered, "We can invite Armienti, but Ronan..."

Leyla texted someone on her communicator before peering up at her. "What about him?"

"He's, um..." Autumn wrung her hands behind her back.

"Come on, now you must tell me. I told you my secret," Leyla pouted, her bottom lip protruding. She reminded her for a split second of her best friend, Lauren. "Please."

"Okay," she leaned in close and whispered into Leyla's pointed ear. "He went back to Earth with my friends to return them home. That's why you couldn't find me. We went on kind of a rescue mission." Although, she couldn't really call them her friends anymore.

Leyla gasped and cupped her hand over her mouth.

"What? I thought your planet was extinct? What about the Grand Supreme? What if he finds out?"

"It's a cover. You can't tell anyone, or everyone is going to be in danger."

Leyla nodded. "I promise. Your secret is safe with me."

* * *

After leaving the banquet hall, they walked upstairs to the sixth floor where the bedrooms were located. As they approached Armienti's bed chamber, giggling erupted, followed by boisterous laughter.

Autumn rolled her eyes. "I don't think he's alone."

Leyla sighed. "He's never alone. He's a disgusting pig who has a new harlot hanging off his arm every other week like a trophy. I'm glad Dante's done with that little phase," she paused. "You've been such a good influence on him. He's really changed. I could tell he had feelings for you from the moment you came here. And quite frankly, I'm sorry I ever doubted you."

She flashed a small smile and wondered. *Could it really be true?* If anyone changed, she had. Her eyes were wide open to the way people could turn on her in a split second and treat her like yesterday's garbage.

Autumn balled a fist and reluctantly knocked on the door.

"Who goes there?" Armienti chuckled through the door. The woman inside giggled like a fool.

"You know who. Cut it out," Leyla stomped her foot against the crimson carpet. "Get out here right now."

The bed creaked and a pair of feet ambled to the door. It glided open slowly, and Armienti stood there wearing nothing but navy spandex briefs. His blue muscles glittered in the hall light.

Autumn's cheeks heated and she glanced away. How embarrassing.

Armienti leaned a hip against the door. "What brings you ladies here?"

"We're hosting a masquerade ball to celebrate Dante's return," Leyla crossed her arms. "How could you not tell me about Ronan? And the humans? What's the matter with you?"

Armienti cupped a hand around Leyla's mouth and her brown eyes bulged. "This is why. Quiet, lest someone overhears your big rattling mouth."

Leyla pulled away, grumbling. "Next you'll tell me Dante was somehow involved in Keyserike's disappearance, the miserable butcher that he is."

Armienti glanced to the side and Leyla gasped. Autumn's heart pounded in her throat.

"Really? How could neither of you tell me this?"

"I'll be there," Armienti winked, dropping the subject. He tilted his head to the side, his golden tresses framing his face. "Masquerade balls are most delightful. You never know who you'll meet."

"You've heard of them?" Autumn's mouth curved. "I'm surprised."

"Of course, I attended one back on Earth. Now if you'll please excuse me, I'm in the middle of some rather important business." He grinned like a jackal, before falling into a bow. "Ladies."

The door slithered closed behind him.

"I swear Armienti is so lazy, all he ever does is entertain and neglect his other duties. My father often complains about him." Leyla groaned.

"What does he say?" Autumn tightened her satin bathrobe.

"He'd rather lounge around court all day and chase beautiful women. That he's only a prince for show and is nowhere near as capable as Dante, although he would like to think himself so. And also," Leyla lowered her voice to a whisper. "I overheard my parents fighting a lot over him recently. I'm not sure why."

They strode side by side through the vermillion hallway before Leyla spoke again. "Anyway, we should figure out what we're going to wear. We don't have much time to prepare ourselves, and I'm guessing you want to make a huge splash at the party. I have the perfect outfit in mind."

* * *

Autumn admired Leyla's bedroom in wonderment. It was a wide-open space with amethyst walls and swirling galaxies that rotated along the ceiling. Hanging mirrored spheres swayed in the warm afternoon breeze. The floor was coated with soft, wall-to-wall fuzzy cream carpeting.

A round magenta bed sat in the center of the room covered with berry velvet pillows and a satin blanket. A pair of French doors leading to a pristine white balcony allowed sunlight to trickle in.

Leyla approached a wall of mirrors and slid them open to reveal hundreds of exquisite colorful dresses. She dug through them and pulled out two that were identical in style with poofy floor-length tulle skirts. They were sleeveless halter tops with wide open backs and deep V-necks that extended to just about the belly button.

Leyla held the magenta dress and handed the midnight-black one to her.

"I'm thinking we could wear these," Leyla said, a hint of excitement playing through her voice. "I have matching gloves as well."

Autumn's fingers ran along the gossamer fabric. "I'm not sure I could pull off a dress like this."

Leyla smiled, reassuringly. "Of course you can. You can do anything you want if you choose to step out of your comfort zone. That's what dreams are made of. All you have to do is believe in yourself."

Autumn reluctantly slipped the gown over her eggplant satin robe. As she glanced into the mirror, she chewed her bottom lip. It fit her like a glove. And for the first time in her life, she looked *sexy*.

"You see, I knew you could pull it off," Leyla winked. "Oh, and before I forget, I know what we can do for masks."

Leyla tore a bottom strip from each of their dresses and poked two eye holes with her fingernails. Autumn stretched it across her face. *Perfect.*

* * *

The remainder of the day flew by in a whirlwind. Autumn talked with Leyla and relaxed in her bedroom while they waited for Emblem and Allegoria to prepare them for the upcoming festivities. Autumn's stomach fluttered with excitement as the time drew nearer.

She had no business being this nervous. She was only seeing *Dante*. It was no big deal.

When Emblem and Allegoria arrived, relief flooded through her, but she quickly noted that they were sweat-slicked and out of breath.

"Greetings, princesses," their chests heaved as they curtseyed.

"Are you all right?" Autumn looked them up and down skeptically.

"Oh, don't worry about us. We're fine," Emblem slid a golden comb from her pocket and a blood-red handkerchief fluttered to the ground. She trembled as she grabbed the fabric and shoved it back inside of her smock.

"We'll hurry. The prince and his entourage should be landing any time now," the twins said concurrently.

Emblem and Allegoria dressed her and Leyla in their glamorous matching ball gowns. Their hair was styled half-up in glittered poufs. A single strip of tulle was secured over each of their eyes.

When Autumn glanced into the mirror, she bit back a grin, absolutely giddy to see Dante and his reaction after he laid his eyes on her again.

"Shall we?" Leyla gestured.

As the door slid open, they encountered Armienti who waited patiently outside. A simple onyx sash was secured over his eyes. He wore his usual black uniform with a royal-purple cape.

When he saw Autumn, his jaw lowered. She glanced away before meeting his gaze.

Armienti stuttered before he spoke. "G-Good evening, I've come to accompany you both to the throne room. We've been asked to assemble there before the festivities." He never broke his piercing stare from Autumn.

She followed them to her least favorite place in the palace. A place where she was sure to encounter the emperor and Valdez. Her stomach churned at the thought of what would occur when they met again.

As they crossed through the maroon hallway, Armienti would *not* stop staring at her.

"Is there a problem? Do I have something on my face?" Autumn brushed her satin-gloved fingertips against her cheek. Now she was officially self-conscious.

"Um, sorry. I'm not so used to you looking so, well, *mature*."

"So, I look old then?" Autumn jested, crossing her arms.

"No, you've blossomed somehow overnight into a beautiful young woman," his cheeks reddened. "Not to say you haven't always been beautiful, but tonight you look especially so."

"Enough Armienti," Leyla rolled her eyes and took her by the arm. "We all know your game and it's tiresome."

They walked ahead at a rapid speed.

Autumn's cheeks heated as she secretly hoped Dante would notice as well.

Seventy-Eight

THE THRONE ROOM was packed to capacity with palace courtiers. They dressed in exquisite gowns and flamboyant masks adorned with jewels, butterfly wings, lace, and feathers. Everyone seemed receptive to the party theme. Everyone except for the emperor, whose face remained maskless. Horizontal lines crept across his forehead as he stroked his midnight goatee.

Autumn took her respective seat on top of the dais with Leyla. Armienti slipped into the dense crowd and melded with the shadows.

"I think he's developed a fondness for you," Leyla whispered into her ear.

She snorted. "I think so too." Deep down she knew it wasn't her imagination the way Armienti had stared at her. It wasn't his first time, but tonight he'd been way too obvious.

The emperor pounded his fist against the arm of his throne, interrupting her thoughts. "Now that we're all assembled, bring forth the rebels."

Her heart slammed against her ribcage. Finally, the moment she'd been waiting for.

Her eyes settled on Dante, who wore his horned helmet in the shade of spilled blood. Although she couldn't see his mouth, she assumed a cocky smile was affixed to his face. How could it not be? He arrived home victorious.

She crossed her legs and bit her bottom lip. Leyla snorted.

Wound around a neighboring soldier's wrist was a chain affixed to the throat of a well-built alien man clothed in a light-gray smock. The soldier yanked him like an animal. Wide-eyed terror spread across his face.

Dried blood stained his clothes, and both of his eyes were swollen. He'd been beaten to hell and back.

Two other men followed, gagged and bound. They groaned in agony, trudging their feet along the velvet carpet.

Autumn had been staring so hard at the rebels, she failed to notice Valdez who walked with a distinct limp and dragged her wounded leg. Her eyes were as cold as sleet. A shiver rattled down Autumn's spine as Valdez fixated on her, cruel mouth twisted to the side.

When the rebels reached the front of the room accompanied by Dante and his entourage, the emperor stood up from his throne and crossed his bulging arms.

Two out of three men fell to their knees, trembling.

The central rebel remained standing.

"Let's not start this again." The soldier holding the leash kicked the back of the rebel's knees and he toppled face forward onto the ground, yanked back by his chain. His face shifted to purple, and gasps erupted around the room.

"That's quite enough." Dante raised a hand and the soldier shuddered before slackening the chain.

"Let this be a lesson to all those who challenge our authority and dare to defy the Grand Supreme," the emperor's voice resounded throughout the room.

The emperor stared at the prisoners, his expression as hard

as stone. "Let me ask you a question. Was this little outburst of yours worth the trouble?"

Two of the three men shook their heads, but the man in the middle remained still and attempted to speak through his dry crusty lips.

Dante loosened his gag and the emperor chortled. "Their ringleader wishes to speak," he said in a mocking tone.

"You sit there high and mighty while your people starve and suffer at your wicked hands. You may have defeated us today, but your reign of terror won't last forever. One day you'll meet your match," the rebel coughed.

The entire room erupted into a boisterous fit of laughter. Autumn sat there, straight-faced. He hadn't said anything funny.

"Is that what they're calling my reign now?" The emperor slapped a palm against his knee and shook his head. "Every sacrifice I've made is for the good of the realm. If that includes breaking your fingers, mining and building our exquisite cities, then so be it. Let's not forget, you exist to serve us."

The rebel spat on Dante's boot, and the soldier whaled the rebel in the back of the head and pressed his shoe against his cheek.

"I've had about enough of you," the soldier said, refastening his gag and whipping him to his feet.

"I guess you didn't hear me the first time, but perhaps you'll hear this, soldier. You'll spend the night in the cells for disobeying my orders and behaving like a wild animal in my court." Dante ripped the chain from his hand.

The soldier glanced at his feet. "Forgive me, sire."

Two guards came and escorted him away.

The emperor's eyes narrowed as he looked upon the rebels. "I hereby find you three guilty of high treason, which should come as no surprise. Normally, our executions are performed at dawn, but with a crime of this magnitude, I won't allow you to live out the night."

The soldiers behind them drew their frightfully large guns, holding them to their heads. The men trembled on their knees.

"Any last words?" The emperor crossed his arms.

Leyla trembled and grabbed Autumn's hand. The charge of the guns zipped through the air. They lowered their gags.

"Long live the Red Cloaks," they uttered before their bodies disintegrated to charred dust.

Seventy-Nine

AUTUMN LEFT the throne room with Leyla, shaken to the core. Dante and his elite special forces spoke with the emperor. She stared at him so long she failed to notice Valdez blocking her way. She swallowed her heart and took two steps in retreat. Leyla's mouth fell wide open.

"Don't you dare think I'll forgive or forget what you did to me," Valdez whispered into her ear. Her voice was laced with venom. "I promise I'll repay the suffering tenfold. When you least expect it, I'll come for you, human filth. I'll gut you like the insignificant piece of dust that you are. I'll take my time though. Slow and steady wins the race."

Leyla grabbed Autumn by the arm, pulling her toward the door. "I'm afraid you imagined whatever you're accusing Autumn of, for she's been with me throughout your entire mission. Perhaps you should have your head examined. You're crazier than I remember," Leyla bit back a smile.

Valdez's jagged wings twitched, and her eyes thinned to slits as Leyla dragged Autumn to the banquet hall.

"What was that about?" Leyla hissed, her entire body

trembling. "You had a run in with Valdez? She's very, very dangerous."

"Never mind," Autumn's stomach churned. Judging by her secrecy, she hadn't told Dante what transpired on Varz. So right now, it was her word against Valdez's.

"There's no never mind. She has you on her list, Autumn. This is serious."

"I know, I know. I'll figure it out," Autumn shrugged.

She had a bad taste in her mouth over this whole ordeal, but she did her best to hide it. She didn't want to spoil the perfectly planned evening.

As they entered the hall, her terror shifted to delight. The ceiling was draped with a sea of cerulean, mauve, and silver silks. Paper lanterns floated over metal tables adorned with silver satin runners. Vases spilled with black roses and baby's breath.

The Empress had done a great job on such short notice.

"Here you go ladies," a pair of hands holding golden bubbling flutes of champagne passed over their heads.

Armienti must've read her mind, because she desperately needed to ease her growing nerves. She sipped her beverage.

Not long into the party, Dante and his entourage arrived. A roaring round of applause erupted around the room. Armienti froze then darted to the opposite side of the hall and mingled with a separate crowd. Several times his piercing eyes met Autumn's.

The way he stared at her with his sky-blue eyes and full tilted lips. She glanced away, hugging herself. Her face flushed.

Autumn finished her drink before reaching for another one, as did Leyla. Her cheeks warmed, and her vision became rosy. Her inhibitions dropped.

As she peeked over her shoulder, a shudder of annoyance rattled through her. Dante still hadn't noticed her. Instead, an exchange took place between him and his father. The emperor attempted to embrace his son, but he pulled away.

"Another job well done. I knew you wouldn't disappoint me," The emperor nudged his son's shoulder. "Now we're one step closer to bringing Keyserike to justice. The coward that he is."

Dante's muscles went taut, and he brushed his hand away. "Thank you, Father." He left him, muttering to himself.

Autumn turned away, fully expecting him to approach her next, but that wasn't the case. He circled the room making his way through a dense gathering of lords and ladies, offering him endless congratulations. It wasn't the lords who annoyed Autumn, it was the ladies who ran their fingers along his arms and smiled and giggled and ate up all his attention.

Attention he should've been showering on her.

She knew her self-worth and demanded his undivided attention. Why was he ignoring her?

He was so annoying, her forehead pulsated.

She deserved it more than them. He hadn't noticed her, hadn't acknowledged her. She lingered like a shadow among a sea of giant guests who were all somehow more important.

As she tightened her grip, a third glass of champagne shattered in her grasp. She didn't know her own strength anymore. Perhaps it was her cue to stop drinking. Droplets of blood trickled onto the floor and into the mesh of her midnight dress. Leyla never uttered a word.

Finally, when she could take no more of being ignored, she hiked up her long flowing dress above her ankles and marched over to him as he told a funny story. Everyone laughed and she remained straight-faced. Women ran their fingers along his arms and chest plaits and giggled with their stupid laughs, making her blood boil.

She cleared her throat and made her way through the

crowd. She sat in his lap, mid-sentence, and laced her satin-gloved fingers around his neck. Her thigh revealed itself.

"I have to have a private word with my husband," she tilted her head to the side.

The women got the hint and scattered into the crowd like flies. *Good riddance.*

Dante twisted his mouth to the side before his lips curved. "Is there a problem?" He batted his long onyx lashes.

"What do you mean is there a problem?" Her blood pressure spiked, and a dizzying sensation overtook her. "Of course, there's a problem. How dare you embarrass me like this."

"I'm not sure what you're referring to," he grabbed a goblet filled with bubbling red wine, swirled it and took a lingering sip. "I'm giving you what you asked for."

"What do you mean, what I *asked* for?" Her molars ground in her mouth.

Dante chucked and rested the goblet on the table. His blue lips hinted at crimson. "I swear, you're always complaining about something. It must be a human trait. I was merely trying to be respectful of your wishes. You asked for space, and you got it."

Her chest hollowed like somebody delivered a fatal blow. "I can see this is all some kind of game to you and I'm a joke," she tried to stand, tears welling in the corners of her eyes, but he held her in his lap. "You abducted me, married me, and now you want nothing to do with me anymore. You didn't even notice I was here. Are you bored of me already, like all those other girls?"

"No, of course not, Autumn. I could never be bored of you," he ran his lips along her throat and a shiver traveled down her spine. He slid his hands to the small of her back. "I noticed you as soon as I walked into the room. I've been watching you all night long. And this dress—"

She leaned over and slipped her tongue into his mouth,

tasting fresh cinnamon. She didn't care who saw. As she ran her fingers through the silken strands of his midnight hair, red dust tumbled and settled in a flurry on the tulle of her dress. They trembled and frantically made out, his hand cupping her cheek, the other pressed along her back. She lost herself, surrendering to his touch.

She pulled away and whispered into his ear. "You're filthy."

He chuckled breathily. "Well, what did you expect? I just came from a war zone."

She grabbed a glass of water from the table as well as a cloth napkin. She he wiped traces of red clay from his face and hands. It wasn't good enough.

She rose from his lap, twining her fingers in his and pulled him to his feet. He kissed her again.

"Follow me," she led him from the hall.

Eighty

ALTHOUGH DANTE DREAMED of making love to Autumn since their time together on Earth, he didn't take the decision lightly. He couldn't help but wonder what changed from the time he was away. *Why did she suddenly want him?* He was a monster and a murderer who'd done nothing to deserve her. Although he tried, he didn't like himself most days.

As he gazed upon her, his hands perspired within his gloves. They stood before his bedroom door, and she bit her bottom lip and grinned the most beautiful grin he'd ever seen. Her cheeks flushed the color of roses, and her moonlit eyes swallowed him whole. He fumbled twice, pressing the code to his room. Suddenly, he couldn't remember it. Dammit.

She slid against him and touched his face with her satin palms. A shiver of desire rattled his core. He could barely think straight. His face warmed like molten lava.

She pulled away and spun on the balls of her toes, giggling. Her poofy dress fell around her ankles and she kicked it to the floor. She sat on his bed, legs subtly opening.

He rushed over and kissed her onto his bed. She laid

against his sheets. He tasted her sweet lips and her mouth as she tugged against his clothes, trying desperately to remove them.

He brushed her hand away. "As much as I want to take you up on your offer. I think you've had too much to drink."

"No, I haven't," she crossed her arms. "You should be the one apologizing to me. You never returned my text, and you left me hanging and worried about you for months. And worst of all you were flirting with those girls in front of me after you made a promise."

"I have my reasons. And no, I wasn't flirting," his face boiled at her accusation. The only girl in the room he noticed was her. He'd been dreaming about her for countless suns and moons.

"Dante, please," she ran her fingers through his hair.

"Obviously, you can't be reasoned with in this state," he chuckled, lowering his mouth to her ear, kissing her lobe. He rested his head against her shoulder.

Her eyes wavered and glazed before she passed out on his bed. He was surprised it took her so long. He tucked her in and kissed her forehead. Afterwards, he pinched his cheeks to ensure he wasn't the one who was dreaming.

* * *

The emperor scoured the banquet hall during the ongoing festivities. He hoped not to see his son with Autumn. It was the most sickening sight in the world. *Human filth*. He groaned as he walked around, his influence slipping through his mighty grasp. The former strength and influence of a god-emperor was non-existent.

Something wasn't right, and it surprised him that he only just now realized it. His son had put everyone in very real danger over his Earth wife.

He feared Keyserike was involved, who was last seen in the lower universes. His gut screamed Dante was responsible for his disappearance.

His eyes settled on Valdez, who walked with a noticeable limp. Her ragged wings settled against her back. Had she crossed his son as well?

Dante was out of control, a danger to himself and those around him.

There was no limit to his selfishness. No limit to his irresponsibility. How could he ever rule?

The emperor only hoped the Grand Supreme hadn't caught on. For if he did, the entire realm risked annihilation over a silly Earth girl.

Eighty-One

WHEN AUTUMN WOKE, every muscle in her body screamed in pain. What had she been doing last night? And why was she *naked* in Dante's bed?

Her cheeks heated in shame. She couldn't recall what'd taken place. All she could remember were the consecutive glasses of champagne she downed, prancing around in a pretty dress, and sitting on his lap and making out with him in front of the entire banquet hall.

Crap.

She balled her fists. If they had been intimate, at the very least he could've waited for her to wake up instead of splitting on her like a one-night stand.

Especially because it would've been her first time.

As she laid there seething, the door slid open, and she threw the dark purple bed sheet around her body. Goose-bumps prickled over her skin from the cool hallway air.

"Oh, wonderful, you're awake. We've brought your breakfast," Allegoria peeked her head through the doorway and grinned. "And afterwards, we'll draw you a bath."

She groaned. "Whatever."

Her forehead pulsated as Allegoria placed a food tray beside her, stacked high with chocolate chip pancakes.

By the time she finished, water flowed like a waterfall in the bathroom. Inside was the largest tub she'd ever seen. Leave it to Dante to have an above ground stone pool overlooking the city. Steam misted across the floor in steady white puffs.

She made her way up the steps, feet sliding over the heated metallic tile, and climbed into the bath.

When Allegoria bent over to grab the soap, a red tail popped out of her pocket again. This time, Autumn tugged at the fabric and the color washed from Allegoria's face.

"What is this?" She scrunched her nose, examining the fabric. It was embroidered with a pair of roses, stars swirling around them.

"Um, it's nothing but a cleaning cloth," Allegoria shoved it back into her smock, stuttering.

"It looks pretty fancy to be a cleaning cloth," Autumn muttered. "It might look better on display."

"Conversing with the help again I see—"

Dante stood in the doorway with his arms folded. A smile wound around his lips. His solid muscles shifted beneath his skintight uniform.

Her face heated. He always showed up at the most inconvenient time. *Why did he have to look so handsome? Dammit.*

"Sweetheart, I trust you were treated well while I was away."

Emblem and Allegoria tensed.

"Yeah, I'm fine," she folded her arms.

But really, she wanted to jump up and down and scream, and demand to know where he was. Obviously, it was somewhere more important than being with her. She was so tired of being everyone's back up choice.

"Good, I think I'll join you. If I recall correctly, you owe me a bath," he winked.

He removed his top and unfastened his royal-purple cape. They fell gracefully to the floor. Autumn marveled at the ripples of his abs, his toned biceps, and the two strange scars littering his chest and ribcage. And his...

Her face heated. She tried not to stare but she couldn't help herself.

"Leave us," he waved dismissively at Emblem and Allegoria. They scurried from the room, closing the door behind them.

She waded in the water as he climbed in. His cerulean skin shimmered in the waves. Every pore on her body set on fire as she stared into his eyes.

"I apologize for not being by your side when you woke up," his amber eyes glinted with sincerity and her insides smoldered. "I was called into a council meeting. You know how that can be."

"Whatever, I don't care," she walked to the other side of the tub.

"*I can tell you're lying. I know you're upset,*" echoed through her head.

"I told you to stop doing that," she protested. "My mind is off limits. If you want to talk to me, just talk."

He glanced away. "Forgive me. You must understand, there's no place I'd rather be than by your side."

He lathered soap in his hands before spreading it over her neck and back and through her hair. His calluses scraped against her skin. Her eyes fluttered closed, lips subconsciously parting.

"Well, you sure had me fooled," she breathed, leaning into his touch. Her inclinations were dangerous.

"How are you feeling after last night?" He nuzzled her ear.

Autumn pulled away. "Wh—why? Did we?"

He submerged himself in the water. "No, you had a little

too much to drink. I would never take advantage of you in that state."

"Well, I would've liked to," she chewed her bottom lip. "Just so we're clear."

"I don't understand your sudden change of heart, I find it confusing," he placed his hand on her forehead and checked her temperature. "Are you feeling okay? You hate me. I'm the villain, remember?"

Her cheeks set ablaze. How could she explain to him that no human would ever want her on Earth, even if she did manage to escape. With her abilities, she'd never be normal again. She was unlovable, and worst of all, dangerous just like he was.

She wanted him, although she couldn't voice her needs. At the same time, she was terrified. She trembled from head to toe.

"I think you're the one who owes me an explanation," he lathered soap through his raven hair. Suds trickled down his back.

She thought about what he could possibly mean. She couldn't tell him her former friends were on their way to Earth with Ronan as they spoke, including her mom's murderer, who she wished she killed instead of forgave.

She concocted another excuse. "I read something interesting about humans in one of the books that you gave me."

His blue cheeks shifted tomato-red. He glanced away as steam flowed over the water. "I didn't realize the Ballad of Sandstorms was in there. I'm sorry, I shouldn't have let you read it, it's way too romantic and idealistic." He smoothed a hand through his midnight hair before going quiet, then he asked, "What did you think of the tale?"

She'd read so many stories; they all blended together. Most were about the history of the universes and alien royalty of centuries past. She could only remember one story involving humans where they were expressly mentioned.

"I enjoyed the Ballad of Sandstorms more than any of the other stories," she ran her fingers along his back. "It was beautiful."

He cleared his throat. "I've always been taught lower life-forms were weak and inferior. That their only purpose in life was to serve and be dominated by higher life-forms. But there was one story that called this into question, involving humans. The tale of Tulia and Lightning," his eyes sparkled. "Thousands of years ago, when Elattions first traveled to Earth, led by prince Lightning, they weren't the least bit impressed, and the humans lived up to the claims. What they didn't count on, or what he didn't count on rather, were the females. They were beautiful and kind, particularly Tulia, who stole his heart. As the Elattions got to know the humans better, they made excellent wives to the warriors. They lived happy, peaceful lives together with the families they created, and evil never prevailed as long as they were together. Everyone was safe and Tulia and Lightning had the most influential reign throughout all of history."

He continued. "That's one of the reasons I was fascinated to embark on a mission to the lower universes and especially to Earth. I spiraled after I lost Maeve, and I feared I could never fall in love again. All I ever wanted was a family of my own, someone to settle down with who actually wanted me around. I felt like Earth was a great place to start, although the nature of my mission was destructive, until I met you," he drifted closer to her. "I know I've made some mistakes, and I should've gone about it differently. I know I was selfish, and I ruined everything. I know how much you miss your family and friends, and I'm sorry about it. I was angry your father wanted to keep us apart and jealous of how close you are to them. I've never had a close relationship with my family, and I don't have any friends," a tear rolled down his cheek and she wiped it away. "I know I don't deserve you. I promise I'll reunite you with your family the first chance I get, I swear it. But right now, it isn't safe. We're being watched all the time."

"What happened to Earth?" She stared into his brilliant amber eyes.

"I recharged my stranded ship and maxed out the force-field. The planet should be safe for another five or so years before it's due for another charge, which I'll gladly provide. I'll go myself. Nobody will ever find out it still exists. Your family and friends are safe, I swear it. I'll do anything to protect them from *him*."

She quivered, pulling him down for a kiss. His story aligned with Armienti's. He finally told her the truth instead of lying or withholding information. Earth was safe, and all he ever wanted was a family. It was her deepest desire as well. She craved stability and familiarity. A place to call home.

He swept her into his arms and propped her on the lip of the tub. The sleepless city hummed. He dragged his mouth against her throat. Goosebumps prickled over her skin. His calloused hands slid down her body and rested firmly against her hips. He leaned over and kissed her, their mouths mingling together before he whispered into her ear. Warm cinnamon breath flowed against her throat. Her toes curled under, and her core tightened from his touch.

"Are you okay? Tell me what you're thinking. I won't pry." He stroked her cheek with his fingertips.

"I want you, and I want this," she finally said. "You're my husband."

"Are you sure?" His lips grazed her lobe before he softly kissed it.

"Yes," her hands grasped the solid muscles of his back, then wandered to the stub of his missing tail. He shuddered from her touch. "I want you more than anything."

He moved closer. She wrapped her legs around his body and ran her fingers through the strands of his ink-black hair. They trembled with desire and anticipation. "I love you, Autumn."

He caressed her neck and her breasts, and she melted into his kiss, losing herself to him. It hurt for a second before the pain faded to pleasure, their quivering bodies entwined. He was slow and gentle and calculated with the way he loved her. All the while the city hummed in the distance.

When they finished, breathless, she couldn't stop smiling. It was better than she imagined. They gazed into each other's eyes in awe and wonder and exchanged kisses and "I love you" s. They climbed out of the tub, and he held her in his arms before they toweled off.

That's when a frantic knock came to the bathroom door.

Dante whirled around as the knocking persisted. He wrapped a towel around his waist and secured one around her body. "Well for heaven's sake come in already."

A servant sputtered inside, falling to one knee, chest heaving. "Forgive me, sire."

"Well, that depends," Dante stroked his chin between his fingers. "You come busting into my wash closet and interrupt me when it's obvious I'm busy."

The servant nodded then stuttered.

Dante chuckled. "I jest."

"Your father—"

His jaw clenched. "Oh, so he's behind this interruption. What about my father? Why has he sent you?"

"He's dead."

* * *

Guillermo Ramon wandered by himself through the crisp fallen leaves of Farrah Falls, or what was left of it since the fire over a year ago. The pale full-moon cast shadows through the barren trees and spilled over the trickling waterfall.

It'd become his nighttime ritual to search the grounds for Dante and his daughter because nobody would believe him no matter how hard he tried to explain the situation.

She'd been abducted by Dante, who was an alien. He'd read the note himself.

He couldn't forget Autumn's admission that he lived in the woods. But *where*? He'd searched every last inch of the forest for clues, and still nothing. There were only trees, rocks, and leaves and not a single animal in sight.

It was like Dante had disappeared without a trace.

On the off chance he did find him, a sheathed kitchen knife rested in his pocket, swinging back and forth as he walked. He planned to use it if the moment struck him right.

PART EIGHT

The Emperor of Nine Hundred and Eighty Skies

Eighty-Two

AUTUMN WATCHED as Emperor Dante I lay peacefully in his bed. Her hands twitched behind her back. She couldn't put her finger on why she still found him so terrifying. He was no longer a threat to anyone. However, the story surrounding his death sounded a bit sketchy.

He went to sleep and never woke up.

Dante spoke with the examiner. He didn't shed a single tear over his father's death. Her stomach knotted. She hoped he wasn't somehow responsible.

She'd heard Dante's threats, and their relationship was a difficult one. Despite the facts, she didn't dare broach the topic. It was neither the time nor the place.

He'd been with her *most* of the morning. Her cheeks warmed as he glanced at her. They shared an unspoken secret. She couldn't allow herself to consider whether he murdered his father. He was different now. Everything was different now.

"Autumn, did you hear me?" Dante asked, his beautiful mouth tilting.

She stared at him, barely registering his words. "Uh, no, sorry."

"We're mourning my father followed by the coronation ceremony. Both events will take place this afternoon."

She nodded, unsure of what each event entailed and didn't think it was the appropriate time to ask.

Leyla burst into the room, cheeks slicked wet with bitter tears. The empress glided into the room after her, followed by Valdez who strode through the door, head held high with her noticeable limp. Autumn swallowed hard, and her throat went dry.

Her spine prickled with fear as Valdez's cold blue eyes roved between her and Dante before snapping to the emperor's lifeless body.

"Pity," she muttered before joining Leyla and Isidora. Leyla draped herself over her father's body, weeping her eyes out. The empress stood beside her, solemn and graceful. Her cheeks were bone dry.

"This is all your fault. I know you're somehow responsible," Leyla hissed at Valdez. Her eyes were red-rimmed and puffed. "Since you've come around, you've brought nothing but death and destruction."

"Why you—" Valdez balled her fists, knuckles cracking. "How dare you speak to me with such insolence, little princess."

Dante ambled over. "Enough, show some respect. His body is barely cold, although he was a miserable man," he mused.

Dante hugged Leyla close, comforting her. He planted a kiss on her forehead. Valdez's eyes thinned to razor-sharp slits. Her wings jutted before resting against her back. A single drop of sweat trickled down Autumn's brow at the awkwardness of the situation. She could sense the hatred emanating from every pore in Valdez's body.

"I apologize," Valdez said in a honeyed voice, straightening her spine. "How rude and thoughtless of me."

Dante held Autumn's trembling hand and they left the room.

* * *

Hours later, Autumn wore a spectacular white floor length gown complete with golden applique flowers. Her hair fell loosely over her shoulders. Dante was clothed in a crisp white uniform. His pristine cape fluttered in the afternoon wind.

A gathering had formed on the rooftop surrounding a spacecraft. A clear casket housed the emperor's body. A bed of red roses proceeded everywhere the procession did, and drones buzzed overhead, broadcasting the event to the furthest ends of the universes.

This time, Armienti stood with Leyla and the empress. His features were drawn and solemn. Valdez, on the other hand, was absent.

No words were spoken, and everyone stared on in silence as the emperor was loaded into the spacecraft by dozens of soldiers clothed in onyx. The craft rose and sped off to the stars carrying with it the end of an era and the beginning of a new reign.

"Long live Emperor Dante the Second," everyone chanted, raising their fists into the air. White rose petals fluttered from the sky.

Dante snapped his white-gloved fingers. "As my eldest male relative who has always been like a brother to me, you shall do the honors," Dante gestured to Armienti whose eyes subtly rolled at the command.

Armienti nodded as a foot-tall titanium crown was brought forth and placed into his hands. He ambled over and put the ornament onto Dante's head. The new emperor steadied it with his hand. Armienti watched Autumn for a moment too long, his blue eyes simmering through her.

"Where's Ronan? I haven't seen him in weeks, and I can't imagine he wouldn't want to be present for this historic event," Dante searched the crowd.

"He's, um—" Armienti stuttered.

"Away on a trip," Autumn interrupted, tilting her head to the side. She was desperate to keep his secret. Even if she could no longer return home for fear of hurting her friends and family, at least Ronan could still find happiness.

Dante's lips curved, apparently buying her excuse as he placed a kiss on her knuckles and then gestured toward his mother. Isidora handed him the golden sunburst crown from her head. The points twinkled with diamonds in the sunlight.

"Kneel," he whispered to Autumn. She felt silly about the whole ordeal. Her cheeks heated. Nevertheless, she fell to one knee, humoring him, and he placed the crown over her unruly curls.

"Now rise." She rose, positioning the heavy decoration on her head. He took her by her hand, "I'd like to introduce Autumn, Empress of Universe 13, equal to me in rank and authority. What she says shall never be questioned. You're to obey her as you obey me and respect her as you respect me. Anyone who treats her otherwise will answer for it."

Whispers spread through the crowd before everyone erupted into applause. "Here, here."

Autumn trembled, making her way through the gathering. Emblem and Allegoria watched on from afar, their hands glued inside their pockets. Her brows furrowed. She wondered if they were hiding something from her.

Armienti bowed, never looking her in the eye. He made a 360-degree change from the guy she danced with at the club and who helped her bring everyone to safety. She recalled him stuttering in the doorway before Dante's welcome home ball with the most shameful expression on his face.

Because of her.

He disappeared into the crowd as she boarded a ship with Dante.

They took their seats and an alarm sounded in dozens of different languages, clearing the skyway of all air traffic.

He leaned over and whispered into her ear, his stern resolve melted. "Are you okay?"

"I'm fine. How are you?" She adjusted her dress as he fastened her harness.

"I'm as good as can be expected under the circumstances."

She squeezed his hand.

"How are you doing otherwise?" he pushed a stray curl behind her ear. "We haven't had a chance to discuss what happened between us."

"Oh, that," her cheeks burned, and her fingers twisted together in her lap. "I'm great. It was, well, great." Not that she had anything to compare it to. She glanced away, her face still on fire.

"I'm glad," his lips curved before he brought them to hers. "I want you to be happy."

The ship hummed and rose over Giarldinia. Hybrids gathered along the walkway in droves. Dante waved through the window, his head held high.

"They want to see you, Autumn, wave. Wave to your people," his white teeth glinted.

She reluctantly raised her hand and waved, feeling silly everyone had come out to see her.

"Wait, I have a better idea," Dante addressed the pilot. "Stop here."

He stood up and took her by the hand. Her mind raced a million miles a second.

Dante floated from the aircraft, and she hesitated, glancing down thousands upon thousands of miles. Her fear of heights was crippling. Although she could fly, her abilities were still unpredictable. *What if she managed to fall instead? She'd be humiliated.*

He offered her a white-gloved hand and she reached for it.

"I promise you're safe," he winked. She nodded and walked through thin air. Gusts of warm summer breeze blew around the buildings. With slow and reluctant steps, she found her stride.

Hybrids cheered, waved, and sobbed; their cheeks slicked wet with tears. Others crossed their arms, eyes shifting back and forth between them, most likely assessing their unusual combination, a pure-blood Elattion emperor and a human empress.

Her heart stopped and she glanced away quickly as she spotted Kyo and the other hybrids from the club. For a moment, their eyes locked and he whispered to the others with scarlet handkerchiefs in their pockets. He recognized her.

Eighty-Three

THE COMING months were filled with celebrations, endless parties, hard sweaty training sessions, and countless nights of lovemaking. Autumn was exhausted but content with her revived relationship with Dante and her new role as empress. However, in the back of her mind, she feared Valdez and the promise she made to her.

The promise to exact a slow and agonizing revenge.

At any moment, the rug could be pulled from beneath her feet, ending her rose-colored fairytale. Not to mention, she'd never see her friends and family again.

While she secretly battled her fears, Leyla continued to sneak out of the palace at all hours of the night, visiting her beloved Kyo who had no knowledge of her true identity.

She was almost as bad as her brother, pretending to be a human for almost a year.

But one warm quiet afternoon, Leyla arrived at the palace bawling her eyes out on the verge of vomiting hysterics. It seemed her luck had finally run out.

* * *

Leyla raced through the palace halls, fists balled, struggling to stifle her oncoming tears. Everyone stared but she managed to avoid their scrutinizing eyes. Nosy courtiers. How she secretly despised being the center of attention and wanted some freaking privacy.

She knew it, she knew it, she knew it. Her brother was involved. Her chest tightened. She couldn't believe he was doing this to her. She'd done everything he'd asked of her and more, and never had to fake it.

Her care for Autumn was sincere, but he failed to hold up his end of the bargain.

She skidded around the corner, knocking into a servant, splattering a whole tray of good food onto the floor.

"Watch where you're going," she commanded. The servant trembled, picking up the mess she'd caused. Deep down she knew she should've said sorry but, under the circumstances, she was unable to think straight.

Dante was in the conference room, all by himself. He picked lint from his crisp oxblood cape, the same one worn by their late father. He read from a hologram shining above the table. Words swirled through the air like a tornado.

Leyla entered the conference room, struggling to catch her breath, then shouted at him. "How dare you? How could you do this to me?" She pounded her fists against the table, causing the hologram to flicker and dim.

He crossed his arms, mouth tilting. For a moment, he reminded her of their late father with his smug expression and razor-sharp features. A chill trickled through her.

Her patience slipped, and she grabbed a planet from Universe 14 and threw it straight at his head. Dante easily deflected and placed it back where it belonged.

"Is that anyway to treat your emperor?" He smiled smugly. "Maybe if you'd actually been training, you'd be able to land a hit on me."

Her fists clenched. "Answer me Dante, answer me right now."

He stood up and laced his fingers behind his back, orbiting the table like the suns. "It's only a meeting, a date really, as humans would call it. It might not lead to anything. Please don't be dramatic."

"Dramatic? I'll tell you when I'm being dramatic—" Leyla's pulse quickened. "You're sending me to an ice world. You broke your promise to me. You said I didn't have to go if—"

"Hardly. The prince is second in command, and he's handsome, unlike his disgusting drooly older brother. But more importantly, he's strong. He can protect you, because obviously you can't take care of yourself."

She crossed her arms and scowled. "I can protect myself. I don't need anyone's help. Especially not some second-string prince."

Dante snorted. "How many times have you trained? Your abilities must be stale and rusty by now."

She cursed beneath her breath. He was right. If only she'd taken him up on his offer to train instead of shopping and being a socialite.

"Well, I don't care. I'm not going."

"Of course you are. They're on their way as we speak. You'll be joining them for their winter festival. Your bags have been packed, and the prince is quite fond of you from what I hear. Just give him a chance."

"He doesn't even know me."

"That will change. Just be open to the possibility. You never know, you might like him, and if you don't, you can come back."

Leyla stuttered. She could barely breathe. She knew she shouldn't but did it anyway. "I know your secret, and I won't hesitate to spill it to anyone who will listen."

She turned on her heel to leave and was frozen in place. A cool tingling sensation overcame her, and she gulped. Now she was in for it.

"What secret do you think you know about me?" His eyes were focused yet wily. Fire burned in the palm of his hand.

She wanted to scream at the top of her lungs, *I know you killed Keyserike*, out of spite. But she refrained. The mention of his name could endanger Autumn's world and her family.

"I-I know about—" Her mind scrambled, searching for a response, and Dante drew closer. "Father—"

"What?" He loosened his grip, and she breathed a deep sigh of relief as she stretched her sore arms. "None of those rumors are true. He died of natural causes. How could you even think I'm capable of murdering our father? I've heard the rumors, but you too?"

"I-I just—"

"Now you're definitely going, no questions asked. You hurt me Leyla. You've sunk to an all-time low."

Warm tears erupted from her eyes and spilled over her cheeks. "I hate you."

She ran out of the room and into the hallway, almost knocking into Valdez, who leisurely ambled, polishing an arrow against her arm.

"One down, one to go," Valdez winked.

Leyla's stomach churned. She couldn't believe Valdez was behind this fiasco. Her lips moved, but no words came out. She needed to find Autumn.

* * *

Autumn laid on the garden fountain lip. Sunshine spilled over her face and loose spray of curls. She read from the stories Dante gifted her. Leyla arrived out of breath. Her hair was a disaster, and her eyes were so red they looked like exploding veins.

She sat up, jaw lowering. "Are you okay?"

Leyla's cheeks were drenched with tears. "Dante wants to send me away. He wants some second-in-command ice prince to court me."

"What?"

"Please, Autumn, please, you must help me. He'll listen to you. I don't want to leave Kyo. I can't," Leyla sobbed against her sleeve. "I don't know what I'd do without him."

Autumn sighed. Kyo was no prize, but she hated seeing Leyla like this—distraught, broken, and teary-eyed. She knew the feeling all too well.

"Don't worry, I'll talk to him."

* * *

Autumn found Dante in the conference room signing virtual fines and death warrants for serious crimes. He'd grown more solemn over the last few months. She supposed his father's passing and new role as emperor weighed heavily on his mind. It was a huge responsibility with no notice. Unless he was responsible for his father's death, but she refused to believe it was true.

She cleared her throat and he glanced away from his work. "I thought I heard you come in," his mouth curved.

"Uh, yes," she fidgeted her hands, and rounded the table resembling the 24 Universes with blinking lights and orbiting planets. "I want to talk to you about something."

As she approached him, she stuttered, unsure of what he knew and what he didn't. She didn't want to get Leyla into any more trouble than she was in.

He admired her with his piercing amber eyes. "I thought

we were past this. If you don't tell me what you need, how can I give it to you?"

"Okay," she sat on his lap and ran her fingers through the loose strands of his obsidian hair.

"I know why you're here," he nipped at her ear. "Husbands are supposed to know these things."

"You do?"

"Of course I do Little Moonlight. Leyla sent you, and you've come to persuade me not to send her away."

He sat her on the conference table and brought his soft lips to hers. His hands rested on her thighs. *I'm open to all types of your persuasion,* he caressed her mind, and she didn't protest. For the first time, she enjoyed it.

They frantically removed each other's clothes, and she laid down, heart racing, legs resting around his waist. They shifted holographic planets into far off universes and set off blinking stars over the blanket of black with each trembling movement they made together. She bit her lip hard as unsuspecting foot traffic passed outside the closed door. All the while, he worshipped her and swallowed her with his eyes.

Afterwards, she smiled so hard her cheeks hurt. He rested his head against her breast, face flushed.

"I don't understand why Leyla won't give him a chance. She always has to be difficult. Sometimes I wonder if she even knows what she wants," he whispered against her skin.

She combed her fingers through his tousled raven hair and debated on whether to tell him the truth. The smell of warm cinnamon consumed her. "I think she does. There's someone else." She finally decided to tell him.

"Wait, are you serious?" He looked up at her. "Who?"

"He lives here on Surge. His name is Kyo."

"I don't understand why this is the first I'm hearing of him. Where is he from, and how long has this been going on?"

She remained quiet, then said, "A little over two years."

"I would very much like to meet him. Tell you what, have Leyla bring this Kyo to me. I'd like to see where his intentions lie."

"ARE you certain that's what Dante said?" Leyla asked hopefully before putting her hybrid disguise in place. She couldn't allow Kyo to know her true identity, at least not yet.

"Yeah," Autumn confirmed. "He wants to meet him." Leyla's heart soared at the thought of Dante and Kyo hitting it off. Still, there were obvious risks.

She texted him, *Meet me on the palace rooftop.*

Almost instantaneously he replied, *On it.*

"Thanks again," Leyla hugged Autumn. "I can take it from here."

* * *

Kyo arrived not too long after Leyla received his message. His aircraft was rickety and dented compared to the sleek obsidian crafts parked on the docks. None of that mattered to her, it was the man inside she loved.

He stepped out with a blood-red scarf secured across his tan, oil-slicked brow. It highlighted his otherwise drab attire.

Her stomach knotted.

"Um, I would take that off," she pointed to the scarf. "It's going to draw unwanted attention. It's not that I don't like it though..."

"What are you talking about?" Kyo quirked a brow. "We're only going to the kitchen, right? I doubt anyone will notice, and even if they do, I'm proud of it."

"No, not exactly," she laced her hands behind her back, chin held high. "We need to talk."

"What, Iris? What's with all the secrecy?" He clenched a fist. "First, I get a summoning message with no explanation. Did you call me here to break up with me? Is there someone else? Out with it already." Kyo became frantic.

"You're, um," she scrambled to find an excuse, rather than tell him the truth upfront. "Here to meet with the emperor."

"The emperor?" Kyo's brows rose. "What does that brute want with me?" He spat on the ground.

"It's hard to explain," she grabbed his hand. "But you must come with me right now. Please hurry."

* * *

Autumn couldn't believe the spectacle Dante made to meet Leyla's boyfriend. He sat on his pulsating veined throne with his arms folded, clothed in a fresh obsidian uniform. If they hadn't been married, she'd be terrified of him. He broke character flashing her a brilliant grin as she took her seat in an equally stunning black bodysuit with a golden, glittering stripe.

"I hope when we have children, they never pull a stunt like this."

Autumn blinked. "Children?" She asked in disbelief. He was thinking about children again. She was twenty with her entire life ahead of her. She wanted to make sure she lived it to the fullest. She still wanted to get her degree and make a difference in other people's lives.

"Uh, you know what I mean," he stuttered, running a hand through his hair, tousling it. "When we decide, *if* we decide."

She nodded, at a loss for words. *Children.*

They were interrupted by a series of gasps and hurried whispers floating around the room. Armienti wandered through the doorway. His eyes widened.

"Leyla, what's the matter with you? How could you come to court like this?" Armienti scolded. "Remember what we talked about."

Dante glanced at him. "You knew?" He asked Armienti, who slowly looked away. "Why am I always the last to find out? I'm the emperor for heaven's sake. Why are you hiding things from me, cousin?"

Armienti remained silent, picking at his gloves.

The expression on Kyo's face was priceless as Leyla's disguise faded to pale blue. Her light brown hair fell over her shoulders like a swimming mermaid.

Kyo's eyes widened.

Dante rose, his late father's crimson cape fluttered over his shoulders. The room fell silent.

"Leyla, this is absolutely unacceptable."

"Wha—why? But you said—"

"I said nothing," Dante folded his arms. "To bring this hybrid weakling in my presence is despicable. How can he possibly protect you?"

Leyla's bottom lip quivered. "I don't need anyone to protect me. He's wonderful. You didn't even give him a chance."

"We both know that's not true."

"With all due respect, it is true," Kyo crossed his arms. The light played off the swirling tattoos on his neck.

A smugness graced Dante's beautiful face. "I'm sorry, is somebody speaking? I thought I heard an insect from across the room."

"What about you and Autumn," Leyla trembled, "She's—"

"A completely different scenario," he took Autumn's hand. "I can protect her. I'd prefer to keep her out of this matter. Our relationship is none of your concern."

Kyo stared at Autumn. "I knew it was you, but I didn't want to believe it."

Dante approached Leyla, and Kyo blocked her with his body.

"If you come any closer to her, I'll kill you."

Dante's mouth curved. "You? Kill me? Well, this I have to see. I'll tell you what, you shall fight me for the woman you love. You love her, don't you?"

Kyo nodded. "Yes, I only wish she wasn't one of you."

"One of who?" Dante stroked his chin with his black-gloved hand.

"A Martyne."

Dante went silent for a moment. "How dare you speak about my family in such poor taste and with the symbol of rebellion wrapped around your head no less," Autumn gulped as he tossed the top of his uniform on the ground. His chest muscles and scars flexed. The room grew hot and dizzying and frantic.

"Beat me in a fight, and you may remain together, no questions asked. If you lose, she goes to be with someone far more worthy than yourself. Do you accept my challenge, or are you too much of a coward?"

"I'm no coward. I accept, but everyone knows you're Dante the Great Conqueror. Your reputation precedes you across the universes."

"True," Dante flashed a dazzling grin, deviant yet calm.

"But someone like you should be able to handle someone like me no problem. At least that's what my informants tell me has been floating around the walkways of Giarldinia. I know all about you and the secret meetings you conduct."

A group of spectators gathered.

"Put your hands up and fight me like a man, Kyo," Dante circled him, one leg crossing over the other. It was the dance of death. "Here's your chance."

Dante crackled a ball of fire in his palm and tossed it at Kyo, who fell to his knees, trembling. Embers sizzled along the gilded wall.

Dante continued. "You don't think I do everything I possibly can for my people and the realm to keep it safe? You don't think I've dedicated my life to this cause? With everything I've had to give up—"

Dante's boots collided with the crown of Kyo's head. Kyo spun around and around, trying to get him off, hands flailing in the air.

"You're right. This is rather unfair, how selfish of me." Dante hopped off and landed gracefully on the crimson velvet carpet, one boot at a time. "To even the match, how about I agree not to use my abilities? We'll engage in hand-to-hand combat, which should be simple enough for someone like you, right?"

The spectators moved closer, and Dante assumed a fighting stance. Autumn bit at her nails again. She had a nagging feeling where this fight was headed, and it wasn't going to be pretty.

"Put your hands up and fight me," he swung a balled fist grazing the side of Kyo's cheek. Kyo winced, stumbling backwards. A red mark blossomed where Dante had struck him. Dante took him out at his feet, and he fell onto his back, squirming. Dante was on him in an instant.

"How pathetic," Dante chortled. "Who taught you how to fight?"

Kyo reached and slid a dagger from his hip and stabbed Dante in the arm. Oozing blood trickled over his hand and all over the floor.

Kyo crawled away and stared at the weapon buried deep in Dante's bicep. His bright red bandana fluttered to the ground. A calm, cruel rage ripped across Dante's face. The metal melted and silver liquid, mixed with blood, dripped to the floor.

"You bent the rules of our little match. I suppose I have permission to bend them as well. After all, all I am to you is bad."

"No, wait. Please, Dante, stop. Don't kill him," Leyla pleaded from the sideline, hands pressed together, trembling. "He was only trying to defend himself—"

While Dante spoke with Leyla, Kyo trembled then froze, his eyes going wide, appearing possessed. He swiped another knife, lunging at Autumn's throat. Frigid steel ripped against her skin.

Kyo snapped out of his daze. "Sorry, I didn't mean to—"

She slammed her eyes shut at the deafening sound of bones popping. When she opened her eyes again Kyo's body was twisted and airborne. He landed in the hall with a thunderous thud. He rolled on the floor and groaned.

Leyla wailed, running after him as the guards dragged him off. Dante spit on the ground and embraced Autumn who stared in silent shock. His arm oozed over her clothes.

At that moment Valdez ambled through the door, a cruel smile plastered on her face. When Autumn blinked, she vanished.

Eighty-Five

"ARE YOU SURE YOU'RE OKAY?" Worry seeped through Dante's voice, although he did his best to disguise it.

Autumn was almost harmed, again. If only he didn't get caught up in a pointless fight with a hybrid with a big mouth and even bigger cause. It was an unfair fight from the start to prove a point but in the end, he couldn't control himself. His blood boiled with the unbridled urge to fight and dominate.

Leyla, making everything more difficult than it had to be. She always has to be this way.

"Dammit," he muttered to himself, still in disbelief Kyo made an attempt on his mate's life. It was like he was crazed.

"What?" Autumn peeked out from the bathroom before tying her hair in a high ponytail.

"Never mind."

She shut off the light and ambled over.

"I'm fine," she joined him in bed, wearing her satin cloud shorts. She smelled of lavender. His mind wandered off to forbidden territories. She was his other weakness.

When he reached to touch her hair, she placed Mr. Hiss between them. He purred rolling, with his soft pink underbelly exposed. It was deliberate. She needed her space after what had transpired, and he couldn't blame her.

"I think you overreacted earlier," she yawned, and stroked Mr. Hiss with her fingertips. "I could've defended myself. If anything, you were the one who took the hardest hit. And poor Leyla."

Poor Leyla, he was tempted to roll his eyes.

"Why didn't you then?" He rested his head on the pillow and admired her in the shadows. A bandage wrapped around his arm, but it made no difference. The way she stared at him with those large doll-like eyes he could tell she was disappointed in him.

How he hated disappointing her.

"Well, I feel I underreacted," he closed his eyes but then opened them again, sensing her piercing moonlit gaze. "I should've killed him."

She blinked. "There you go with the killing again. Violence isn't the answer. You don't need to add anyone else to your death toll."

"When it comes to you, I'll kill anyone who gets in my way," he said. "I'll burn any city, destroy any planet, or conquer any universe to keep you safe. And you know what, Autumn, I'm not sorry for it. I brought you into this mess and it's my job to protect you. I'll protect you until the day I die."

Her lips flickered. "You sound like my dad."

The guilt rippled through him. He sure did.

* * *

The following morning, Dante was awoken by Autumn's infuriating maids. He disliked them but could never quite put his finger on why. They were odd, to say the least. They worked in silence and never looked his way, too terrified to make eye contact like everyone else.

But he didn't have time to ponder them. It was an important day.

"Come on, Autumn. We don't want to be late."

* * *

Autumn arrived with Dante in the throne room. Her coils were slicked in glittered gold.

The dowager empress was accompanied by Leyla who wore all black, like she was being sentenced to death. Her deep brown eyes were red-rimmed and sunken. Her lips were cracked, and her hair was disheveled.

She trembled, falling to her knees, weak from exhaustion and crying too much. It wouldn't surprise Autumn if there wasn't a single tear left in her body. She went to approach her but then hesitated.

Dante crossed his arms. "This is how you choose to present yourself to a prospective mate? I went through a lot of trouble arranging this meeting. He'll flee back to his planet at the pathetic sight of you."

"For heaven's sake, Dante, show some compassion," Isidora stroked Leyla's back. "Your sister has been through a lot—"

"And we haven't? An attempt was made on Autumn's life, twice now. It's one date and one winter festival. Quit being so dramatic. Nothing is set in stone."

"He was only trying to defend himself," Leyla's voice cracked. Snot rolled in her nostrils. "Maybe if you hadn't attacked him and just sat down and had a normal conversation, none of this would've happened—"

"Maybe if you hadn't been perusing around with a known criminal disguised as a hybrid, none of this would've happened." Dante countered.

"You're a fine one to talk," Leyla spat. "At least he has a

dream for a better life. The rules never seem to apply to you. I'm sorry, Autumn." Leyla looked at her with pleading eyes. Autumn could tell she was dying inside, having made that same look many times herself.

Dante's brow furrowed. "I won't hear another word of this nonsense," he snapped his fingers and a servant approached and bowed. "Pretty her up. We haven't much time."

Leyla was brought into a side room where she was bathed, perfumed, and dressed in a spectacular plum bodysuit. She reemerged almost like normal.

Almost.

"Well, well, well, what do we have here?" Valdez strode through the door, jagged wings dragging along the floor. Splatters of blood decorated her obsidian toga. Autumn's stomach churned.

"All set for your little voyage, I see."

Leyla folded her arms. "Screw you, you she-devil. Go back to your own planet. You've long since overstayed your welcome."

"Leyla," Dante hissed. "Enough."

"It's all right," Valdez, grinned, sending a shiver shooting down Autumn's spine. For the first time, she noticed Valdez's canines were pointed like daggers ready to sink into someone's pulsing throat. She walked with a noticeable limp, the one Autumn had inflicted on her. "Who knows, one day maybe we'll all be one big happy family."

"I'm never going to forgive you for this. You had better watch your back," Leyla said to Dante. With that, she was ushered through the door by a sparkling white-haired off-planet ambassador. Autumn's stomach churned. The entire situation made her sick.

Eighty-Six

"IS THERE any way Leyla can come back?" Autumn hoped as she ambled with Dante. Her communicator had been blowing up all day long and into the evening since her departure. Leyla made no secret of her unhappiness with non-stop obscenities and threats directed toward her brother.

"I'm afraid it's for her own good. My mother shall join her if all goes according to plan." Dante squeezed her hand. Autumn twisted her mouth to the side.

"But why?" she protested, but he never answered.

Her heart sank deep in her chest. And just like that, her only friend on the planet was gone.

They headed to the banquet hall for yet another celebration, although Autumn didn't feel the least bit jovial. Since the day they were crowned, the festivities had been endless and far worse than the house parties she endured back home, with a thousand times the attention.

Dante's pride at his new station bordered arrogance as he graced the hall with his magnificent presence. His late father's cape trailed behind him with every stride. A six-point, foot tall titanium crown sat on his head.

She, on the other hand, was like a deer in the headlights as Empress. The attention made her jittery and uncomfortable. Speech class was nothing in comparison. This was far more terrifying.

She followed Dante making their obligatory rounds, clothed in a forest-green diamond-encrusted gown. A gilded sunburst crown topped her mess of glittered curls.

At that moment, she missed Leyla more than ever. She would've known how to navigate a situation like this—no problem.

Tables were decorated with gilded satin runners. Decadent meats, cheeses, and exotic fruits were piled high on platters. Solid gold fountains poured bubbling milk chocolate. Everyone drank from golden goblets without a care in the world.

She made her way with Dante to the head table. They took their respective seats. It was strange with only the two of them there. His entire family was missing, including Armienti.

She sighed and glanced around the room quietly observing the banquet.

Dante turned toward her. "There's no need to be nervous."

She snorted. "Is it that obvious?"

Dante chuckled. "Painfully so. You've been trembling the entire evening, and you haven't said two words or touched any of your food."

Her hands quaked in her lap, moving against her will, and her cheeks blazed. "Oh."

"You'll get used to it. All the attention, I mean," he tilted his head toward her throat and kissed it. "You look particularly alluring this evening, perhaps after the festivities we can go somewhere to be alone."

Her thoughts scrambled with excitement as he placed his hand on her thigh.

The main door to the hall flew open, slamming against the wall. A thunderous bang followed. Her eyes widened. *What was all the commotion about?*

Guards dragged a young woman into the room who appeared more or less her age. Her short hair was ice-blonde and fell loosely over her pointed ears. She twisted and kicked, her gray shift sliding in the guards' grasps.

Dante folded his arms and examined the young woman. "What's the meaning of this?"

"She was caught red-handed committing a serious offense." The guards replied with their monotone voices.

Dante waved his hand. "Let me cut you off right there. I never see prisoners while I'm eating."

The guards dragged the squirming young woman away.

Dante grabbed a goblet of wine before turning toward Autumn, "Shall we?"

Eighty-Seven

AS AUTUMN FOLLOWED DANTE, her hands twitched. The banquet hall emptied out. The residents of the palace were a nosy bunch who wanted to be a part of every little bit of drama. She sighed.

By the time they arrived in the throne room it was packed to the brim. Dante took his seat and she sat beside him.

He swirled the goblet of wine in his palm before taking a lingering sip. When he removed his mouth, his lips tinted the shade of red blood. She stared ahead and her heart thundered in her chest.

"Bring her forth," Dante commanded.

The guards tossed the barefooted woman on the ground. Autumn jumped at the sound of the impact.

"Easy," Dante said to the guards.

The young woman pushed herself to a shaking stand.

Dante crossed his legs and took another sip. "You can stay right there. Please do enlighten me, what is this all about?"

Her stomach tied itself in a hard knot. She wasn't sure she wanted to know.

Dante continued, his mouth flattening. "Have you nothing to say for yourself?"

"I have plenty to say, m'lord, but I don't suspect you'll listen."

"She speaks," he chuckled. "Try me."

"Well, I—"

"Out with it already," his mouth fell flat.

"I stole from one of your royal supply ships," she admitted, straightening her spine. "And then, I took a homemade explosive device and blew up the cells at the edge of the palace wall."

"So, you're a thief and a rebel who's foolish enough to plead guilty to her own transgressions?" Dante set his goblet on the floor. "Why? What would possess you to do something like this?"

"Well obviously I was hungry," She paused for a moment. "And you stole from me first."

He rose and folded his arms. "Watch it. What exactly have I stolen from you?"

"My brother Kyo can no longer provide for my family. He never came home, and he was last seen here."

"You're Kyo's sister?" His eyes flickered. The young woman began sobbing. Her cheeks were slicked wet with tears.

She reached and pulled a gun from beneath her tattered smock, aimed it, and fired a blue stream of swirling energy straight toward his face. With a flick of his wrist Dante deflected the attack and melted the gun in her hand. She screamed as the weapon sizzled against her flesh. She fell to her knees, blowing on her skin.

"You're just as foolish as your brother. First you break into my home and then you attack me? I'm afraid you've sealed your own fate," a fireball crackled in his palm. "I don't have time for this nonsense."

The young woman screamed and tried to run away but she was dragged back by the guards.

The hairs on the back of Autumn's neck rose. She couldn't sit quietly anymore in this disastrous situation.

"This is awful, don't do this," she pleaded.

"She dug her own grave and now she shall lie in it. You saw what she tried to do, and she stole from us to boot. It can't go unpunished."

"She was hungry and frustrated. She's looking for her brother and having a bad day. Please, don't do this."

He stared at her, his amber eyes flickering. "My decision displeases you, Autumn?"

"Yes."

"Very well then," he retracted the flame.

Every last inhuman eye in the room was fixated on them, watching and waiting.

"After some careful thought and consideration, I've decided to commute the prisoner's sentence. I've decided to be merciful."

"You really have grown soft, haven't you?" A voice cloaked in shadow echoed from across the room.

Valdez slithered over, polishing her talons against the hem of her crisp obsidian toga. Mischief radiated from every pore of her body. "Weak and nonsensical behavior like this leaves you open to the possibility of an attack and the end of an alliance, but I suppose you've never taken that into consideration." Gasps erupted all around them. "You do whatever your doe-eyed mate asks of you. It's clear who calls the shots. Can you even still perform your duty, Dante the Great Conqueror?" She batted her spindly lashes then grinned.

Autumn shot up from her seat. "We don't care what you have to say, Valdez, you're not welcome here after everything you've done." She trembled from head to toe, unable to stop the words as they passed through her mouth. "I think you should leave."

Valdez's wicked lips curved into a smile. "Is it true, Dante? You don't want me here anymore? Shall I inform the Grand Supreme of your sudden change of heart? That you've grown soft and wish to end our four-hundred-year alliance? I wonder how he'll handle the news? A weak emperor, whipped by a human."

Autumn placed a hand on her hip. "Maybe you'd like to share your little secret too…"

Valdez's blue eyes bulged in her skull. "That's quite enough out of you, human."

Dante entered a state of deep thought before his expression hardened like stone. "Rather than excuse her, bind her to a pillar and give her ten lashes. That should do it."

"Make it twenty," Valdez suggested, ripping her eyes away from Autumn. "Better yet, how about thirty. She stole, destroyed the cells, and fired a gun at an emperor."

"Thirty it is."

"And every time she makes a noise, we'll start back at one," Valdez's mouth twisted.

Dante took his seat and raised his goblet calling for more wine. He was eerily calm, considering the severity of the situation.

Autumn gasped. "I can't believe you're going through with this—"

He propped his chin on a fist. "My decision in the matter is final."

The prisoner was dragged and bound to a pillar. The smoothness of her back was exposed. Thirty cracks echoed through the room accompanied by bone chilling screams. They finally came to a stop.

Autumn cupped her hands over her mouth as the bile in

her gut rose. The young woman laid unconscious against the blood-stained pillar.

The room emptied as the excitement came to an end. Dante leaned over to speak to her, but she jumped up and sprinted away. She was so disgusted by him. She went to her bedroom and pushed past the guards, slamming the door shut.

She could barely see straight, could barely breathe. She couldn't stop the residual screams from ringing through her skull. She had to leave, had to get out of here. What Dante had done was unforgivable.

Eighty-Eight

AUTUMN THREW her sunburst crown across the room and unzipped her extravagant dress. She raced to the closet and pulled out a few bodysuits and shoved them into her cross-body bag. Mr. Hiss emerged from beneath her bed yawning and stretching. He trotted over, his pink fuzzy tail swayed with every step.

"You're coming with me," she swept him in her arms and turned on her heel. Her communicator and digital books remained on the table. She no longer needed them where she was headed. She was getting the heck out of here.

A loud knock rattled against the door, and she ignored it, making her way toward the balcony. She'd fly wherever she had to, as long as it wasn't here.

Dante teleported through the door and entered the room regardless. His vermillion cape fluttered in the warm summer breeze.

"Are you going somewhere?" He assessed her from head to toe.

She levitated, holding Mr. Hiss against her breast. "Obviously, and you can't stop me."

"I knew the day would come when you would leave me," he stared at his black-gloved palms before meeting her gaze. "I did the best I could. I granted the prisoner mercy like you asked—"

"Get away from me. I can't stand to look at you," she made her way back into the bedroom and headed toward the main door. She had to get away from him and his pathetic excuses.

"I'm not going anywhere until you tell me what the problem is. Perhaps I can fix it."

She folded her arms and sighed. Mr. Hiss buried his face against her chest. "Valdez has to go. I don't feel safe with her lingering around. The way she controls you and how she treats others is disgusting," she paused. "What happened downstairs wasn't mercy. It was totally barbaric. That girl was hungry and from what I can tell, there's no shortage of food around here. And what you did to Kyo—"

"What about Kyo? In case you've forgotten it's my duty to enforce the law. I'm the emperor."

She rolled her eyes. "Thanks for reminding me."

He folded his arms and cocked his head to the side. "In any case, I did their kind a great justice. They're just hybrids."

She gasped. "You call that justice? I call it heartless. It was an unnecessary display of power," she trembled with ire. Mr. Hiss sprang and ran beneath the bed. "The laws you preach apply to everyone but you. You're a thief and a murderer. A hypocrite. I can't even stand to look at you. You disgust me. And if this is how you feel, then we don't understand each other at all."

The energy in the room became hot, thick, and furious, but on the exterior, Dante remained calm and calculating.

"I'm a thief and a hypocrite, am I now? I don't hear you complaining when you benefit from the spoils of my back-breaking work. Where do you think all the finery you've grown so accustomed to comes from? I never hear any complaints about that. You lay back and reap the rewards," a fireball burned in his palm before he retracted it back into his hand. "Who do you think paid for your extravagant wedding? Who do you think is keeping your planet safe and would kill anyone to keep it that way?"

"Save it, it's all your fault I'm here to begin with. You never think about anyone but yourself. You ruined my life and my future."

He glanced away. "I know," he admitted quietly.

"What bothers me the most is you're becoming more and more like your father every day. "Her eyes welled with tears. "And here I am feeling bad and missing you already, and I haven't even left. What's wrong with me?"

She reached over to touch him, and at the last second, he brushed past her and stormed over to the door and ripped it open. Light flooded through the room. Armienti stood outside his fist balled, mid-knock.

Dante chuckled, shaking his head. "What on earth are you doing here, cousin?" His eyes widened with a wily furiousness.

Armienti stuttered and blinked. "I-I was just—"

Dante twined his fingers behind his back. "Allow me to rephrase the question. What business could you possibly have with my wife at this hour in her bedchamber?"

Armienti remained quiet and glanced away. His golden hair tousled to the side.

"That's what I thought. This little obsession of yours has gone on long enough. You always want what you can't have. No matter how hard you wish, you'll *never* be me."

Dante darted over to the table where her two snow globes sat, one with a scene from Alice in Wonderland and the other with a silver-spired castle in the snow. He grabbed the castle and shoved it at his cousin, snowflakes swirling in a whirlwind of white.

"Don't think I don't know this present was from you. It has you written all over it. You're useless and pathetic. Now get out. I don't want to see you around here again."

Armienti mumbled something incomprehensible under his breath, turned on his heel, and left.

Dante closed the door and inhaled. "I apologize. Where were we?"

She grew silent, save for the sound of her breath. Her mind scrambled like an egg.

What did Armienti want from her, and why didn't he know better than to visit her in her bedroom?

She hesitated, heart pounding against her ribcage.

What was she doing? Something had to be wrong with her. She saw her dad's face when she bid him goodnight for the last time, the way Dante hurt her friends, and the threat he posed to the universes and to Earth. All she saw was red-hot fury, but ultimately, she couldn't deny her feelings for him. She couldn't help herself.

The energy in the room stabilized.

"I've always wanted to believe you were capable of better, that you could be different, and we could be endgame, but you keep disappointing me, Dante. I can't even put it into words how much you disappointed me."

"Endgame?" His lips flickered then fell flat. "Don't I provide you with love? Why can't that be enough?" He stroked her cheek with his black-gloved hand.

"It is, but—"

"I know there's something you want more. Something you're desperate to have. Something I deprived you of because I was selfish and stupid," he paused. "I knew I could never measure up to your standards. Like I explained before, it isn't the way the universes work. Only the strongest and most ruthless survive."

Screams from the girl earlier accosted her and she shuddered. She couldn't get Valdez's wicked face out of her mind.

Dante sat on the edge of the bed, his face buried in his palms. He radiated with regret.

She ran her fingers through the soft stands of his hair. "I'm tired of fighting. I'm taking a shower."

He never looked up or responded, so she left him and walked to the bathroom. She undressed and stood beneath the steady stream of warm water. Golden glitter from her hair swirled in a twinkling spiral down the drain.

After a few minutes, two heavy footsteps entered the room, followed by the swing of the shower door. Her face warmed as she admired him. Droplets of water trickled through his midnight hair and across his chest and scars.

"I'd like to finish our conversation," he lathered soap through his scalp.

"Okay?"

"I'm going to let Valdez know she's overstayed her welcome. You're right, and I'm wrong. It's time for her to leave. She's done enough damage, and I don't care what the consequences are."

She stood on her tiptoes and brought her lips to his. Their tongues danced in each other's mouths, before she pulled away, craving more of him.

"Also, I think it's time that I return you to Earth and make good on my promise."

"What are you talking about?" Her jaw dropped. "Is it because I—"

"Your father misses you and searches endlessly for you at Farrah Falls. He cries your name out in his sleep."

Her heart clenched, and her cheeks slicked wet with tears. "How do you know?"

"I left trusted soldiers behind, and they provide me with regular reports of his whereabouts. Your friends as well.

They're not handling your disappearance any better. I'm sorry. I know it's all my fault."

* * *

Dante held Autumn in his arms, flushed with warm humiliation. He was the one who made her suffer, because he was selfish, because he wanted a family, and most of all, because he wanted to be loved. He knew he had to send her back, having made every excuse to keep her here, but still he worried how he'd get her to return to him after all was said and done.

What if she decided not to keep her promise to him? The promise where they shared their lives together. He secretly hoped she'd invite him to come along with her.

"As much as I miss my friends and family, I'm not sure it's the best idea," she twisted her fingers together again, and he calmed them with his own. "What if they think I'm a freak, or I accidentally kill someone again with my abilities? I'm a danger to everyone, including myself."

"You could never be a freak, Autumn," he brought his lips to hers and she shuddered as he dragged them to her throat. "And even if you are a freak, who cares, you're all mine."

He fell to his knees, running his fingers against her hips. "I hope you'll return to me, my love, you challenge me to be a better man. I need you by my side." He paused, regretting the words before they left his mouth. They could only spell trouble, but he was desperate to make everything right. "This time, bring your father back with you. He's more than welcome in my home. I want us to be happy as a family."

"Our home," she corrected him, running her fingers through his hair, sending shivers down his spine.

"Our home," he smiled as he kissed her, caressing his hands against her soft skin. Warm droplets of water ran against their bodies. Her fingers gripped his back. How he enjoyed her sweet lips and being the only man in her life.

Mouths entwined, he propped her against the beading shower wall, gazing into her eyes. She wrapped her legs around his waist, quivering, her delicate body in his hands. He wanted her to feel how much he loved her, how much he'd miss her when she was gone. How desperate he was to have her in his life. How he hoped she could choose him of her own free accord.

Afterwards, she leaned in close and whispered in his ear. Her voice sent shivers crashing down his spine. "Please stay with me, I don't want to be alone tonight."

He rested his head on her shoulder. "I wouldn't have it any other way."

Eighty-Nine

FOR THE FIRST TIME, Dante hadn't lied.

Autumn woke the following morning wrapped in his arms. She bit back a smile, admiring his chest gently rising and falling. Her fingers grazed his solid abs and deep jagged scars.

Although she had to go home, she felt guilty for wanting to stay with him for just a little bit longer. The warrior, the conqueror; the man she loved.

She leaned over and kissed him, rousing him from his sleep. His mouth curved as he laid his eyes on her, returning her affection. Her skin erupted in goosebumps as his calloused hands ran through her hair and over her body. She trembled in his embrace.

"I love you," he breathed against her neck, resting his head on her shoulder. He ran his fingers through her coils. "I wish—"

A loud knock came to the door disrupting them, and she wrapped the sheet around her naked body. His mouth fell onto a tight flat line. He sighed.

Emblem and Allegoria bumbled inside carrying tray after

tray filled with cheeses, fruits, steaming floral tea, and her absolute favorite, gooey chocolate chip pancakes.

They placed the trays on the table. For a moment, the excess food reminded her of the girl from the night before whose bones protruded in all the wrong places and whose back was bloodied and covered with marks.

"Good morning," Autumn forced a smile, blinking hard trying to forget the girl's crying face.

"Good morning, Autumn," they answered, their sweet chipper voices in sync. Their eyes widened with terror as Dante rolled over and rested an arm around her waist.

He snorted. "You can leave now. I'll never understand why it takes both of you to complete the workload of one servant. You're so utterly lazy." He rested his head against the pillow.

They curtseyed and scrambled from the room. The door slid closed behind them.

Autumn rolled her eyes at his rudeness and complete lack of consideration for their feelings.

She poked his arm, running her finger against a pressure point. He jumped. "That was mean. They have names, you know, and they're my friends, the only friends I have since you sent Leyla away." Her heart sank a little bit as she wondered what Leyla was up to.

His mouth twisted. "Forgive me. I was under the impression all servants had one name: *servant*. And as for Leyla, it was necessary."

"How did you feel when someone treated me like crap? I remember your overreaction." She rolled her eyes. "Why not show Emblem and Allegoria an ounce of the same care?"

He ran a hand through his hair. "I'll try to be nicer but sometimes it's difficult with them. I'm sorry, there's something about them I can't stand. We should eat before our food gets cold. There are many preparations to make before your departure."

They popped open their trays and Autumn's heart skipped a beat as she smelled her chocolate chip pancakes. They reminded her of her dad, who she couldn't wait to see, but then, once again, the girl's gaunt face flashed through her memories. Her sunken eyes and pale skin, her bony body, and ill-fitting tattered clothing. Autumn was enjoying her breakfast when she was somewhere starving.

After their meal, Dante dressed and threw on his uniform and cape for the morning meeting he was responsible for hosting solo.

"I'll see you soon, sweetheart. If you need me, I'll be in the conference room." He kissed her forehead and turned on his heel, cape fluttering.

She laid back in bed and stared at the pristine white ceiling in silence. She fixated on the unfortunate events that'd unfolded the night before. The pain and suffering inflicted on Kyo's sister at the hands of someone she loved. And that remorseless *witch*, Valdez. Her forehead pulsated. How she wanted to give her what she deserved.

Before she left for Earth for who-knows-how-long, she had to find a way to undo the wrong that'd been committed, all because the young woman was hungry and searching for her brother.

She grabbed her sleek teal communicator and paged Emblem and Allegoria.

"I need to speak with you immediately," she texted.

In a flash, they entered the room. "How may we be of service to you?" Their eyes darted around. Autumn could only suppose they were searching for Dante.

"Don't worry, he's gone. I want to apologize for the way he treated you."

"Honestly, we're used to it." Emblem shrugged. "It makes no difference anymore."

"You shouldn't have to be," she crossed her arms. "So, again, I'm sorry."

There was a long quiet pause. Aircraft hummed through the city in the distance.

"I called you both here on official business, but I'd like for it to be our little secret."

"A secret, you say? How can we be of service?" Allegoria's brows rose.

Autumn frowned. "I'm sure by now you've heard of yesterday's incident."

They nodded. "Yes, of course we have, along with everyone else in the universes. The unfortunate event was broadcasted."

Her stomach knotted. *Oh no.* She couldn't imagine the situation getting any worse. Everyone had witnessed her humiliation.

"Now everyone refers to the emperor as Dante the Terrible."

Allegoria elbowed her sister. "Bite your tongue, Emblem. You shouldn't speak disrespectfully about the emperor to his wife. She might—"

Autumn rolled her eyes. She was so *not* surprised. "It's okay, I promise I won't say anything," she paused for a moment, gathering her thoughts. "Do either of you know the woman's name?"

"No."

"Okay, here's what I need you to do," she leaned in close. "Ask around the palace, but please be discreet. I want to know her name and address. Bring the information to me and I'll compensate you for your trouble."

"Okay, we can certainly try," their voices chimed like sunshine.

"Thank you, I really appreciate your help."

After their conversation, she put on a teal bodysuit with a

gold metallic stripe. Her hair was gilded in a single French braid ponytail. This was the last time she'd wear anything as extravagant, and she hated to admit she was going to miss it.

Emblem and Allegoria left to complete the assignment she entrusted them with. As she went to follow, she spotted Armienti lingering in the hallway. His cornflower eyes and loose blond hair shined in the light.

"Might I have a word with you, Autumn?"

"Are you sure it's a good idea that you're here, after—"

"It'll take but a moment."

She scanned the hallway. "Um, all right."

The guards let him through and into her bedroom. The door slid closed behind them.

"So, what's up?" She crossed her arms, assessing him.

"I don't quite know how to say this, but there's a rumor floating around the palace about you."

She stared at him quietly before speaking, "Well, what is it?" Her hands fidgeted behind her back.

"They heard a lot of screaming last night and they say Dante placed his hands on you, which, if it's true, it's a new all-time low, even for him."

Her brows furrowed and her mouth twisted to the side. "No, he would never do that. He's been nothing but gentle," she said. "We did have a misunderstanding, but it never came to violence. You shouldn't always believe everything you hear. Thanks for your concern though."

His lips curled and his blue eyes smiled at her. "I'm glad to hear you're doing well. May I ask how everything else is going with you, you must be elated with your new title?"

"The attention is a bit overwhelming, but luckily I'll have a break from it soon."

"How so?"

She whispered. "I'm returning to Earth."

"Well, if I might say so, you carry your crown with such

beauty and grace I've never seen on an empress before. It's like you were destined for this role."

"Thanks," she crossed her arms. "I think."

"If you ever need a friend to talk to, I'm always here."

"Thanks again, Armienti. I'll see you around."

She opened the door to let him out of the room and he stopped and turned around. "Here, your zipper is down, allow me to get it for you." He placed his hands on her back and pulled her zipper up. She wasn't sure how she neglected to pull it up earlier.

Her cheeks warmed. "Thanks."

She closed the door again and slid to the floor, mortified to hear everyone's opinion of Dante. All she could do was hope Armienti could put the nasty rumor to rest, but it was nothing compared to *Dante the Terrible*.

She craved a distraction. No, needed it. She headed outside to the back garden of the palace, her digital books in hand. She planned to make her last day on Surge matter.

Ninety

THE WEATHER WAS GORGEOUS, as usual. The twin suns shimmered like diamonds in the cloudless blue sky. Autumn rolled onto her stomach and read at the entrance of the Great Maze. Cobalt grass swayed in the breeze.

Not long into her story, she heard a pair of uncoordinated footsteps approaching at a rapid speed. The guards cocked their metallic guns.

Allegoria arrived, struggling to catch her breath.

"Let her pass," she gestured.

"Did you find something?" Autumn lowered her voice so the guards couldn't hear.

"Yes, one wine bearer knows the woman personally," breath spilled through Allegoria's mouth.

"You have her name and address then?"

"Yes, Lady Autumn, her name is Treble Spriggs. Her address is 50,000th Street, Building 307 million, Apartment 85."

Autumn stared at her. *What the heck?* She'd never heard such a bizarre address in her entire life.

"Come again?" She shrugged.

Allegoria repeated herself, and Autumn was sure it was in fact a real address, as unbelievable as it sounded.

She hugged Allegoria. "I'll give you and your sister each a heaping sack of rubies," she recalled the chest she and Dante received for their wedding. At least she could put the money to good use.

"Are you sure?" Allegoria gasped. "That's equivalent to a little over three years of our regular salary."

"Yes."

"Thank you," tears welled up in the corners of Allegoria's eyes. "You're most gracious. This will really make a difference in our lives."

She smiled. She had no problem with the amount, but now she had to figure out where the money was kept without Dante finding out.

* * *

When Autumn reentered the palace, she relieved her guards for the time being. She was officially on a secret mission and didn't want to risk it somehow making its way back to Dante.

She turned the corner. *Holy crap*. It was just her luck that he was in the middle of a hearing.

He sat on his throne chin propped on a black-gloved fist. His eyes were closed as he rested his feet on a pintuck cushion. A golden goblet sat on the floor.

It seemed he drank more since he was crowned emperor. The stress of his new position probably ate away at him.

She chewed a nail in her mouth as she waited for the hearing to be done. When she began to cross the room, she pretended she didn't see him. But he approached her regardless.

"Where is it you're in such a hurry to go off to?" His amber eyes twinkled like golden starlight as they met hers.

She melted inside. "I—"

"And where are your guards?" He scanned the room. "I don't recall relieving them from their duty?"

"I gave them the day off. I don't need a babysitter," she placed a hand on her hip and hoped she seemed convincing.

He kissed her forehead. "Of course you don't."

"I'm headed to the kitchen to thank the chef for the delicious breakfast he made us since you asked…"

Dante folded his arms. "What's bothering you, really? You don't think I know by now when you're acting off?"

The hairs on the back of her neck rose. She broke out in a cold, dizzying sweat. "I—"

"You're still sore about how I addressed your sluggish maids, Emblem and Allegoria, is it?"

"You learned their names?" Autumn stared at him in shock. "When?"

"Yes, I did. And I assure you no harm will come to them while you're away. I know you enjoy them. You have my word, even if they deserve to lose their stations."

"You're right," she squeezed out a smile. "That's exactly what's bothering me." In reality, it was far from the truth.

"I like to know when you're troubled and when things are on your mind. I wish you were more comfortable talking to me. You should go find the chef. Your departure isn't too far off."

She brought her lips to his, trembling a bit, bested by her anxiety again. When she turned to leave, Dante watched her walk away—like he had something to tell her, but it escaped him.

* * *

The kitchen was down a flight of dark winding crimson steps. She often smelled food coming from here, and it was a place where none of the royalty or nobility of the palace ever trekked.

The kitchen itself was bright, clean, and industrial. Dozens of chefs labored wearing light-gray jackets, pants, and cone hats.

She stood in the doorway and crossed her arms. "Um, excuse me."

Everyone stopped. All eyes assessed her, and gasps erupted throughout the room. "It's the empress," everyone fell on one knee.

"I'm sorry to bother you, but I need your help," she laced her fingers together.

"We assure you, you're no bother at all," a chef spoke. "Especially the way you stood up for us in the past."

She surveyed the room, then continued. "Please pack several large containers with cheese, fruit, vegetables, and meat. Any sort of food you can think of."

The chefs scrambled to prepare the order and packed baskets filled with decadent food and treats. Golden bottles of champagne were added to the order.

In no time, they presented her with four steel baskets, each decorated with a burgundy velvet bow.

"Do me a favor and leave them by my aircraft on the dock. Thank you."

The chef left, doing as she instructed, and she was grateful he didn't ask any questions. After all, she wasn't prepared to answer them. Only one more stop remained before she departed to the mysterious address. A lump formed in her throat. It was the most complicated of all and she was running out of time.

Ninety-One

THE PALACE TREASURY was opposite the conference room and made apparent by a pair of balance scales etched into the door in gold, overflowing with gilded rubies. Large twisting Ivarkian symbols sat underneath the image. Although Autumn couldn't read them, she knew she had found the correct location.

Inside was a room decorated with celestial stained-glass windows and an oval table spilling over with treasure gifted and stolen from other worlds.

Exquisite crowns and tiaras laid on dress forms covered with fur and cloaks. Natural light shimmered through the windows in a kaleidoscope of color.

She was approached by a man with wrinkled blue skin. His gray hair and body was concealed beneath a hooded obsidian cloak, secured at the waist with a bronze tassel.

"How may I be of service to you, your Imperial Majesty?"

"I need you to prepare twelve satchels of rubies for me," she reached into her pocket and handed the man Dante's two access chips she'd never returned to him after his mission.

"That's quite the hefty sum, my lady," his crinkled eyes

widened. "I'm assuming this transaction has been approved by the emperor?"

"Yes," she cracked her knuckles and twisted her fingers inside her palms.

He grabbed twelve velvet pouches, hanging from the edge of the table, and then hesitated. "Hold on. Let me double-check with him."

She whipped out her communicator. "I'll save you the trouble," her trembling fingers hovered over the buttons. "I'll be sure to let him know you questioned me. We all know what happens when he gets angry."

"No, wait, it's quite all right," his wrinkled lips curved, hands waving. "Forgive me. I'll prepare the bags as you've instructed."

He walked away, holding the pouches. A single droplet of sweat rolled between her shoulder blades. *Holy crap*, what a close call, one she was grateful she didn't have to explain to Dante.

The treasurer held the weighted sacks. "Is there anything else I can assist you with?"

"No, but thank you." She snatched the bags from him.

When she left, satchels of rubies filled the bags to the brim, and she could've sworn he uttered *shrew*.

The docks were warm as sunshine spilled across the concrete. Luckily, the baskets of food were right where she asked the chef to place them.

She loaded her aircraft, sure to put her helmet and gloves on. A few moments later, she was off into Giarldinia.

She merged onto the skyway, full speed ahead. Although she glided past thousands of other zipping aircraft, they were sure to keep their distance—likely due to the royal crest etched onto her faux license plate. She snorted.

At the rate she soared, she hoped to return in time for her departure, so Dante would be unaware of her doings.

Her heart sank a little as she wished he could come home with her.

Then—

Her communicator vibrated again, and again, and again. *Holy crap, it was him.* She fumbled the device in her hands and ignored it at least a dozen times.

She couldn't risk him discovering her whereabouts.

"Autumn, where are you?" She heard in her mind but managed to suppress it.

Relief flooded through her. She was halfway to her destination, as her aircraft operated on auto fly.

The rich jewel tone buildings decreased in size and color to the muted hue of beige. They appeared dilapidated and neglected. Soot tarnished their finish, and shards of glass were smashed all over the sandy ground. Mountains of stinking garbage were piled everywhere.

Dozens of hybrid children rolled through the trash wearing tattered light-gray rags. Beggars wandered the streets barefoot. Her jaw lowered. The area looked nothing like the rest of Giarldinia.

As she descended, she spotted street number fifty thousand. Her aircraft settled on the dirt ground, dust and rubble sprayed. She took deep controlled breaths as she plotted her next move. She never considered how she would carry everything all by herself.

Her communicator bleeped again, and this time she turned it off.

As she went to exit, an obsidian royal aircraft landed on the ground beside her. Her skin erupted in sweat.

Someone had been following her the entire time, and she hadn't bothered to pay attention.

Her tongue twisted as she concocted a lie to explain why she was all the way out there to begin with. For some reason, her mind drew a blank.

The pilot removed their helmet and placed it onto the seat.

"What are you doing here?" Her brows furrowed.

Ninety-Two

GUILLERMO RAMON WANDERED through the barren forest of Farrah Falls. Winter had come. Snowflakes danced through the wind and settled on the slick rocks and along the stumps of the trees destroyed in the great fire a year ago. Crescent moonlight sparkled along the sticks. The sky was sprayed with stars.

It felt like a hole had formed in his chest. He couldn't find his daughter, no matter how hard he searched. It'd been over a year since her disappearance.

He'd combed through every square foot of the forest, or at least he thought, and still no sign of her or of Dante. His teeth clenched. How he planned to teach that boy a lesson once he found him.

He ambled past the frozen falls to an area he'd sworn he'd been to in the past, but this time, it was somehow different.

Fallen tree trunks crisscrossed along the ground, appearing to have landed at a singular point in time. However, it wasn't the tree trunks that caught his eye, it was the swirling tornado of mist that spun from the ground and flowed through the sky. Beneath it, he caught a flash of a black angular structure that was larger than life.

In an instant, it vanished into the night. His shaking fingers gripped his flashlight.

"So that's where he's hiding her."

* * *

Armienti stared at Autumn with a glowing smile erupting across his mouth.

"I could ask the same of you. What on Earth are you doing all the way out here in peasantville?" He ran a black-gloved hand through his golden hair, the strands sparkled like rays of sunlight.

"Why did you follow me?" Autumn's fists clenched at her sides, steadying her weight.

He ignored her question, then continued. "Dante has gone positively mad searching for you. He's tearing apart the palace as we speak."

"Did you tell him where I was headed?" her voice wavered with concern.

"No."

She shoved a nail into her mouth, and her mind scrambled a million miles per hour.

"Since you're here now, I could really use your help." She pointed to the baskets in the backseat of her craft, before handing a few to him to carry. She wasn't going anywhere until she completed the task at hand.

"Who's all this for?"

"Treble Spriggs."

Armienti shrugged. "I apologize, that name doesn't ring a bell. However, it does sound low-born."

"Stop being such a snob and help me." She grabbed ten

satchels of rubies and left two on the seat for Emblem and Allegoria, like she'd promised. She planned to give ten bags to Treble to ease her family's suffering in her brother's absence.

His eyes widened. "Where did you get that from?"

"Never mind, just come on."

She turned on a heel and scanned the buildings for number three hundred and seven million, when she spotted the numbers on the front of a demolished building. The rich peach exterior had been polluted with ash and soot.

"I found it," she sprinted, heart speeding in her chest. Armienti followed her into the desolate structure. The floors were littered with heaping trash and every ceiling light was smashed to oblivion, allowing natural light to shimmer through the shattered windows. Many of the doors were boarded tight and the walls were decorated with fading graffiti.

They searched and searched and searched, making their way up several flights of crumbling steps. Eventually, they reached the floor where the eighties were located.

"Autumn, I can't fathom who resides in such a horrifying place. What's this all about?"

"Will you shut the heck up," she scanned the hall. Her adrenaline raged. She did not need the third degree, especially with Dante searching for her. "Nobody invited you to come."

He grumbled beneath his breath when, finally, she spotted apartment number eighty-five. Her hands fiddled while she stood in silence before the lime green door.

Knock, knock, knock, she pounded against the steel, to no answer.

"You need to use more force," he grumbled, raising a fist. His violent knocks echoed through the empty hallway.

Low, hurried whispers erupted on the opposite side of the door. Somebody was home.

* * *

Autumn had been missing for hours. She'd failed to respond to Dante's communicator messages. And there was no response through their bond.

It was as if she'd disappeared into thin air.

Wherever she was, she hadn't left for Earth. Dante had her room and belongings packed on the pretense she was going on holiday, Mr. Hiss in tow. Nobody needed to know her true destination, except for a select few. She'd be traveling in invisible mode.

He'd scoured every last centimeter of the palace. Something was awry, he could feel it in his gut. His stomach twisted with anxiety. It was only a matter of time until he became physically ill.

He collapsed on his throne. He had to compose himself. He was the emperor now, for heaven's sake. Any sign of weakness could open him up to an attack.

Valdez sauntered into the throne room, braiding her long jade hair. She wore an obnoxiously short toga skirt; like nothing had happened.

Dante inhaled, holding his breath for a moment too long.

"What's got you all stressed?" She batted her spindly lashes. "Any way I can help?" She placed a hand on his knee that he promptly brushed off.

"I can't find Autumn," he muttered into his palms. "Have you seen her, perchance?"

"No, and quite frankly I'm not surprised."

His vision blurred with red. "What are you talking about?"

"Oh, nothing," she shrugged, playfulness underlining her voice. "Really, it's nothing."

His fingers clawed, bending the steel arms of his throne. They cracked beneath his might. "Well, it doesn't sound like *nothing*. Do you know something I don't?"

"It's just that—" Valdez approached and took a seat beside him on the throne. She crossed her legs, and tilted her head to the side, trying her best to be charming but having known her his entire life, he could see through her facade. "This isn't the first time she's not been truthful with you."

"How so?" His brows furrowed. As far as he was concerned, she was the most truthful person he'd ever known. She was loving and kind, with one agenda—to help others.

"She was on Varz."

"What?" He rose, crossing his arms. He furiously paced the dais. His mind scrambled. "You lie, she was here the entire time with my family. She would've told me otherwise."

"No, I assure you she wasn't," she picked at her flawless manicured talons, mouth tilting to the side. "She freed her human friends and sent them away with Ronan. Who can truly say what transpired."

It meant Armienti must've known as well, and as far as he could recall, he hadn't seen him either since yesterday when he caught him prowling around her bedchamber. Damn it all to hell.

He gathered himself and inhaled a deep trembling breath changing the subject. "This is long overdue. Get out of my sight. Ever since you've shown up, there's been nothing but problems. I want you off Surge, effective immediately. And if I discover you lurking in any of my territories, we're going to have a real issue."

"I know you don't really mean that, Dante. You and I have known each other for a long, long while," she winked. "Plus, I've known about Earth all along. That's where the humans are headed. They have nowhere else to go."

"Earth?" His fists trembled at his sides. "How did you find out?"

"I'm not as foolish as the others to believe your outlandish story. I know you'd do anything for that girl, at any cost, although I can't figure out why. She's nothing but a disgusting human. I also know, because of her, you murdered Keyserike, but he was a useless weakling anyhow, so it's not a huge loss."

Valdez paused for a moment, then continued. "You should stick to your own kind. What you need is someone with power and influence. Someone to compliment—"

Dante snorted. "Someone like you? Save your breath."

He ran a hand through his hair. "Who else knows about my indiscretion?"

"Nobody yet, and we can keep it that way. If we join forces, we can overthrow the Grand Supreme. We'd be unstoppable. But apart, we're no match for him."

Something deep inside of him snapped and hurled a crackling ball of blue fire straight at her face. Her eyes widened. Even she couldn't anticipate his move.

She screamed as it melted her magnificent clothes and singed her skin. Her long, jade braid fell in a heap on the floor. The room smelled of burning hair and flesh.

He realized the magnitude of what he'd done when her eyes met with his. They sparkled like two blue murderous daggers.

"That was a dire mistake."

"Get out of my sight. You're no longer welcome here. You've caused enough trouble and enough pain," he loomed. "If you so much as mention Autumn's name again, or go anywhere near her, I'll kill you."

Valdez stormed out of the room, limping and concealing her face with her hand. He could've sworn she whimpered.

"It's about time that selfish she-devil tyrant was on her way."

Dante whipped around, the flame still sizzling in his hand. "Oh mother, I didn't realize we weren't alone."

His mother placed a palm on his shoulder. "You're never alone my dear, someone is always watching over you, and right now Autumn needs you more than ever. You have to find her."

Ninety-Three

AUTUMN STOOD there as the door creaked open, revealing a short, slender boy with olive skin and oversized hazel eyes. A red bandana was fastened around his forehead, which he ripped off after seeing her and Armienti.

"You, you're Empress Autumn," he averted his eyes to the ground, stupefied. "And you're Prince Armienti."

She nodded. "Yes."

His cheeks reddened. "I'm sorry, I don't know how to act in the presence of royalty."

"I always get nervous meeting new people too," her mouth bowed. "How do you know who we are anyway?"

"I saw your wedding on broadcast. Everyone knows who you are."

"Oh, that's right," her cheeks flushed. "Um, can I ask what your name is?"

"I'm Kittlen Spriggs, Your Majesty."

"Nice to meet you Kittlen." A knot fastened itself in her throat. Without a doubt, she was in the right place.

"Would you like to come in?" He gestured into his home.

"Yes, thank you."

They made their way into the apartment. The space was dark and musty and cramped. Clear barriers laid over the broken windows, fluttering in the late afternoon breeze. A tiny kitchen sat nearby with tarnished mint-green cabinets. On the right were battered seating cushions. Mold spanned a large part of the wall, creeping in spindles across the ceiling.

"This place is disgusting," Armienti whispered into her ear. "I can't wait to leave and get back to cultured civilization."

"Stop it. Don't be rude," she hissed, her brows knitting. "Is Treble here?" She glanced at Kittlen hopefully.

"Oh, is that why you're here?" Kittlen fidgeted his hands, stuttering. "So you know, she learned a valuable lesson about stealing from our emperor and firing a gun at him. She'll never do it again, I promise."

She nodded, terrified to mention Kyo's name. Enough suffering had affected this family.

"Can you please get her? I need to have a word."

Kittlen nodded mechanically and left the room, followed by a series of groans and whispers erupting from the back of the dwelling. And finally, a loud gasp.

When he returned, he informed them, "She'll be out soon."

"Can I get either of you something to eat or drink?" He pointed at the sparse cabinets.

"Don't worry about it, thank you." she replied, clutching the baskets of food and champagne, nauseous with anticipation. There was no telling what type of condition she was in. As far as she was concerned, she was lucky to be alive.

Treble emerged wearing the same light-gray smock from the night before. The fabric was streaked with dry blood stains. She limped, with a noticeable hunch. Autumn struggled not to drop the baskets on the floor and put a hand over her mouth. The horror of it all.

Armienti crossed his arms, spine straightening. "I know

you. You're the thief and the assailant everyone is talking about."

Autumn took the heel of her boot and kicked Armienti square in the shin. "Stop it already, you're embarrassing me."

He hopped up and down and slammed his mouth shut.

"I want to thank you, Empress Autumn, for pleading mercy on my behalf. If you hadn't, I'm not sure where I'd be," Treble stared at her feet. "I'd also like to apologize for stealing from you and the emperor, busting the cells, and firing a gun at him. What I did was wrong. I realize that now. I'm lucky to be alive."

"Don't apologize for being hungry. If anything, it's a failure on our part." Autumn placed the baskets at Treble's feet as she was too weak to lift them herself. The satchels of rubies spilled on top. Her eyes widened.

"Thank you, Empress Autumn, you're more than gracious." Tears welled along Treble's lashes. She reached to hug Autumn who was mindful of the scars littering her back. The embarrassment and torture she suffered at the hands of her husband and Valdez was beyond humiliating.

"If you ever need anything, don't hesitate to contact me." Autumn handed her a piece of paper with her communicator number on it and turned to leave. She'd be gone for a while but was more than willing to lend a helping hand.

"Would you like to stay for supper?" Kittlen gestured toward the kitchen. A dented pot simmered on the stove.

"Thank you, but we really should get going." Autumn's eyes settled on Armienti who was texting someone on his communicator. "What's wrong?"

"Special forces are storming the city searching for you. Dante's leaving no stone unturned. He won't rest until you're home."

Crap, she gulped.

"Please stay for a little while," Treble interrupted her

thoughts with her weak yet melodic voice. "It's not every day we get to meet someone famous. It'll probably be the one and only time we'll ever get this chance."

"Okay," Autumn agreed, her mind scrambling in a million different directions. In some way, she felt responsible for Treble's suffering, and if this was the only way to make it up to her then so be it.

Dante would have to wait.

They sat at a rickety steel table. Treble joined them, taking her seat as slow as molasses. Autumn cringed, still unable to fathom the amount of pain she was in. The scars on her back would probably be permanent.

Kittlen struggled to carry four bowls to the table of plain broth and a crust of bread. Armienti jumped up to help him. It was the first time he was decent all day. She could throttle him for his rudeness. They placed the food on the table and ate. Armienti was uncharacteristically quiet.

"This is delicious," Autumn sipped her blue tinted broth.

"Uh, yes, it's very good," Armienti said into his bowl. Autumn glowered. *He'd better stay on his best behavior.*

"What was it like growing up as a princess on Earth?" Treble asked, struggling to eat her meal, hand trembling.

"I wasn't born a princess. I had a job serving food, went to school, and lived in a regular house."

All the things she wanted back, desperately.

Treble squeezed out a smile "Really? I didn't know. I thought you were born royalty."

"No," Autumn glanced subtly at the time on her communicator. She had to wrap this up fast without seeming rude. Messages were flowing into her inbox like water.

"Really, is that so? How impressive, Empress Autumn." Armienti batted his eyes and she rolled hers in return.

Autumn nudged his arm, and Armienti snorted into his soup.

"Maybe it's why everyone loves you so much. All the girls I know want to be just like you. Pretty and kind, with such beautiful curly hair," Treble gushed.

"Thank you," Autumn's cheeks warmed against her will.

Autumn paused, almost afraid to ask. "What do they say about the emperor?"

Treble grew silent, her fingers sliding against her fork, before shooting Kittlen a pleading look.

"Don't worry, I promise it won't get back to him."

"I can't say. To do so would be treason," Treble replied quietly.

"I promise you'll be okay. Nobody is going to hurt you again." Autumn placed her hand on Treble's.

Kittlen interrupted, swallowing his soup. "They say he's all powerful and has never been defeated in a fight. He's a sadist who drinks the warm blood of his victims."

"They also say he's ruthless and cares nothing for the welfare of his people. He spends his days enslaving foreign planets," Treble reluctantly mentioned.

Kittlen continued. "It's rumored he arranged for the murder of his own father."

Treble nodded. "People feel bad that someone as wonderful as you was forced to marry a beast like him."

Autumn soaked up all the horrible information. Although her heart wrenched as she listened, at the same time, she wasn't surprised. Dante had built quite the reputation for himself throughout the years. No thanks to the Grand Supreme and Valdez hanging around the palace all the time.

The bitch had to go.

Life deteriorated since she decided to come around.

"Thank you for being honest." Autumn pushed out the most convincing smile she could muster. But still, her chest hollowed.

* * *

After all was said and done, the twin suns set in the sky, casting shadows over the massive cityscape of Giarldinia. Thick dark smoke flowed in the distance.

An entire day had passed since Autumn went searching for Treble Spriggs and located her at the far end of the city. Since embarking on this trip, she missed her dad more than ever, seeing Treble's family and how much they relied on and cared for one another. She was anxious to get back to Earth. Hopefully he'd still love her the way she was.

If matters weren't stressful enough, she'd have quite a bit of explaining to do to Dante, but that was the least of her problems.

"Thank you again for your hospitality," she waved to Kittlen and Treble. "Remember, if you need anything at all don't hesitate to ask."

"Thank you," Armienti muttered, for the first time sounding polite.

They exited the apartment building, leaving the siblings behind. It was full-dark outside, and the sky glittered with misty stars.

She inhaled and thick smoke invaded her lungs. Her mouth fell ajar at the sight of Giarldinia. Fire churned in the distance. *Holy crap*, her heart sped.

She raced to her aircraft with her key in hand, desperate to put an end to the panic and chaos. But Armienti cut her off.

"Where are you headed to so quickly?" He batted his eyes and tilted his head to the side.

"I have to get back before Dante destroys the city searching for me," she rubbed her hands over her eyes as they blurred then refocused. She must've been more tired than she thought. "I'm going home to Earth. There's a ship waiting to take me." She reminded him.

Armienti stroked his chin with his fingertips. "Are you sure that's a safe idea?"

"If it's safe enough for Ronan, it's safe enough for me," she said matter-of-factly. "It's my home and I can't wait to return."

He nodded as his eyes scanned the ruins.

She turned around and saw nothing but dust, crumbled buildings, and garbage. *Oh, the smell.*

She pinched her nose. "What the heck are you looking at?"

"Nothing," he shook his head. "I just wanted to say what you did for that family was very kind, and in retrospect, I'm sorry for the way I behaved. I should've been more sensitive to the situation. I know I came off as rude."

She nodded. "It's fine, don't worry. I'm sorry, I really have to get going."

"No, it isn't, and I'm sorry. I'm a product of my environment but I know it's no excuse for my behavior."

She opened her aircraft, then hesitated. Her eyes blurred and she blinked away the fog. He lingered close by.

"You never told me why you followed me here," she was almost afraid to ask.

He ran a black-gloved hand through his golden tousled hair. "Well, you see, I like to know where you are at all times," he said. "And you needed my help, so it was a win-win situation."

"What do you mean, *you like to know where I am at all times?* You don't have to watch out for me." Goosebumps splintered down her spine.

That's what she had Dante for, who she grew more desperate by the minute to get back to. There was no telling what he was up to.

"Believe me, I understand you're my cousin's mate. I try to be respectful, but—"

She pushed past him to get into her aircraft. "I'm sorry,

but I have to go." *He was sounding more deranged by the second.*

With the door open, she palmed her communicator and read through a few of the hundreds of missed messages from Dante, ranging from concerned to super desperate. Rather than address every single one, she texted him a single message. Her fingertips trembled against the screen. It went through.

Armienti grabbed her communicator and crushed it with his palm.

"What are you doing?" She gasped.

"I'm afraid you're not going anywhere."

Ninety-Four

AUTUMN'S HEART hammered in her chest as Armienti wrapped a hand around her wrist. "Let go of me, let me go," she struggled, screaming in his grasp.

She kicked him square in the face and he stumbled backwards, tripping over his own two feet. He groaned as he landed in the sand in a pile of golden hair and gorgeous eyes.

Rather than wait for her aircraft to start, she jumped into the air and flew toward the city.

"Crap, crap, crap, crap, crap."

Her heart pounded. She had no way to contact Dante for help. Her communicator was gone. When she turned around, Armienti was flying after her, hot on her tail. His purple cape fluttered in the wind.

Another dizzy spell hit her, and she slowed down, her body lowering in the sky.

Then she remembered their bond. She hated when Dante used it, but now she desperately needed it to contact him. She closed her eyes and attempted to soothe her mind and concentrate.

"Dante, Dante, are you there?" She shouted to no answer.

When she opened her eyes again, she collided with a hard object. It rattled her core so hard she bit her cheeks. Metallic blood trickled over her tongue and teeth.

She searched, but there was nothing in her way. For a moment she managed to steady herself but then fell from the sky. Down, down, down, into the bottomless pit of the city. She struggled to control her abilities. A wave of nausea hit her like a brick.

She focused and hovered through the air. Everything moved in slow motion. *Armienti must've put something in her soup. The blue tint.*

A sharp jutting pain stung the middle of her shoulder blades. She turned and swung, but her fist was caught in a palm. Talons dug into her skin, causing streaks of blood. Her eyes widened as they met Valdez's feral glare. Her luxurious jade hair was half its usual length, her extravagant clothes were ripped, and raw burn marks singed the right side of her face. She smelled like she'd been barbecued.

"You think you can get one over on me again, human filth? Our last encounter was nothing but beginner's luck."

Valdez took her knee and slammed it into Autumn's gut. Breath spewed from her body, and she tumbled through the air. She managed to regain her senses and charged. Valdez chuckled, easily dodging her attacks.

"Freeze."

Autumn stopped mid-air like a fly caught in a spider's web, struggling and screaming for anyone's help. But nobody came. Her body went limp. A warmth spread across her muscles as they became weak and uncoordinated.

Valdez grabbed her by her glittered hair and slammed her face-first into the steel sidewalk. Blood trickled down her nose and mouth, she rolled over onto her side and gagged.

Valdez straddled her and punched her again, and again,

and again. Her balled knuckles wailed against Autumn's bones. She struggled to block, her vision blurring to black.

"This wasn't part of our agreement," Armienti pulled Valdez from her. Her eyes widened. "We've attracted enough attention. We should really be going."

Hybrids gawked from the sidewalk, frozen with fear. Valdez blinked and they disintegrated into black dust.

"I'm keeping a promise *I* made," Valdez turned and rammed her boot into Autumn's rib cage followed by the crunching of bones. Autumn cried out, as stars danced across her vision. She struggled to breathe.

Valdez grinned. "I won't stop until I hear her beg for her miserable human life." She rammed her boot against another one of her ribs, snapping it.

"Come on, seriously, stop. We must get going."

"All right, all right." Valdez raised a hand. She took Autumn by the collar and pressed her mouth to hers, digging her long, pointed tongue down her throat. She gagged.

"Pleasant dreams." Sweet numbing venom seeped into Autumn's mouth before everything went dark.

* * *

Dante soared over Giarldinia. His mother was close behind him. Endless raids conducted by his soldiers yielded nothing but the destruction of his home city.

Maybe Autumn was right. *He was a monster.* It shouldn't have to come to this. But she was missing and by gods so was Armienti when he needed him the most. Although, he regretted yelling at him the night before.

Unless—

He panicked, his heart thundering in his chest. He couldn't help but wonder if somehow, he was responsible for her disappearance.

"Oh, Armienti," he ground his teeth in his mouth. "When I get my hands on you, there will be hell to pay."

His blood boiled in his veins. He was desperate to find Autumn. She had to be around here somewhere, but then again, the city was endless.

Dante's communicator beeped and he froze. He fumbled it in his hands and slid the screen up.

"I want you to come with me to Earth. I'll miss you too much if you don't. I lo—" the text read.

His mouth flickered but then flattened as the message cut off. She wanted him to accompany her to Earth; his chest warmed. By now, he was positive everyone in the universes had heard about his betrayal.

Valdez wasn't known for being discreet. It was only a matter of time until his master learned of his deception and came to collect the debt he owed. He'd be ready though, as ready as he could possibly be to defend Autumn and Earth until his dying breath.

"The south side is clear," his mother said.

He nodded. "Thank you for helping me. I don't know what I would've done if I had to go about this alone."

"You know I'd do anything for Autumn," his mother reassured him.

Dante crossed his arms. "I swear, I'm going to kill Armienti when I get my hands on him if he's at all responsible for her disappearance."

And for making him worry and fear the worst. Just like Maeve. He relived the panic he experienced when she vanished. He covered his mouth as he recalled the horrifying state she was in when he discovered her. When he closed his eyes, he saw her charred skin and smelled her burning hair.

She'd breathed her last breath in his arms. A lump formed in his throat and his fist clenched. They had to work harder and faster. They had to find her lest she met the same fate.

Tears welled in his mother's large brown eyes and streamed down her cheeks.

"What's wrong? Why are you crying?" His brows furrowed as he placed a palm on her back.

"Promise you won't hurt him, promise me," she held his hand to her wet face. He pulled away and crossed his arms.

"I'm afraid I'm not going to make a promise I can't keep, not even to you."

"Please, you must keep it for me, please. Armienti isn't your cousin, Dante. He's your brother."

Ninety-Five

AUTUMN SHIVERED IN THE SHADOWS, her breath flowing in a white mist. She winced as she struggled to sit up. Her right eye was tender and swollen shut. A thick layer of crust glued her lashes together making it impossible for her to open it.

Where am I? She surveyed her surroundings as best she could. Blackness crept along the walls and through the corners of the room in spindles and swirls.

How long had she been out?

The metal floor was cool beneath her palms. Stray stars skittered across the tiny rectangular windows in an endless galaxy. When her vision refocused, she caught the dark lingering silhouette of Armienti.

Her teeth ground in her mouth.

"Why did you do this?" She balled her fists, trembling with fury, but in the process overexerted herself and landed back onto the floor. She groaned and threw a hand to her chest as her broken ribs shifted and crunched.

The way the light from the passing stars played through

the dark, they highlighted the glass of her clear enclosure. She was trapped like an animal.

"It's nothing personal," he glanced away. Rays of wispy gold fell over his face. "I'm here to collect a debt."

"What kind of debt?"

His expression grew solemn. "A debt that's long since been owed to me."

She struggled to stand and landed on her backside, gasping for breath. A cold dizzying sweat overtook her. Nausea set in.

"Well, what's this have to do with me?" Her stomach knotted.

"I told you I'd call upon you for a favor in exchange for your friends' safety and safe passage to Earth, did I not? I held up my end of the bargain, and now it's your turn to hold up yours."

"What are you talking about?" Her voice grew dry and weak. She spoke in little more than a whisper.

"Every emperor needs an empress by his side," he winked. "An emperor is only as strong as his second half."

Her heart flew to her throat. "What about Dante?"

He had to be worried sick about her by now and there was no telling what he was up to in her absence.

He shrugged. "What about him? He's dead to me."

"You," she lunged at him as hard as she could but almost knocked herself out as she collided with the clear divider and landed on the floor. She rasped a breath. "This is how you treat your own family?"

"Look at what he did to you, and to me. He's selfish and dangerous."

He ran a black-gloved hand through his golden hair before he continued. "I promise, I'll let you out once you simmer down. It won't be long now," the corners of his mouth flickered with strange delight. He turned on his heel to leave but then hesitated. "If you like, I can heal your wounds. It doesn't have to be a miserable ride."

"Get away from me," she hissed and waved her hand with a trembling fury.

He nodded. "Have it your way. I know eventually you'll come around. I can be as loving, if not more, than he was. You'll see. Please allow me to prove myself. Oh, and Valdez thinks she's going to kill you. That was part of our agreement, and she took a hit for it on Varz so you'd trust me but there's no way I'm going to let her hurt you. I'll set her straight."

Armienti walked away and Dante's crimson cape fluttered over his shoulders. She fell to her knees and warm bitter tears rolled down her cheeks followed by a puddle of vomit.

After she drowned in her own sorrow and cried herself to sleep, she became angrier than she'd ever been in her life. Desperation coursed through her, followed by red-hot rage. Because of Armienti, she'd never see Dante or her family again, and she was going to make him pay.

From the Publisher

Thank you so much for reading The Midnight Prince!

We hope you enjoyed the journey and characters as much as we loved bringing them to you. **Please leave a review on Amazon** and Goodreads while the story is fresh in your mind. Reviews are writing fuel for authors and help their books get into the hands of other hungry readers. If you're a big fan of speculative young adult and middle-grade fiction, we invite you to join our street team. Get copies of our books in advance, early access to covers, and other freebies!

Stag Beetle Books
  www.stagbeetlebooks.com